The Art of
Standing Still

ALSO BY PENNY CULLIFORD

Theodora's Diary

Theodora's Wedding

Theodora's Baby

The Art of Standing Still

Penny Culliford

a novel

ZONDERVAN®

ZONDERVAN.com/
AUTHORTRACKER
follow your favorite authors

The Art of Standing Still
Copyright © 2007 by Penny Culliford

Requests for information should be addressed to:
Zondervan, *Grand Rapids, Michigan* 49530

Library of Congress Cataloging-in-Publication Data

Culliford, Penny.
 The art of standing still / Penny Culliford.
  p. cm.
  ISBN-13: 978-0-310-26559-7
  ISBN-10: 0-310-26559-2
  1. Theater—Fiction. 2. Women journalists—Fiction. 3. England—Fiction.
 I. Title.
 PR6103.U46A88   2007
 823'.92—dc22

2006030876

Internet addresses (websites, blogs, etc.) and telephone numbers printed in this book are offered as a resource to you. These are not intended in any way to be or imply an endorsement on the part of Zondervan, nor do we vouch for the content of these sites and numbers for the life of this book.

Interior design by Beth Shagene

Printed in the United States of America

06 07 08 09 10 11 12 • 23 22 21 20 19 18 17 16 15 14 13 12 11 10 9 8 7 6 5 4 3 2 1

Acknowledgements

MY THANKS AND APPRECIATION FOR ALL THEIR HELP WITH THIS BOOK GO TO
Mike Tyler, Kit Bird, Alan Lyons, and Samuel Valentine for inspiring me with their experiences of the York Mystery Plays To Lucy
Brinicombe and Peter Unsworth for helping me to understand
the workings of a local newspaper and Peter Cornwell for showing
me inside a police station and so cheerfully answering my bizarre
and gruesome questions. To Debi Simmons for musical advice. To
Wintershall Estates, Surrey, for helping me to visualise the performance and for advice on costumes, and the Alexanders at Home
Farm for inside information on cattle farming. Finally, my gratitude
goes to my editor Diane Noble and to Sue Haward for reading it and
helping me to make it make sense.

*Christ is already in that place of peace, which is all in
all. He is on the right hand of God. He is hidden in the
brightness of the radiance which issues from the everlasting
throne. He is in the very abyss of peace, where there is no
voice of tumult or distress, but a deep stillness – stillness,
that greatest and most awful of all goods which we can
fancy; that most perfect of joys, the utter profound,
ineffable tranquillity of the Divine Essence. He has
entered into His rest. That is our home; here we are on
a pilgrimage, and Christ calls us to His many mansions
which He has prepared.*

CARDINAL JOHN HENRY NEWMAN

*Be still, and know that I am God;
I will be exalted among the nations,
I will be exalted in the earth.*

PSALM 46:10

Act One

Scene One

IT WAS THE SPLASH THAT WOKE JEMMA DURHAM.

She thought at first that it was a swan or one of the other water birds landing upstream, but the muttering and muffled cursing certainly didn't belong to any kind of waterfowl. She sat up and checked her alarm.

'Two forty-eight,' she groaned. 'Who in their right mind ...?'

It was still pitch black. Wary of drawing attention to herself by switching on the light, she tiptoed to the galley end of the narrowboat and edged back the curtain. She peered outside, blinking back sleep.

Silhouetted in the moonlight, stood a person. He – or she – was dressed in dark clothes and leaned out precariously from the towpath. Jemma held her breath. The figure appeared to be holding a long pole, perhaps a branch or a boat hook.

She watched, intrigued yet horrified, as the figure dragged it through the water as if dredging the river. Or maybe searching for something.

Jemma returned to bed and tucked her knees under her chin. She wondered if she should call the police. What would she say? 'There's someone mysterious poking around in the river with a long pole?' She could imagine the laughter.

She couldn't lie still, not with the splashes and muffled mutters from across the river. She returned to her sentry post at the window. Half of her brain wished they would go away so she could get back

11

to bed. The other half hoped they would fish up a dead body or something – anything that she could transform into a story for the *Monksford Gazette*, fry up, and present on a plate to her editor in the morning.

The figure seemed to be getting frantic, thrashing around with the pole in the water. Curiosity completely overwhelmed her. She pulled on her coat and Wellingtons and quietly unlocked the door. The water lapped slightly against the *Ebony Hog*'s hull as she climbed up the ramp. She sneaked along the grass next to the towpath, avoiding the gravel surface so her footsteps wouldn't be heard.

As she crept closer, hiding in the shadow of the elder bushes and willow trees, she heard him utter a curse. A dog barked nearby. Jemma froze and held her breath.

The figure, she was sure now it was a man, straightened, listening.

They both stood motionless for what seemed like years. Then, to her horror, she heard a familiar tune. The phone in her pocket had started to ring. She unzipped her coat, groping frantically to silence it. But it was too late. He dropped the pole and ran with long strides up the towpath towards Todbourne Heath.

A car door slammed and an engine fired up. She stood, dismayed, as the sound grew more distant. She heard the car accelerate along the Fordbrook Road; then it was gone. Jemma looked up the river and saw the abbey illuminated in the moonlight. The dog barked again; then all was silent.

She glared at her phone. What kind of idiot rings someone at that time in the morning? She flicked through the menu.

Richard's number.

Jemma didn't know whether to be furious or worried. One thing for sure – her cover was blown. That was the end of her surveillance operation for tonight. And she was none the wiser about who she had seen and what he was doing.

She turned and walked back up the towpath, not caring now how much noise her feet made on the cinder surface.

Back aboard the *Ebony Hog*, she stared at her phone. She hadn't spoken to Richard since 'the note.' He had made his feelings perfectly clear. She threw it into her handbag and lay down in bed. The events at the river and Richard's call jostled in her mind, and neither was likely to allow her the luxury of getting back to sleep.

No point lying there worrying; she needed get up and do something – anything. In college, she had written many essays in the early hours, and more recently, she had seen the sun rise several times while completing articles. She crawled out of bed again and put the kettle on. There wasn't much she could do about the stranger's 'night fishing trip', but she could find out what Richard was up to.

She extracted the phone from her handbag and took a deep breath as she pressed the call-back button.

'Hello.' Richard's voice sounded slurred.

'What do you want?'

'Jems ... I'm sorry.'

'Sorry for what? Sorry for leaving me or sorry for ringing me at three in the morning.'

'It's just that I miss you.'

'Oh, you miss me, do you? You wouldn't be missing me if you'd stayed. How's that tart you left me for?'

Silence.

'Have you been drinking?'

More silence ... except for his irregular breathing. It sounded as if he was crying.

'Jems ... I'm all on my own here.'

'Good. Then you know what it feels like.' Jemma pressed the off button and threw the phone back into her bag. She flopped down on her bed, no nearer sleep than before.

So, he was all alone? Well poor him!

❧

ON REFLECTION, JEMMA DECIDED THE NEXT MORNING, DRIED COW PATS WERE definitely preferable to fresh ones. She wiped her heel on a tuft of grass and picked her way, with increased care, through the field towards the makeshift arena.

She should not have sacrificed practicality for fashion. Had she thought deeply enough about it, she would have realised the hazards associated with a 'cow-pat throwing contest' would be of a bovine residual nature. If anyone had asked her advice on what to wear, she would have recommended Wellington boots every time. And she would have done well to heed her own advice. But Jemma preferred giving advice to taking it. Anyway, it was too late now. She hadn't time to go home and change. The contest was in full swing and she didn't dare miss a throw.

She caught a glimpse of Saffy Walton, the photographer, zooming in on a grinning man who was holding a bovine pancake aloft as if it were the World Cup. Being on an assignment with Saffy Walton was rather like being trailed by a slightly bewildered gerbil. Oh well, it was going to be one of those days.

Jemma checked her bag – notebook and pen; handheld recording machine, though she preferred shorthand; bottle of mineral water (still, not sparkling), and the note. The note from Richard that she found on her table in the galley last week. The one that she had read over and over, but the words still seemed to say he was leaving and not coming back. It was written on a piece of paper torn from an envelope. Surely two and a half years deserved at least a piece of narrow ruled, if not vellum. She stuffed the crumpled scrap to the bottom of the bag. Then he had the nerve to phone her last night!

'Come on girl, you've got a job to do.' She waved a fly from her face and set off smartly across the field – as quickly as her impractical footwear would permit.

Jemma believed in self-motivation. If she told herself she could do something often enough, she would come to believe her own words. And it seemed to be working. So far she had spent only an hour on the phone to Lou, alternately sobbing and shouting, another hour stuffing Richard's belongings into several black sacks while listening to breaking-up songs on a late-night radio station, and had, this morning, after several fitful nights' sleep, gone shopping.

The taupe-suede kitten-heel boots were a bribe to herself, like chocolate to follow nasty medicine. They had called to her from the shop window – and they went beautifully with her soft beige corduroy skirt. They had cost nearly half a week's wages, but she could surely justify the expense. She had worn them to prove she was over Richard. It didn't seem to be working.

To her irritation, she noticed that Saffy was wearing sensible green Wellingtons with her baggy jumper and jeans. Her corn-stalk hair was sticking up in all directions. She looked as if she had just crawled out of a barn. Typical local paper! Jemma never quite fitted in with that image – she just wasn't a tweed-cap, green-gilet-wearing country hack. To her, the job with the *Monksford Gazette* was merely a stage, a step, a tread on the stairway to the national dailies.

The realization, however, that the darling little suede boots were infinitely more suited to the paved serenity of 'Fleet Street' than a field somewhere southeast of Monksford, just served to make Jemma more irked. Only the thought that Richard would have hated them stopped her taking them off, stuffing them into her bag, and carrying on in her socks. That and the fresh cow pats.

'And the winner of the under eighteens with a throw of three metres, twenty-four is Harry Denholm,' crackled the public address system. 'If the next contestants for the freestyle throw – the over fifties – would please step up to the mark.'

The grass in the arena had been flattened by the people of Monksford who had turned out in force to support the event. It was wise to keep in with the locals, so Jemma nodded a greeting to those she recognised. Who knows when the next town scandal or piece of juicy gossip might find its way to her?

It appeared that all the great and good of the town had gathered to watch desiccated cow dung being tossed into orbit. It served to prove what Jemma had long suspected – that not much happens in the town of Monksford.

There seemed to be a lull in the proceedings – that, or maybe there was never more excitement than this – so Jemma headed towards the tea tent for a coffee. She yawned. Perhaps the caffeine would cancel the effects of her sleepless night. Tired and grumpy was not the best frame of mind to attend this event full of fragrant local colour.

'Bound to be that disgusting instant stuff,' she muttered to herself, trying to avoid the potholes and muddy places on the grass. A short woman with ginger hair came out of the entrance to the tent and almost bumped into Jemma, slopping her tea on Jemma's boots.

'Watch out!' Jemma shouted. She was about to let rip with a tirade of choice words when she noticed the woman was wearing a dog collar.

'Oh, I'm so sorry.' The woman said as she started to mop at Jemma's feet with a paper serviette.

'Ruined! And they cost me a fortune,' Jemma said. The boots, like her day, seemed doomed.

'I can't apologise enough. I'll pay to have them cleaned. Make sure you send me the bill.'

'I will.' As if a few pounds would make her feel any better.

The woman wrote her address on a scrap of paper, and Jemma took it. 'Reverend Ruth Wells,' it read and gave the address of the vicarage. To her amazement the woman smiled.

Jemma did her best to smile back, 'Thanks – no, really. It is kind of you.' She thrust the paper into her pocket and went into the tea tent. She was pleasantly surprised to find a pot of percolated coffee sitting on a warmer and a large jug of fresh creamy milk. A jolly caricature of a farmer's wife with a flowery frock and a terrible perm served her cheerfully.

She took her coffee and found a seat outside the tent. The tables were covered in blue-and-white checked cloths, each with a china vase holding a posy of wild flowers. The sun was warm on her face and the coffee tasted heavenly. Farmers with chocolate éclairs shared anecdotes with ladies with large-brimmed hats and strings of pearls who delicately nibbled their clotted-cream scones.

Jemma looked around. A young policewoman in uniform stood by the entrance to the tent, sipping from a blue-and-white striped china mug. Should she say anything about the nocturnal shenanigans by the river? A group of teenage boys swaggered past. Jemma remembered their photographs on the *Gazette's* 'Shop a Yob' page. They 'accidentally' bumped into the policewoman, slopping her tea. She yelled in protest, and the group ran off, with the policewoman in pursuit. Jemma's heart beat a little faster at the whiff of a newsworthy story. She jumped up, leaving her half-finished coffee on the table, and scrabbled in her handbag to find her notebook.

She squinted in the brilliant sunshine outside the marquee. The WPC stood at the gate with her hands on her hips as the lads sauntered up the lane, turning around to shout the occasional curse.

She returned her notebook to her bag. 'Youths Spill Constable's Tea' would make a lousy headline.

Jemma made her way back to the arena, passing women in flowing summer dresses, twin-sets and pearls, and hats that would not be out of place at Ascot.

At least she wasn't the only one to commit a fashion crime. A woman in a short tight skirt, high heels, and enough foundation on her face to plaster a wall caught Jemma's eye. She tottered around on the arm of a middle-aged man who was wearing a dark business suit. Her pencilled eyebrows zigzagged in irritation as she stumbled over the rough grass. She clung to his arm like a lifebelt. Sweating profusely, he scowled in the September sunshine, and then paused to wipe the sweat from his coarse face. Jemma recognised them as Councillor Alistair and Mrs Amanda Fry. As she took them in she made a mental note: visits to farms – no short skirts, no pinstriped suits, and definitely no kitten heels.

At last, someone to interview! Her heels embedded themselves in the soft turf as she half ran, half staggered, towards a pen where Fry and his wife were admiring a large Jersey cow.

'Jemma Durham, *Monksford* ...'

'I know who you are.'

Jemma thrust her hand out to the man, who shook it reluctantly. 'Excuse me, Councillor Fry, can you tell me why the council overturned the previous decision not to build a road through Monksford farmland?'

'No comment,' Fry snapped.

'Well, in view of local and national protests and evidence from environmental groups ...' Jemma pressed.

'I said, "No comment."'

Fry strode past her and steered his faltering wife towards the exit. Jemma couldn't help wondering if Amanda Fry's unsteadiness was entirely due to her footwear.

She shrugged and tucked her notebook back into her bag. Opportunities are there to be seized. Too bad if they slip out of your grasp.

She located the man she assumed to be Bram Griffin, the organiser of the event, leaning on a gate. She picked a path across the field, skirting round the cow pats and narrowly avoiding the gossip-laden attentions of Mrs Grimsby-Johnson and her Bell Ringers Social Group.

Bram Griffin was wearing a green gilet and wellies. Rather incongruously he was also wearing a large white cowboy hat. She suppressed a grin. He looked like *Horse and Hound* meets the Village People.

'Good afternoon, Mr Griffin.' She held out her hand, hoping this time for a friendlier response. 'Jemma Durham, *Monksford Gazette.*'

'Delighted, Miss Durham. Are you enjoying the contest?'

'I can truly say I've never attended anything quite as – ' she searched for the right word ' – extraordinary.'

Bram Griffin beamed with delight. 'Of course you know the best technique to get the cow pat to go the farthest?'

Jemma shook her head. She didn't know, and she didn't wish to know.

He told her anyway. 'You see, you got to lick your fingers first ...'

Jemma shuddered and pretended to write it down.

Saffy scuttled over and started to set up her monopod. 'Why can't she get a proper one with three legs?' muttered Jemma. 'Excuse me, Saffy. I haven't finished.'

'Oh, oh ... I'm sorry!' Saffy fumbled with her lens cap. 'I'll ... er ... come back when you're ... um ... done.'

She dropped the lens cap and went down on her knees, still clutching her monopod in one hand, and fumbled in the grass. Bram Griffin looked heavenward as if checking for signs of rain that might spoil his white Stetson, then shuffled his feet, replacing a clod of earth with the rubber heel of his boot. Jemma sighed. Poor Saffy, clumsy, socially inept, and what a start in life when your parents decide to land you with the name Saffron Walton. Jemma quickly dismissed the thought that Saffy's parents might once have spent a night of abandon in North Essex.

Jemma said, 'Let me hold that,' and took the camera.

'Oh, thank you,' Saffy said. 'Just one moment, I'll be out of your way.' She snapped the muddy lens cap back in place, a few blades of grass poking out like flower petals. Finally, she tucked her monopod under one arm and scuttled off to find someone else to annoy.

'Mr Griffin,' Jemma cooed. 'I'm so sorry for that interruption. Now if I might ask you where you got the idea for a cow-pat throwing contest ...'

Monksford Gazette   *Thursday September 8*

A PAT ON THE BACK FOR LOCAL FARMER

By Jemma Durham

A local farmer has found an unusual use for the by-products of the 200 plus dairy cattle on his farm – a cow-pat throwing competition. Bram Griffin, 55, welcomed the public to his Monksford farm last Saturday to compete for the £100 prize and a Golden Cow Pat trophy.

The cow pats are dried in the sun, then thrown, the winner being the person who tosses the cow pat the farthest.

'I got the idea during a trip to Oklahoma last year. After all, we have enough of the raw material lying around,' Mr Griffin said.

'There are several techniques, including throwing it like a Frisbee and pitching it like a cricket ball.'

The event also benefited local children's hospice charity, raising over £300 from entry fees and a charity auction.

Mr Griffin said, 'It was a great way to have fun and do some good in the community at the same time.'

Overall winner, Joshua Wood, 32, intends to donate his prize to the hospice.

There are plans to make the contest an annual event.

Scene Two

RUTH WELLS RUBBED HER EYES AND STRAIGHTENED THE KINK IN HER ACHING back. It was getting dark, and she reached across the desk to switch on the anglepoise lamp, trying not to send the piles of sermon notes, parish council agenda, and back issues of *Church Times* cascading onto the floor. Dimitri, startled by the noise, quit his spot on the filing cabinet, jumped down, and after a long, luxurious stretch of his stripy back, rubbed around her ankles.

She glanced at her watch. It was getting late. Three hours had flown by, and she needed to feed Dimitri, snatch a bite to eat, and bring in the washing before tonight's meeting. Working on the plays wasn't supposed to take her this long. It was only supposed to be a bit of fun, a hobby, a diversion, not something that would take over her life. She had originally planned to modernise all forty-eight plays in the cycle, then halved that number when she realised how long it would take. She concentrated on her favourites, those she could imagine being performed, but even that venture had taken her the best part of two years.

Dimitri seemed to think his supper was still an over-optimistic flight of fancy, closed his green eyes, and settled by the door for another forty winks.

Ruth stared at the screen. Just one more stanza, then she would prepare for the Deanery meeting. Ruth studied the manuscript and almost wept at Mary's words.

> Sich sorow forto se,
> My dere barn, on the,
> Is more mowrnyng to me
> Then any tong may tell.

Ruth typed slowly, stopping often to flick to the glossary at the back of her copy of *The Canterbury Tales*, regretting she hadn't paid more attention during her English class. Middle English, like Latin, seemed pointless when she was at school. Now she realised how much she would have benefited from both.

> Such sorrow do I see,
> My dear child, on you,
> Is more mourning to me
> Than any tongue can tell.

She clicked on the *save* icon. That would have to do for tonight. She would allow herself half an hour before breakfast to try to make it scan and read properly. She had long ago given up on forcing the lines into rhyme, simply to coax them into making sense to the contemporary ear. She had made a point of reading the modernised texts of the York plays and was startled at the similarity to the Monksford text. She wished she had the expertise, scholarship, and dedication of Beadle and King or good old Canon Purvis, but all she had was the will to do her best. After all, this was only Monksford, where nothing ever happened and a lost cat would make the news.

She shut down the computer and went into the hall to put on her coat. She picked up the newspaper from the doormat, glancing at the headline before she tucked it straight into the recycling bin. A sudden weariness overwhelmed her, and she flopped onto the antique pew that ran the length of the vicarage hallway. She saw her reflection in the mirror, and she felt old and dowdy. Her ginger hair, which Mother used to call strawberry blonde, was cut into a practical bob, and her round face made her look friendly and approachable, the sort of person others could confide in. And people were always telling her what a lovely bright smile she had. She would be forty-eight next birthday but people said they couldn't believe she was out of her thirties.

Unless, of course, people were lying.

Ruth had never felt young, slim, and attractive, even when she had been. Now she saw a dumpy middle aged woman with ginger hair and frumpy clothes and empty eyes.

'Dumpy Frumpy sat in the hall,' she sang to herself, then laughed out loud. Dimitri turned his back. She followed him to the kitchen and opened a tin of something purporting to be rabbit and game. He didn't complain. She went outside and threw her notebook, directions to the church in the village of Leaton Maynard, and her Bible onto the passenger seat of her battered Ford Fiesta. She returned to the house, turning the key in the oak door but leaving a light on in the hall, 'for the burglars' as her mother used to say. Ruth hoped the burglars would be grateful.

She eventually found St Gregory's Church, through a graveyard, up an alley, down an unlit country lane in a village in the middle of nowhere with totally inadequate signposts.

She was late as usual. Everyone was already sitting down in the pews, and heads turned as she came in. She hurried to a side table with an electric kettle and a stack of biscuits on a plate. She poured lukewarm water on some instant coffee granules – nothing was going to prevent her from getting her caffeine fix – then reached automatically towards the biscuits. Scottish shortbread petticoat tails, her favourite. But then, everything was her favourite. She pulled her hand back. If she was already feeling dumpy and frumpy, biscuits certainly wouldn't help. She hesitated a moment. The secretary gave a little cough. Ruth's hand shot out and she took two. *Oh, who cares if I'll never look like Jerry Hall*, she thought.

An ancient priest in a dusty black coat, who looked as if he had been resurrected for the occasion, opened the meeting with a solemn and sonorous prayer, then got down to business. Ruth glanced at the empty pews. Even the promise of free coffee and biscuits had not been sufficient to lure most of the local clergy from their sofas. The agenda itself looked less than scintillating, and the pervading smell of damp and musty hymnbooks made her wrinkle her nose in aversion. She smiled briefly at Canon Gregory Grindal, who was sitting, as usual, as far away as possible from the female clergy. *Perhaps if he ignores us, he thinks we will cease to exist*, she thought. She squirmed to find a comfortable position on the pew. Finally she settled with one elbow on the pew back and her cheek resting on her hand. The discussion of youth work around the parishes just about held Ruth's attention, but when it came to the treasurer's report and the feedback from General Synod, Diocesan Synod, and Bishop's Council, she could feel her eyelids drooping. The coffee wasn't doing its job.

The next thing she knew, a hand gently touched her shoulder.

'We occasionally offer shelter for the night, but I really can't recommend the pews. And I'm sure your bed is much more comfortable.'

Ruth sat up and wiped her hand across her chin, worried she had been dribbling. She recognised the man who stood over her: The new Deanery secretary.

'I'm so sorry! It wasn't as if I was bored or anything, it's just that I've been working quite hard, and I'm translating this play in my spare time and . . .' Ruth realised she was burbling and stopped. The man was smiling at her.

'I know the feeling.' The man's smile widened, and a little place in her heart warmed. He had kind blue eyes under bushy eyebrows.

Ruth quickly gathered up her agenda and notebook. The pages were still blank. Her report back to the church council would be interesting.

'I'll see you to your car. It's a bit gloomy out there.'

Ruth was an expert at getting to her car alone in gloomy churchyards. Since St Sebastian's one security light got vandalised last winter, it could win awards in Gloomy Churchyard of the Year competitions. But it was nice for someone to care enough to volunteer to walk with her. For a moment she thought he was going to offer her his arm, but he didn't. She waited in the porch while he extinguished the lights and locked the church door. A harvest moon hung in the sky, and a tawny owl shrieked as they picked their way along the rough gravel path.

'So, you're writing a play?' he said.

'Not writing it; just translating.'

'From what?'

'Middle English. It's the Mystery Play Cycle they found. Didn't you read about it in the papers?'

He shook his head. 'A mystery play, eh? Does anyone get horribly and brutally murdered?'

'Not that kind of mystery.' Ruth smiled. She wasn't sure if he was serious.

'Oh, you mean the "Mysteries of God".'

'Yes, that's more like it. In the fourteenth and fifteenth centuries many towns acted out stories from the Bible and other religious drama. York, Wakefield, Coventry, Chester … all had them.'

The man smiled and nodded. She still wasn't sure if he was serious. She carried on anyway.

'The city folk performed them in the streets, usually on the feast of Corpus Christi. The local guilds would take on different plays in the cycle: shipwrights building the ark, bakers being responsible for the Last Supper – all masters of their crafts – "mastery" plays, which is where the word "mystery" comes from.'

'I see,' he said.

Ruth was on a roll. Usually she could see a glazing of the eyes, a stifled yawn, when she reached this point, but he seemed fascinated. 'Turns out Monksford had its own cycle of plays. They think the manuscripts were hidden in the abbey until it was ransacked during the Reformation, then transferred to St Sebastian's where they'd lain for more than three hundred years. I'd heard the plays existed, but no one knew where the manuscripts were.

'Even if they had survived the dissolution of the monasteries, they were lost. They were rediscovered in the 1850s after a fire at St Seb's. The manuscripts were then kept in a vault in the old council chambers, near the town hall. The chambers were emptied a couple of years ago – just before they were demolished to make way for the new ring-road.'

He smiled. 'Actually, I'm pulling your leg. I was there when they found the manuscripts. Recently, I mean, not in the 1850s.'

They both laughed.

'You were in the chambers?'

'Yes, I was supervising the removal of old documents. I'm on the Town Council.' He held out his hand to her.

'Alistair Fry,' they said in unison.

Ruth realised that she had seen him in photographs in the local newspaper. He had stood virtually alone to object to plans to build the road through Monksford farmland. The groundswell of public opinion was enough to earn him the honour of being hailed as a local hero. Victory for the anti-road campaigners seemed assured but a last-minute vote by the other council members had reversed the decision, and the road went ahead. Fry and his supporters had been devastated, and work on the road had started.

'Sorry about the road,' Ruth said, not quite sure why she was sorry.

'Yes, I can't believe they all turned on us at the last minute. There's another bit of rural England interred under asphalt. Puff!' He waved his hand like a conjuror. A flash of pain crossed his face, as if he had knocked an old injury. Ruth felt a surge of compassion. She wanted to reach out to comfort him, but she didn't. He shrugged. 'C'est la vie!'

Ruth studied him in the moonlight as best she could without tripping on the rough ground. She had always imagined that moonlight softened the features, but it seemed to cast shadows on Alistair Fry's face, roughening his complexion, brutalising his features. He was wearing a tailored dark suit and a camel coat. His briefcase looked like Italian leather, not that Ruth knew what real Italian leather looked like, but this was how she had imagined it. Whenever she dreamed about having a husband, this was how the fantasy looked:

rugged, dependable, and prosperous. Lawyer, Town Councillor and secretary of Deanery Synod – here was a man who liked to sit on committees.

Ruth also remembered that Councillor Fry had a wife. Mrs Fry was as much the household name as her husband but for very different reasons.

Her cheeks warmed as she realised she was staring at him. He smiled that smile again, and her heart gave a little flip. Was he deliberately flirting? Ruth couldn't tell. But she knew that he was married, and she was a priest so there was nothing doing either way. They had reached their cars, his near the lych gate, hers several yards down the lane. He started walking with her, but she dismissed him with a wave.

'I'll be all right now. Thanks.'

'The pleasure has been all mine.' He turned back to his car. 'Good luck with the play.'

'Thanks,' Ruth called after him. She unlocked her car and sank into the driver's seat and turned the key in the ignition. The loneliness overwhelmed her. She was grateful that it was so dark. No one could see the tears burning down her cheeks.

Scene Three

JEMMA ARRIVED EARLY AT THE OFFICE ON FRIDAY MORNING. SHE WANTED TO make a good impression. In fact, she would be happy to make an impression of any kind. Since that slime-ball Richard dumped her and crawled off to his cesspit – who cared where – with some little heifer ... Jemma took a deep breath and started again. Since Chief Reporter Richard Sutton moved on, there was a vacancy, along with a pay rise, just waiting for the right person. And only one little exam away. One little exam that would be another rung on the ladder, another step nearer her dream job.

It wasn't that Jemma had a problem with Mohan Dattani; it was just that he treated her as if she were invisible. At first she had thought he treated everyone that way. Then she noticed he went out for drinks with the subeditors, invited the advertising department to his birth-day party, and even allowed drippy Saffy Walton to simper around him at pubs and parties. But not once had he invited Jemma.

Then there was Richard. Mo and Rich had been best pals. Mohan was almost as upset as Jemma had been when Richard left. Almost, but not quite. Jemma couldn't possibly replace Richard as Mohan's drinking buddy, and Mo obviously thought she wasn't good enough to fill Richard's shoes as chief reporter.

She would show him.

When a young father lost his wife and two of his children in a house fire, who was it that sat for hours in the coroner's court, listening to all the stomach-churning details? Who went to interview him when no one else would do it because they couldn't bear to face the raw grief and turn it into a sympathetic article? Who suggested the campaign for Christmas presents for him and his remaining child, an act that resulted in them being showered with gifts, even a Caribbean holiday? She was more than a journalist; she had helped rebuild two people's lives and had given a whole community the opportunity to feel good.

By the time Mohan and the rest of the department arrived, Jemma had convinced herself she was a cross between Gandhi and Lois Lane.

'Good morning,' she called cheerily as Mohan passed her desk. He headed towards his office without replying. Fortunately she had a plan. She reapplied her lipstick, undid another button on her blouse, poured a cup of freshly perked coffee, and knocked on Mohan Dattani's office door.

'Come in.'

Jemma leant over Mohan's desk and placed the mug of coffee in front of him.

'Thanks.' He looked surprised.

'I was making one, so I thought ...'

'Oh, Jemma – ' Mohan coughed and tapped his own shirt '– your, um ... button.'

'Thank you,' Jemma said. 'Must put a stitch in that buttonhole. Wouldn't want to draw attention to myself like that.' She buttoned her blouse up to her neck and sat defiantly in the seat opposite.

Before she could speak, he jumped in.

'Jemma, I'm glad you're here. I've been wanting to talk to you.'

'Yes, I was hoping I could catch up with you too.' This was her chance.

'What did you want to see me about?'

'It can wait. You fire away,' Jemma said.

'I've been watching your work recently ...'

She raised an eyebrow.

'... and I can't help noticing you're getting a little ... stale.'

She frowned. This wasn't what she had expected to hear at all. 'Stale? What's that supposed to mean?'

'Well, take your report on Bram Griffin's charity event in yesterday's paper. It seemed a little …' he looked at the ceiling, searching for the right adjective.

'Scatological,' suggested Jemma, thinking of the ingrained stains on her boots.

' … lacklustre,' said Mohan.

'It was a cow-pat throwing contest, not a Royal Wedding,' she said. 'What did you expect me to say? I got all the facts down, didn't I?'

His expression was one of disappointment mixed with pity, like a teacher explaining to a child the importance of bringing the correct equipment to a geometry lesson.

'Did you even turn up at the event?'

'Of course I did!' Jemma's face burned with indignation. She had the stains on her boots to prove it.

'I honestly couldn't tell from your article. It wasn't evocative. There was no atmosphere.'

'I spent most of my time trying not to tread in the "atmosphere".'

Jemma's little joke fell flat. Flat as a cow pat.

'You don't believe me do you?'

The coffee was getting cold.

'Believe you … ?' He gave a little laugh.

Jemma was regretting the coffee but not as much as she was regretting entering Mohan's office in the first place. If she had been of a more delicate disposition, she would have been crumbling by now.

'I'm just saying I need more from you. I care about your career, Jemma, but I care more about producing something that people want to read. They want someone who can hear the heartbeat of the community and reflect that on eighty black-and-white pages.' He paused, Jemma suspected, for dramatic effect. 'To that end I have a little plan …'

'Just get to the point, please, Mohan.' She didn't care if her irritation was starting to show. She had already shelved the idea of asking about Richard's job.

'Look at this.' He pushed a piece of paper across the desk. It was a press release, the kind that usually hastens its way straight into the wastepaper bin. Jemma scanned down the page.

'"Medieval mystery play" ... "community theatre" ... "great opportunity".' She handed the letter back to Mohan. 'Lovely, but what does it have to do with me?'

'Well, they've updated this old religious play they found. It's of great historic and local significance, a link straight back to medieval Monksford.' Jemma wondered if he had spent a previous life writing guidebooks for tourists. 'And they're auditioning actors to play the parts of the Bible people ...'

'Yeah, I read that bit.' Jemma folded her arms and sat back in the chair.

'Well, I thought you could take one of the parts then write about it for the paper.'

'A weekly column, you mean?'

There was a gardening column, a local events column, and a car repair column, each written by an ex-Fleet Street hack well beyond the age for retirement. Ten minutes ago Jemma was one step closer to the nationals, now she was a step nearer the scrap heap.

'What do you say? The readers would love it.' Mohan spread out his hands, smiling serenely.

'I think it's a terrible idea!'

'Why?'

'I came here to be a reporter. All I've had so far is grotty supermarket openings, road protests, horrible deaths, boring council meetings – oh, and the highlight, a cow-pat throwing contest, of all things.'

'Jemma, this is Monksford, not downtown Miami. This is what we do here, and these mystery plays are important. If you find the whole thing so tedious, might I suggest that you are in the wrong job? And judging by yesterday's article, perhaps you feel the same way?'

'No!' protested Jemma, seeing 'Fleet Street' and all her dreams slipping through her fingers like Swarfega.

'Then you'll go to the audition.'

'Are you asking me or telling me?'

'I'm asking you.'

Jemma took a deep breath. 'No way! Absolutely no way.'

He leaned forward, placing both hands on the desk. 'All right then, I'm telling you. Jemma, you are to audition for a part, get the part, act in the play, and write about your experience. You did drama as part of your English degree, or so it says on your application form.'

'Mohan, this is unfair. You can't force me to do this.'

'Of course I can't, but ...' He paused. 'I'm suggesting that you do it. It would be good for the community, good for the paper, which is good for me and good for you. Everyone benefits.'

Mohan rested his elbows on the desk, linked his fingers, and waited for Jemma's response. If there had been a white cat in the room, he would have been stroking it.

'How would it be good for me?' Jemma asked.

'It would indicate that you might be ready to start thinking about a promotion.'

'This is blackmail!'

'No, no! You should know better than that, Jemma. Call yourself a journalist? You must use words accurately. Blackmail involves money changing hands. This is not blackmail!' He gave a little snorting laugh. 'Technically this is extortion – "obtaining money or favours by intimidation, violence, or misuse of authority".'

Jemma opened her mouth, then closed it again. She wanted to flounce out of the room, slam the door, and start throwing things, but a monumental sulk might not be the approved method of handling this sort of employment dispute. She could always phone the union later.

'Okay, what you're saying is that I've got to do this if I want the senior reporter's job?'

'Put it this way: you need to demonstrate to me that you are ready for the added responsibility, and this would be a good way to do it.'

'What if I audition and don't get the part?'

'Then I know you're not trying very hard.'

'You've made up your mind about this, haven't you?'

'The contact number is at the bottom.' He pushed the paper over to Jemma again.

She picked up the letter, and with a look that said everything, she stood and walked out.

'HOW CAN HE DO THAT?' JEMMA THUMPED HER FISTS ON THE TABLE.

'Steady. He's your boss, he is supposed to be able to tell you what to do.' Lou calmly drained the last of her wine. 'Besides, getting involved in the mystery play would be good for you. Get you out, help you to meet people.'

'You make it sound as if I'm in need of therapy! I meet loads of people at work, and I'm hardly ever in the office. How much more gregarious can I be?'

'I don't mean meet "people"; I mean meet *people*, male people.'

'Ever the matchmaker. Look, I couldn't possibly think about anyone else at the moment. Besides I'm enjoying being young, free, and single.' Jemma raised her glass. 'Here's to spinsterhood.'

They clinked glasses.

'Except I'm not free, am I? I'm stuck doing this play because Mohan says so. That is beyond the call of duty.'

'Just smile sweetly, do the job … then clobber him with your overtime claim.'

'Excellent idea, with just one drawback,' said Jemma.

'What's that?'

'They don't pay overtime.'

'In that case, I'd better get the next round, you impoverished young hack, you.'

'Just another cola, please,' said Jemma. 'I'm driving.'

Lou looked heavenward and headed over to the bar with its mock-Tudor beams and horse brasses. The idea of getting plastered appealed to Jemma, but she really was driving, and she had work in the morning, and the feeling of sleeping on a boat, with the movement of the water was not a pleasant one if you were intoxicated. She had learnt that from experience.

The Fruiterer's Arms wasn't the most fashionable pub in Monksford, but it was friendly, did a good evening meal for under a fiver, and they had an admirable selection of real ales, which Richard liked … Jemma felt the slap of realisation. They had only come here at Lou's suggestion. They could have gone to any pub in the area. How, then, had they ended up here with memories as deeply ingrained as the smoke on the embossed ceiling? She wanted to run. Was it impossible to go anywhere without being reminded of Richard? When he first left, she thought of him constantly so the pain was always with her, but now she would go minutes, even hours without thinking about him, then suddenly – wallop! Her eyes stung, but she couldn't blame it solely on the farmer sitting behind her, his pungent coat, and equally pungent pipe tobacco.

Lou returned with the drinks. 'What's the matter with you?'

'Feeling a bit claustrophobic, that's all. I think I'll go home.'

Lou laid her hand on Jemma's arm. 'I brought you here to cheer you up, and you're not leaving until I do.'

They were in for a long haul then.

THE REFLECTIONS OF THE LIGHTS ALONG THE RIVERBANK QUIVERED SLIGHTLY as a cool breeze stirred the water. Jemma pulled up the handbrake and clicked the security lock shut on her steering wheel. She opened the boot and took out the torch she always carried, then crossed the towpath to where the *Ebony Hog* was moored. The river seemed calm and quiet, and there was no sign of anyone on the towpath. She heard a rustle in a nearby elder tree. She held her breath. A blackbird flew out, squawking, and she exhaled with relief.

The full moon was veiled in misty cloud. She glanced over to the twinkling rows of amber streetlamps in Monksford. She could see the two streams of lights: one red, receding, and one white, advancing along the bypass; and in the distance, the industrial estate with its state-of-the-art meat packing factory, illuminated like a football stadium. It was quiet, now, by the river, except for the rumble of traffic along the bypass and the water gently lapping on the boats' hulls.

She stopped and took a deep breath; the autumn smell of bonfires hung in the air, the outrider signalling winter's imminent arrival. She would need to buy extra gas to keep the central heating running through the winter. Shining the torch, she carefully climbed up the ramp and onto the deck. She fumbled for her keys and unfastened the padlock. Shutting the door behind her, she sighed with relief. She was home.

Jemma put on the kettle for tea, found the letter about the auditions, and opened her laptop. She typed 'Mary Magdalene' into the search engine. Her drama teacher had always encouraged her to research the character she would be portraying. She needed to get inside Mary Magdalene's head if she was going to play her.

The Internet connection was running slow. She sat back with a sigh, thinking she could have waited until she got to work tomorrow. But like a Boy Scout she wanted to be prepared even though last month her phone bill came to nearly as much as her mooring fees.

'Bingo!'

There was certainly no shortage of information about Mary Magdalene on the Internet, and before long Jemma learnt that Mary was one of Jesus' most significant female followers and that he had cast seven demons out of her. She was one of the women who witnessed his crucifixion and saw him laid in the tomb. Mary was the first one to witness his resurrection.

'So, Mary Magdalene, what were you really like?' she whispered.

Jemma glanced at her watch. The clock at St Sebastian's concurred by striking midnight. Jemma stood up and closed her notepad.

At the end of nearly an hour, she knew less about Mary than when she started.

Was she the woman caught in adultery? Some sources claimed so, but there was no proof. Had Mary been a prostitute, and if so, why was she hanging around with this holy man? And why had he bothered to spend time with her? Surely the Son of God would have no time for women of that sort. What about his reputation? And that was assuming their relationship was purely platonic. She also found a lot of other material from various groups that claimed that Jesus had married Mary, fathered her children, and that they had come to live in Europe. But as far as Jemma could work out, that information wasn't corroborated.

As for the seven demons ...

Jemma shut down the Internet connection and folded the screen on her laptop. She started to undress for bed, her thoughts still whirling, grumbling, as she moved the three black bags from the bed onto the floor. She gave each of them a kick for good measure. How dare he clutter her space with his remains? When she had rather unceremoniously dumped his book, spare contact lens case, toothbrush, and shaver, as well as several jackets and jumpers and a pair of trainers, into black bin-bags, she wondered if there was any permanent reminder of their relationship. True, the hot water tap didn't leak any more, but that was all. Two years of their lives and her single keepsake was a tap washer. The only place he remained was in her mind, and if she had her way, he would soon be evicted from there too. Anger welled up inside her. She couldn't stand this clutter, the evidence of two wasted years, any longer. She had to get him out, now. Out of her life, out of her boat, and out of her head.

She couldn't decide which would be worse: Richard coming to get his things or taking them to his new place herself. The latter was out of the question, as she didn't even have his address. Part of her really wanted to just take them to the side of the boat and gently tip the contents into the river. Instead, she gathered them up and grabbed the keys. She squeezed the bags through the narrow cabin door and hauled them up onto the deck. The temptation to ditch them overboard resurfaced.

With the torch under one arm and both hands full, Jemma struggled down the ramp and across the towpath. House clearance in one's pyjamas in the early hours was an odd sight, she was certain. If someone did step out of the shadows, and she shivered at the thought, it was too dark to witness the deed. She dragged the bags over to where her car was parked and stuffed them into the boot of her hatchback, struggling to get it closed.

'I hope they get stolen,' she muttered.

With a shiver, Jemma held the torch out in front of her and followed its unsteady beam back to the river. The dew on the grass soaked into her slippers. She carefully skipped over a muddy patch. A noise behind her in the bushes made her jump.

'A fox,' she said aloud, just in case it wasn't.

Like a child running down a dark corridor from the bathroom, she sprinted up the ramp onto the *Ebony Hog*. She bolted the door behind her and leapt into her bed, pulling the covers up around her head. For the first time in months, she wished Richard was there. She could snuggle up to him, and he would soothe away her fear.

Her breathing slowed but her skin prickled, and the volume on her senses seemed to have been tuned to 'high'.

'A fox,' she said again, more quietly this time. She had left the rubbish bin on the deck and expected to hear it being overturned at any minute.

Nothing.

Then she heard the footsteps. They crunched slightly on the gravely path. Even footsteps, the long stride and flat heels of a man. No particular hurry, but not dawdling either. Perhaps a late dog walker.

The footsteps were getting closer now. Jemma struggled to swallow her fear.

She tried to take a deep breath, but her chest seemed full. She tried to exhale, as if she could breathe out this irrational fear. The tightness gripped her chest, and the breath would hardly come.

The footsteps still approached. Then they halted. Right beside her ear.

She kept motionless. Perhaps he was stopping to light a cigarette or to get his bearings. She heard him walk back a few paces, towards the stern then back again. Was he waiting for someone ... or searching for something?

Finally the footsteps moved on, upstream towards Monksford. She heard the metallic clang as they crossed the bridge. Jemma could breathe again.

Trembling slightly, she inched her way out of the berth and edged down to the galley. She grabbed the largest and sharpest knife in her collection and, gripping the handle, lay back in bed, listening ... always listening.

Then she heard it, a single loud splash, a short distance upriver. Too big to be a pebble and too small to be a body. Her nerves jangled like a wind chime as she strained to hear the faintest sound. Had the man come back to search the river? This time, it didn't sound like someone searching, but like something being dropped into the river.

Only silence filled the night. She lay awake for what seemed like hours, listening, grasping the knife.

JEMMA WOKE WITH A START. HER HAND STILL CLUTCHED THE HANDLE OF THE knife, and the sunlight that streamed through the crack in the curtains glinted on the blade. Her knuckles were stiff and her head ached. She slid the knife back into the drawer, filled the kettle, and put on a jumper. Autumn was definitely on its way. Gingerly she pulled back the bolt on the door and stuck her head outside. The towpath no longer seemed threatening. Raymond Jones, Jemma's nearest neighbour, was standing on the deck of his boat, the *Endeavour*, shaving.

Jemma looked up and down the towpath. She wasn't surprised to find there was no sign of the stranger from last night.

'Morning!' Jemma called to Ray.

He answered with a wave.

She ducked back inside the *Hog* and quickly dressed. Once outside, she walked to the place where she calculated the splash had originated and studied the greenish water. There were no broken twigs, no places of flattened grass. It was a favourite spot for anglers, and she often found their discarded tackle. Even now, a luminous orange-topped float bobbed just out of her reach. The gravel path displayed no footprints, and the mud by the water's edge had too many prints to identify a single one.

Besides, she didn't know what she was looking for. All she had heard was a splash. It could have been a worker returning from night shift, throwing away the egg sandwiches his wife had lovingly made him and he didn't have the heart to tell her he detested. It could even be, Jemma thought with a touch of cynicism, a jilted lover disposing of their ex's worldly goods in a fit of pique. Yet her instinct, which she liked to think of as journalist's intuition, could not accept these rational explanations. What others interpreted as prying, Jemma thought of as a highly evolved sense of curiosity.

She walked along the bank until she reached the *Endeavour*. 'Ray, did you hear anything unusual last night?'

'Pardon?' said Ray. 'Hang on a minute, I'll just get my hearing aid. I wasn't expecting visitors.'

That answered Jemma's question. She stayed another quarter of an hour, discussing mooring fees and the cost of heating; then she made her excuses and returned to the *Hog* to get ready for work. She would have to put her curiosity on hold, at least for now. This time her assignment was to report on an open day at the Animal Sanctuary. It seemed Mohan was determined to mire her completely in the agricultural life.

This time Jemma wore Wellington boots.

Scene Four

RUTH SNEAKED OUT HER NOVEL, A ROMANCE – A WONDERFUL ANTIDOTE TO THE intensity of the mystery plays – and found the right page. She opened it, bending it back on its spine so Elsinor Heartman's name was less obvious and the couple in a passionate clinch on the front was not quite so visible. Ruth glanced up to see if anyone had come in to view the Harvest decorations, wondering if, for appearance's sake, she would rather be discovered reading the Bible or kneeling in prayer. Ruth hesitated for a moment then returned to *Love's Passionate Embrace*. If any of her parishioners had a problem with that, they would have to take it up with Elsinor Heartman!

The church seemed to glow in the late September sun. A shaft of sunlight stabbed through a break in the clouds and shattered the stained glass into fragments of light that gilded the nave. The brass on the altar glinted for all it was worth, as if it had a long cherished ambition to be mistaken for gold. The varnished wheat-sheaf loaf glowed golden too. Then the sunlight was gone. A grainy dullness returned to St Sebastian's, and Ruth heard the rain fall once again on the slate roof and wondered if she should check for any new leaks.

She looked around the church. She would have liked it to stand open all year, but the threat of theft and vandalism restricted it to special occasions – Christmas, Easter, and Harvest – and then someone was required to be on duty, to welcome visitors and maintain security. This time that someone was her. To be honest, she enjoyed the peace and quiet, and it afforded her the opportunity to do something very rare and precious in her busy life, time to sit and read. Bored with her novel, she closed it and walked around the chancel, admiring the adornments. The large pumpkin; the orange, yellow, and white chrysanthemums, their heads as big and round as footballs; the produce, some homegrown, some shop-bought, crowding the altar steps and every ledge and windowsill; the swathes of hop-bines – all boasted of God's abundance to Monksford. Ruth's heart swelled with pride at the generosity of the people of the town. Soon the church would be in a position to give a gift back to the community – the gift of a play.

There was a clatter outside, and Ruth guiltily tucked her book under a parish magazine that lay next to her on the pew. The door swung open, and three women, all with tight grey perms all but hidden under plastic rain hats entered. They shook their umbrellas over the rush matting. Ruth hurried over to them, holding the umbrella stand.

'Oooh, thank you, dear. It's raining cats ...'

'... and dogs ... out there.'

Ruth nodded her head as the women spoke, almost in unison, two of them finishing off the phrase for the other one.

'Welcome to St Seb's, ladies.' She swept her arm in an extravagant gesture before launching into her tour-guide speech. 'Extensively rebuilt in the nineteenth century following a fire, there has been a place of Christian worship on this site since Norman times ...'

She started near the door at the stone font, then led them up the aisle.

'These brasses commemorate those who died in the First World War, and this window, showing the raising of Jairus's daughter, was a bequest from the Freeman family.'

She pointed out the oak lectern, carved as a giant eagle, its wings extended, supporting the Bible, which was open to 2 Corinthians, chapter 9. The shorter of the old women stood on the platform. 'Oh, look at this! "Each man should give what he has decided in his heart to give, not reluctantly or under compulsion, for God loves a ..."'

'" ... cheerful giver."' The other ladies chimed. All three giggled, and Ruth guided them past the box that bore the legend 'St Sebastian's Church. Please give generously to the parish fund.' Ruth was disappointed to note that the Bible passage had no effect. The ladies listened and nodded appreciatively at Ruth's commentary. They paused near the harvest produce.

'Ooh, aren't there some lovely ...,' said one.

'... gifts,' finished the other two.

'And the flowers! Don't they look ...'

'... beautiful.'

Ruth conducted them up the aisle, towards the chancel arch, then back to the font near the door. She stood in full view of the donations box, shook each of them warmly by the hand, and invited them to next week's service. Short of wrenching the box from the wall and rattling it in their faces, Ruth didn't know what else to do to promote the restoration fund. They ignored her intimations and reclaimed their umbrellas.

'We knew your mother you know. Isn't it a ...'

'... pity.'

'And you're a such a lovely girl, isn't she a lovely ...'

'... girl.'

Ruth sat down again and tried to resume her reading, but her thoughts kept drifting towards Alistair Fry. They had a tendency to do that too often these days. Was she starting to develop some kind of feelings for him? A crush?

A middle-aged vicar and a married man – ludicrous. She offered the ridiculous thought to God, then felt ridiculous for even having thought it.

She had seen those headlines – 'Vicar Runs Off with Sunday School Teacher.' And she had joined in the collective tutting and head shaking. Funny that there never seems to be headlines screaming, 'Vicar Stays with Spouse of Twenty Years' or even 'Vicar Preaches Fantastic Sermon.'

She prayed a little more, then tried to analyse her feelings. Was it a physical attraction? There was no denying he was a handsome man, in a rugged sort of way. But no, she wrinkled her brow. Then it hit her. It was because he took notice of her. He made her feel she mattered.

She had spent her whole life being invisible – the good student, the loving, dutiful daughter, the supportive friend, the vicar. Sometimes she felt like running away, just disappearing, and she wondered just how long it would take anyone to realise she was gone. A few hours? Two days? Several months? Would they ever notice?

In the weeks after her mother had died, she felt like a grey ghost moving around her house and parish. She had refused to take time off deciding, against the advice of the Bishop, it would be better if she kept busy. In truth, she remembered very little of those weeks. It was as if she had died, not her mother, and just her essence, cold and insubstantial like a cobweb, remained.

People had shown their concern in a polite and distant way, bringing flowers and cards, asking how she was coping, but there was no one to hold her when she sat weeping in the night.

Meeting Alistair, having him offer to walk her to her car, taking an interest in the play, made her feel special. Ruth knew that romance was out of the question, but what about friendship? More than anything else, Ruth wanted him to be her friend. She picked up her book again. Didn't the picture of the hero on the front look just a little like Alistair?

A blast echoed around the church like machine-gun fire. Ruth's first instinct was to drop to the floor. Before she could move, another burst rattled the stained glass of the beatitudes window. Why would anyone with a machine gun attack the church?

Then anger took over. She threw down her book and dashed to the door. It flew open, almost knocking her off her feet. A group of six teenage boys barged past her into the church.

'Excuse me, you can't come in here.' Ruth's indignant voice echoed off the cold stone.

'Yes, we can. It says so on the notice outside. "All welcome".'

She should have considered the wording more carefully, perhaps settling on something more pointed such as: 'All except teenage thugs and batty old ladies welcome.' Unfortunately, as a parish church, exclusivity was not an option. The boys had split up, one was rifling through the stack of hymnbooks, one was in the pulpit shouting out a mock sermon, two were lounging in the pews, one had vaulted over the communion rail and was behind the altar, and still another looked as if he was trying to eat the flower arrangement. Ruth shook from a combination of rage and fear.

'Would you leave now, please!' Her voice sounded weak and shrill. The lad in the pulpit mimicked her. None of the boys moved from their stations.

The boys in the pews had taken out cigarettes and were about to light up. Ruth took a deep breath, reminding herself not to take it personally. After all, they didn't understand what they were doing. They meant no real harm. She lowered her voice and gripped the pew end tightly, to stop shaking.

'Excuse me,' she said, more forcefully. 'I'm afraid you can't smoke in here.'

'Why not?' The boy in the grey hooded sweatshirt and navy baseball cap squinted up at her, lighter in hand.

'This is the house of God,' as if that would mean anything to these boys. 'And you're not allowed to smoke in here.'

'Says who?' The boy was obviously not going to take notice of Ruth.

'Says the vicar, and that's me.'

The boy in the pew next to him, wearing a red hooded sweatshirt and a white baseball cap, swore at her. He spat out the expletive with such venom that Ruth, who considered herself broadminded and not easily offended, had to blush.

There was a crash. The boy at the altar, navy hooded sweatshirt, black cap, had knocked over one of the large brass candlesticks. She pictured the dent and groaned quietly.

'Can you come away from there, please?'

'I didn't do nothing,' the boy said.

The boys in the pew had lit their cigarettes and were flicking ash onto the Victorian tiled floor.

The boy that had been in the pulpit was now sitting in the font. He laughed. 'How do you flush it?'

Ruth's anger was now at boiling point. She fumbled in her pocket to find her mobile phone. This was outrageous; they were defiling God's house – no, worse than that – they were ridiculing everything she believed in. She started to dial 999. Her fingers hovered over the last digit. They were mocking God and doing it very convincingly.

When Jesus stood before Pilate the crowds mocked him. As she had translated those words for the play, she wondered how it was possible to show such utter contempt towards another human being, let alone towards the Son of God. Hearing similar words as they spewed from their lips, here in the church, shook her to the core.

She looked into the boys' faces, so young but already so much hatred in their eyes. She frowned. There was something familiar about them.

She hesitated, studying them more closely. Then it came to her. They had all attended the local primary school where she had regularly spoken at assembly.

The one at the altar, the ginger-haired one, was Danny Milner. The one who had sat in the font was Andrew Coates. She didn't remember the names of the two boys smoking in the pews, but the one who was carefully dismantling the flower arrangement next to the vestry was Ryan Martin. They had all been cheeky, lively, freckle-faced little boys. Ryan had played Joseph one year in the school nativity play. They didn't look sweet now.

Ryan's father had committed suicide five years ago. Ruth led the funeral service. Little Ryan had looked so lost among the mourners, his big eyes frightened and confused, not sure if he was allowed to cry. Now he was no more than a vandal, probably with several petty crimes behind him and a future in prison.

She had to intervene. She tucked the phone in her pocket and walked over to him.

'Hello, Ryan,' she said.

Ryan dropped the dahlia he had plucked from the arrangement. 'H-how did you know my name?'

'I don't know if you remember me; I'm Reverend Wells. I used to come to your school.'

Ryan shrugged, then sidled towards the pair of smokers. Safety in numbers, she thought, as she followed him.

'How's your mum now, Ryan?'

He spun round, stung by the question. 'Fine,' he said a little too quickly.

'I was worried about her, you know. Well, I was concerned about all of you.' Dirty tricks, but all of it was true, and her worries were justified.

Ryan's mates started sniggering.

'Shut up!' He punched them both. For a moment, Ruth feared that a full-scale fight was going to break out.

'I was especially worried about you, Ryan. I wondered how you would cope after your dad . . .' If Ryan could have become liquid and oozed off the pew, his expression said he would have. 'You and your mum would both be welcomed in church at any time – ' She was interrupted by a crash. The boy at the altar had knocked over the side table. She couldn't tell if it was accidental or deliberate, although she suspected the latter.

'You know we've had a lot of problems with vandalism at this church.'

'It wasn't us! We never done nothing!' Ryan said.

'I didn't say it was.' A plan flew into her mind. She smiled and shot a prayer of thanksgiving heavenward. 'What do you think about Jesus?'

The boys sniggered again.

'No, I'm really interested,' she said. One of the boys gave an answer she pretended not to hear.

'He was that dude in the Bible,' Danny Milner said. Despite appearances, perhaps he had been awake during her assemblies.

Ruth resisted the urge to hit them with the whole gospel. 'That's right,' she said. 'And some of the stuff he did was pretty amazing, even by today's standards.'

The boys, sensing a sermon coming on, started to migrate towards the door.

'Wait, boys,' she called.

That wasn't part of her plan. Ten minutes ago, she would have given anything to rid the church of them. Now, more than anything, she needed them to stay. She went towards the door and stood blocking the way.

'Hang on. I don't want you to go yet. How would you like to be in a play?' The boys couldn't have moved faster if she had shouted, 'Fire!'

Ruth knew the phrase 'a volunteer is worth more than ten pressed men', but she had made up her mind.

'Listen, we need people to act in our play. I want people to be in the crowd. All you have to do is shout and – '

The boys streamed out of the door and through the graveyard, heading for the lych gate.

'I'll pay you!' Ruth yelled, hoping they wouldn't notice the note of desperation in her voice.

Two of the boys carried on, but Andrew, Ryan, Danny, and one of the smokers, stopped and turned round.

'How much?' asked Danny.

'Five pounds each.'

They laughed and carried on walking.

'Ten,' she called. They didn't turn round. 'Fifteen quid each – my final offer.' She would worry about getting the ninety pounds later.

Suddenly she had their interest.

'And we don't have to do none of that holy stuff, right?' Ryan said.

'Right.' Though Ruth had no idea what that 'holy stuff' was. 'I'll give you a fiver each if you turn up at the auditions on Tuesday and the other ten when the show's finished.' The boys nodded and swaggered off through the lych gate, probably calculating how many cigarettes they could buy with their earnings.

She breathed a deep sigh and put her hand against her chest. Her heart was beating a samba rhythm. She had done it. Not only had she got the boys to leave the church without calling the police, she had drummed up an angry mob (well, a tiny percentage of an angry mob). She went back into the church, swept up the cigarette ash, picked up the brass candlestick that miraculously was not dented, and straightened the altar cloth ready for the next onslaught of visitors.

The mob was sorted. Now the only problem was the rest of the cast.

RUTH GLANCED LEFT AND RIGHT, THEN HURRIED ACROSS THE HIGH STREET, running the last few yards as a delivery van swept past her. She unfurled the bundle of posters under her arm and pulled one out: 'Monksford Mystery Plays – Come and Join In.'

She needed as much publicity as possible for the auditions. She felt sure that Ronnie Mardle was already grooming favoured members of Monksford Operatic and Dramatic Society, MOADS for short, and was desperate for free rein. She withdrew the key and opened the glass-panelled doors on the village notice board. She looked over her shoulder, then unpinned the notice for the Women's Institute talk entitled 'Hang Gliding for the Over Seventies' and replaced it with her poster.

'What's that, then?'

Ruth turned, startled, to see an elderly man wearing a flat tweed cap, a gabardine raincoat, and enormous spectacles standing behind her.

'It's about the mystery plays. Monksford is reviving its own medieval tradition. They show the creation of the world, Noah's flood, the story of Christ, and the last judgement.'

'Well, I don't think it's right.' He put his hands on his hips and jutted out his stubbly chin.

Ruth frowned. 'What's not right?'

'Messing with Bible stories. Turning them into a spectacle. Is nothing sacred?'

Ruth rubbed her hand over her mouth to hide her smirk. 'These are sacred plays. They're very old, you know. They date from the thirteen hundreds. The people of Monksford used to perform them on the feast of Corpus Christi. It was before ordinary people had copies of the Bible.'

'How does that work then?' The old man blinked owlishly.

'Well, actors take the parts of the people in the Bible stories, and instead of reading them, you watch them being acted out.'

He shook his head again. 'It's not right. Have you got a man playing Jesus?'

'We hope to have.'

The old man turned puce. 'It's not right! You can't have Jesus looking like an ordinary man – he's the Son of God!'

'The Son of God did look like an ordinary man – as far as we know. "For us and for our salvation he came down from heaven: by the power of the Holy Spirit he became incarnate from the Virgin Mary, and was made man." There's no reason to think he looked any different from any other Jewish men at that time.'

'You can't have Jesus looking like a Jew!' Bubbles of spittle formed at the corners of the old man's mouth.

'But Jesus was a Jew!' Ruth could see she was fighting a losing battle. A small crowd was gathering.

'Well, it isn't right. It's blasphemy. It's idolatry. "Thou shalt not make unto thee any graven image, or any likeness of any thing that is in heaven above, or that is in the earth beneath, or that is in the water under the earth."'

He was breathing rapidly now, and a vein in his neck pulsed. Ruth worried he would have a heart attack. 'A judgement will be upon you, mark my words ...,' he spluttered.

'I'm sorry you feel that way Mr ...'

'Giddings.'

'Mr Giddings, we're sticking very closely to the Bible accounts, so I hope it won't be blasphemous. And we're not worshipping the actor playing Jesus, so it has nothing to do with idolatry.'

'Well, it's just not right!' Mr Giddings gave a final glance at the poster, shook his head morosely, and shuffled away into the Post Office.

Ruth sighed and smiled weakly at the onlookers. The auditions were just the first step. The responsibility for the performance weighed heavily upon her. She would delegate the day-to-day tasks to Harlan Westacre and Ronnie Mardle, but it made her uneasy – as if she were selling her children. She wanted the whole production to belong to her and hated having to share it. Once she had opened those ancient texts, a bond had formed. Ruth and the mystery plays had become inseparable.

She couldn't deny that Ronnie, the operetta producer, and Harlan, the choir mistress, possessed talents she didn't. She would just have to grit her teeth and get on with it. Much as she wanted to, she couldn't do it all alone. One offer of help that was slightly easier to accept was from Alistair. She had just finished arranging a meeting with Ronnie and Harlan a few days before, when the phone rang. His deep voice had soothed her and a thrill shot through her.

'How is it going?' he had asked.

'Harlan and Ronnie are driving me mad, I can't find anyone to play God, and I'm two baritones short for the choir; apart from that, everything's rosy.'

'I can't sing,' he had said, 'and I'm no Laurence Olivier, but I'll do whatever I can.'

'Well, you've already managed to secure a pretty hefty financial contribution from Monksford Town Council. We're having a preliminary meeting tomorrow night. We're desperate for help with admin, and,' she said, her tone coy, 'we need a treasurer.'

'Nothing would give me greater pleasure.'

Ruth smiled. Alistair would be the perfect antidote to Harlan, the black widow, and Ronnie, the human marshmallow. The crowd had drifted away. She gathered her posters and drawing pins and stuffed them in a carrier bag. She took a final look at the poster and headed across the road to the general store.

Now, to buy some biscuits. Ginger creams or bourbons? Or both?

DIMITRI WOVE ROUND HER ANKLES, ALMOST TRIPPING HER, AS RUTH TRIED TO elbow the lounge door open. Just as she managed to push the handle down without the cups sliding off the tray or the milk slopping, the door opened, and she almost fell through. Dimitri ran to claim his territory under the radiator. Harlan Westacre tutted impatiently and jumped up to steady the tray.

'Almost lost that lot,' she said. 'Here, let me take it.'

If it had been anyone else, Ruth would have been grateful for the offer, but Harlan had a knack of making Ruth feel uncomfortable, even here in her own home.

'I can manage, thanks,' she chirped.

Ruth had read it was possible to tell a false smile from a genuine one because a false one only makes the mouth smile while a real smile lights up the eyes too. As she grinned at Harlan, she fervently hoped Harlan hadn't read the same article.

'Is it Lapsang?' Harlan asked.

'It's fair trade.' Ruth poured the tea, trying not to let her hand shake. She handed Harlan a mug that had come free at the petrol station.

Harlan wrinkled her nose. 'It's so difficult to get the stains out of cheap earthenware, isn't it?'

Ruth wished she had unpacked the best china.

'Hmmm, wet and warm.' Harlan wiped her lipstick smears from the mug. Dimitri sidled up and rubbed his head against Harlan's legs. Cats were poor judges of character. She shooed him away.

Ruth offered the plate of biscuits. 'Bourbon or ginger cream?'

Harlan shook her head vigorously, her wind-chime earrings tinkling like a clarion. Of course, Harlan wasn't a biscuit eater; Ruth should have known. You don't get pencil thin and granite hard from eating crème-filled biscuits. *Never trust a non-biscuit-eater,* Ruth reminded herself. She knew that small talk was the order of the day, but her talk was so small that it masqueraded as total silence.

She craned her thin neck forward. 'So, Ruth, how was Harvest this year?'

Ruth swallowed hard. *Yes, we had Harvest, no thanks to you,* was the answer on the tip of her tongue. Harlan's sarcasm detector was probably set to 'Seek and destroy', so Ruth restrained herself. 'We had hoped you could provide some girls to supplement the choir as usual ...'

'Naturally,' Harlan said. 'I'm disappointed, but with the choir festival on Saturday and Christmas coming up, I'm afraid we had other priorities. Such a pity as we've just finished a unit on choral music, and the girls have recently been working on Rutter. Still, we hope to do something special for Christmas. Should help to make St Sebastian's carol service something unique this year. You know, lift it out of the ordinary and humdrum.'

Ruth's hackles were up, but she bit her tongue, kept her voice steady and her expression neutral. 'Sounds lovely.' Ruth performed another smile.

'Of course,' Harlan said, 'the mystery play must have suitable musical and choral interludes. In fact, here is a draft score.' She waved a sheaf of papers under Ruth's nose. Ruth couldn't admit that she didn't read music.

'It's a modern arrangement. I wrote it myself, naturally.' Harlan said.

Ruth's argument about authenticity was doomed from the start. For one thing, Monksford no longer possessed the traditional guilds to perform the play. For another, she had no intention of dragging carts around the town as stages for the performers.

To Ruth's relief, the doorbell rang. She excused herself and rushed into the hall. She could see Alistair Fry's form distorted by the patterned glass, and her heart seemed to stop for a moment. She straightened her jumper and smoothed her hair. Dimitri joined her in the hall. She opened the door.

'Alistair, so glad you could come.' She smiled.

'You sounded as if you could do with some moral support.'

She was about to volunteer to take his coat and to offer him tea or coffee when Ronnie Mardle huffed and puffed his way up the path, and Ruth felt duty bound to abandon Alistair and welcome Ronnie. She let out a little sigh of regret as she opened the lounge door to let Alistair through to Harlan's lair.

'Ruth, my love.' Ronnie grabbed her by the shoulders and planted a slightly slimy kiss on each of Ruth's cheeks.

'Ronnie, how are you?'

'Been better, dear, been better. Where's your loo? Got a touch of … you know.'

Ruth didn't know, and she definitely didn't want to know. 'Up there and first left.' Before the words were out of her mouth he had jogged up the stairs, his bottom wobbling with each step.

She resisted the urge to wipe the kisses off and went through the kitchen to put the kettle on to boil again. She poked her head into the lounge. To her relief, Harlan and Alistair seemed to be involved in amicable conversation. She could see Harlan's earrings swinging like chandeliers in a wind as she laughed at Alistair's jokes. She wanted to be in there laughing too, not stuck in the kitchen like a serving wench. She felt a warm hand on her shoulder. 'Just to let you know, dear, you're out of toilet paper.'

'Thanks, Ronnie, I'll change the roll later.'

'I'll go through, shall I? Can I take anything?'

Ruth shook her head, and they both made their way through to the lounge, Ronnie making a beeline for Ruth's favourite chair. It had been Mother's chair and she felt rather possessive about it. She perched herself uncomfortably on a dining room chair. Dimitri settled at her feet.

'Alistair was just telling me that he has persuaded the council to put up five thousand pounds towards the cost of the production. Isn't that marvellous?' Harlan said.

It certainly was; they all nodded in approval.

'And I'm assuming the church will be putting up a similar amount . . . ,' she added.

Ruth managed not to laugh out loud. Five thousand might replace the missing tiles on the roof or stop the woodworm in the bell tower or pay for Mr Briggs to go private for his hip operation, but fritter it on the mystery play? There was no way they could possibly raise five thousand pounds. They didn't even make fifty in last week's collection.

'I was thinking more in terms of providing manpower, free meeting, and rehearsal rooms, abundant tea and coffee and, of course, a spiritual input,' Ruth said.

'Oh.' Harlan's well-plucked eyebrows shot up.

'As treasurer, I'd like to say that I think a financial contribution from St Sebastian's would be completely inappropriate,' said Alistair. 'I hope Ruth won't mind me saying so, but she has come close to wearing herself ragged with the hours upon hours of work she has put into undertaking the translation of the text. And that doesn't include the time spent organising the publicity, calling the auditions, and arranging the rehearsals, and all that on top of her parish duties.'

Harlan gave a little snort. Ruth ignored her. Nothing could take away the sudden warmth in her heart from his approbation. Alistair had supported her – no – more than supported her, he had endorsed her, been her advocate. She squirmed on her hard chair; the struts were digging into her back, and her behind was becoming numb. She watched Ronnie, his fat rump overhanging the seat. He didn't need soft cushions; he had sufficient padding of his own.

As the meeting went on, Ruth grew increasingly uncomfortable and increasingly resentful. Not only was it the most comfortable chair in the room, and not only was it her chair, but she had planned to save it for Alistair, the only reason this evening was bearable … She checked her thoughts. She just had to stop thinking about Alistair in this way. Like a schoolgirl with a crush …

'… sixty giggling schoolgirls, all with a crush on the latest "pop idol" is not my idea of solemn or portentous.' Ronnie Mardle seemed to be conducting his own imaginary orchestra as he spoke. His arms swung in wide arcs, and Ruth was starting to fear for her crockery. 'This play calls for something with more of the sense of the numinous, something more majestic, orchestral – '

'Nonsense!' Harlan's scrawny neck stretched out like a turkey's, and her earrings oscillated furiously. 'My girls are as disciplined and proficient as any professional group of musicians. My choirs have won awards and received acclaim from the highest quarters. What are you bringing to this production – a glorified chorus line? They'll turn the whole thing into a carnival, a circus!'

'How dare you!' spat Ronnie. 'How dare you compare my highly trained cast with your bunch of simpering, frivolous bobby-soxers.'

'Actually, a festive atmosphere would be in keeping …,' Ruth began.

Harlan bulldozed through Ruth's words. 'What are you suggesting? That MOADS are let loose on it? Heaven forbid!'

'The *Monksford Gazette* described our *Camelot* as "breathtaking and stunning",' countered Ronnie.

'That meant they couldn't breathe for laughing and felt as if they had been hit with a sledgehammer.'

'You poisonous old witch! If you think your troupe of singing gnomes can possibly provide anything with sufficient gravitas – '

'At least they can sing in tune, unlike the band of half-witted, talentless has-beens and wannabes that constitute the Monksford Operatic and Dramatic Society.'

'Ladies and gentlemen …' Alistair held up his hands to silence the pair. Then he turned to her, looking perplexed. As if now that he had obtained silence, he didn't know quite what to do with it. There had been no chance to forewarn him, besides it would have been difficult to explain this elaborate ritual, this war dance, in a way that wouldn't make her appear deranged.

They always started off like this. The truth was, both Harlan's choir and Ronnie's actors and singers would do a terrific job, she just couldn't tell them that, at least not in front of the other. She had once tried to avoid the confrontation by arranging two separate meetings, one for Harlan and one for Ronnie. Her efforts had failed miserably and served only to convince each that some kind of conspiracy was going on. Far better to let them slog it out first.

'I can see I'm not required here.' Ronnie stood up petulantly. 'Ruthie, darling, you have my number if you need me.' He flounced into the hall. Ruth shot Alistair a glance, then followed Ronnie out. As Harlan continued to sound off to Alistair, Ruth closed the door behind her and mustered her most beguiling tone for the job of placating Ronnie, whose feathers were not just ruffled, he was close to pecking himself bald. She could only hope that tomorrow's auditions would prove easier going.

Scene Five

JEMMA LAY ON HER BERTH, GAZING AT THE WOODEN CEILING. SHE WAS FURIOUS with Mohan for dragooning her into auditioning for the role and furious with herself for accepting. Could she have refused? Not without seriously damaging her career as well as her credibility with Mohan. No, she was resigned to the column and the audition for the lousy play.

She rolled over, pulled a script off her desk, and read it aloud once more, just to establish it in her mind. Everyone had their own technique for learning words. When she was at university, the students had discussed how best to memorise a script. She had favoured recording it on tape, then playing it as she went to sleep, hoping the lines would embed themselves subliminally in her brain.

She had thought hard about what to perform for her audition piece. She again considered her options as she flicked through her drama folder from university. The Bible was too obvious. Besides she didn't understand it. She contemplated Elizabeth Proctor's speech from *The Crucible* – too controlled, Blanche from *A Streetcar Named Desire* – too hackneyed. And *Abigail's Party*, well! Then she thought of Shakespeare, one of Viola's speeches from her favourite play – *Twelfth Night* – and ran though the words in her mind.

'I left no ring with her; what means this lady? Fortune forbid my outside have not charm'd her! She made good view of me; indeed, so much ...'

As fervently as Jemma tried not to engage with the mystery plays and tried not think about her firmly twisted arm ... still, she was the sort of person to give it her all. If she had to be part of this play, she had to do it well. Mohan didn't seem to have countenanced the possibility that she wouldn't be cast in the role of Mary Magdalene, and, to be honest, neither had she.

She had always got the lead role, right from her nursery school. She wasn't going to be a stand-around angel. No, for Jemma, nothing less than the Virgin Mary would do. Her ambition extended far beyond her career. She was competitive, that was just her nature. Sports, careers, relationships. Perhaps that was why she hit the ground so hard and jumped to her feet again so quickly when Richard left. At this moment, she agreed with Olivia, and fully intended to avoid love 'like the plague'. The pun made her smile.

A screech of brakes brought her bolt upright. Then footsteps, running along the towpath. She shot to the window. It was too dark to see. A car door slammed. She threw open the hatch and a pair of headlamps blinded her as a car shot towards her, mounting the strip of grass and threatening to cross the towpath. Instinctively, she put her hands up. The engine screamed as the car reversed. The gears crunched and the car sped across the car park. Her view was obscured by trees. She heard the tyres crunching over the gravel of the car park, then take off up the lane. She stood fixed to the spot, hardly daring to breathe. All was quiet again outside.

Something strange was afoot, she was sure of it. Still she couldn't go to the police. She had no description of the car or the people in it and no evidence of a crime. Perhaps she would tell Mohan. Perhaps he would think it worth investigating, or perhaps he would laugh and dismiss it as paranoia.

'I wish Richard was here.'

Instantly, she slapped that thought in the face. Whatever happened, Richard was the last person she needed. She lay on her bed again, this time, cocooned in the quilt.

She listened for the car to return, but all she heard was the screech of a barn owl and the water lapping gently, lapping, lapping . . .

Scene Six

JEMMA EVENTUALLY FOUND A PARKING SPACE HALFWAY UP THE HIGH STREET. Slowly she unclenched her hands from the steering wheel and exhaled. First, an accident on the bypass delayed her for nearly an hour; then the traffic had been almost at a standstill at Monksford General Hospital.

It had been nothing but traffic jams since the 'highway improvements' last August. The new road, which led through the revamped industrial estate – now Monksford Business and Retail Park – was supposed to have been the panacea to all the town's problems. But rather, it had caused even more ills. It cut an ugly wound through the Kentish farmland and took passing trade away from the town centre.

As she rummaged through files, crisp packets, and empty drink cans, looking in her car for her script and her bag, a blue van drove past, narrowly missing her half-open door.

'Watch it!' she yelled. The driver shouted back something that Jemma couldn't hear. She slammed the car door and locked it. She glanced at her watch. Already five minutes late.

She ran along the pavement, dodging pedestrians and telegraph poles. The pale blue van was parked just a few feet from the entrance to the church hall. Jemma, irked the driver had found a space so close, a space that should have been hers, repressed the urge to kick the tyres. A dark-haired man climbed out of the driver's seat. He smiled at her. She scowled back.

'I'm sorry about nearly taking your door off,' he said, still smiling.

'Yeah, okay,' muttered Jemma.

'You going for a part?' He nodded in the direction of the hall.

'Yes, my boss is making me.' She answered. 'You?'

'My vicar's making me.'

She couldn't help smiling back. Was anyone taking part in this play voluntarily?

'What's your audition piece?' she asked as he held the door open for her.

'I just thought I'd read a bit from the Bible. After all, that's what it's all about.'

'So, you're not an actor?'

'Hardly,' he laughed. 'I've never been on the stage before. I work at Abacus.'

'The do-it-yourself shop?'

He nodded. 'You?'

'I studied drama at college but now I'm a journalist.'

He raised his eyebrows.

'Keep it quiet. I thought I'd go incognito, you know. Tell the story behind the story.'

'I'd better watch what I say.'

'The chances of anything of interest happening are pretty remote. This is Monksford, after all.'

'You don't sound very keen on the idea.'

'I've been killing myself all week learning my piece. I wish I hadn't bothered. It's my editor's idea to write a weekly column.'

The man held out his hand. 'I hope you get it. If that's what you want.'

She smiled. 'Good luck to you too. Break a leg, as they say.'

Jemma walked into the hall and felt as if she had blundered into the middle of Oxford Street a week before Christmas. It was packed with people, milling around, talking, laughing. She spotted a harassed looking woman sitting at a desk. Resisting the urge to barge to the front, she joined the queue. In front of her were a jester, a Morris dancer, a nun, and several surly looking teenage boys. The woman at the desk took their names and assigned them to different parts of the room. She appeared to be handing the teenage boys five-pound notes. *This is good, we get paid too!*

Finally it was Jemma's turn. The woman looked up and smiled at her.

'Jemma Durham. I'm auditioning for the part of Mary Magdalene.'

'Hello, are you the reporter?'

Jemma nodded. So much for undercover journalism.

'I'm Ruth Wells, the vicar. That …' she gestured towards a small, plump man in a pink pullover and wearing small round glasses 'is Ronnie Mardle, and over there is Harlan Westacre. She'll be auditioning you.' She nodded towards a thin woman with dangling earrings. 'If you'd like to wait over there, we'll try to get organised as soon as we can.'

'Lot of people here.' Jemma did a mental count for the article.

'Yes, I'm delighted at the turnout – oh, will you excuse me?' She stood up and beckoned to the man Jemma had met on the way in. 'Josh! Over here.' He smiled and waved. He really did have a very nice smile.

Jemma crossed the hall and joined the other potential Mary Magdalenes near the piano. The familiar burning of ambition ignited inside. She studied the competition. There were four other women. Two looked well over sixty, so Jemma dismissed them. A dark-haired woman sat demurely with her ankles crossed on a blue plastic chair. Another woman, vaguely familiar, a blonde with a short skirt and high heels, was on her mobile phone, speaking loudly with animated gestures. She wore an ankle bracelet, large hooped earrings, and far too much makeup. Jemma wondered if she was attempting to portray the shadier side of Mary Magdalene's reputation.

'Alistair, you're late!' the woman screeched into her phone. 'You've made me look really stupid, standing in this hall, waiting for you. I've got better things to do.'

Amanda Fry! Of course. Jemma hadn't recognised her sober. The woman glanced around at the stares and lowered her voice.

Jemma pulled her hairbrush from her bag and groomed her hair, brushing out the kinks, and letting it hang smooth and straight, like a dark curtain to frame her face. The scrawny, bird-like woman the vicar had pointed out earlier approached the motley quintet. She carried a notebook and pen.

'Evening, ladies. I'm Harlan Westacre, and I'll be putting you through your paces tonight. Right, who's first?' She glanced at Jemma, but one of the older women put up her hand.

'I'll do it.' She jumped to her feet and grabbed a CD player. 'Where do you want me?'

Harlan gestured towards a corner of the hall. The woman turned on the CD and proceeded to sing 'Tomorrow' from the musical *Annie* in a wavering soprano. Jemma covered her mouth with her hand to hide a smirk.

Harlan was kinder to the woman than she deserved and pointed out Ronnie Mardle for her, suggesting she talk to him about a possible future in amateur operatics.

The second woman muttered her way through Lady Macbeth's 'out damned spot' speech while Harlan made notes. At the end Harlan thanked the woman and said she would be letting her know. Jemma knew she meant she wouldn't be letting her know.

Harlan smiled at Jemma, who stood up, took a breath to still herself, as she had been taught, and proceeded with her monologue. As she spoke Viola's words, a hush descended around her. She tried not to notice heads were turning. She was good and she knew it. At the end there was a smattering of applause, and Jemma was tempted to bow.

'Brava!' cried Harlan, scribbling notes on her pad. The mousy-looking woman stood up and whispered something to Harlan.

'Are you sure, dear?'

'Yes, I'm sure,' the woman said and scuttled for the door.

'Well, Jemma Durham. It looks as if you've got the part.'

'What about her?' Jemma glanced towards Amanda Fry, who was still on the phone.

'Excuse me.' Harlan waved her hand in front of Amanda's face.

Amanda put her hand over the mouthpiece of the phone. 'What?'

'Are you going to audition for the part?'

'I'm waiting till my husband gets here.'

'Why, is he auditioning for the role of Mary Magdalene too?' Harlan smiled.

'Can I have all the Jesuses over here, please?' Ronnie Mardle's precise enunciations drowned out Amanda's snide reply. Half a dozen men climbed on the stage, and the audition started.

Harlan drew Jemma to one side. 'I'm sorry, I'd give you the part like a shot, but I've got to make it look fair. Alistair Fry is a vital link in this project – financially, if you get my drift. Without him and his filthy lucre, we'd be up the creek.'

It wouldn't look fair if the part went to Amanda Fry just because she's the Councillor's wife either. But it wouldn't surprise Jemma if it happened.

Jemma sat down to wait. She pulled out her notebook and began scrawling shorthand across the page.

'Joshua? Joshua Wood next please,' Ronnie called out.

Josh climbed the steps on to the stage with a Bible in his hand. He was visibly shaking, and his face looked pale despite his tan. He swept his dark hair out of his eyes and swallowed hard. His discomfort made Jemma want to turn away.

'Off you go, Joshua,' Ronnie said.

Josh Wood opened the Bible and cleared his throat. '"Then Jesus went with his disciples to a place called Gethsemane, and he said to them, 'Sit here while I go over there and pray.' He took Peter and the two sons of Zebedee along with him, and he began to be sorrowful and troubled. Then he said to them, 'My soul is overwhelmed with sorrow to the point of death. Stay here and keep watch with me.'"'

The richness of his voice combined with the poignancy of the words had an electrifying effect on the people in the hall. The 'Pharisees' in the corner became silent, the 'Romans' by the broom cupboard watched intently, and Harlan Westacre stood with her hands clasped, captivated by Josh.

'"Going a little farther, he fell with his face to the ground and prayed, 'My Father, if it is possible, may this cup be taken from me. Yet not as I will, but as you will.'"' He stopped reading and looked up. 'Shall I go on?'

'No, I've found my Jesus!' Ronnie clapped his hands and jogged onto the stage to pat Joshua Wood on the back. 'The rest of you can go. I need look no further.'

The other men gathered round Ronnie, grumbling their complaints.

'You can all be disciples!' Ronnie announced with an extravagant gesture. The men didn't seem mollified, but Jemma had to agree, the part couldn't possibly have gone to anyone else.

Josh closed the Bible and, wiping his hand across his face, climbed down from the stage.

Jemma went over to him. 'Congratulations. You were very good. I thought you said you'd never been on the stage before.'

'I haven't. I was so terrified I thought I was going to throw up. Couldn't you tell?'

'Not at all.' Jemma fibbed.

'Besides, it was a bit different from acting, you know, just saying words. That meant something.'

'The Bible?'

'Yes, it's ... real.'

'Is it?' Jemma had never thought of it as any more than an old collection of stories.

'Even as Jesus spoke those words ... he knew what would happen. He knew he would die. In the garden, the bit I read, he asked his best friends to wait with him while he made the hardest decision of his life. He wanted some support from his mates, but when he went back and checked on them they'd fallen sleep.'

'That's awful!'

'It really happened. He had to choose whether to go through with it – the cross and certain death – or to quit. And he made that decision alone.'

'What did he choose?'

Joshua smiled. 'He chose the cross.'

'I knew that!' Jemma reddened a little. Of course she knew that Jesus Christ died on the cross. People complained about how badly Religious Education was taught in schools, but even she knew about the cross! She just never heard it explained so clearly. He had made it sound as if it happened yesterday. As if it was something he had read in the newspaper.

'Attention please.' Ronnie Mardle clapped his hands. 'Could I have all the Judases over there, please, and if you've already been cast in a part, please make sure you've given your name to our lovely vicar, the Reverend Wells ...' Ruth gave a little wave from her desk by the door.

'... and if anyone's interested in coming tomorrow night, we're doing the Old Testament. Bring along your stone tablets. We're in need of a Moses.'

'Looks like I can go,' said Josh. 'What about you?'

'Still waiting to hear. One more audition.' She glanced at Amanda Fry, who was still on the phone.

'I hope you get the part,' said Josh. This time it was his turn to blush a little. 'I'd like to see you again.'

Before she could answer, he turned and walked out of the hall, almost bumping into Alistair Fry. Alistair greeted Ruth, then came over to Amanda, who finally finished her call. He kissed her lightly, once on each cheek, then held up a hand and apologised to Ronnie.

'Glad you could make it.' A hint of sarcasm crept into Ronnie's voice. 'You're too late for Jesus, I'm afraid, but we're still a Judas short, if you want to try out for that.'

Harlan turned to Amanda. 'Are you ready now?'

'Changed my mind,' she said and tottered over to join her husband.

Harlan came up to her and put a bony arm around Jemma's shoulders.

'Well done, Mary Magdalene. Make sure Ruth's got your address and phone number, and we'll give you a date for the first rehearsal. You can pick up your script too. Welcome aboard.'

Jemma grinned. Then she reminded herself that she didn't want the part. Not only did it mean a night or two out every week, unpaid, but the indignity of a weekly column.

Then again, there was Josh Wood. Maybe there were compensations after all.

JEMMA DROVE HOME WITH HER HEAD SPINNING. THE FIRST REHEARSAL WAS A week on Thursday. She had got a part in a play she wasn't interested in, had to write a column she didn't wish to write, all to please a boss she found irritating. To cap it all she felt her heart tugging her towards another relationship. This was definitely the last thing she wanted to happen.

She pulled up in the car park alongside the river and leant her head against the steering wheel and closed her eyes. She let out a deep groan. First Richard and now this. How could it happen?

She felt like this only once before, when she was eleven. She was on holiday with her father, her uncle, and her cousin Brad. Brad at fifteen was like a two-year-old Labrador – the body of an adult with the mind of a puppy.

They had stayed in apartments on Corfu, and Brad became obsessed with water sports: speedboats, jet skis, paragliding, and scuba diving.

One afternoon, when the adults were taking their siesta, he had procured the keys to his uncle's speedboat. 'Come on Jemma. Let's see what you're made of. I've hitched up the towrope. You get the water skis. I'll just go and start the engine.'

Jemma had frozen, rooted to the spot.

'Not chicken, are you?'

No one called her chicken, especially not that spotty brat.

She climbed on the skis for only the second time in her life, and they took off around Agios Georgios Bay at breakneck speed.

Terrified, she clung to the tow handle. Afraid to hang on and but even more afraid to let go. As she bounced round the bay, panic overcame her pride.

'Stop, Brad! Please stop.'

He chose to ignore her. She was trapped. Held by the rope that was both peril and lifeline. The pain in her shoulders and arms was excruciating, but she clung to the handle.

Then her father shouted from the shore. She gritted her teeth. And prayed. Finally Brad slowed down, drove the speedboat close to the beach, and she felt safe enough to let go. Kicking off her skis, she swam to safety, where her white-faced father and uncle were waiting. As she rose from the water, shaking more from terror than the cold, she vowed never to take on anything she couldn't control.

Now that she was an adult, she insisted on driving herself everywhere, she cut her own hair, and she refused to visit a doctor unless she was at death's door.

No one ever told her to 'get a grip'. Her grip on her life, her emotions and her destiny was Herculean. Until now. She tried to pinpoint the start of her current predicament. She leant back in the driver's seat and opened her eyes. And screamed. Two eyes stared back at her through the windscreen.

She closed her eyes again for a moment, willing the apparition to go away. She took a deep breath and then, once more, squinted at the windscreen. This time the face took shape.

'Richard!' She lowered the window. 'What are you doing here?'

'Nice to see you too.'

'What do you want?'

'Don't worry. I haven't come to ask you to have me back. I've just come for my stuff. I left it as long as I could.'

'I know.' Jemma studied his unshaven face and bloodshot eyes. He could certainly do with some of his clothes and toiletries. 'I packed them all up for you.' Jemma wound up the window and got out of the car. She opened the boot and nodded at the black bags.

'Take them,' she said.

'Thing is,' he hesitated, 'I haven't got the car.'

'Where is it?'

'In the repair shop. I had a bit of a disagreement with a Ford Mondeo.'

'Let me guess. You were in such a hurry to get away from me you weren't looking where you were going?'

'Jems, don't. Please.'

'Don't call me that!' Jemma slammed the boot shut and started walking towards the *Hog*.

'Look, I'm sorry to disturb you at this time of night. In fact, I'm sorry that I've had to come back at all. I didn't want you to see me like this.'

'Like what?' Jemma turned and looked at him in the moonlight. His clothes were crumpled and his hair was unkempt.

'I ... I haven't been well.'

'Bring out the violins!'

'I went to the doctor and everything. He said it was stress. He gave me some tablets.'

'So? What do you expect me to do about it?'

'I just want a bit of understanding. A bit of sympathy.'

'Like you gave me when you dumped me. You didn't even let me down gently. You didn't try to talk to me. You didn't give me the opportunity to try to sort this out. You just left me a letter – no, not even a letter. A note. A note written on a scrappy piece of envelope. It looked like something you'd found in the bin! Do you know what that says to me, Richard? That our relationship was garbage. It wasn't worth the effort while we were in it, and to end it you used something I wouldn't even use to write a shopping list. You were always very keen on the symbolic. Well that just about says it all.'

'I'm sorry.'

'No, you're not. We could have talked. You could have spoken to me. Just one word – '

'I didn't know how to say goodbye.'

'There, you just said it. It wasn't that hard!'

'There were things ... things that made it difficult to stay.'

'So what was her name? No, don't tell me. I don't want to know!'

'It wasn't like that. Please, Jemma ...'

'No!'

They had reached the moorings, and Jemma fumbled for her keys.

'Could I come in for a moment?'

'How could you even ask that?'

'Thing is ... I've got nowhere else to stay. I had to leave the flat ...'

'I don't believe this!' She unlocked the padlock and switched on the lights. She felt chilled from the night air.

'Can I at least have a coffee? Please?'

He looked pathetic. And if this new girl had thrown him out ...

She took a deep breath. 'Okay, just one coffee and you go.' Jemma filled the kettle and turned on the heater. The small cabin would soon be cosy. She looked at the spare berth. Perhaps one night ...

Her mobile phone rang. She tucked it against her shoulder while she continued to spoon out the coffee granules into two mugs.

'Hi, Jemma. It's Josh. I hope you don't mind me ringing. Ruth Wells gave me your number.'

'Oh Josh, hi! No that's fine.'

'I just wanted to say that I was really pleased that we'd be working together on the play.'

'Yes, but all those words to learn ...'

Richard opened the door. 'I'd better go.'

Jemma put her hand over the mouthpiece. 'Where will you sleep?'

Richard waved his hand, dismissing her concern.

'Let me know when you've found somewhere to stay, and I'll bring your stuff round, right?'

Richard nodded and left. Jemma felt a blast of cold air as the door opened and closed. She shivered.

'Is everything okay?'

'Yes, everything's fine now.'

THE PLAY'S THE THING

It was with some trepidation that I made my way to St Sebastian's Church Hall for the auditions for the Monksford Mystery Plays. The plays were discovered in a vault last year, and I caught up with the Reverend Ruth Wells, who has modernised the plays from their *Canterbury Tales* language, transforming them into something that wouldn't be out of place in an Eastenders script. This busy village vicar has managed to combine her bustling parish life with reviving these ancient plays, which became a labour of love for close to two years. Despite the medieval origins of the plays, Ruth Wells hopes there will be something for everyone.

I asked Reverend Wells about her aspirations for the project. 'We're hoping the whole community can become involved,' she said. 'We have found some terrific actors among local people. This is an opportunity for the church and community to work together.'

The auditions attracted several hundred adults and children from Monksford and the surrounding villages, and the main parts were cast.

I questioned Reverend Wells about the decision to cast the plays using purely amateur talent. 'My ambition is for it to be a production for the people by the people. We're hoping to put Monksford on the map.'

Councillor Alistair Fry has secured much of the funding for the production from the town's leisure-and-arts budget. 'Culturally and historically,' he said, 'these plays are very important for Monksford. In times of change and modernisation and uncertainty, they provide an anchor to the past.'

And for the record, yours truly, local journalist Jemma Durham, has been cast in the role of Mary Magdalene. Over the coming weeks I'll be letting you know how I get on and bringing you the inside story on the Monksford Mystery Plays. Now where did I put that alabaster jar?

Scene Seven

IT WAS STILL DARK WHEN RUTH ARRIVED AT BROADOAK GREEN FOR THE THIRD time that year. Instead of the spectacular sunrise she had hoped for, the gunmetal grey October sky became progressively paler until she realised its slate colour, that almost matched the roofs, was as light as it was going to get.

She pulled her jacket around her as a bitter east wind cut along the river and threaded its way between the buildings. Ruth stood with her back towards the Monksford Business Centre. It was a squat, square 1960s monstrosity, which crouched in front of the river like a shabby dog. At least it afforded her some shelter. She tried to ignore the racket coming from the nearby dispatch depot and closed her eyes, imagining the area as fields. This was the very spot where the waggons, which had been used to perform the original Monksford Corpus Christi plays, would have been stored.

She stood as still as one of the broad oaks that six hundred years ago had encircled the green, and she strained to listen, hoping she might hear an echo from the past.

The rumble of the wooden wheels over the cobbles, then a shout from the guilds' men. She imagined their bright torches. The horses snorted and stamped. A man in a dark blue coat called out, 'You builders, stand here in readiness. The sun will soon be up, and the folk are at present gathering for the pageant.'

A cry of 'torches, torches' brought a clutch of boys hurrying forward. One lad, wiping the sleep from his eyes, let the flaming torch drop. The man in blue cried out, 'Give heed to that straw, boy! If that were to catch fire you'd not see the morrow.'

The musicians tuned the strings of their vielles and blew their sackbuts and cornets. Singers commenced their chants in disorderly fashion. Eventually the sound melded from a cacophony to a recognisable tune. The faint drizzle that hung in the air clung to their clothes and made the horses appear to steam. The man in the blue coat held a loosely bound manuscript. ''Tis time. Heed me well, I will see no drunkenness, rebel, or disobedience this day. Now forward, to the glory of God and the praise of Our Lady.'

The first waggon creaked as it moved off. The players and musicians followed to a drum beat and chant as the procession wound its way towards the river, across the bridge, and into the High Street and the first station where they would re-enact the creation of the world.

The harsh sound of a pneumatic drill jolted Ruth back to reality. The workers on the construction site – luxury three- and four-bed apartments with river views – had started early.

RUTH HOPED THE COMPRESSIONS OF HER SPINE WOULDN'T LEAVE HER WITH permanent injury as she bounced and rocked over the ruts in the track leading to the high field at Hope Farm. She had just come from a neat farmhouse with window boxes, fake Bargeware wheelbarrows, and empty watering cans, where she searched outbuildings and hallooed into barns for what seemed like hours. Finally a farmhand appeared who directed her to the top field towards Highwell Wood.

Bram Griffin was leaning on a gate gazing towards Monksford when Ruth found him.

'Mr Griffin,' she called as she climbed out of her car, 'you are a hard man to track down.'

He turned and cracked a smile, offering her a weathered hand.

'Marvellous view.' Although with the new road and the industrial estate its peace had been shattered and its beauty scarred. 'Who knows how much longer we'll be able to admire it.'

Bram Griffin grunted in reply. The lines around his eyes seemed deeper and his hair seemed greyer. Two years before, he had lost almost all his herd from the foot-and-mouth epidemic and had come close to losing the farm. Ruth had offered her support, but, unlike the rest of Monksford farmers who happily poured out their own woes, Bram had remained tight lipped. Ruth had fully expected to hear he had taken himself off into the woods with his twelve-bore.

But Hope Farm had survived. She marvelled at the dairy herd, calmly grazing by the copse and, in the small lower field by the river, a flock of British milksheep. They looked like a child's drawing – little clouds with four legs – but renown for the quality and quantity of their milk. Fluffy white cotton-wool in the lush green pasture.

Not only had Bram and his farm survived, they were positively thriving. The turning point seemed to be his trip to the States last year. He left a depressed Kentish farmer and came back a cowboy with a white Stetson and a penchant for telling terrible jokes. Last Sunday, after the service he had complained about being woken too early by his old cockerel crowing at four in the morning. 'Still,' he had said, 'there's only one sure way of stopping your rooster waking you early on a Sunday morning.'

'Oh, what's that?' Ruth had asked.

'Eat him for supper on Saturday.'

Bram had left the church still chuckling. But today was different. Today Bram looked a worried man.

'How are you, Mr Griffin?'

'I'm great.'

'Things are going well then?'

'Just fine and dandy.' He let his gaze drift over her shoulder.

'The road, though, it must have affected you. It cut right through your land.'

'The cows ain't complaining.'

Ruth could see she was getting nowhere so she tried a different tack. 'It's very kind of you to let us use your farm for the mystery plays.'

Bram shrugged.

'I'm just worried it will disrupt your routine. The cycle takes all day, and you'll have cars and people trouping round your fields. We'll have to lay on catering and toilet facilities, first aid ...'

'That doesn't matter.'

'We – I mean St Sebastian's – will organise all that of course, but I wanted to check with you. Make sure you really didn't mind. We would have loved to do it on waggons through the streets of Monksford, but that just wasn't practical. Besides, I'm sure the council would never give permission for the roads to be closed.'

'You're probably right.'

'We finished the casting last night, and it's finally all shaping up. We've got a smashing young man playing Jesus. He's only just joined the church. In fact, he's only just become a Christian. But he's so enthusiastic, and he really looks the part – his mum came from somewhere in the Middle East. And we've appointed our Mary Magdalene. She works for the local paper. Good actress though. She's done it before. And you'll never guess who's Judas ...' She paused.

His expression said he couldn't care less who was playing Judas.

'Alistair Fry!' Ruth threw her head back and laughed. 'But only because no one else turned up for the part.'

Bram looked steadily at her. Ruth could not read what was behind his eyes.

'Well, I've kept you long enough, Vicar. I'm sure you need to get on. Besides, I've got to go into town.'

'Bram,' she called to his back. Without turning he continued striding across the field back down to the farmhouse. 'Bram, do you mind if I have a look around? I want to check on the locations.'

He turned suddenly. 'What for?'

'Well, I just want to make sure everything's all right. Do you remember we talked about it? The creation in the upper field, Noah's ark and Moses down by the river, the birth of Jesus in the old barn, and the crucifixion and resurrection in the abbey ruins. I need to think about getting the staging constructed.'

'Now? The play's months away.'

'All this will take time. For one thing, I need to get someone in to look at temporary footpaths. I was going to drive it, to see if I can get some idea of distances.'

'You can look round here and go up to the barns, but I don't want you down by the abbey today.'

'I'm sorry it's not convenient, Bram. It's just that I don't get much free time, and I was hoping to get it all done today.'

'You can't go down there – I've been spraying. Best to leave it a couple of weeks for the chemicals to clear.'

'Oh, okay.' Ruth did her best to sound compliant.

Bram grunted and carried on. Ruth walked back to where she had parked the car. Spraying? She was no farming expert, but Bram's dairy farm had only a little pasture and a field or two set aside for hay. She couldn't imagine what he would be spraying.

She climbed in the car and drove down the hill to the top of the upper field. The pastureland dropped away below her, like raked seating in a theatre. The flat area at the bottom would be ideal for the staging. The autumn wind buffeted her as she struggled to close the car door, threatening to send her sprawling.

'Hello!' she shouted to no-one in particular. The wind snatched the sound away before it left her lips.

Even in balmy June, they would need a powerful public address system for the actors' words to be heard. She tried to picture the audience spread over the field. It seemed enormous; even so she wondered if it would fit the whole town. That's if anyone turned up at all. She smiled. Judging by Bram's silly cow-pat contest, Monksford folks were only too happy to travel the mile or two out to Hope Farm. She trusted that a medieval religious play would exert a similar, if not greater, draw than watching dried cow dung being launched into orbit.

She set her trip counter to zero, then bounced over the rough grass to the bottom of the field. Nought point three eight miles. She jotted the figure down and climbed out of the car again. It was more sheltered here, which was good. She made her way across the rough grass and leant on a dilapidated wooden gate between this field and the next. She made a note to ask for the area to be mown, or at least grazed, before the event.

She turned towards the river. The skeleton of the abbey ruins stood cold and dark against the heavy sky. She strained her eyes to see anything unusual about the forbidden field. It looked perfectly ordinary; just more coarse pasture, with a new barn of wood and corrugated steel. Why didn't Bram want her to go in there? She felt a little guilty ignoring Bram's injunction, but she had come to see where the plays would be performed and she was determined to do just that.

Then she remembered; if she took the road to Todbourn Heath, there was an entrance to the towpath near the old mill. And she could reach the abbey without having to cross Bram Griffin's land. True, she wouldn't be able to measure the distance, but she could inspect the site. That would do for today.

She drove along the deeply rutted track, the Friesians gazing at her with mild curiosity as she passed. She slowed when she reached the farmhouse and parked on the concrete next to a green milk churn painted with gaudy and symmetrical posies. Without waiting to see if Bram had gone out, she walked to the old barn and peered through a gaping hole in the ramshackle door. Delightful. It held a collection of decaying, rusting Massey Ferguson tractors. But the barn was large, and the farmyard would provide ample standing room for the audience. Once the barn was cleared and a raised platform built, it should do beautifully.

Ruth climbed into her car once more, and instead of turning left towards Monksford, she turned right and headed towards the hamlet of Todbourne Heath. Distracted by rioting ducks on a small pond, she braked sharply. Just around the bend, Bram's cattle were crossing the road for their evening milking. She thumped the steering wheel in frustration. It would be dark soon, and she had no great desire to be poking around in a spooky old abbey. She refused to believe the legends of ghostly abbots and headless monks, but she did know for a fact that it was a favourite haunt of local drug addicts and a congregation of Goths.

Finally the last black and white rump disappeared down the lane, and the old stockman gave her a lethargic wave. She drove on, turning left, then left again by the river. She parked on the grass and then made her way to the towpath by the river to consider the best setting for Noah's ark.

The canal narrowboats were moored along the river, painted in muted shades of blue, green, and black, with their names in red and gold lettering on their cabins. She walked past the *Ruritainia*, the *Ebony Hog*, *Endeavour* and the *Lucky Lady*; stopping to admire the trough of flowers on the deck of the *Noble Maria* and having a chuckle at the wit who had named his boat *Viagra*.

She passed the abbey and continued towards Monksford. Bram Griffin's lower field, the one that bordered the river, contained his milking sheep. Their smooth-fleeced heads looked as if they had been added on to their plump woolly bodies as an afterthought. She watched them, standing, eating, walking on a few paces, and eating again, no sign of intelligence or even curiosity in their yellow eyes. They were just machines to produce milk and wool.

She was always puzzled by the Bible's analogy that humans are like sheep. She would rather be almost anything than one of these bimbos of the animal world. Absolutely nothing between the ears. Would Bram be prepared to move them out so that the ark could be constructed and so that the audience could watch the show unimpeded? Actually, the sheep looked so dim they probably wouldn't even realise.

One corner of the field had been sectioned off with metal stakes and plastic tape. Perhaps this was the area he had sprayed. Ruth scrutinised it. It just looked like pastureland, the same as the rest of the lower field. She couldn't see any crops or any evidence of spraying. Besides, that close to the river he couldn't possibly use toxic chemicals. Too much danger of it seeping into the watercourse. She glanced at her watch. It was getting late, and she still hadn't visited the abbey.

The abbey stood resolutely beside the river, its sandstone pillars silhouetted in the dying light. Ruth felt something pulling her towards them. The abbey had been built just before the first recorded performance of the mystery plays. Perhaps the monks from the abbey had been involved in the scripting. She felt a bond with those first scribes, imagining how they sweated and laboured over the task of recording those wonderful, terrible, words.

> I am gracious and great, God withoutyn beginning,
> I am maker unmade, all might is in me;
> I am life and way unto welth-wynnyng,
> I am foremost and first, all I bid know it be.

The three enormous arched windows curved above her. She made her way to where the chapel would have been, found a patch of soft grass between the fallen stone, and knelt down. She thought of the centuries of dutiful prayer and profound praise that echoed off these stones. She remained as still as possible, barely breathing, with her eyes closed. She tried to still her mind too – stop the whirling, dancing thoughts that threatened to intrude. If only she could keep still, eliminate all voluntary movement and thought, if she could completely surrender, then she would hear God speak. 'Be still, and know that I am God ...,' wrote the psalmist. If only she could be perfectly still ...

Peace seemed to emanate from the gentle golden limestone. Just as the sharp edges had been eroded by the weather into smooth curves, so time had eroded its bloody history into soft memories. She breathed in. The pleasant smell of wood smoke filled the air, and Ruth felt a tingle that started in the back of her neck and soon engulfed her body. It was as if God himself had just walked past.

Ruth stayed in prayer until the darkness descended and the air grew chill. The knees of her trousers were damp. She stood up stiffly, brushed the grass from her knees, and pulled her jacket around her. Then she started back towards her car. Two bright lights swung into view, dazzling her. She halted, temporarily blinded, and leant against a partially demolished wall. The car stopped and she heard a door open, then slam. Suddenly the old abbey seemed a threatening place, the home of dark menaces. She stayed, for several minutes, hidden by a pillar.

She heard footsteps along the towpath and then a splash.

Scene Eight

'NO!' JEMMA CLAPPED HER HAND OVER HER MOUTH. SHE HADN'T MEANT TO
express her frustrations aloud. She smiled feebly at her colleagues
who had turned to stare from their cubicles, and they lowered their
heads and continued with their work. Mohan shook his head and got
up to pour himself a coffee.

Jemma had been working from home over the last few days,
where her outburst may have alarmed a few mallard but no more
than that. She had decided it would be judicious to show her face
in the office today, to try and redeem herself with Mohan as well as
demonstrate she was getting on with her work. Although her job, by
its nature, involved working outside the office – either on assignment
or composing the articles at home – Mohan always regarded his staff
with suspicion.

Jemma returned to the article she was editing for her column.
She was working to make it sound lighthearted, but insightful, appealing to all ages, but neither 'youf-speek' nor fuddy-duddy. Mohan
had asked her what an alabaster jar had to do with anything. With
an air of superiority, she told him to look it up in the Bible. She knew
he wouldn't.

She had redrafted the first paragraph of her second article three
times but all she could think about was Josh Wood – she could have
written a whole full-page spread about him. She could have started
with his eyes, deep brown and fringed with dark lashes; his hair,

jet black, shining a little too long perhaps; his smile with the little dimple in his left cheek; his hands strong, yet gentle …

'Jemma, are you listening to me?' Mohan was standing behind her. 'Are you hung over or was it just a late night?'

'I was thinking!' She realised too late, and with considerable embarrassment, that her computer had got bored with waiting and switched itself to standby.

'Fire at the retail park, do you want it?'

'Sure!' Jemma leapt up and snatched her bag and notebook. She tapped her foot impatiently while Saffy Walton searched for her camera.

At last, a welcome relief from the column and something interesting finally happening in Monksford! She had become rather an ambulance chaser of late. Bad news set her heart pumping faster, and disaster cheered her up no end. Bad news was so much easier to write about than dull preparations for some centuries-old plays.

'I hope no one's hurt,' Saffy said as Jemma pressed on the accelerator.

Jemma dodged the speed cameras along the bypass. She wouldn't wish anyone injured either – at least not seriously. In a town where lost pets make the headlines, a fire was a journalist's godsend. She could see plumes of black smoke over the town. A fire engine streaked past them with its blue lights flashing and sirens screaming.

The traffic was being diverted off the bypass at the Millstoke Road. Jemma slowed near the policeman directing the traffic, stopped, and lowered the window.

'*Monksford Gazette.*' She flashed her press badge.

'Sorry, Miss, I can't let anyone through,' he said.

'But I'm a journalist! I have a piece to do on the fire.'

'We're in the process of evacuating the area. We can't let anybody near until the fire brigade has given it the all clear.'

'I'm not anybody! The people of Monksford have a right to know what's going on.' She sounded pompous, but she didn't care. With this Jobsworth, it might just do the trick.

The policeman refused to budge. 'That's a DIY store. They have flammable liquids, paints, even butane and acetylene down there. I will let you through when we can be sure the whole lot's not going to blow up. The people of Monksford don't want to see a journalist splattered all over the county, now do they?'

Jemma wound up her window and turned to Saffy. 'We'll see about that.'

'But if it's not safe ...' Saffy's face turned pale.

Jemma turned down Millstoke Road then left into Backcliffe Lane. She pulled up in a gateway that led to a field.

'This'll do. Come on.'

Jemma was half way over the stile before Saffy had removed her equipment from the boot. Jemma kept close to the hedge as she crossed the field and came to the point where the road had been cordoned off. She scooted round behind the policeman who was explaining the diversion to another motorist. There was a wire fence then a steep bank of chalky soil sprouting patches of newly planted grass, the slapdash landscaping stage of the construction. The smoke made her splutter as she skidded down the bank of earth towards the retail park. She could hear Saffy choking behind her, and she slowed slightly to let her catch up.

'I'm really not sure about this,' Saffy said.

'Come on, we'll make the front page.'

'Just as long as we don't make the obituaries,' Saffy sniffed.

She offered Saffy her hand as they reached another wire fence at the bottom. The wind seemed to have changed direction, and the smoke was drifting away from them, towards the industrial area. They scurried round to the front of the furniture superstore, where fire engines, police cars, and ambulances lined the street.

She stood upright and slowed her walk, trying to make herself look official, as if she had every right to be there. Saffy followed suit. The police had roped off the area, and the staff from the shops and stores stood grouped in little knots, talking quietly. Some had foil emergency blankets around their shoulders. Managers with clipboards were doing a roll call of staff. One woman sat on the kerb sobbing softly.

She ducked under the tape and ambled up to a firefighter in a yellow helmet. Saffy followed, trotting behind like a poodle.

'Excuse me,' Jemma said, 'do you know what happened?'

'Looks like some flammable liquids went up in the warehouse of the DIY store. Too early to say how it happened.'

'Was anyone hurt?' Saffy asked.

'They managed to get everyone out as soon as the fire was discovered. I think there are a few minor injuries.'

'Do you think you'll be able to put it out?' Jemma fluttered her eyelashes a little.

'We're trying to keep it away from the other shops and industrial units at the moment. We've had to evacuate the meat-processing plant.'

Jemma glanced over at the huddle of Asian women in white overalls. A weasel-faced man Jemma recognised as Colin Riley, the manager of the meat-processing factory, stood glowering at the edge of the group.

'When did it start?' Jemma surreptitiously jotted a few notes in shorthand. Unfortunately, the firefighter noticed her notebook and turned on her.

'Are you press?' He glowered at her.

'Sort of,' confessed Jemma.

'Then you can call our press office. You're not even supposed to be in here.'

'If I could just ask a couple more questions . . .'

'Shove off! I haven't got time to waste answering stupid questions.' He held up the tape, and Jemma and Saffy ducked back under. He returned to the fire engine, eyeing the two women with suspicion.

'Come on.' Jemma beckoned to Saffy. They skulked a few yards past the fire engine, and Jemma stooped back under the tape. They were at the front of Abacus DIY where they could make out smoke and flames coming from the rear of the store. The gigantic green and yellow sign bearing the legend 'Abacus DIY – You Can Count On Us' looked rather forlorn. It would need more than a few nails and a litre or two of emulsion to restore Abacus to its former glory. She sneaked past another firefighter who was watching the proceedings from a safe distance.

'You can get a really great shot from here,' Jemma said.

Saffy looked doubtful but browbeaten; as usual, she acquiesced. She snapped a few shots while Jemma scouted around for someone more willing to be interviewed.

They returned to the relative safety of the roadway near the ambulances. So, there had been some minor injuries. Experience had taught Jemma that people with 'minor injuries' were usually at the centre of the action and possessed interesting theories about the incident – theories that time and composure hadn't restrained. They were usually only too willing to speak. The shock of the crisis loosened their tongues nicely. She looked for Saffy who had taken herself up the bank and affixed the telephoto lens on her camera. Jemma made her way around the groups of employees who were huddled together for protection from the autumn mizzle. Saffy joined her. A woman was shouting at one of the policewomen.

'My bag, I need to get it! What about my phone ... and my keys! I'm supposed to pick up my little girl! I need to phone.'

The policewoman was doing her best to calm her. She wouldn't make a good subject for interview. To her irritation, Jemma noticed Saffy reaching into her own bag and handing the woman her mobile phone.

Jemma looked into the open back of one of the ambulances. A rather desolate-looking old man sat with an oxygen mask over his face. One of the ambulance crew was attending to him. The other crewmember leaned nonchalantly against the open door.

'Is he going to be okay?' asked Jemma.

'Are you a relative?'

'No, not really.'

'Then I can't tell you anything.'

'Any idea how it started?'

The man shrugged. 'Ask the fire crew.'

'Oh, they said to ask you.'

The paramedic looked at Jemma over a pair of imaginary spectacles. She began to wonder if she was losing her touch. She scrutinised the people standing in the car park for a glimmer of interest, but everyone looked as if they had rather go home.

She marched up to Colin Riley and introduced herself. He scowled back. 'Excuse me, Mr Riley, do you have any comment to make on this situation?'

'Only that it's cost me the best part of a day's production.'

One of the ambulances inched forward, and Jemma had to leap out of the way. Saffy appeared at her elbow. 'Can we go back now, I really need the loo.'

Jemma looked skywards and sighed. She resisted the urge to ask her why she didn't go before they came out. Honestly, working with Saffy Walton was like working with a six-year-old.

'Must be the cold,' Saffy said.

'Get any good shots?' Jemma said, changing the subject.

'I think so,' she said. 'How did you do?'

'Waste of time,' Jemma said, and they returned to the car.

BACK AT THE OFFICE, THE ARTICLE ABOUT THE FIRE PROVED AS DIFFICULT TO write as the column. She nearly didn't bother calling the press office. She could count fire engines herself. Then she thought better of it. As she had failed to get even one eyewitness interview, she would have to try to include a statement from the Divisional Officer. She sat down at the computer to write the article. It was full of glib clichés; she knew Mohan would have a field day. At least Saffy had furnished her with a half-decent photo.

BLAZE AT ABACUS DIY

More than 50 fire fighters were called to a fire at the Abacus DIY store in Kennett Way, Monksford yesterday.

Kent Fire and Rescue Service Control Centre received the first call to the scene at 10.34 on Thursday morning. Two specially equipped vehicles arrived from Monksford fire station. The premises, on the newly built Monksford Retail Park, were found to be well alight with a serious fire in the warehouse. The fire service used jet and a hydrant, and an aerial appliance was also on the scene, and the fire was soon surrounded. Crews wearing breathing apparatus searched the building and, despite earlier reports, found no one inside.

The officer in charge of the incident, Senior Divisional Officer Gary Winchester said, 'Crews have done an excellent job in bringing the fire under control so quickly. We were concerned that other retail units may have become involved. In the event, everyone was evacuated and only minor injuries were sustained. The building has, however, suffered serious damage and we have asked the building control officer to attend and assess the safety of the structure.'

Police and fire investigators have returned to the scene of the fire today but the cause of the fire is not yet known.

MOHAN LOOKED UP FROM THE ARTICLE. 'IT'LL DO.'

Jemma eked out a smile.

'How's the column going?'

'Fine, first rehearsal tonight.'

She was desperate to ask him if there had been any reaction from the first article but was equally desperate not to sound desperate. She seized the proofs as soon as the subeditors had checked them. Mohan looked over her shoulder.

'What do you think?'

'Layout's good. Not sure about "Curtain up". Not particularly accurate – no curtains on a farm.'

Mohan disregarded her comments. 'Gives it a nice theatrical feel.'

She did like the little masks of comedy and tragedy that topped her column and the photo of St Sebastian's to one side. What she wasn't quite so happy with was the photo that Saffy had taken of her. With all the wild-eyed, washed-out, spaced-out qualities of an embarrassing snapshot, it would have made a good passport photo.

She reread the article in print and allowed herself a little contented smile. Its truthfulness and proficiency would have pleased even her grandfather. Perhaps she would send it to him.

When she had accepted, a little too gratefully, with hindsight, the job of staff reporter at the *Gazette,* her first assignment had been to report on a protest meeting about a proposed centre for the arts. With her new notebook, pristine ballpoint, and eagerness cranked up to fever pitch, Jemma had arrived to find one young man with blond dreadlocks, two elderly women, a chap with a West Highland terrier, and a middle-aged man in a pinstriped suit.

Hardly a protest meeting, although one woman was carrying a homemade banner. In an effort to remain professional, she duly interviewed everyone concerned. Once they started talking, their fears were quickly allayed, the woman rolled up her banner and everyone returned home happy, leaving Jemma to manufacture an article, one that wouldn't cause the population of Monksford to fall asleep in their cornflakes.

She rose to the challenge and wrote with passion and clarity, and with a few well-placed words, the odd bending of the truth here and there, she turned a nonevent into an occasion. She allowed herself a little smidgen of pride. She felt like a real journalist.

After it was published in the *Monksford Gazette,* she'd driven to Yorkshire to show this, her very first proper article, to her grandfather. She sat in front of him, feeling like a child who had just given her parents her school report. She watched his face, searching for his reaction, desperate for the old Yorkshireman's approval.

Finally, he folded the paper and gave it back to her. 'It's a very fine article, lass.'

Jemma knew that already. She didn't need an assessment of its technical competence; she needed to know that he liked it.

'Would you have accepted it? Would it have been good enough for the *Yorkshire Mail* when you were there?'

'Aye, as I said, it's a fine article. Is all of it true?'

'What do you mean by true?'

He chuckled. 'I mean did it all 'appen as you've written it? Did people actually say what you've quoted? Did you double-check their names? And if one of them people that was there read it, would they say, "Yes. That is how it was"?'

Jemma squirmed. 'Sort of.'

'There's no substitute for honesty in this business. Oh, I know journalists have a reputation for making it all up, but the best journalists, the very best, are the ones people know they can trust. They're the people folks pick up the phone and talk to when something happens. Integrity – that's what matters, and it's even more important when you work in the town where you live.'

Jemma blushed. She knew that when those two elderly women, the guy with blond dreadlocks, the man walking his Westie, or Councillor Fry, picked up their copy of the *Monksford Gazette*, they certainly wouldn't recognise that 'packed meeting' where local residents 'raised their voices in protest'.

'Oh, and never use the word "probe"; that's what gynaecologists do, and boats are launched, inquiries are not.'

'So those words never appeared in the *Yorkshire Mail*?'

' "Not on my shift," as they say.' He laughed and the laugh turned into a crackling cough. He reached for the oxygen mask beside him and inhaled as deeply as his damaged lungs would allow.

'Be truthful, accurate, and fair. Truth is often more boring than fiction, but it's your duty to be truthful. And if someone tells you something in confidence, don't break their trust, however good the story. They will never come back to you if you do. You may get a story that sells papers, but will you be able to live with your conscience?'

'Surely, there are some occasions ...'

'Truthful, accurate, and fair. If he's behaved like a scoundrel, and you have the evidence, call him a scoundrel. Ain't nothing wrong with that.'

'I think I understand.'

'And another thing, don't drink, not while you're writing. You hear stories about the genius of the alcohol-soaked Fleet Street hack. Don't you even think of trying it. Only the really clever ones get away with writing while they're inebriated, Jeffrey Bernard and his ilk. If you try it, you'll write rubbish, I can promise you that.'

Jemma wasn't very impressed with the 'compliment' but she knew he was right.

'And never smoke either.' His face split into a broad grin. 'I learnt that the hard way. Didn't affect my writing but by 'eck has it affected my life.'

Jemma had taken his advice. At least, most of the time. Mohan and the subeditors had even complimented her on the freshness of her writing. *Avoid clichés like the plague*, she chuckled to herself.

JEMMA TOOK A LITTLE EXTRA CARE OVER HER MAKEUP, TOUCHING UP HER LIP gloss and brushing her hair to a sheen. Tonight she would finally stand on stage opposite Josh. She had spent her lunch breaks poring over her script and evenings watching the others rehearse, but tonight was her turn, play number twenty-four of the cycle, where Jesus visits the house of Martha and Mary.

At the last rehearsal, Ruth Wells had pointed out that Mary, the sister of Martha and Lazarus, almost certainly wasn't the same Mary as Mary Magdalene. But Jemma barely paid attention. She was thinking of all the time she could spend admiring the magnificent Josh.

Besides, they all seemed to be called Mary back then, so what was the difference?

She arrived early at the church hall and immediately scanned the room for Josh. He wasn't there so she took out her notebook and found a disciple to interview. The disciples seemed to have been chosen for their abundant facial hair, rather than any outstanding acting ability. Unfortunately, she got cornered by a disciple with bad breath who was keener to tell her about his ferret-breeding programme than he was to discuss the play.

The door swung open, and a sheepishly grinning Josh entered with a young woman. Jemma bristled. Who was she? Then she noticed Josh's hands were wrapped in bandages. The disciples, John the Baptist, and Lazarus stopped their conversation and rushed over to him. Jemma joined them.

'Hey, I've never been mobbed before! Wow, I know how Brad Pitt feels!'

'What happened to you?' asked Jemma.

The woman standing next to him laughed. 'Hero of the hour, aren't you, Josh?'

Josh shrugged and gave the woman a peck on the cheek. 'Thanks for the lift Loraine, I'll see you tomorrow.'

She placed a bag on a chair and waved as she left.

'What happened?' Jemma repeated.

'There was a fire at work this morning. I'm surprised you hadn't heard.'

'But I was there! I didn't see you.'

The man playing Simon Peter stepped closer. 'Too busy rescuing people, probably.'

'I didn't really rescue anyone,' Josh protested. 'In fact, all I did was try to put out the fire. It was a totally brainless thing to do.'

'You put the fire out?' Jemma's mouth hung open. How had she missed all this?

'No. I *tried* to put the fire out. The Kent Fire and Rescue Service did the job properly.'

'Did you see how it started?' Jemma was in 'news-hound' mode.

'No. I think perhaps someone had sneaked out for a crafty cigarette. There are notices everywhere, but you know, I'd probably have done the same a few years ago. We store all sorts of chemicals in the warehouse – paints, paint strippers, aerosols ...'

'Good job you noticed it, the whole place could have gone up,' John the Baptist said.

'I did spot the smoke,' Josh said, 'but it was probably only a matter of time before the alarm was raised – it's a DIY store, we sell hundreds of smoke detectors.'

'So what did you do?' Jemma licked her fingers and turned to a clean page in her notebook.

'Well, I yelled for someone to call the fire service; then I grabbed an extinguisher.'

The questions came thick and fast. Jemma couldn't keep up with who was speaking.

'Is it true you rescued a bloke?'

'Sort of,' Josh grinned.

'He's a hero!'

The audience gasped. Josh just shook his head. 'I didn't do anything, really.'

'Was he all right?'

'Was the fire out?'

Josh held up his hand. The crowd was all calling out at once.

'How's the man now?'

Harlan Westacre walked through the barrage of questions, tapping her clipboard to gain their attention. 'Gentlemen and ladies, if I could have your atten — ' She gaped at Josh and clapped her hands to the sides of her face. She reminded Jemma of Munch's *The Scream*. 'Great Scot! What happened to you?' The rehearsal was delayed another five minutes while Josh told his story to Harlan.

Jemma put her hand on his shoulder. 'Please, can I have an exclusive interview tonight? Please? Oh, please, say I can.' She sounded like a whining child; she didn't care. 'I'll buy you a drink afterwards.'

'I don't know about an interview, but I like the sound of the drink.' Josh grinned and climbed onto the stage.

Jemma sat down and jotted notes on what she had already gleaned from Josh, taking only a vague interest as the actors read through their lines. John the Baptist and the man whose sandals he was not worthy to tie were discussing who should baptise whom.

FIFTEEN MINUTES AFTER THE REHEARSAL ENDED, JEMMA AND JOSH MADE THEIR way through the saloon bar at the Fruiterer's Arms. While Jemma collected her cola and Josh's orange juice from the bar, Josh made his way to a small oak table in the corner by a window. She sighed as she headed towards him a few minutes later. Orange juice and cola? They were not exactly going to be in for a wild night.

'I don't suppose you could get me a straw, could you?' Josh sounded slightly pathetic. He was in a helpless state, and she hoped it would translate into an interview. Although the paper didn't employ night staff, she could email the draft, head in early, and have the revised article on Mohan's desk by nine, making the deadline easily. 'A straw? Be happy to,' she said, smiling, and headed back to the bar.

'So, let's have the full story.' Now seated across from him, she pulled open a packet of crisps. She offered the open packet to Josh, only realizing too late she would have to feed him should he decide to eat one. She breathed a sigh of relief when he shook his head.

'Well, I'd just come back from my break and was heading into the warehouse when I first saw the smoke. I'd gone in to restock with paint stripper. At first it didn't seem too bad. Just some smoke coming from the cage where we put the wastepaper and card. I raised the alarm and grabbed an extinguisher; then I realised someone was there, between the cage and the shelves. An old man, slumped against some paint tins. To be honest, I thought he was dead.' Josh paused to take a drink.

Jemma realised she had been so absorbed in his tale that she had forgotten to make notes. 'Go on.' She pulled her chair closer and sat with her pen poised above her notebook.

'If you're sure I'm not boring you.'

Jemma shook her head. 'No way!' This would make great copy.

'I'd no idea who he was – he doesn't work there or anything – so I grabbed hold of the cage and pulled it to one side so I could get him out. Of course the metal cage was hot.' He held up his bandaged hands. 'That's how I did this.'

Jemma winced. 'Does it hurt?'

'Er ... yeah!'

It was a stupid question, and she tried to cover it with another, more sensible question. 'So what happens next?'

'I'm not sure. I suppose the fire service will investigate. I don't think I'll be back to work for a few days.'

'How will you manage?'

He shrugged. 'I'm sure Loraine will lend a hand – literally.'

'Girlfriend?' She could have kicked herself for being so obvious.

'No, a neighbour. We help each other out. And you're driving me home. I'm very grateful for that.'

'Yeah.' Jemma wished she could take the rest of the week off to be with Josh so he could be even more grateful. Two things prevented it – Mohan, and it was too soon after Richard even to think about another relationship.

'Do you mind if we go soon? I'm getting a bit tired. I've had an eventful day.'

They walked back to Jemma's car, and she helped to fasten his seatbelt. She drove him down a narrow lane on the west side of Monksford, just off the High Street, on the other side of the bypass. He nodded towards a red brick terraced house. She circled the car and opened the door for him; then they walked to the gate that separated the tiny front garden from the road. A light shone through a window near the front door.

'Do you live with your parents?' she blurted.

He smiled. 'No, light switch on a timer. We sell them at Abacus. Or we used to.'

'Of course,' she said, then gave him a clumsy kiss on the cheek and hurried to the car.

'Sorry,' he called. 'There's one more thing you're going to have to help me with.'

'What?' She spun around. What horribly personal and excruciatingly embarrassing task did he have in mind?

'The key. I can't open the door.'

Jemma felt her cheeks warm as she reached into his jacket pocket, withdrew a bunch of keys, and unlocked his front door.

There was an awkward pause. In the normal run of events, Jemma would have expected him to invite her in for a drink, perhaps a coffee. One thing would lead to another, and she would creep out at six thirty in the morning, just in time to return home to shower and change before work.

He didn't invite her in. She was both disappointed and relieved. He must have been tired after his heroic escapade. She was still thinking about him when she arrived home and began rewriting the article.

LOCAL HERO

A worker at a DIY store took customer service to a new level yesterday when he saved the life of a man in a blaze at Abacus DIY in Kennett Way, Monksford yesterday.

Kent Fire and Rescue Service Control Centre received the first call to the scene at 10.34 on Thursday morning. Brave employee, Joshua Wood, 32, had already got the fire under control and had managed to rescue the injured man who has not yet been named.

'The fire didn't look too bad,' claimed Mr Wood. 'I raised the alarm and grabbed an extinguisher, then I realised there was someone there, between the cage and the shelves, an old man, slumped against some shelves. To be honest I thought he was dead.'

The fire service arrived to ensure the fire was completely extinguished. Crews wearing breathing apparatus searched the building and found no one else inside.

Both the injured man and Mr Wood were taken to Monksford General Hospital, where Mr Wood was treated for burns to his hands.

'He's a hero!' claimed a local resident. The Fire Service has recommended Mr Wood be nominated for a bravery award.

Police and fire investigators returned to the scene of the fire yesterday, but the cause of the fire is not yet known.

JEMMA PRESSED THE SEND BUTTON, AND HER ARTICLE RUSHED THROUGH cyberspace to the PC on her desk at work. All she needed now was a photo of Josh. It was too late to ring Saffy; she would catch her in the morning.

Smiling, Jemma got ready for bed. Things were definitely looking up. Her mind drifted, lulled by the gentle movement of the water and the occasional splash. Water fowl? Or was it the man in the dark coat and the pole with the strong hook on the end, a few hundred metres upstream?

Scene Nine

RUTH RAN HER FINGERS THROUGH HER HAIR IN FRUSTRATION. 'ALISTAIR, I APPRECIATE
what you are saying. The Middle English is very beautiful ...'

Alistair took a deep breath and began to recite,

> 'Sirs, a tokenyng in this tyme I schall telle yoou vntill,
> But lokis by youre lewty no liffe yoe hym lenne:
> Qwhat man som I kys that corse schall ye kyll,
> And also beis ware that he will not away – I schrew you
>   all thenne.'

Ruth listened to his soft, rich voice as he spoke Judas's words of
betrayal. When he had finished, she said kindly, 'It's just that, well,
it's a bit highbrow – you know, exclusive.'

An emotion she couldn't identify shot across his face. Irritation
perhaps? Sadness?

'They were written in the common language, for the people,' he
said. 'Tradesmen performed the mystery plays. All right, some of the
guilds were pretty well-to-do – the Merchant Adventurers and the
like, but most of them were typical working-class men. Of course,
the women didn't perform.' He gave Ruth a wink. 'The plays weren't
highbrow in the slightest!'

'I know that, Alistair.' Ruth wondered if he was serious, or if he
was teasing her again. 'This is a modern audience – they won't understand it.'

'Don't you think we're in danger of underestimating them? You know, looking for the lowest common denominator?'

She thought of the good people of Monksford. In her experience, there was absolutely no danger of underestimating them. The lowest common denominator couldn't possibly be too low or too common. Besides, the hours – no, weeks and months – she had spent translating it into modern English ...

She swallowed down her rising anger. She thought he supported her. He had certainly never expressed any misgivings; nor had he ever offered to help with the modernization.

'This is a wonderful opportunity to experience history come to life,' he said. 'These plays are like time capsules. Medieval Monksford resurrected.'

'It's not just the history!' Ruth swallowed her indignation. 'What about the spiritual aspect? Most of the audience never set foot in a church. This is a chance to share the good news with them. This was their purpose in the first place.'

'Watch out, Vicar, your dog collar's showing!' he said.

She looked away to hide how much his jibe hurt her.

The door of the hall swung open and Josh Wood entered. He appeared uncomfortable, holding his bandaged hands away from his body, a carrier bag suspended from each wrist.

'Sorry,' he said. 'Taxi was late. I'm rather at the mercy of other people's transport at the moment.'

'That's okay.' Ruth smiled. 'Glad you could make it. Alistair and I were just talking.'

Alistair gave a noncommittal grunt.

Rather uncharacteristically, Ruth seized the opportunity to stick the knife in. She liked Alistair, but today he had annoyed her. No matter how fond she was of him, she was fonder still of the plays that had occupied her every spare moment for the last two years. 'Alistair thinks we should perform the plays in their original language.' Her bluntness surprised her, but to her satisfaction, Alistair started to backtrack.

'I didn't say that all the plays in the cycle should be performed in Middle English, just that it was a pity to lose the resonance of the ancient words. We're breeding a spoon-fed, dumbed-down society where celebrities are our gods and *The Sun* is our literature. The symphony orchestras play only film scores, and the West End critics pan everything unless it contains ex-soap stars taking off their clothes. Education is all media studies and Information Technology with no room for the classics, and even in church – ' He stopped abruptly. Ruth knew what he was going to say next. He was going to complain about the modern liturgy and Bible translations. He might even start on female vicars!

'Go on, Alistair.' Ruth could feel her cheeks burning again. 'You were just about to tell us what's wrong with the church.'

'I was just going to say – ' Alistair rubbed his palms down his trousers – 'that people don't attend in the way they used to. We can no longer assume a common Christian heritage in this country.'

Nicely sidestepped.

'What's your opinion?' Alistair looked at Josh, who shot a glance at Ruth.

He looked like a schoolboy, afraid to give the wrong answer, in case his classmates laughed at him. 'I think that Jesus told his stories in the language that the people around him could understand. What's more, the first Bibles – '

'Wycliffe and Tyndale,' Ruth filled in for him.

' – were in the common language. I think we have a responsibility to make sure our performances are easily understood.' He glanced from Ruth to Alistair. 'But that's just my opinion. And I think Ruth's done a great job updating them. And I don't think I could learn them in that old-fashioned language, even if I could understand it. It might be fine for the medieval merchant tailors and goldsmiths, but not for blokes that work in DIY shops.'

Alistair's expression said he was no longer bantering. 'Our language is desecrated, our morality belongs in the gutter, and our countryside ruined ...'

A fine veil of perspiration broke out on his forehead. Ruth had never seen him like this before, so angry. They had touched a nerve. She found herself praying for wisdom, recalling the words from the Proverbs: 'The wise in heart are called discerning, and pleasant words promote instruction.' She needed to find the key to his reaction. She couldn't face fighting about the script, and she couldn't afford to have Alistair walk out. Then it came to her. She knew what was behind his tirade.

'I'm sorry about the road,' she said gently. For the second time Ruth found herself apologising for the bypass. 'I know how hard you fought to stop it.'

Alistair fell back in his chair, looking as if he had been hit in the stomach. 'It's mutilated the town … and there was nothing I could do about it.' He hung his head.

Bingo, thought Ruth.

'It's made the rush hour easier,' Josh said brightly.

Alistair glared at him. Ruth placed her hand gently on Alistair's arm.

'We're here to read through the play. Alistair, if you'd like to try improving on my efforts, you're very welcome. I mean it.'

'Thank you.' Alistair placed his hand over hers. 'I think you've done an admirable job. I'll try my utmost to do it justice.'

The two actors read their parts before walking through their moves, their voices echoing around the church hall. A chill went through Ruth as Alistair said the words; 'The man that I kiss is the one you should kill.' And once again she wanted to weep at the injustice of the betrayal of one man by another, one to whom he had been so close.

MUCH AS RUTH LOATHED THE IDEA, SHE KNEW SHE WAS OBLIGED TO VISIT THE other rehearsals. She would have to sit there while Ronnie or Harlan mangled her text and directed the cast in a way guaranteed to set her teeth on edge.

Ruth arrived early at the Edwardian grammar school to watch the choir rehearse. She followed the chatter and giggles of teenage girls – the angelic choir, she assumed – to the classroom on the second floor. The hallways smelt of disinfectant. It reminded Ruth of her own schooldays.

'Ah, Reverend Wells, come in.' Harlan beckoned to her.

In an effort to keep Ronnie and Harlan separate as far as possible, Ruth had allocated the music in the Old Testament section to Ronnie and the New Testament to Harlan.

'How's it going?' Ruth asked.

'Very well indeed. We're about to start, so you can hear for yourself.' She clapped her hands.

Most of the girls continued their conversations. There were plump girls, black girls and Asian girls, short girls and tall brunettes. There was even a redhead with glasses. Unfortunately, there were no boy angels.

She made her way to the back of the classroom and sat at a desk facing the whiteboard. Harlan asked a couple of girls to push the small upright piano away from the wall and angle it so she could peer round at the girls. She positioned herself, perched on the piano stool like a bird, and commenced the warmup exercises.

Ruth lamented that none of the original music had survived from the Middle Ages.

'Ah,' Harlan had once said, defending herself, 'I heard about a musician connected with the York Mysteries who studied ancient paintings and managed to construct a piece by examining the sheet music held by a choir of angels in an ancient painting. How's that for resourcefulness?'

As the choir began, it was obvious Harlan had not gone to the same trouble. At first Ruth thought the choir was carrying on with warmup scales and arpeggios; then she recognised some of the words.

'Glory to God in the highest and peace to men on whom his favour rests.'

But the melody! It would have made Schoenberg sound positively conventional. She tried not to let the pain show on her face as the beautiful words had the life squeezed out of them by the appalling tune. Ruth could honestly say she would rather have listened to amorous tomcats than Harlan's choir.

Now Ruth's discomfort shifted focus. She needed to tell Harlan what she thought of it – and she needed to be honest. Harlan ran through a couple of passages, singing out the notes and demonstrating high and low notes to the girls by making horizontal chopping movements with her hands, as if she was a rather indecisive lumberjack in the process of felling a sapling, unsure of how high up the trunk to make the first cut.

When the seemingly interminable song at last ended, Harlan sidled over to Ruth. Behind her, the girls chatted loudly about their boyfriends and the latest episode of their favourite soap.

'Well, what do you think?' Harlan's eyes shone and her pendulous earrings almost brushed her shoulders as they swung.

Ruth paused to take a deep breath. Before she could get the words out, a crash distracted them both. One of the girls who had been perched on a desk fell to the floor with a shriek. Her giggling friends tried to pull her to her feet. Harlan hurried over to check on the girl and re-establish discipline. That done, she returned to Ruth.

'So glad you liked it,' she said. 'That awful man – ' Ruth assumed she meant Ronnie – 'maintained that you couldn't have a contemporary setting for ancient words. "Nonsense," I told him.' She shook her head vigorously, entangling her earrings with her hair. 'It's been such a fantastic opportunity, not only for me as a composer, but also for the girls to get away from all those trite pseudomedieval ditties.'

A scuffle broke out among some young ladies in the front row. Harlan again propelled herself out of her chair and homed in on the debacle. Ruth took the opportunity to slide out of the room, closing the door quietly behind her.

Back in her car, she tried to think logically. From the start she felt a sense of connection with the plays, yet the whole project had now taken on a life of its own. She could no more claim ownership of the plays than she could the sea or the wind or God himself. She had a choice. She could let the plays have their head, or she could attempt to rein them in and make them behave.

A choice? Why then did she feel so helpless, as if she could not stop the plays from running amok.

Scene Ten

JEMMA COULDN'T DECIDE WHETHER TO TAKE A COPY OF HER ARTICLE IN THE *Gazette* to the rehearsal to show Josh or whether to play it low-key and modest, assuming he had already seen it. Finally she peeled the front page off the current issue, folded it neatly, and tucked it into her handbag. That way all eventualities were covered.

When she arrived at the hall, Ruth looked flustered, sitting in her director's chair, speaking urgently into her mobile phone. Jemma sidled up to Ronnie to find out what was going on.

'John the Apostle has been seconded to the Frankfurt office for three months; St Peter is on holiday for a week, and Lazarus has the flu. Says he is at death's door!'

That would be handy, Jemma thought. *Then the part wouldn't tax his acting skills too much. Still, it might be a bit of a tall order for Josh to resurrect him ...*

'Thanks, Alistair,' Ruth said into the phone, 'I knew I could rely on you ... yes, we will just be reading in ... by half past seven; yes, that would be wonderful. Thanks so much. You've saved my life.' Ruth flipped the cover of the phone closed.

Jemma assumed Ruth had to drum up replacements and stand-ins at short notice, but Alistair! There was something about the illustrious Councillor Fry that made Jemma's hackles rise. It wasn't that she didn't like him; it was just that ... Jemma couldn't put her finger on what was bothering her. Perhaps it was that 'reporter's nose' again.

The door swung open and Josh entered. The bulky bandages were gone, and his palms were covered in flat white dressings. Some of the sore, reddened skin on his fingers showed. Jemma felt relieved; he was obviously on the mend. She wanted to rush to him and cradle those hands and kiss his fingers. But before she could walk across the room to make polite conversation with him, Ruth intercepted him, presumably to explain the lack of disciples. Josh glanced at Jemma and she smiled at him. He quickly looked away.

The door clattered open again and Alistair rushed in. He was still wearing his navy three-piece pinstriped suit, but his maroon tie with the Monksford town crest was askew and his top shirt button was open. Ruth's face brightened when she saw him and she quickly abandoned Josh to welcome Alistair.

Josh stood alone. Jemma wanted to go to him, but she felt herself blush as shyness overwhelmed her. This was not an emotion she usually experienced, not since she was a little child. But here it was, keeping her feet cemented to the floor. She half wanted to walk over and show him the article. Her other half wanted to run and hide in the toilet. She didn't have the opportunity to do either.

'Right!' Ruth clapped her hands. 'Let's get started. In your positions, please. Jesus over here and Woman Caught in Adultery over here.'

Jemma and Josh climbed onto the stage along with her four accusers.

'Of course there's no biblical or historical precedent to think that the woman caught in adultery and Mary Magdalene are one and the same. But from a production standpoint, it's just such a small role it's hardly worth getting anyone else in.'

Jemma nodded. She knew this. *Why does she have to go through this every time?* Her irritation rose as she prepared to be dragged on by her accusers. *It's as if she feels the need to justify everything. To me, perhaps? Or to her God? What does it matter?*

Rough hands took hold of her arms and dragged her across the stage. They threw her at Josh's feet. She glanced up and looked pleadingly at him. Josh was staring down at her. There was something cold in his eyes. He wasn't acting.

'"Lord, no man has condemned me,"' Jemma said.

'"And because of me, be ashamed no longer. Of all your sins I make you free. Look no more to sin's assent,"' Josh said.

For all the forgiving words, Jemma sensed a barrier between them that had nothing to do with either of their roles.

Even so, this was one of the scenes she found the most difficult to understand. So the girl had had a few boyfriends; she had been about a bit. Why would they want to kill her?

They played through the scene again and again until Ruth was satisfied; then they moved on to the raising of Lazarus with Alistair standing in for the indisposed corpse. Jemma played Mary, this time with a different coloured scarf on her head, to signify, as Ruth was at pains to point out – again – that Mary Magdalene and Mary the sister of Lazarus were not the same person.

Part of the middle of the play text had been lost, giving the whole scene a jumpy feel, like a badly edited movie. Jemma wondered why Ruth had included this fragment. Then she realised that it was almost certainly for her benefit. They spent a little while talking about how to fill the gaps in the play.

'Well, I know it's not completely authentic, but I've taken the Bible story, tweaked it a bit here and there, and slotted it into the original play.' The inconsistencies irked Jemma's writer's sense. If only she could get her editing pen to that script ...

Finally they stopped for a break. She smiled over at Josh, who turned his back to her and left the building, letting in a blast of cold, damp air before the door slammed close. Jemma pulled on her coat and followed him out.

'Hi,' she said, placing her hand on his arm. 'Are you okay?'

He shrugged out of her grasp. 'Why did you do it?'

'Do what?' She frowned.

'Write that article. What do you think you were playing at?'

'What do you mean?' She tried to stay calm, to not raise her voice.

'All that hero stuff! Why did you do it?'

'I thought you'd be pleased!' Jemma was shouting now.

'Why? Why would I be pleased? I just can't believe your nerve. You took my comments and splashed them all over the front page of the local paper. I thought you wanted factual information. Instead you've turned me into a ... I don't know ... a celebrity.'

'I didn't misquote you, did I?'

It was Josh's turn to shout now. 'That is not the point!'

'Then what is?'

'I'm not a hero; I didn't do it for publicity ...'

'Then why did you do it? Pure altruism? Or did the DIY store pay you a bonus?'

Josh turned, red faced, and headed back towards the hall.

Jemma followed. She wasn't going to let this rest. She had done nothing wrong. In fact, she had done him a favour.

'Josh – don't you walk away from me.' She caught him by the arm and pulled him outside. 'What is your problem?'

'Firstly, it was not heroics. I just did what anyone with a scrap of compassion would do. Secondly, you have used things I told you privately, and thirdly ...' He looked down at his feet. 'I thought you cared enough about me, I thought you'd got to know me well enough to realize that I wouldn't want all this attention, all this glory.'

He looked up and Jemma searched his brown eyes. Her anger was diminishing but she still needed to make her point.

'I understand what you're saying,' a phrase she used when she didn't understand what someone was saying, 'but, this was news. Best of all, this was good news – '

'Good news!' His voice rose an octave with incredulity. 'My work-place almost burns down, a man nearly dies, and I get my hands burnt – superficial and deep dermal burns the hospital said. There may be some permanent scarring they said. Great news, let everyone rejoice!'

'The fire got put out and nobody died. All right, you got hurt, but you'll heal.'

'Thanks very much!'

'No, hear me out. If you had any idea of what comes in to news-paper offices, if it's not boring or trivial, it's the most heartbreaking stories of suicides, lives ended in horrific road accidents, or murders. Some days I wonder what kind of world we live in. Sometimes what I hear and see, and what I have to investigate and write about makes my heart sick. Sometimes I have to go home and shower, just to get the feeling of degradation off me. Then we get a story like this, a story of ... well, hope. You did a good thing, Josh, and the public need to know about it. People need hope. I managed to persuade my boss to run that story as the front page. Do you know what the alternative was?'

Josh shook his head.

'It was the story of a woman of ninety-eight who was attacked in her own home. She was robbed of sixty pounds, her pension and sav-ings, and left shocked and bleeding. A neighbour found her later that day but she died in hospital from her injuries and from shock. That's what happens in Monksford.'

'Isn't it important that people know about the old lady too?'

'Of course, and the story did go into the paper, along with in-formation from the police about how to keep safe. It just wasn't the first thing they saw when the paper dropped through their letterbox. You did something special, Josh, and no, I don't think just "anyone" would have done what you did. You rescued someone. You saved their life. And you put your own life at risk to do it. To my mind, that's no small thing.'

She took him by the shoulders. 'Please, Josh, don't be angry with me.'

'I'm not angry. It's just that there are more important things.'

'More important than saving a man's life?'

'"For whoever wants to save his life will lose it, but whoever loses his life for him will find it."'

'What's that supposed to mean?'

'Look it up.'

'What?'

'In the Bible – Matthew 16. You have got a Bible, haven't you?'

Jemma growled in frustration. 'Don't you dare throw Bible verses at me. If you want to talk to me, you can explain properly in words I can understand.'

'How's this? I am not a hero. Jesus is. I don't want to be on the front of the *Monksford Gazette*. I want him to be. I don't want people talking about me. I want them talking about him. What I did was nothing. Zero. Compared with what he did. I prolonged one man's earthly life for possibly a few years. Jesus forfeited his life so we could live forever. Do you understand?'

'No.' said Jemma. She was getting cold, standing out here discussing metaphysics with this man. 'Besides he's been dead for two thousand years!'

'No, he hasn't!'

'Of course he has! It's there in the play. You should know. Christ's death on the cross.'

'No, you should know. What about his resurrection and appearance to Mary Magdalene.'

'This is all real to you, isn't it?' Jemma studied Josh's face. He wasn't just acting in a play; he was living another man's life.

'Yes,' he said softly.

'Look, I'm sorry I used your story like that. I should have asked first.'

'Yes, you should have.'

'I've apologised. I meant it.'

'Okay, just don't do it again.'

'Well don't go rescuing anyone else from burning buildings.'

Josh shook his head. 'I meant I don't want to see anything else about me emblazoned across the local press.'

'I promise.' Before he could stop her, she gave him a peck on the cheek. He looked startled and put his hand to his face, as if she had slapped him. She turned and walked into the church hall. She didn't look back, because she didn't want him to see the smirk on her face.

The second half of the rehearsal went better than the first. Josh had relaxed, and there was more warmth between them. Ruth had grabbed a Bible, and they blocked out the scene where Martha and Mary took Jesus to Lazarus's tomb. Some mourners were cast in role, and the company performed the shortest yet most profound verse in the Bible: 'Jesus wept.'

At the end of the rehearsal everyone looked happier. Alistair and Ruth seemed deep in conversation, the woman playing Martha had flown off to relieve babysitters, and the disciples and Jewish leaders had disappeared to the Blue Bell.

'Do you want to join them at the pub, or do you want a lift home?' Jemma asked Josh.

'Home, I think.' He sighed. 'I'm back to work tomorrow. Not that I can do much with these.' He looked at his hands with the white dressings covering both palms.

Jemma drove down the High Street, but instead of continuing to the bypass she turned left into the Todbourne Road.

'I think you've taken the wrong turn,' Josh said.

'I don't think I have,' said Jemma.

'You were supposed to be taking me home.'

'I am, you just didn't specify whose home.'

'Stop the car!'

'Josh, what's the matter?' She pulled up to the kerb, flicked the key to silence the engine, clicked the catch on her seatbelt, and turned to face him.

'You know exactly what the matter is.' He swivelled in his seat to face her.

'My home is very nice,' she wheedled.

'Jemma, what are you playing at?'

As if he didn't know, thought Jemma. 'Well, I like you and I think you like me ... and I thought we could go back to my place for a coffee and ...'

'And what?'

'You know.' She furrowed her brow. Was he being deliberately stupid? 'Do I need to spell it out?'

'You're doing it again, aren't you?'

'What?'

'You're assuming you know what I want. I thought after our conversation earlier that you'd understand.'

'Don't I?' She placed her hand on his knee. He moved it back to hers.

'You have absolutely no idea who I am or even what's important to me, and frankly, I don't think you care enough to find out.' He turned and stared through the passenger window.

Jemma sat there for a moment with her hand over her mouth. If she hadn't, her jaw might have dropped and left her sitting there, gaping like a goldfish in the Kalahari. What young, good-looking, red-blooded male in his right mind would turn down an offer of ... That was it!

'I'm so sorry. You're gay. I didn't realise ... I just thought ...'

'I am not gay!' He glared at her. 'Why do people assume that just because I'm not jumping into bed with everything in a skirt that I'm gay? Five years ago I would have taken you up on your offer – like a shot. A year ago, maybe, even six months ago I would have given it serious consideration, but not now. I've changed.'

Jemma was just about to ask, 'From what into what?' when he started to speak again. He took her hand and looked into her eyes. 'I know it's just not right for me to do that any more. Oh, it's not that I don't want to. It's a matter of respect. Respect for you, for me, and for what God wants.'

Jemma felt her anger rising. How dare he patronise her like this, and how could he be so arrogant as to say he knows what God wants?

'What about what I want?'

He looked away.

Who was he? Mr Morality? Practically perfect and a mindreader too? She refastened her seatbelt and started the engine. Her tyres squealed as she hauled on the steering wheel and executed an inelegant seven-point turn, just missing the opposite kerb. They sat in silence as she drove, foot to the floor, along the High Street. She didn't slow down for the speed camera. She was beyond caring. A sixty-pound fine couldn't make her feel any worse. When they arrived outside Josh's house, she jammed on the brakes so firmly their noses nearly touched the windscreen.

She leapt out of the driver's seat, slamming the door hard. After she went round to the passenger door and wrenched it open, Josh climbed out. He had hardly closed the door before Jemma revved the engine and took off down the road. She didn't slow down on the way back, bringing the car to a sliding halt with the assistance of the handbrake on the gravel next to the towpath.

Her mobile phone rang. She let it. It might be Richard. Or Josh.

She might as well have brewed a triple espresso for all the sleep she would get tonight, but instead, she tucked herself into bed with a mug of camomile tea. Two seconds later curiosity overcame her and she checked her voicemail. It wasn't Richard; it was Josh and the message was only two words: 'I'm sorry.'

Jemma lay in bed, replaying the conversation. He had talked about respect. She wasn't sure how refusing to sleep with someone showed that you respected them. And the God stuff! People who were Christians must have sex, surely? Does God not like it? Her RE teacher at school was at great pains to point out that God had created sex and made it beautiful, even commanding Adam and Eve to go out and reproduce. Perhaps God had changed his mind since then. She rolled over and switched off the bedside lamp. The moonlight on the water projected ripples on the ceiling. She watched the undulating pattern, trying to fall asleep, but a series of thoughts flowed through her consciousness, each one, as it moved downstream, being replaced by another, until she felt as if her mind would be washed away by the current.

Josh's apology had softened her anger, but as she thought about it, she realised it wasn't him who needed to say sorry. She imagined the roles were reversed. If any man made the same assumptions she had just made, she'd have labelled him as a lech.

She pressed the call button. There was a long delay before Josh answered. She wondered if she had woken him.

'Hi, it's me.'

'I thought it might be. You took your time calling back.' He didn't sound sleepy.

'I've been thinking.'

'And what have you been thinking about.'

'Us.'

'Oh.'

Jemma couldn't make out what 'oh' meant.

'I just wanted to apologise for coming on to you like that. You're right. We should take things more slowly, get to know each other properly. Before ...'

'Before what?'

'Josh. Stop playing games will you? You know exactly what I mean. We're both adults here.'

'We are.'

'I said, stop it! It feels like you're judging me.' Her anger rose again.

'Jemma, I have never judged you. And I'm sorry if anything I've said has made you feel ...'

'Look, I know I've slept with men. It doesn't make me a bad person.'

'I never said it did.'

'It's all right for you. I don't suppose you've ever done anything wrong. Just don't accuse me ... of ... of ...'

'What did I accuse you of?'

'Nothing. Nobody has accused me of anything. It's just me.' Jemma's brain was reeling. 'Look, Josh, I'm tired. I'll call you later. Goodnight.'

And before he could say anything, she pressed the button and ended the call.

Scene Eleven

RUTH WAS HEARTENED THAT SO MANY OF THE COMMUNITY OF MUNKSFORD HAD become involved in the plays. But so much of her time was taken up with the mysteries that she had time for little more than the weekly services and the occasional deanery and diocesan meeting. When Peter, her bishop, asked to see her, she feared the worst. Even as she brewed tea before his arrival, her hands shook, and when the front door bell rang, she jumped.

The Right Reverend Dr Peter Croxted filled the doorway. As usual, he was five minutes late. He took her hand, and she felt his beard brush her face as he kissed her on the cheek.

'Peter, come in; make yourself at home.'

Dimitri opened one eye. Bishop Peter tickled him under the chin with one sausage-like finger, before folding his huge frame into Ruth's largest armchair. She handed him a mug of tea. He fished in his briefcase and pulled out a packet of chocolate biscuits.

'Jenny thought you might need these.' He opened the packet and spilled the contents on the tray.

'Tell your wife she's a star,' Ruth said.

'Are you sure you're all right, Ruth?' His face was suddenly serious. 'You look rather tired, and it's not long since your mother ...'

'I'm fine, Peter. I just feel a little ... guilty. You know, "messing around" with the plays and neglecting the ministry.'

'Why do we do this job, Ruth? To attend endless meetings or to share the Good News of Christ?'

Ruth smiled. 'Sometimes it feels like the former! But I do have a sense of vocation.'

Peter's eyes twinkled. 'Glad to hear it! And the plays?'

'All part of it. It sounds funny, but I believe God can use these plays to change people, the cast and crew, the people of Monksford, and to change me.'

'Good. I share your vision – taking the gospel outside the walls of the church and into the community. That's what it's all about. In a way I envy you. As long as you keep things ticking over in the parish. I'm looking forward to being in the audience. A few years ago, I would have been up there on the stage.'

Ruth couldn't hide her surprise.

'Oh yes, I've done Shakespeare, Ibson, Brecht. I once had a major part in A *Midsummer Night's Dream*. I've been told,' he leaned towards her conspiratorially, 'that my Bottom was to die for.'

Half an hour later, she waved goodbye to Bishop Peter, locked her front door, and headed for St Sebastian's.

Inside, she picked up her digital camera, nudged the vestry door, and went into the church. The east side, which had escaped the fire of 1852, contained what she had been told was the most beautiful medieval stained glass outside York Minster. She had to agree.

She gazed at the east window, a scene of Christ's crucifixion dating from the thirteenth century, studying the image of torture and triumph, of pain and victory. It showed the Roman soldiers, not wearing the traditional *lorica segmentata*, crested helmet and tunic, but dressed as medieval knights. Next to it was the Annunciation window with the Virgin Mary in a green gown with a brown cloak. Her hair hung loose and uncovered, to signify she was unmarried.

Ruth sighed with disappointment. Dreary weather had caused the sun to fail in its duty to illuminate the coloured glass, so she checked the flash was switched on and pressed the shutter button. On the screen, the beautiful, ancient scenes looked dull and flat. The images that, at times, had the power to move her to tears resembled a badly coloured painting-by-numbers set.

Returning to the vestry, she printed out the photographs, then held them up and studied them one by one. 'So this is what you wore in your Corpus Christi pageants, is it, medieval Monksfordians?'

They did not answer. Their images, more permanent than photographs, more luminous than oil paintings had been vitrified and preserved – a moment caught in fragments of coloured glass. But they could speak only through their stillness.

She had begged, borrowed, and hired costumes from local Shakespearean societies and a drama club near Canterbury that regularly staged productions of the *Canterbury Tales*, but she still needed to have most custom made.

In response to Jemma's plea in the *Monksford Gazette*, a woman called Eliza Feldman had left a message, in the wavering voice of the very old, on the vicarage answering machine. Ruth jotted down the address on a scrap of paper and set off for Todbourne Heath to visit Eliza.

As she left Monksford, a watery attempt at sunshine spilled over the horizon. 'You're too late,' she muttered.

The Todbourne Road joined the bypass at a roundabout. There had been yet another accident. The traffic was snarled up and Ruth had to push her way round the cars to get across. The other side of the bypass, when the traffic had cleared and the road ran parallel to the river, Ruth wound down her window and breathed in the country air. Although it was bitterly cold, she couldn't bear to be confined in the car.

Since listening to the voice message, she had worried about what she assumed was Mrs Feldman's religious background and how she might react to the plays. As she drove, she prayed. 'Father, thank you for Mrs Feldman and her offer to assist with the costumes. Please help me not to say or do anything that might offend or upset her, and may she become closer to you by hearing the story of your Son. Amen.'

As she drew up at Primrose cottage, she realised her assumption had been correct when she saw the Mezuzah attached to the frame of the lilac-painted door. She took a deep breath and rang the doorbell.

She glanced at the garden as she waited for Mrs. Feldman. The tiny front lawn was immaculately manicured and the shrubs were already arrayed in their winter outfits of bright red berries. A robin landed on the garden wall and studied Ruth intently. She stared back but the tiny bird in its scarlet waistcoat must have taken offence, for it flew abruptly away and sat on the roof, fluffing its feathers. The door opened slowly, and Ruth could see a small, white-haired lady who seemed to be wearing a large patchwork quilt.

'You must be Ruth,' she said. 'I'm Eliza. Please come in. I won't take your jacket; you may need to keep it on.'

She followed Eliza into a tiny sitting room, full of overstuffed furniture in Chintz prints. On the wall over the fireplace was a beautiful tapestry, woven in myriad colours of wool. The words were in Hebrew. Eliza caught Ruth looking at it.

'It's a blessing on this house,' she said.

Ruth smiled, and Eliza indicated a chair. 'Won't you sit down? Tea?'

Ruth nodded, and the old woman shuffled out to the kitchen. Ruth noticed she was indeed wearing a quilt. The grate was empty, and the room was freezing. Ruth rubbed her arms vigorously. She wandered round, trying to keep warm, looking at the vast array of ornaments – china figurines, pewter mugs, knitted dolls. In one corner a huge sewing machine sat on a table. Bags stuffed with fabric scraps were everywhere. She shivered and rubbed her arms again. She could see her breath.

'Sorry, it's got a bit chilly in here since the boiler went out.'

'It is a little,' Ruth said. 'Is someone coming to fix it?'

'Well, I asked my neighbour, but he got called away on business. Mrs Jones, next door on the other side, is ninety-three and has arthritis in her hands. I don't really know anyone else.'

'What about a plumber or a boiler repairman?'

'I don't think it justifies calling someone in. I do have it serviced regularly, you know.'

'How long has it been broken?'

'Oh, I'm not sure it's broken; the pilot light's gone out. Mind you, I'll have problems when the cold weather comes if I can't get it started.'

The little head and legs protruding from the cocoon of quilt, the tiny sticklike ankles, and porcelain skin, the hair, fine and white as thistle-down, made Eliza Feldman look as if a strong breeze would blow her away.

'Would you like me to take a look?' Ruth feared her gallantry might be misplaced, but if it was as straightforward as Eliza had suggested, at least she could try.

'Oooh, yes, please.' She led Ruth through to the doll-sized kitchen. An enormous wall-mounted boiler hung, cold and sulking, in one corner. Ruth recognised the make; they had had the same kind in the house where she grew up. She remembered well her mother pulling open the door and grumbling as she used a spill to unblock the gas jets and relight the pilot. With a terrible foreboding that she just might blow up the entire street, Ruth tugged the door open and poked around as she remembered her mother doing. She blew into the jets, remembering to shut her eyes as the dust rose into a cloud. Finally, she carefully lit a wooden spill from the gas cooker and prayed as she turned the knob. The gas lit with a pop, sputtered, and went out. Ruth tried again. The same thing happened. She sighed.

'Perhaps you'd better stick to preaching sermons, vicar,' Eliza said.

Ruth nodded in agreement. 'Look, there's a member of our congregation who's a gas fitter, semi-retired. He'll come round and sort it out, and he won't charge you a fortune, I promise.'

Eliza looked relieved. She poured the tea, and they both took their mugs into the sitting room. Ruth cupped her hands around hers in an attempt to thaw out her fingers. 'Now,' she said, 'you contacted me to offer to help with the costumes for our waggon plays.'

'That's right. I was a dressmaker for nearly fifty years. I've made ladies and men's bespoke clothes and theatrical costumes. I've even done some work for film studios. As you can see, here's my machine. And I've got plenty of time … well … actually, I haven't got much time.'

Ruth frowned.

'I've got cancer you see. It's in my lungs and my bones now. I take tablets and they check up on me every month, but there's nothing can be done.'

'Oh, I'm so sorry,' Ruth said. Her stomach lurched. It was too soon after Mother.

'Don't be sorry. I've had a good life. Now I want to do this last thing. Something to be remembered by. "Because your love is better than life, my lips will glorify you. I will praise you as long as I live, and in your name I will lift up my hands."'

'A psalm of David?'

'That's right, and God will give me the breath and strength to complete this task.'

Ruth looked at this frail, birdlike lady. 'Before you agree, there's something I need to discuss with you.'

'Fine! Discuss away.' The old lady folded her hands in her lap.

'I don't know how much you know about the mystery plays. They're very old – dating from the fourteenth century. The first few plays show how God created the world, then the fall of man, Noah's ark, and Moses. Then it goes on to the story of Jesus' life and death …'

'Yes …'

'Well his trial, persecution, and crucifixion are quite graphically portrayed.'

'What is your point?'

'Well …'

'Spit it out, girl!'

'People have said that it could appear, antisemitic. You know, the Jewish High Priests – the villains, being responsible for Jesus' death.'

To Ruth's amazement, Eliza threw back her head and laughed.

'I don't see how that's antisemitic. I know the baddies in your Christian stories are Jews. But don't forget, the goodies are all Jews too.'

Ruth breathed a sigh of relief. She handed her the photographs and promised to drop over the measurements. Finally, she left Eliza Feldman's tiny, freezing little house, but not before she had chopped a gargantuan pile of logs and kindled a roaring fire in the grate. It was the least she could do.

She whispered a prayer of thanks, allowing herself a moment's relaxation, then realised that she was due to see Harlan Westacre after lunch. She had the sinking feeling that meeting couldn't possibly go as smoothly.

SHE MET HARLAN AT TWELVE THIRTY IN DONATELLO'S, A PRETENTIOUS LITTLE coffee bar in the High Street. The leather sofas, cherry-wood floors, and swing music were supposed to lend the place a little urban chic; instead, it just made it look as if it was trying too hard. Harlan was perched delicately on one of the expansive leather sofas, her buttocks hardly denting the cushion. She was embracing a cappuccino mug the size of a birdbath. When she spotted Ruth, she jumped up. 'Darling, what can I get you? The Choco-Cream Frappuccino with a dash of toffee-nut syrup is just divine.'

'Just a black coffee, thanks.'

'Oh, if you're sure.'

Ruth nodded. 'Absolutely.' The truth was, she would have loved to try one of Donatello's exotic concoctions, but she didn't want Harlan to be the one to introduce her. She wanted to assert her firmness, and she was starting with the beverages. Of course, she was just about to violate the principle of 'if you're going to criticise something, you'd better make sure you can offer something better.' She had come empty handed, and when engaging in combat with Harlan, this put her at an immediate disadvantage.

Harlan fired the first shot. 'So what did you think of the choir?'

'Well ...,' began Ruth.

The waiter approached the table. Harlan ordered Ruth's coffee.

'The music was quite something, wasn't it?'

'It certainly was!'

'I wrote it myself, you know. Well ... arranged it. The themes are taken from ancient monastic chants.'

Could have fooled me. The waiter came with her coffee. She took a sip. It was hot and strong and nearly stripped the skin off the roof of her mouth.

'They've worked so hard to learn it. It's not easy stuff you know.' Harlan forced a smile.

Ruth suddenly had the urge to shoot herself in the foot, just to render herself *hors de combat.*

'You didn't like it did you?' Harlan's chin jutted forward, ready for a fight.

'I wouldn't say I didn't like it exactly. It's just that I felt, given the costumes and the language and the setting ...'

'Go on.' A challenge! She placed her mug carefully on the table and leant back, her arms folded.

'That it might be a little, well, modern.'

Without a word, Harlan collected her bag, drained her coffee mug, and marched out of Donatello's, leaving Ruth with the bill.

'That went well,' Ruth muttered to herself. She pulled her mobile phone out of her bag and pressed a button. Alistair's slightly gruff voice answered.

'Have you had lunch yet?' Ruth asked.

'No, not yet, why?'

'Do you know Donatello's in the High Street?'

'Yes.'

'Good. If you can get here in the next ten minutes, I'll treat you to a ciabatta.'

Ruth ordered another coffee and waited for Alistair. He came through the door quarter of an hour later, red faced, and slightly breathless. Ruth felt rather flattered that he had hurried to meet her.

'Houston, we have a problem,' she said as Alistair settled himself in the armchair and picked up the menu. 'Harlan.'

Alistair raised his eyes heavenward. He listened patiently as Ruth struggled to put into words the hideous tunelessness of Harlan's composition. 'I wondered if you'd be able to go and see her this weekend. I'd do it myself, but I think I'd be the last person she'd be prepared to listen to.'

'I'm sorry; I can't this weekend. I'm seeing the children.'

'Children!'

This came as a surprise. Ruth hadn't realised he and Amanda had any children. Somehow he didn't seem the paternal type.

'Yes, from my second marriage. Rory's twelve and Stefan's eight. I do try to get over to see them as often as I can. Of course, the other three are off my hands now. Christa's living in Denver, Marcus is married, and Lulu's just finishing at university. Thank goodness for that, an end to tuition fees, at least until the other two start.'

Ruth sat there open-mouthed.

'Yes, Amanda's my third wife.' He gave a sigh. 'I sure know how to pick them!'

Ruth was lost for words. Fortunately, the waiter came over, and Alistair ordered lunch for them both.

Alistair was in full flow. 'I'm sorry you had problems with Harlan. Mind you it makes me feel a bit better about Ronnie.'

Ruth winced.

'Not good news there either, I'm afraid,' Alistair said.

'What happened?'

'Well, Ronnie too has gone for a modern slant on the music. Except ...'

Ruth leaned forward. 'Except what? He's been allocated the Creation of the World, The Fall of Man, Noah's Ark, and Moses and Pharaoh. Where could he go wrong with that?'

'He decided to link it with songs from Broadway shows.'

'He did what?' she screeched.

Couples at neighbouring tables looked round, alarmed. People did not usually raise their voices in Donatello's. Even the waiter looked shocked as he brought their sandwiches.

'He did what?' Ruth repeated in a whisper.

'He's got them singing "Oh, What a Beautiful Dawning" when God says "I bid in my blessing you angels give light," "You'll Never Work Alone" for the creation of Adam and Eve and ... "I'm Gonna Wash That Man Right Out of My World" just prior to the flood. I didn't wait around to see what he'd done to Moses.'

'You're not serious! I thought he was joking when he suggested "Mack the Knife" as an introduction to the story of Abraham and Isaac.'

Alistair's face told her he was indeed serious. She drooped her head into her hands. 'What are we going to do?' she groaned. 'The whole thing's going to be a complete farce!'

When he didn't answer, she looked up. He shrugged and glanced at his watch. 'Sorry, Ruth, I have to get back to work. He scooped up his sandwich and threw a twenty-pound note on the table.

'Hey, lunch was supposed to be my treat!' she protested.

'I think you've got enough on your plate,' Alistair said and left.

Ruth finished her ciabatta and tiramisu; then as twenty Korean businessmen entered and started reorganising all the furniture, she decided it was time to pay a visit to the library. Perhaps their music section would hold something she could use to arm herself for the next round of the battle. Besides, she could do with the walk – all that coffee had made her twitchy. That and Alistair's three marriages.

Her car-park ticket was running out, which was an excellent excuse for abandoning the library until tomorrow and heading out of town to check on her favourite scaffolder. Rajinder's (Est. 1981) was situated on a small industrial unit on a farm just outside Monksford. 'Raj' Rajinder had been carrying out building work and repairs to St Seb's for as long as Ruth could remember. When the mortar on the Norman tower had started crumbling and a brick nearly ended Mrs Warboye's career as churchwarden, Raj had been round the same day to shore up the structure and start repairs.

All this happened shortly after her mother died, and Ruth was grateful for Raj's efficiency and compassion. He not only made tea for himself and his employees, but he often brought her one too as she worked, usually close to tears, in the small vestry. Without that little act of kindness, that shoring up, she too might have crumbled and collapsed completely.

She smiled at the memory as she parked in the yard and skipped over the puddles to reach the little office. A blast of warm air greeted her. A tall man in a blue turban stepped out of a back room and shook Ruth warmly by the hand.

'Raj, lovely to see you.' At least she knew she wouldn't get any unpleasant surprises from him.

'Ruth, as always, it's a pleasure. I hope the church tower isn't falling down again, and I sincerely hope it isn't a case of "bats in the belfry".'

'Closer than you think!' Ruth laughed. 'No, I've just come to talk about next June – the mystery plays. Well, the budget has been finalised, and I thought maybe we should discuss the arrangements. Obviously, you'll need to measure the sites yourself, but I went there the other day and took a few notes. I thought I might give you a rough idea of what I'd like done for the money, then you can laugh and tell me what I'm really going to get for the money.'

Raj smiled. 'Go ahead.'

Ruth told him, and he did indeed snort a laugh.

'I tell you what. There'd be no problem at all, me constructing a stage down at the abbey. You won't need seating in the lower field if it's as steep as you say, but I'll put a platform there. You'll ask people to bring blankets and picnic baskets? So perhaps I could build a seating stand near the barn.'

'That sounds marvellous.'

'And I won't charge you for labour, just for the hire cost. And I'll let you have that at a discount.'

'That's very kind Raj, but I don't want to put you out of business.'

'Ruth, you're a good customer. And with you, I know I'll always get paid on time. I can't rely on everyone. Also, you are a woman who knows God. That is very important to me.'

'When are we going to see you and Surinder in church?'

'When we see you at temple, I think.'

'I have been to your temple. You had an open day. I had a lovely meal and chatted to Mrs Kaur for ages. She knew my mother.'

'I remember.'

'So it's your turn.'

Raj's smile faded.

'What's wrong, Raj? I hope I haven't upset you. You don't have to come to church.'

'It's not that. I'm worried about Surinder.'

'What's the matter? She's not ill, is she?'

'No, but she might as well be, the amount of time we spend at the hospital.'

'So, what's wrong?'

'We've ... we've been trying for a baby, for nearly six years. Nothing happens. We're having tests. It looks as if we may have to undergo fertility treatment.'

'Raj, I'm sorry. Look, if there's anything I can do.'

'Could you pray – to God?'

'Of course! Would you like me to come round and see you both?'

'Yes, we'd like that. You've been good to me, Ruth, and I hope I've assisted you. I thought ... well, I thought that by helping you put on this Jesus play, that God might be merciful to us and grant us a child. Do you think he will?'

'I don't know, Raj, but I do know that he rewards faith.'

'Yes, I believe that. You shall have your scaffolding – as much as I can give you, and I will have your prayers.'

'Deal! Thank you, Raj.' Ruth shook his hand again. She wanted to hug him, but she was aware of eyes watching. Of course she would pray; she would pray for a child for this lovely couple. She would also pray that they would come to know the source of their hope, the living God, through the Lord Jesus Christ.

Scene Twelve

IT WAS WITH TREPIDATION THAT JEMMA PREPARED TO ATTEND THE REHEARSAL.
It was not so much the rehearsal itself – Noah's ark – but it was the prospect of meeting Josh afterwards for the first time since she had tried to seduce him. She knew she had blundered in, and she knew to expect debris. Broken trust, fractured feelings, and the sense she could make things worse rather than better.

'You know nothing about me!' The accusation that caused her least pain at the time but stung the most afterwards. He was right. She knew his name, his address, his occupation, and his religion – application-form knowledge that gave her no insight into Josh, the man.

And she resolved to change this. Tonight.

The rehearsal was more entertaining than she had imagined. Noah's wife, a pantomime dame of a woman, complete with a rolling pin, was wonderfully stubborn, refusing to enter the ark and terrorising her scrawny husband.

'Sons, help me hold her down, she doesn't realise what danger she is in!' cried Noah, ducking blows from the rolling pin.

'Please, mother, stay with us,' begged her son. He clung to her apron strings as she spun round, brandishing her weapon.

'No! I must go home, I have pots and pans, ladles and spoons to pack. And I mustn't forget those little metal things for squeezing lemon wedges.'

Jemma suspected Ronnie had been taking liberties with Ruth's text – but it made everyone laugh.

'Dearest, why must you make more trouble for us?' Noah said.

'Noah, you never let me know where you were, out early and back late, and you left me at home twiddling my thumbs.'

'Ay, well, I was doing God's work.'

'Oh, yes, and what makes you think you're going to get away with it? I swear I'll give you the hiding of your life.'

'Darling, I beg you, be still. You cannot argue with God's will.'

Eventually, Noah prevailed, but Jemma wouldn't like to have spent forty days and nights on a boat with her. She roared with laughter when God sang, 'I'm Going to Wash That Man Right Out of My World' after pronouncing judgement. Then she noticed Ruth was sitting with her head in her hands.

'A modern touch to an ancient story that will allow contemporary audiences to relate to the virtues of a bygone age.' She scribbled in shorthand. She was enjoying herself so much that she almost forgot about meeting Josh.

She had spent most of the morning trying to read the Bible to impress him but only managed to skim the first hundred or so pages.

It had started well, 'In the beginning God created the heavens and the earth ...'

She loved the suddenness, the power of it. The idea that God spoke and it all happened. At school, she had of course learnt about the 'Big Bang' and the stupendous forces that had formed the universe, but she never thought there was a supreme being, a creative mind, behind them.

She recognised the story of Adam and Eve, Noah's ark, and Moses, then it all seemed to get confusing, with rules and covenants. She decided, then, the only way to begin to understand what she was reading was to take a small section at a time. So she had tried it again.

The Lord said to Moses: 'When a person commits a violation and sins unintentionally in regard to any of the Lord's holy things, he is to bring to the Lord as a penalty a ram from the flock, one without defect and of the proper value in silver, according to the sanctuary shekel. It is a guilt offering. He must make restitution for what he has failed to do in regard to the holy things, add a fifth of the value to that and give it all to the priest, who will make atonement for him with the ram as a guilt offering, and he will be forgiven.'

It didn't help. She looked up the reference on websites and still felt none the wiser. It seemed to mean that if you do something wrong and don't realise it is wrong, you have to kill a sheep and everything will be all right. 'Totally weird,' Jemma muttered.

The overwhelming conclusion she reached was that the Bible was virtually incomprehensible – full of old stories and rules. The one thing she learnt from the websites was that Christians couldn't agree on anything. She felt sure if you put two Christians in a dark room, they would spend the first hour arguing over whether to switch the light on or not.

Still, she had managed to find out that today was All Saints' Day. Jemma had no idea what Christians do to celebrate the day, but perhaps Josh would be impressed.

When Ronnie finally uttered the words, 'It's a wrap', and everyone had cringed, Jemma took a minute or two to brush her hair (sleek and glossy), adjust her dress (short), and check her makeup (fresh and subtle) before driving to the Fruiterer's Arms. Josh was already waiting at a table in the corner and stood up to greet her with a peck on the cheek.

'What would you like?'

She requested cola, and he ordered a pint of orange juice topped up with lemonade.

They sat at the table near the fire.

'You look very nice this evening.'

Good, he noticed. She lifted her glass. 'Happy All Saints' Day.'

Josh looked puzzled at the toast but lifted his glass, and they clinked.

'All Saint's Day? Since when ...?'

'Just because I make a point of knowing my important church festivals ...,' Jemma said. The gesture was not lost on Josh.

'What's brought this on?'

'What?'

'Well, today, there's hardly any leg on display, no cleavage to speak of, and I discover you're au fait with holy days. Is this the Jemma I know? Next you'll tell me you're not going to try to get me into bed.'

Jemma felt her anger rising. If this is the reward she was going to get for making the effort, then he could stuff it. She picked up her glass of cola and tossed the liquid into his face. Then, mustering her dignity, she marched out of the pub, much to the astonishment of the regulars, leaving Josh, soaked and sticky, sitting with his mouth open and a lap full of ice cubes. *At least the locals got a bit of entertainment tonight,* she thought as she stomped to her car. Unlike Lot's wife (a story she liked though she did think God was a little hard on the poor woman) she didn't look back, but drove straight to the *Ebony Hog.*

The first thing she did was to pour a glass of cola. Why should she miss out on her beverage just because Josh needed to be taught a lesson?

She swigged her fizzy drink as quickly as possible without getting hiccups, still fuming at Josh. A car slid to a halt on the gravel the other side of the towpath. She allowed herself the luxury of peeping out of the window. It was dark. The only illumination came from the one light, paid for and erected by the river's residents for security purposes. And so the vandals and car thieves could see what they were doing. She strained her eyes to see. It was a dark blue estate car, not Josh's light blue van.

She switched on the computer. Typing up her notes and starting this week's column would be a good distraction. If Josh did turn up, she wasn't sure what she would say to him. Although there was a little digital clock in the bottom left-hand corner of her computer screen, she took off her watch and laid it on the desk next to her laptop, a practice her grandfather had suggested.

'Them editors will have you working all the hours God sends, give them 'alf a chance. Make sure you know exactly how much time you're putting in after hours, then if anyone says you've taken too long on a job, or you want to nip out to the bank, or leave a bit early one day, you can say to them, "I've already worked four hours twenty six minutes outside me scheduled time this week. Surely you can't begrudge me ten minutes?" Of course you haven't got a leg to stand on legally, but you'd be surprised how many back down if you give them a to-the-second reckoning on all the extra work you've done.'

She hadn't plucked up the courage to try this with Mohan, but she had with her first editor, a buxom woman called Margaret with an over fondness for frilly blouses and too much mascara. She managed to concentrate for seven and a half minutes before she heard another vehicle pull up. She peeped out again. This time it was a pale blue van – Josh. She sat down pretending not to notice and carried on typing. There was a tentative knock on the door. She ignored it.

'Jemma, can you open the door please?'

She sat by the computer, watching the second hand tick round. The knock came again.

'Jemma, I know you're there. I saw you looking out of the window.'

In spite of herself, Jemma started to giggle at the absurdity of the situation. She clamped her hand over her mouth so Josh wouldn't hear her.

'Please let me in, Jemma. I'm soaking and rather sticky. It's freezing out here and it's starting to rain.'

'Good,' she called to him. 'That will wash the cola off.'

She heard him turn to go and, figuring she had made him suffer enough, she opened the door and called out. He jogged back through the drizzle and gratefully ducked through the hatch. Jemma handed him a towel.

'Thanks,' he said.

'Are you okay?'

'Yes, just warn me next time you're going to do that, so that I can take off my leather jacket first.'

'Do you want a wash?'

He frowned dubiously.

Jemma put her hand to her forehead. She wanted to scream.

'There's a lock on the bathroom door, and I promise I'll leave you in peace.'

He gave a sheepish grin and disappeared inside with the towel. She heard yet another car pull up. Looking outside she could just make out the shape of a Land Rover. She filled the kettle and put it on to boil, then flicked through her CD collection. She wanted music, but she didn't want to set a mood. She found a classic U2 album she hadn't played for ages and slid it into the computer. With so little space on the boat, even her electronic gadgets had to be multipurpose. Josh opened the bathroom door. His hair was wet and he carried a soaking towel.

'I used your shampoo. I hope you don't mind.'

Jemma didn't mind at all.

'Tea or coffee?' she asked. Then added with a grin. 'Or a glass of cola?'

'Tea, please.' He threw himself on one of the sofa-benches that ran the length of the cabin. 'Blimey, I haven't heard this track in a while.'

Jemma went through to the galley and finished making the tea. When she came in to hand him a mug, he was thrashing away on air guitar.

'Old habits die hard,' he said.

'You go ahead, enjoy yourself.' She sat down on the sofa bench opposite. 'I'll watch.'

'You've embarrassed me now,' he said, not looking in the least embarrassed.

'Have you eaten?' Jemma asked.

'Yes, thanks,' replied Josh.

'I haven't. Do you fancy a walk to the chippy?'

'All those deep-fried carbs!' Josh pulled a face. 'I'll cook you something if you like. I'm a superb cook, even if I do say so myself.'

'I don't think I've got much.' Jemma considered the contents of her fridge: some mouldy cheese and half a liquid cucumber more than likely. 'And the galley can be a bit of a challenge if you're not used to it.'

'You say that, but I can rustle up a meal out of more or less anything.' He opened the door of her compact refrigerator and stuck his head inside. When he emerged, he had a look of disgust on his face. 'Jemma, do you know what the date is on these eggs?'

Jemma shrugged. She assumed they were months out of date.

'And what is this?' He held up something green and limp and slightly hairy. 'This is evidence for the theory of evolution if ever I saw it. It's a completely different life form than when in went into that fridge. This is not a kitchen – this is a biohazard!'

Jemma shrugged. She'd never claimed to be Nigella Lawson. 'Looks as if it's the chippy after all.'

They both put on their coats. Jemma grabbed an umbrella then locked up.

'Can't be too careful around here,' Jemma said.

'Certainly not,' said Josh. 'You can't take any chances with that gang of felonious water voles and the notorious burgling otter brothers on the loose.'

'What are you going on about?'

'Of course they got a seven-year stretch. For holding up a bank.'

'A bank. What bank?'

'The river bank!'

Jemma groaned. 'Right, you've had it. No chips for you.' She ran ahead down the towpath.

'We'll see about that.' Josh gave chase and caught up with her effortlessly. He put his arm around her shoulders. It was a gesture of friendship rather than anything more. But Jemma liked it and had to battle with herself to resist the urge to turn and kiss him. She didn't want to spoil the moment. They strolled down the towpath, sharing Jemma's umbrella.

'You're into health food then?' she said.

'I like to try to keep fit. I eat plenty of fruit and vegetables, fish, and a little meat. I don't drink or smoke now, but I jog and go to the gym regularly. And my job keeps me fairly active.'

'You make me feel like a slob as usual,' Jemma said.

'Sorry. I didn't mean to do that.'

'Perhaps I am a slob. I mean, who else do you know who drives from their home to their garage, eats chips seventeen times a week, and has vegetables in their fridge for so long that they change species?'

'It's those little quirks that make you so appealing. That and your meddlesome nature.'

'Meddlesome! Excuse me! That's my "journalistic nose" you're referring to. Like a bloodhound, me. First sniff of a story, and I'm there like a shot.'

He stopped and scrutinised her face. 'But what made you choose that as a career? Do you feel that is your destiny? Is that what you were created for?'

'That's a difficult question. Yes, it's something I feel drawn to. My granddad was a journalist. I suppose you could say it's in the blood. My ambition is to be like him. He's my hero.'

'The job, is that why you came to Monksford?' he asked.

'Yes, but I want to move on. Get a job at a national newspaper, travel. I've never been one to stay in one place for too long.'

'Is that why you live on a boat?'

'That was the original idea. I suppose I don't feel ready to put down roots.'

They turned off the towpath and right onto Todbourne Road. Jemma paused on the humpback bridge that crossed the river. It had stopped raining so she put her umbrella down.

'And what about you? Is working in a DIY shop your "destiny"?'

Josh smiled. 'I don't think so. I'm still trying to work out what God wants me to do with my life.'

Here he goes again. Conceited enough to think he knows what God wants. As if God would bother with worms like us when he's got a whole world to run.

They turned the corner and started up Monksford High Street. Josh was walking fast, and Jemma had to jog to keep up. She tried not to let him see she was out of breath. She was right; she was a slob. Using the car less and walking more would help. And reduce the amount of take-away food she was eating – but not tonight. The queue for Charlie's Chippy was spilling out the door onto the pavement. They joined the end.

'So how did you end up at Abacus DIY? Did God put you there?'

'I suppose he did in a way. When I got back to England, I needed a job. My parents live in Maidstone. I wanted to be close, but not too close.'

'You've lived abroad?'

Another of Jemma's ambitions. The nearest she had got to 'abroad' was a boozy fortnight in Ibiza or Faliraki.

'Sort of. The Balkans.'

They reached the front of the queue. Jemma ordered battered cod and chips with vinegar and mushy peas. She was delighted that Josh also ordered chips and was even more delighted when he paid for the meal.

They carried their food outside, swaddled in white paper, sending steam into the icy air as they pulled back the paper and began eating with their fingers.

'You were telling me you lived in Eastern Europe. What were you doing there?'

'I was in the army at the time. Only a private. I wanted to see the world, but all I ended up seeing was the back streets of Sarajevo and Kosovo.'

'Is that why you left?'

He stopped eating and looked at Jemma. His face darkened, and she began to wonder if this line of questioning was a mistake.

'No, I left when I became a Christian. I just couldn't do it any more.'

'Do what?'

He started walking again. Faster. Jemma was getting left behind.

'Do what?' she called. She had had enough of trying to carry on a conversation while he disappeared into the distance. She sprinted to catch up with him, and she linked her arm through his to slow him down. 'I thought there were loads of Christians in the forces. Fighting for Queen and country; isn't that supposed to be a noble calling? The church walls are covered in memorial plaques for those who gave their lives for their country.'

'Perhaps ...'

'So, why did you leave?'

Josh crumpled his paper and slam-dunked it into a rubbish bin as he passed.

'I couldn't stay in a job that might require me to kill people,' he said.

Jemma hadn't had him down as a pacifist.

'You mean the Ten Commandments – "Thou shalt not kill"? Isn't that about murdering people? Defending our country from enemies, surely that's a good thing, a heroic thing.'

They reached the bridge over the river. Josh stopped walking, much to Jemma's relief. He leaned on the edge of the parapet, studying the dark river, its current carrying debris downstream.

'And who are our enemies? People like us, defending their country from *their* enemies. Jesus told us, "Love your enemies and pray for those who persecute you, bless those who curse you, do good to those who hate you." I can't see that you can kill them if you love them. They were people, just people.'

'Yeah, and those people were slaughtering each other. You were there to stop them.'

'We didn't stop them though, did we? We just killed a few more. Made it worse.'

'Surely there were other duties, peacekeeping and all that. What about other countries?'

'No, it was time to move on. I just about lasted my four years. I applied for a discharge as soon as I could. I couldn't stand it any longer. I saw so many of my friends go ...'

'Were they killed in action?'

'No, only one got killed by a landmine in Sarajevo. Another hanged himself, and of the others, two were given a medical discharge for psychiatric problems and one drank himself to death.'

'So you thought "blow that for a game of soldiers".' Jemma laughed. Josh didn't.

'I can't describe to you what it was like.' Josh's voice had changed. His words sounded thick and flat. She laid a hand on his back.

'I ... I didn't mean to upset you.'

He didn't reply, but she knew he was crying. A mixture of compassion and distaste filled Jemma. She didn't know what to do. What kind of man bursts into tears on you in the middle of a discussion?

'I didn't mean to pry. I guess you're right about me being a journalist. Meddlesome, that's what you said.'

'It's not your fault,' he said wiping his eyes with the back of his hand. He started walking again, almost running. By the time she caught up with him, he had reached the car park and was fumbling in his pocket for his keys. 'I'm sorry. I never intended to offload on you. What do you think of me? I thought I was over it. It's just every now and then ... I feel so stupid. Look, I'd better get home.'

'No! I mean, no, please don't go. We can go back to the boat and talk if it would help. Besides, I still haven't finished my chips.' She held up the crumpled paper.

'Jemma, you're a lovely girl, and I really enjoy your company, but tonight, you've just seen me make a complete idiot of myself. I'm cold, damp, embarrassed, and I want to go home. Talking won't get me anywhere. I just have to get over it. I'll see you at the next rehearsal ...'

There was a huge splash. Jemma and Josh looked at each other, frozen for a moment, then he took off at a run towards the river. 'Get a torch!' he called over his shoulder.

Before she could move, Jemma heard footsteps on the other side of the bridge – heading straight towards her. Within a heartbeat, a man barged past her, but not before almost knocking her into the canal.

She recovered her balance, jumped onboard the *Hog*, and grabbed a flashlight. She shone it towards where the man had disappeared into the gloom of the car park.

'No!'

She had lost him.

'Hurry up with that torch,' Josh called.

She ran across the bridge where Josh stood, scanning the murky river. He snatched the torch and swung it round like a search beam. Nothing.

A shiver ran through her and she froze. The sound of footsteps, this time on the far side of the river. A rustle in the bushes. Footsteps again, now running in the car park. Josh swept the torch beam in a wide arc. An engine started and revved. Headlamps dazzled them; then tyres spun on the gravel and an engine whined, reversing at high speed. Another splash from the river. Josh aimed the torch again.

'Look,' shouted Jemma. 'There's someone in the water.' She pointed towards the bank, where reeds thrust their blades out of the muddy river. Josh threw his coat on the bank and kicked off his shoes. He waded into the icy river, gasping as the freezing water stole his breath. Jemma dropped the torch and grabbed a life ring. She threw it towards Josh's voice.

'Light!' he yelled. 'I can't see a thing!'

She picked up the torch again and held it in both hands, trying to keep the beam steady. Josh had reached the body and, with one arm tucked through the life ring, struggled to haul it to the opposite bank.

'Can't you pull it out this side?' called Jemma.

'No ... bank's too steep.'

As she ran across to help him, she could hear Josh's teeth chattering. Finally, he reached the edge, and she took hold of the man's shirt and pulled while Josh pushed his body and legs. They managed to manoeuvre him on to the bank and Josh clambered out.

'Is he dead?' Jemma asked.

Josh rolled the man on his back and listened for breath. The man's hair and face were dark with blood. The blood had washed off his clothes, but his head and face were still fairly dry. Perhaps the blood was a good sign. Dead men don't bleed.

'Is he dead?' she repeated.

'He will be if we don't get help soon. He's not breathing.' Josh felt the man's neck for a pulse.

Jemma dialled the emergency services while Josh started to work on the man's chest and airway. Doors of neighbouring boats flew open and soon a crowd of people offered blankets, sweet tea, and brandy, and suggestions of how best to help the victim. Josh sent away all but the blankets.

Jemma's heart was pounding so hard she thought everyone could hear it. How could this be happening in Monksford, in her town, on her river? Then her reporter's sense kicked in, making a mental note of all the events, people, time, and places, and committing as much as possible to memory. Whatever happened, this was going to make a great story. How Josh would cope with being the hero twice in as many months, she was not quite so sure.

Ambulance sirens wailed in the distance as Ray Jones arrived with a hurricane lamp, far more effective than Jemma's faltering torch beam. She held it above her head. The man was wearing a blue checked shirt and jeans. He had blond hair, matted and stuck to his head. Blood streaked his face, obscuring his features. Whatever Josh was doing seemed to be working. The man stirred and his eyelids flickered a little. Skye Wortham from the *Lucky Lady* arrived with some warm water and a tea towel. She started to mop at the victim's face and head.

The man's eyelids fluttered, then opened. His lips moved as he tried to speak. Jemma moved in closer to hear was he was saying.

The man whispered a name. The name was 'Jemma'.

Scene Thirteen

RUTH SAT AT HER DESK, SORTING THROUGH THE BOX OF PHOTOGRAPHS SHE had found in Mother's room. Most of the early ones were black and white: Her parents at a dinner dance, her mother in a satin gown with a wide skirt and a shawl collar, her father in a double-breasted suit. Her mother had curled her copper-coloured hair, and her father was smiling shyly.

Her parents' wedding day, mid-January with snow on the ground. Her mother, dressed in a navy skirt-suit, the jacket cut full to hide the baby.

The following June, her parents in the garden, her father cradling a bundle swaddled in a blanket, smiling proudly.

A camping holiday, the baby now a toddler, hair in bunches, and another swaddled bundle, her brother, Roy.

Her father astride his Norton motorcycle, Ruth standing proudly next to him, with her hand on the tank. She was about eight, probably the year he died.

Ruth and Roy at the seaside. Staying with Auntie Joyce while mum had Susan. Another holiday, Margate, possibly. Uncle Fred had taken the photo. She and Roy had been fighting and both looked sulky. Sue was about two. Her mother looked pale and exhausted. There was very little help for single parents in those days, even widowed mothers with three small children. No wonder she looked so tired.

Teenage years – hippy skirts and flared jeans, platform shoes. She looked self-conscious. Ruth and some friends at a funfair, standing

142

next to a roller coaster at *Dreamland*. She was holding her friends' coats and bags beside the gargantuan roller coaster. She hadn't quite mustered the courage herself to go on it but watched while Julie and Paul, Caro, and Tim screamed and shrieked. Vicarious entertainment.

Her first dance – at the Palais, wearing a maxi-skirt and a lime green blouse with ridiculously long collars. Ruth had always thought of herself as a fat teenager, but these photos, taken before the days of digital manipulation, refused to corroborate her memories.

Bryan Smith, at twenty, had been her first real boyfriend. She stood next to his car, a Triumph Spitfire, grinning proudly. She would have done anything to have married him, but he never asked. Her mother cried when they broke up. She so wanted to see Ruth walk down the aisle.

Eastbourne, the last holiday she and mother had taken, just after they had found out the final dose of chemo hadn't worked. They wanted to go away, have fun before … before … It had rained all week in Eastbourne.

A biography captured in photographs. An existence of almost, nearly, not quite. There were reservations in every picture. It was as if life came with a caveat. It was never perfect. She had spent her early years wishing her father alive, her teenage years wishing herself thin, and her twenties wishing herself married. Most of her thirties, she had struggled through university and ordination, wishing herself qualified, and more recently, wishing her sick mother well. That wish hadn't come true either. Now she was qualified and ordained and resigned to the idea that she would never be thin. Watching her friends and siblings on their second and third divorces she was glad she had never married. She and Dimitri made a good couple; very few demands on either side.

What was life all about? Perhaps she was better off as she was. Perhaps this half-life, with a little pain and not very much pleasure was preferable to the emotional roller coaster that had driven more than one acquaintance to alcohol, drugs, or suicide. Did it matter that she had never screamed with terror or felt the wind in her hair? She helped people. She had a faith that sustained her, good friends, and a job that was worthwhile. And her hobbies – golf, gardening, and now the mystery plays that had taught her so much and brought so many interesting people into her life. On top of all that, she was well thought of, a pillar of the community, a brick, a good egg.

Tears ran down her cheeks. Suddenly it did matter. It mattered very much. She had been 'Miss play-it-safe' all her life; now, at forty-eight, she longed for danger. Finally, nearing the menopause, she felt she was just reaching puberty. She must be a late bloomer. The thought made her smile. She tucked the photographs back in the drawer and tidied her desk. She would book a haircut and, against all her frugal, utilitarian principles, a manicure and a facial. She reached for a tissue and wiped her eyes. It wasn't too late for a new start. Life begins at forty-eight.

SHE LIKED TO BE FOUND ON HER KNEES PRAYING IN CHURCH. NOT IN SOME KIND of pharisaical way, but so that people knew that she prayed. Prayer is something so personal, so silent and solitary, that no one can tell that you are doing it at all. In the same way that someone can only tell you're breathing when you sigh or snore, they can only tell if you pray aloud (only practical in a worship meeting) or if you show it by your body language. Ruth was surprised at how much spending some time in prayer had cheered her up. She seemed to have so many more people to pray for these days. There was Raj for a start; and Eliza Feldman; Josh and that reporter, Jemma; Ronnie and Harlan and how she was going to tell them about the music; Bram and his farm. That was in addition to all the usual people and things she prayed for. She ended with the Lord's Prayer, got up, and turned round to find Alistair Fry sitting in a front pew, watching her.

'Oh! You startled me!' She put her hands to her chest.

'Sorry, I didn't mean to scare you.'

'How long were you there?'

'I arrived somewhere between Mrs Wainthrop's shingles and "Our Father".'

She had not prayed aloud. How did he know? He was holding a parish magazine, open to the page 'for your prayers'. Of course she would pray the Lord's Prayer, everyone did. Even so, she felt odd that he knew what was happening inside her head. It both comforted and frightened her.

'What do you want?' Her heart had stopped racing, but she couldn't help feeling angry. It was almost like being stalked.

'You.'

'Pardon?'

'I want you. Come on, we're going out.'

What was he thinking? He took her hand but she pulled it away.

'What about Amanda?'

'Oh, she didn't want to come.'

'You asked her?'

'Of course!'

'You told her you were taking me out?'

'She thought it was a good idea, said you'd been working too hard and could do with a bit of pampering. Unfortunately, she had to go to Ashford this morning and said she wouldn't be back in time.'

'Are you sure?'

'Absolutely. Come on, I've packed a picnic; I even polished the car this morning.'

'A picnic, but it's the middle of November.'

'Which is why I've included a flask of oxtail soup, warm pasties, and apple pie with custard. Besides, the sun's shining and it's not that cold. Anyway, I want to talk to you.'

'What about?'

'We have a little problem that needs sorting out. Or should I say two little problems – Harlan Westacre and Ronnie Mardle.'

Ruth groaned.

'That's what I thought. So we're going out, blow the cobwebs away, and put the world to rights. Well, a very small corner of it anyway. What do you think?'

Ruth grinned. 'Why not.'

The midnight-blue Mercedes was polished like a mirror. Ruth really could see her reflection in it. It distorted her and made her look even plumper than she really was. Her confidence almost deserted her, and she was ready to call the whole excursion off. But she had made herself a promise. She wasn't going to let life pass her by; she would seize it with both hands. She was going to ride that roller coaster.

'Where shall we go?' asked Alistair.

'Not too far. I've got a busy afternoon. How about by the river?'

'Can't you think of anywhere more adventurous than the river?'

In truth she couldn't.

'Come on, what's your favourite place?'

'Around here?' She thought for a moment. 'The abbey ruins. Very atmospheric. Especially if we're going to talk about the Mysteries.'

'Hmm, about as exotic as the river.' Alistair's voice betrayed a hint of irritation.

'But I like the abbey ruins. You asked me where I wanted to go, and I told you. We don't have to go anywhere if you don't want to. We could have the picnic here in the graveyard.' She folded her arms, surprised at her assertiveness.

'Okay, Monksford Abbey it is.' He held the door of the Mercedes open for her, and she climbed into the passenger seat. She sank into the sandy-coloured leather upholstery. The car smelt clean and fresh, unlike the rancid smell of rotting fruit and general grime that seemed to pervade her car.

'Nice car,' she said.

'Thanks. I didn't have you down as the materialistic type. I wouldn't have thought you'd have been so easily impressed.'

'When you drive a 1988 Ford Fiesta, believe me, this is impressive.'

They drove the mile from St Sebastian's to the abbey in near silence. Ruth studied Alistair as he drove. He seemed tense, his jaw clenched. He looked tired, and the lines around his eyes seemed a little more pronounced. In her fifteen years of listening to people, Ruth had learnt to read their faces. If she hadn't known better, she would have assumed he was a worried man. His knuckles were white as he gripped the wheel, and he muttered under his breath as he applied the brakes to avoid Mr Giddings, on his bicycle, who swerved out into his path.

'Is everything all right, Alistair?'

'Of course.' He laughed. 'I'm away from the office and the chambers, the sun's shining, and I have the company of one of my best friends. What could possibly be wrong?'

He parked the car on a strip of grass. A flock of Canada geese flew up from the river and passed overhead, making a terrible racket. Ruth put her hands over her ears. 'Worse than being on the flight path from Gatwick!'

She helped Alistair unload the hamper and a rug from the car. The wind was freshening and the sky had darkened. The limestone abbey ruins seemed to have taken on a silvery sheen that made them stand out in sharp contrast to the dark grey clouds. She shivered.

'Let's find a sheltered place. Look – over here behind these stones.' He spread the rug on the grass in a little alcove, sheltered on three sides by the remains of the abbey walls. Ruth sat on the ground, pulling her coat close and hugging her knees. Alistair sat next to her and opened the hamper. The feast was just as sumptuous as Alistair had promised with sandwiches of gammon and mustard and roast beef and horseradish. The pasties had been wrapped in foil then placed in an insulating bag. Alistair handed one to her, and she unwrapped it and bit into it gratefully. He poured them both a mug of oxtail soup.

'What are we going to do about the quite hideously, disgustingly awful mockery that passes as music in our lovely medieval masterpieces?' he asked.

'More's the point, how are we going to deal with it and still have Ronnie and Harlan talking to us at the end of it?'

'Do we care if they're still talking to us?'

'Yes, Alistair, I do care.'

'Yes, of course.'

Ruth picked up a hot chicken drumstick and waved it at him like a baton. 'The best way to make anyone change their mind is to make them think they thought of it themselves.'

'Ah, psychology,' Alistair said.

'Precisely.'

'And,' Alistair picked up his own drumstick, 'we could do it by suggesting an alternative. Something so toe-curlingly appalling they'll fall into line and do what we want. Did you find any more suitable music in the library?'

'Yes. Some lovely medieval choral stuff. It would be just perfect.'

'Great. Well done. Now how could we persuade them?'

'We could record their music and play it back to them so that they can hear how dreadful it sounds.'

'We could, but they hear it when they rehearse. It sounds dreadful but they don't seem to notice.'

'What about getting Ronnie to Harlan's rehearsal and Harlan to his?'

'World War Three!'

Ruth laughed. He was right, though. And that would be the end of the mystery plays.

'I love it when you laugh.'

Ruth felt her cheeks warm.

'I mean it. It brightens my day.'

'Your day won't be very bright unless we hatch a plot to sort this mess out.'

'Hang on! I think I've got it.'

'What?'

'We could choose some outrageously inappropriate song. "The Birdie Song" or something similar and insist they incorporate it ...,' he said.

'Or we could just take along this beautiful CD, say we appreciate the work they're putting in but that the two sections Old and New Testaments are just too dissimilar, then politely hand them the manuscripts.'

'We could. Then what?'

'We run for cover.'

They both laughed. Ruth gazed over at the river. A mist was gathering. It felt good sitting here with Alistair. They shared a sense of humour, he listened when she talked, he was handsome – in a rugged sort of way. But he was just so ... married. She took a deep breath and dragged her thoughts back to reality.

'So, how were the children, Alistair?'

'They were fine, thanks. I went to see Rory play in a Rugby match. Stefan lost a tooth, so I got to be tooth fairy. Do you know the going rate for teeth these days?'

Ruth shook her head.

'Two pounds for incisors and canines, two pounds fifty for molars. Can you believe that?'

'I used to get sixpence.'

'So did I!'

'Stop. You're making me feel old.'

'You're not old. You're gorgeous.'

She couldn't help smiling at his outrageous flattery. 'So did Rory win his match?'

'Sadly not. And we had to drown our sorrows in strawberry milkshake at the local burger bar.' He gave a sigh that seemed to come up from the soles of his boots.

'You miss them, don't you?' She put her hand on his.

He nodded. 'I don't feel as if I've ever been a proper dad. Oh, I have a good time when I visit, and I'm sure the kids enjoy it. But every day I'm with them is like Christmas day; everyone's on their best behaviour, trying to be polite, walking round on tiptoes. I mean, it usually involves me giving them presents. I've never done the ordinary things that dads do every day – tucking them in, reading to them.'

'What about the older ones?'

'Christa was four and Marcus was two. Louisa hadn't even been born. She was seven before I saw her for the first time.'

'I'm sorry. Why did you leave?'

Alistair looked like she had slapped him in the face. 'I didn't, they did.'

'Your wives left you. Why?'

'I – I don't want to talk about it.' He started to toss the remains of the picnic into the basket. 'It looks like rain, or perhaps snow. We'd better get back.'

'I'm sorry. I didn't mean to be nosy.'

'Both of them, Joanne and Nikki, they both went off with someone else.'

'That must have been dreadful for you. At least now you've got Amanda.' She drained her soup mug as Alistair made his way back to the car. 'Alistair!' She caught up with him and handed him the mug, which he put in the boot of the car.

'We don't have to go back just yet, do we?' Ruth smiled up at him, but his face remained grim.

'I suppose not.' He locked the car and walked towards the towpath. It had started to drizzle, and a grey mist hung over the river. The flock of geese returned and flew low. As they walked towards the town the light grew dim, even though it was still early afternoon. Ruth felt cold and stiff from sitting on the damp ground. Even through the thick blanket, the chill seemed to have pervaded her bones.

'As I said, I'm sorry I brought up the subject of your ex-wives. It's just that you looked so ...'

'Old?'

'Worried. Alistair, you can talk to me you know, if there's any-thing bothering you. As you said, we are friends.'

'It's Amanda.'

'What's wrong with her?'

'I can't help thinking she's going to leave me too.'

'Why would she do that?'

'I don't know ... The signs are there.'

'What signs?'

'Little things. The phone rings and when I answer the caller hangs up.'

'Sales calls. I get them all the time. It's a dialling machine that calls lots of numbers. If you're not the first to answer, it just cuts off.'

'Buying new clothes, having her hair done.'

'She's just trying to please you, or herself.'

'And going out. Oh, I don't expect her to stay in all the time ...' He laughed. 'And I'm not the jealous controlling type that won't let her out of my sight or make her account for every second.'

'So what makes you think there's anything peculiar going on?'

'She's never there when I call. Her phone's always switched off. She's out most days ... and a lot of evenings. She complains that I don't pay her enough attention; then when I try to arrange some-thing, like today, she's "going out".'

'That doesn't mean – '

'It's all falling apart again. I can see it. I can read the signs. Don't tell me I'm wrong; it's happened to me twice before. I should know.'

Ruth laid a hand on his shoulder. The distress had contorted his face and he was breathing heavily.

'Calm down, Alistair, it may not be what you think.'

He sat on a bench and held his head in his hands.

'You're right, of course. I've just got myself into a state over this. I'm not eating properly, I'm irritable, I can't sleep. I try to convince myself it's not happening again, that it's different this time. But ...'

'Have you tried getting help from the church?'

'My own church? No, I can't talk to them, too much to lose. That's why I'm talking to you.'

'I am not "the church"!' Ruth stood up and walked farther along the towpath. Houseboats were moored along the towpath, their muted colours – deep blue, bottle green, and black – blending with the dark water of the river.

When she stopped next to the *Endeavour*, Alistair stood up and joined her. 'I didn't mean it like that. I meant as a friend.' He took her by the shoulders and turned her to face him. 'If it hadn't been for you and for our friendship over the last couple of months, I think I would have gone mad.' He kissed her very gently on the cheek then pulled her close to him and hugged her tight.

She breathed in the scent of his cologne, felt the rough wool of the jumper on her face, his strong arms around her, and thought she would melt. She looked up into his blue, blue eyes. He kissed her again, this time full on the mouth. He kissed her long and hard and deep. She didn't resist.

ON THE DECK OF THE *EBONY HOG*, JEMMA STOOD AND WATCHED IN AMAZEMENT as the Councillor kissed the Vicar passionately on the lips.

Act Two

Scene One

IT WAS ONLY ONE KISS BUT IT CHANGED RUTH'S LIFE.

Christmas and Easter passed in a blur. Ruth found ways of keeping herself busy; it hadn't been difficult. She managed to keep her thought life under control – just – and mostly managed to avoid Alistair.

Rehearsals were tense. When she saw Alistair, her heart raced, and she was convinced everyone could see the electricity arcing between them.

He caught her alone a few days after their kiss. 'Ruth ...' He tried to take her arm. She walked into the church-hall kitchen. He followed. She stood by the sink and pretended to make tea. He turned her round to face him. His eyes were tender, almost tearful.

'We have to talk – '

'No, we don't, there's nothing to talk about.'

' – about what happened.'

'I told you, Alistair. Nothing happened.'

She opened the door, almost knocking Harlan over.

'Ruth, I need to see you about the Nativity chorus. It's just too ... angelic.'

She led Harlan to an orange plastic chair and sat across from her, leaving Alistair to finish making the tea.

As the weather grew warmer, she spent more time by the abbey, thinking and praying and marvelling that they seem to have got away with it.

One day, she walked by the river and sat on the soft the grass at the abbey ruins. She stroked the velvety turf and lifted her face to the warm sun, reliving that moment when she knew another human being loved her. She had felt more cherished, more wanted and desired than at any other time she could remember. Since that kiss, her prayers had been a mixture of guilty outpourings and solemn promises. But then, hadn't her prayers always contained the mix of guilt and promise?

Even as a child she felt love was based on good behaviour or academic achievement, and when her mother grew old and ill, Ruth felt needed, but need didn't always translate into love. Not love without condition anyway. And then there was Dimitri. Unconditional love? Hardly. The little tame tiger loved her so long as there were tins of food in the larder.

'Father, I know that you love me. I know that in my heart, but I can't help feeling that even your love comes with strings attached. How could you still love me knowing what I have done – what we have done?' She tried to remind herself that unconditional meant just that – without condition. She had even looked it up in the dictionary, as if seeing it in black and white would help her believe it: 'complete and not limited in any way'.

Guilt hit her hardest when she read out the words of the confession 'For failing you by what we think and do and say; Father forgive us.'

'Am I really forgiven, Father? I committed adultery. Not in the physical way, but in the mind, many times, and I know that Jesus considered it just as bad: "You have heard that it was said, 'Do not commit adultery.' But I tell you that anyone who looks at a woman lustfully has already committed adultery with her in his heart."'

She couldn't bear to think about it any longer. She looked at her watch and stood up, brushing the grass from her skirt. She wanted to stay outside on a day like this, not in a cold, dusty church, with all its trappings. She did not want to be reminded that she was the Vicar and could not entertain fanciful thoughts about married men. She walked briskly, kicking a loose stone along the pavement. Kicking something made her feel better.

'Father, the worst of it is, I can't actually say I regret the kiss. As much as I know it was wrong, I'm not sorry it happened. It made me feel so needed, desired ... loved.'

Feelings of guilt almost overwhelmed her. Of course, she repented many times, but the fantasies kept coming back. She loved Alistair and he loved her, and that's all there was to it.

She ran through scenarios many times in her mind. She imagined that Alistair had left Amanda, and he asked Ruth to go away with him. She tried to picture their life as a couple, but whenever she attempted it, her imagination drew a blank. She literally couldn't imagine it. It was simply beyond her.

The other possibility, which kept playing out like a repeat, was that people would find out what had happened. 'Father, you know I am weak. I'm just a human being. I can't do this. It's too difficult. Why can't we be together? I could get another job. I would still try to do your will. His marriage is a disaster anyway. Would it really be that bad?'

She came to St Sebastian's solid oak door, unlocked it, and stepped inside. Shafts of summer sunlight cut through the dusty air. She shivered.

'It was just one kiss! It's not as if I instigated it or planned it – it's not as if I had even wanted it to happen ...' Ah, that was not quite true. She may not have put it in so many words, but she had, deep in her heart, wanted his lips to touch hers. And she was not surprised when they did. 'It was not my fault!'

Maybe not, but she should not have let things go that far, and she should not have enjoyed it! No, if anyone found out, if the incident was reported to her church council or to the Bishop, she would be in big trouble. She shuddered at the thought of the disappointment she would see in Bishop Peter's eyes. He was understanding – but not that understanding. Her only course of action had been to avoid

Alistair, to pretend he didn't exist. To make sure, absolutely sure it wouldn't happen again.

She went into the small office-come-vestry. There were messages on the answering machine. They would have to wait. She sat at her desk and shuffled through the pile of post. She would open them later. Right now her mind was too busy wandering, and she couldn't concentrate.

She remembered how she had felt when, as a child, she tried to get her bicycle along the narrow drive of their house past her father's car. Her father was at work, and she had been too impatient to wait for him to get back from the station. She had taken the bicycle out of the garden shed and started to wheel it down the drive. The gap between her dad's new shiny Wolseley and the fence was narrower than she thought and the pedal left a bright gash in the paintwork on the door and down the wing.

She was so mortified that she ran away. She cycled to the woods and hid in the hollow carcass of an oak tree. She had wished death on herself, hoped lightning would strike her, anything except going to confess to her dad. She searched the wood for a cave, somewhere she could shelter, living all alone, surviving by foraging for berries and trapping wild animals.

She pushed the chair back and wandered into the sanctuary, still lost in her memories.

Of course, she had known that she couldn't live like that. When it started to get dark, she had returned to the house, pushing her bicycle. She went indoors to find her parents and her brother Roy sitting at the dinner table. Everything seemed normal. Dad looked the same as always. Was it possible he hadn't noticed? That made it worse. The usual chat about what they had done during the day accompanied the meal, but Ruth could hardly swallow the shepherd's pie. Eventually she put down her knife and fork and confessed.

'I know,' her father said.

She couldn't pay financially for the repairs to the damage, but pay she did. She paid in disapproval, in the lack of trust her parents afforded her. She had blotted her copybook and never quite earned back her parents' confidence. A quiet man, he almost stopped talking to her, and every time he looked at her, she sensed his disapproval of her for desecrating that shiny paint. Her father died not long after, so she had never had the opportunity to prove herself to him as an adult.

Just as her father had ceased talking to her years ago, God too had been strangely quiet since the kiss. She had ranted and shouted and pleaded, but he said nothing.

Now as she knelt in prayer in front of the altar, she studied the stained-glass window of Christ enthroned in heaven. 'What should I do, Father?' she asked aloud. As usual the Lord remained silent.

Ruth stretched, got up, and wandered round the church. She had thought she had mastered the art of standing still, but now she seemed to be spinning, faster and faster. She circled round, matching her physical movement to her inner turmoil. She scrutinised the faces of saints and apostles, prophets and angels in the stained-glass windows, the scenes seeming to blend in her mind with the scenes from the mystery plays.

She turned round, faster and faster, spinning like a child, until she felt dizzy and the colours were a blur. She grabbed hold of a pew and waited till the world stopped revolving. She stared at the window depicting Elijah at the mouth of the cave and read the Latin inscription: *Zelo zelatus exercituum sum pro domino deo* – 'I have been very zealous for the Lord God Almighty.' The irony made her smile. She had been zealous in her role as producer of the mystery plays, but was her zeal for the Lord? She still felt like finding her own cave to hide in.

She remembered coming to the church for the first time as a curate. Old Tom Bedford, the churchwarden, had showed her around. He read the Latin inscriptions and provided his own translations.

'*In omnibus labor*; that means, "Go to work by bus" ...' Ruth had laughed, but Tom remained deadly serious. She never got to know him properly as he had died before she took up the post. She still wasn't quite sure if he really thought that's what it meant.

'... and this one 'ere: *Zelo zelatus exercituum sum pro domino deo* means summink like "exercise zealously, though some prefer dominos".'

Directing the plays was one area, at least, where she felt some sense of control. The rehearsals had gone reasonably well during the winter and the spring. The actors remembered their lines, Ronnie and Harlen had eventually acquiesced over the music. The next few weeks would entail polishing the performances and putting all the final touches in place.

Enough navel gazing; she needed to visit Eliza Feldman. She had been communicating by notes, carried back and forth by one of the choir members who lived nearby. Ruth had included Eliza, as well as Raj and Surrinder, in her daily prayers but hadn't seen them for weeks.

THE FRONT DOOR WAS OPEN A CRACK WHEN SHE ARRIVED AT ELIZA'S COTTAGE. She knocked and went inside. Eliza was sitting in an armchair with a white angel costume on her lap. The full skirt covered the lower half of the tiny woman and cascaded down on to the floor. Eliza was bent over it, stitching away furiously. She didn't appear to notice Ruth's entry.

'Mrs Feldman? Eliza?'

She didn't seem to hear. Ruth knelt on the floor beside her chair and placed her hand on the old lady's arm. Eliza Feldman looked up at her with weary eyes. Ruth gasped. Eliza hadn't been exactly ample when Ruth had seen her in the winter, but now she had shrivelled to a husk. Her skin appeared too large for her body and seemed to hang in loose folds. Her face had a yellowish tinge and her lips looked slightly blue. Although the day was warm, Eliza was wearing a thick cardigan. Her fingers moved constantly. Even when they weren't stitching, it seemed as if they were trying to.

'The door was open. I did knock.'

'Oh, hello, Ruth. Yes, I leave it open for Joan, my neighbour … She's been helping me with a few bits and bobs … tidying, cooking …' She struggled for breath, pulled herself upright in the chair, and gasped.

'How are you?' Ruth felt like kicking herself. Eliza Feldman was obviously dying.

'Yes, dear. I'm doing very well … I've finished five angels and I'm just stitching the hem of this one … I have two more high priests to do then the Mary of Magdela. I want that one to be fitted really nice and tight – I know what kind of a girl she was.'

Eliza winked. Ruth didn't comment on the possible effect of Mary's conversion on her fashion preferences.

'I'll ask Jemma to call round one evening for a proper fitting.' She looked at Eliza. 'You don't have to do this, you know. I can get someone else to finish them off.'

Eliza's eyes blazed with anger. 'How dare you!'

'What?' Ruth was stunned by her reaction.

'Let me put in all the hard work and then at the last minute take it all away from me.'

'I didn't mean – '

'Use me, wear me out, then discard me! What kind of a way is that to treat someone?'

'Mrs Feldman – '

'Eliza,' snapped the old woman.

'Eliza, I'm so sorry if it sounded as if I was dismissing all that you've done. That was the last thing I meant to do. I'm so grateful for all your work; your skill, your commitment, and, of course, the beautiful costumes – they're just magnificent.' She took Eliza's hand. 'It's just that I can see that you're very ill, and I don't want this to be a burden to you.'

'It is not a burden. This is what keeps me going. Do you not understand?'

Ruth shook her head.

'Last May, they gave me six months at the most ... Back in March, they said I'd be lucky to last till the end of the month. Now it's May again and I'm still here. Every morning it gives me a reason to wake up, and every evening I pray it won't be my last ... When the pain gets strong, it gives me something to take my mind off it. When the sickness means I don't feel like eating, I remember I need to keep my strength up ... Don't you see? God has given me a job to do, and I'm jolly well going to finish it. Then I can die in peace.'

The speech seemed to exhaust her, and her head lolled back against the chair.

'Thank you,' Ruth whispered.

Leaving Eliza to rest, Ruth went into the kitchen to see if she could make herself useful. She dried up some cups on the draining board, filled the kettle, then peeped in the cupboards, which were nearly empty. She added shopping for Eliza to her already too-full list of things to do today.

After brewing the coffee she took two cups back into the lounge. She stopped, dead still, at the sight before her. Eliza Feldman was slumped forward in her chair, her breath rasping. Ruth quickly sat her upright and took her pulse; she could barely feel a flutter through the old woman's parchment skin.

Praying hard, Ruth ran out to her car and grabbed her phone to call the emergency services. She ran back up the path, tapping numbers furiously. She stopped by the gate to give the operator all the details. A large woman with dark curly hair was standing in Eliza's garden.

'Are you Joan?' Ruth asked.

The woman nodded. 'What happened?'

'It's Mrs Feldman. She's having trouble breathing. I've called an ambulance.' Without waiting for the other woman to speak, Ruth rushed back into the tiny house and knelt on the floor next to Eliza. She barely noticed that Joan had followed her in.

'Oh, she won't like that.' Joan said finally.

Ruth frowned, still keeping her eyes on Eliza. 'Won't like what?'

'Going to the hospital. She doesn't want to go.'

'She needs medical treatment. There's no alternative.'

The old woman's chest rattled as she tried to breath, as if to confirm Ruth's diagnosis.

Joan shook her head. 'She's been quite clear about that. She doesn't want to die there.'

She doesn't want to die at all, not yet. 'I'm sure they'll know what to do for her.' She looked up at Joan and softened her voice. 'The woman's face was etched with concern. 'Don't worry. I'm certain they'll take account of her wishes.'

'She's seen what happens. They'll get her in there, pump her full of drugs till she don't know what day of the week it is, then, when no one's looking, they'll stop feeding her and she'll die alone. She wants to be here, in her own house, surrounded by friends.'

Eliza stirred slightly, and Ruth sent Joan to get a glass of water.

'What happened?' Eliza's voice was just a hoarse whisper.

'Don't worry,' Ruth said. 'I've called an ambulance. Help will be here soon.'

'Bring my sewing,' Eliza gasped.

Just minutes later a knock sounded at the door and two green-suited paramedics hurried in and manoeuvred themselves around the furniture to get to Eliza. Joan ducked into the kitchen while Ruth explained what happened. After giving her a quick examination, the paramedics gently lifted her into a carrying chair and took her to the ambulance. Ruth gathered up the angel costume and the sewing basket, lying next to the chair. She called out instructions.

'Would you mind locking up and checking that everything's switched off? And can you bring a bag with her toothbrush, night-dress – oh, and don't forget her glasses. I can call in and collect it tonight. And I can take you to see her if you like. I should think they'll keep her in for a few days.'

'If not for good.' Joan stomped back into the house to do Ruth's bidding.

Ruth followed the ambulance to Monksford General Hospital. She waited with Eliza who was seen almost straight away, then transferred to a cubicle. Her dog collar probably helped speed the process along. She had learnt that lesson when her mother was in hospital. With her cassock on, she was treated with respect, as a spiritual leader, not just dismissed as the frumpy, middle-aged daughter of the patient.

She sat beside Eliza's bed and filled in the admission form as best she could. Eliza lapsed in and out of consciousness. The nurse had fitted her with an oxygen mask, which, when she could speak, made it very difficult to understand what she was saying. When the doctor came, Ruth left them alone and went to get herself a cup of coffee from a machine down the corridor. She took a swig then winced – golden roast with a hint of gravy. When she got back, the doctor was waiting for her.

'Are you next of kin?'

'No, I'm a friend.'

'She's a member of your congregation?'

'Actually, no. She's Jewish.' Ruth could see the doctor's irritation rising. She realised the dog collar was cutting no ice with him. 'Look, she has no other relatives. I've been visiting her occasionally, and we've been getting quite close. The only other person is her neighbour who will be in this evening. Do you need me to sign anything?'

'No, she's been able to consent to treatment herself. I just want to make sure someone can be with her. Would you do that?'

'Yes, of course.' Ruth did not consider herself squeamish, and she had lost count of the number of times she had sat beside patients as they fought to stay alive. She had witnessed many battles and watched people lose as well as win, but she was not comfortable here.

She tipped the rest of the coffee into a washbasin and stationed herself on a plastic chair close to Eliza Feldman's trolley. She took the old lady's hand. Eliza opened her eyes and smiled briefly, then drifted off to sleep again. Ruth looked around the cubicle. The walls were painted a soothing duck-egg blue and the mottled blue curtains had been drawn on two sides, leaving only the end at the foot of the trolley open. There was a washbasin, a yellow clinical waste disposal unit, and a light with an extending arm on the wall. She could hear a child screaming a few cubicles away.

The realisation of how much she hated hospitals came as a surprise to Ruth. Her senses were filled with all the usual things: the smells, the sights and sounds associated with sickness and death, the memories of her mother's last few weeks. But something else gnawed at her, a feeling that she wasn't quite in control. It was if she had to abide by the rules of a game she didn't fully understand, and when she felt obliged to ask, the answer always seemed patronising. Besides, she was never quite sure whom the rules were intended to benefit.

Although it was over a year ago, her mother's time in Monksford General was still fresh in Ruth's mind. The restrictions on visiting hours made the pain of seeing her mother so unwell worse. If she had just watched an episode of *Coronation Street* and was dying to discuss it with her mother, who was bound to have been watching the same episode, she couldn't just turn up. She had to wait for visiting time, by which time, the freshness, the urgency would have passed and neither would care any more. She often made up some life-and-death excuse and visited her anyway. 'Uncle Vanya has just died' or 'my cousin Rachel has left her husband,' she would tell the staff nurse, hoping she hadn't studied English literature. Her mother had rather enjoyed the subterfuge.

She had once tried to cheer her mother up by painting her fingernails bright pink. When she visited the next day, the nail polish had been removed. Hygiene regulations; her mother had been informed. They couldn't even enjoy a number seventeen, a thirty-four, two forty-ones and spring roll from the Happy Wok.

Ruth had just completed arrangements for her mother to be admitted to the local hospice when she died. It would have been a place where Ruth could visit whenever she wanted, where she could have painted her mother's nails whatever colour took her fancy. The staff encouraged families to watch their favourite soaps together, and best of all, a copy of the menu from the Happy Wok was pinned to the patients' notice board.

After she died, Ruth sat alone, with the curtains closed, watching their favourite television shows. Occasionally she turned to her mother's empty chair, with a comment on the tip of her tongue, a joke they could have shared; then she would realize, and the grief would overwhelm her again.

A nurse tapped her on the arm.

'Would you come outside, please? The doctor would like to talk to you.'

Ruth was prepared for bad news; she stood straight, bracing herself.

'Reverend Wells, Mrs Feldman is very poorly.'

'I know that. How long? Hours, days?' She wondered if she should contact Eliza's rabbi.

'It's hard to say, a few weeks, possibly six months, but I doubt she'll see Christmas.'

A half-witted comment, considering Eliza's background, but Ruth was shocked. 'You mean she's not going to die tonight?'

'I shouldn't expect so.'

'But her breathing.'

'She has advanced cancer ...'

Ruth wondered if the doctor had taken a degree in the 'blindingly obvious'.

'Fluid has collected around her lungs, compressing them and making her breathing difficult. We need to drain away the fluid. I'll do that now. Then I'd like her to spend the night in hospital. She's also dehydrated, but I can't find any sign of infection. We'll check her blood – she's almost certainly anaemic – and transfuse her if necessary. I also want to look at her pain control medication and prescribe her some nutritional drinks for when she finds it difficult to eat. If she's feeling better, she can go home, probably in a few days, perhaps a week or so.'

The doctor smiled and turned away.

'Then she's really not going to die?' she called to his back.

He looked over his shoulder. 'Reverend Wells, we're all going to die. It's just a matter of when.'

Ruth sank into the chair with relief. Eliza was sleeping. Ruth didn't want to wake her, nor did she want to leave without saying goodbye. It was half past five. She was hungry and thirsty after missing lunch and the Bovril flavoured coffee hadn't helped. She shuddered. Disgusting!

She spotted a nurse through her six-feet-wide window on the world and informed her she was going to the restaurant.

'If Mrs Feldman wakes up, please tell her I won't be long.'

The nurse shrugged. And Ruth followed the warren of corridors to the restaurant where staff, visitors, and outpatients could buy food. Ruth ordered a plate of fish and chips, poured herself a glass of cola and looked around for a table. The restaurant was surprisingly busy but she spotted a free table at the far end, next to the window.

She quickened her step, so that no one beat her to it. She staked her claim by setting down her glass on the table and her sweatshirt on the chair. She wished she had brought a book to read. Perhaps she could buy a newspaper at the shop. Setting off in search of the cutlery and vinegar, she stopped in her tracks when she saw Jemma Durham, sitting at a table with a cup of tea and a sandwich.

'Jemma! What are you doing here?'

'Oh!' Jemma looked startled. 'Hello, Ruth.'

'Would you mind if I join you?'

Jemma hesitated, then shook her head and shifted her handbag off the chair onto the floor.

Ruth collected her belongings and decamped to Jemma's table. Although she saw Jemma almost every week at rehearsals, she rarely conversed with her. Jemma usually arrived late and was often the first to leave, with or without Josh. Even at tea break, Jemma always seemed to be either fluttering her eyelashes at one of the disciples or sitting in a corner scribbling in her notebook. It was almost as if she was avoiding her. Gripped by paranoia, Ruth had once glanced at the notebook when Jemma had left it lying open on a chair. To her chagrin, the notes were in shorthand, so she, like everyone else, had to wait until the weekly free newspaper dropped through her letterbox to read Jemma's column. So far, the column had all been truthful, witty, and sometimes complimentary. Correspondence had started appearing in the letters column, and a full-page ad promoting the play cycle had prompted a rush of inquiries.

'Jemma, I didn't expect to see you here. Is everything all right?'

'Not really.'

'What's the problem?' Judging by Jemma's expression, Ruth had the feeling that she should have asked this question weeks ago.

'It's Richard. My boyfriend – ex-boyfriend.'

'But I thought you and Josh were ...' Ruth didn't know how to finish the sentence.

'We were, sort of. Then this happened. I felt I should be there for Richard.'

'What happened?'

'Didn't you hear about it?'

Ruth shook her head. Jemma hadn't mentioned it before.

'Last November someone attacked Richard, hit him on the head, and threw him in the river.'

Ruth sat back, gaping. 'That's awful. I didn't know.' She tried to make it her business to know what was going on in her parish.

'We kept it pretty quiet. One of the advantages in working for the press, I suppose. Josh helped pull him out. He was unconscious. They didn't think he'd live.'

'How is he now?'

To her surprise, tears came into Jemma's eyes. 'Not great, still unconscious. PVS they call it, and they don't know if he'll ever wake up properly. The longer he's unconscious ...' She blinked a tear away and took a deep breath as if willing herself to be optimistic. 'He's having therapy, and he's starting to make a little progress. He can open his eyes occasionally and respond to bright lights. He pulls faces and makes sounds, but it's as if he's in a deep sleep and no one knows how to wake him up. I try to get in every day. Talking, playing loud music, massage – it's all supposed to help. I even bring in garlic and kippers, some people react to smell.' She smiled and blew her nose.

'And is it working?'

'I think so. I wish it happened like it does in films – the patient suddenly wakes up and everything's okay.'

'I'm sorry, Jemma. I had no idea.'

'There's no reason why you should.'

'But I see you and Josh nearly every week. I could have – '

'Helped? I doubt it. No offence, but there was nothing you could do. And I asked Josh to keep it quiet, so don't blame him.'

'I won't.' Ruth smiled.

'Actually, he's been great. A real friend. He comes by the hospital to see Richard and pray for him.'

'I'm sure that makes a difference.'

'He is getting better.' Jemma sounded as if she was trying to convince herself as much as she was trying to convince Ruth. 'It's very slow ... And they say it's unlikely he'll make a full recovery.' Jemma took a swig of her coffee and grimaced.

'Coffee or unidentified brown gunge?'

'It's better than the stuff out of the machines.' Jemma stood up to leave. 'I'll see you around.'

Ruth gave a little wave and returned to her fish and chips. There had been one question she wanted to ask Jemma but hadn't plucked up the courage. Who could have done such a dreadful thing to Richard?

Scene Two

JEMMA GENTLY PLACED THE HEADPHONES ON RICHARD AND TURNED UP THE volume. Motorhead wasn't everyone's cup of tea; she wasn't even convinced Richard actually liked heavy metal, but he had seen the band once in concert, and he wore their T-shirt. Her personal brand of physical therapy would either kill or cure.

As usual, his eyes flickered as the opening chords of 'Ace of Spades' ripped through his eardrums. Jemma took his hand and started the rough massage therapy, as she had been shown, to try to stimulate him out of the coma. He really was getting better, squeezing her hand when she spoke, smiling while Josh prayed for him. She longed for the day when he would recover fully. If that day ever came.

Mohan was devastated when he found out Richard had been injured and was anxious to splash it all over the front page of the *Monksford Gazette*.

'Let's catch the low-life scum that did this despicable thing!'

It was Jemma, prompted by Josh, who had persuaded him not to. She had promised Josh he wouldn't get the hero treatment again, and it would be impossible to run the story without details of Josh's rescue. It had ended up as a one-paragraph insert on page two.

'Passers-by rescued a man from the river at Monksford on Thursday evening. The man, Richard Sutton, 32, remains unconscious in Monksford General Hospital. Police are appealing for witnesses to what appears to be an attempted mugging.'

170

The police had asked lots of questions at the time, interviewing both Josh and Jemma, who could tell them very little, and eventually reached the conclusion that it really was a mugging gone wrong. Jemma was not convinced.

'So, Miss Durham. Tell me again exactly what you saw.'

'I didn't *see* anything. It's what I *heard*.'

'And what was that?'

'Splashes.'

'Splashes.'

'Yes. On a number of occasions, usually in the middle of the night.'

'And do you have any idea of the reason for these splashes?'

'No. But they were strange.'

'In what way strange?'

'Mysterious, peculiar. And I'm sure there's been someone fishing around in the river.'

The constable looked down his nose at her.

Jemma felt confused. It all sounded so stupid when she tried to explain it.

'Oh, I don't know!'

'Now Miss Durham. If we could get back to a description of the car you saw driving away from the scene.'

'It had headlights.'

'Headlights. Well that narrows it down, considerably.' The young constable's tone was heavy with sarcasm.

In the days after they discovered him, Jemma returned to the place where they had pulled Richard from the river to search for clues. The police hadn't found anything, so she didn't expect to either. The river's residents saw to it that rubbish left on the bank side or thrown in the river itself was quickly cleared. It was cleaner than most of Monksford itself. A cola can barely touched the ground before Skye Wortham whisked it away and recycled it.

Jemma tried looking for footprints, but there were so many that she didn't know where to start. She examined the flattened-down reeds, but nothing indicated what had happened. She started to believe the mugger theory. Just one thing still bothered her. Why had Richard been there? Had he come to see her? Highly unlikely – they had no unfinished business. She had finally returned all of his possessions when she heard that he had moved to Maidstone, so he had no reason to be near the river in Monksford. And it didn't seem that he could enlighten her in the near future.

She looked up as Josh entered the room. His hair was longer now and starting to curl on his shoulders and his beard had thickened.

'Hi,' said Jemma.

'Hi.' He stooped to kiss her softly on the cheek. Her heart gave a little flip.

'What's the CD?'

'Motorhead.'

Josh grimaced and turned it off. He removed Richard's headphones. 'How is he today?'

'Much the same.'

'He's probably deaf as well, now. As if he didn't have enough problems.'

'The doctor said that loud music . . .'

'Joke!'

'Sorry . . .' Jemma rubbed her temples.

'What's the matter?'

'I saw Ruth Wells today.'

'You see her every week.'

'I know. But she spoke to me today. I couldn't look her in the eye. I didn't know what to say.'

'Does she know?'

'Know what?' Jemma frowned.

'You know – does she know that you know?'

'Josh, this is starting to sound like a rather bad comedy sketch!'

'Does she know that you saw her and Alistair Fry kissing?'

'Shhhh! Keep your voice down.'

'Well, does she?'

'I ... I don't know.'

Jemma resumed her massage, kneading Richard's upper arms and shoulders. His skin reddened as she pummelled him. Richard grimaced and pulled away from her grasp.

'It seems to be working,' Josh said. 'He's definitely responding more, moving around.'

Jemma pounded his thighs.

'Hey, I'm glad it's him you're taking it out on, not me.'

'I'm not taking it out on anyone. It's therapy.' The tears stung her eyes. Josh took her hands.

'Why didn't you expose them?'

'I nearly did. It was my first instinct. After all, "Local Councillor in Steamy Clinch with Lady Vicar" is a local journalist's dream story. It would probably have been picked up by the national tabloids – they love that sort of thing.'

'It could have been your ticket out of Monksford.'

Jemma nodded.

'What stopped you?'

'I suppose ... because it's not just a story, is it? It's people's lives. I tried to think through the consequences, like ripples. Alistair would have to leave the council. And he's done so much for Monksford. It could destroy his marriage, that's another life affected. And as for Ruth – well, she would lose her job for sure and that would affect hundreds of people. They don't deserve it. Do they?'

Josh shook his head. 'I suppose not.'

'What would you do? What's more important – that they get punished for what they did, or that they be allowed to get on with their lives. Do the people of Monksford have a right to know the truth?'

'Difficult questions.'

'I know this sounds silly, but it came to me, when we were rehearsing that scene – you know, the one where I'm the woman who's been caught between the sheets with someone else's husband. I'm standing there and you're kneeling at my feet and you're saying, "Woman, where are those reckless men, that were so keen to make their accusations? Who has condemned you?"'

'And all her accusers disappear because they've all seen the sin in their own hearts?'

'And I'm thinking, who am I to condemn Ruth and Alistair? I've done things I shouldn't have. Everyone has. But how would we feel if our mistakes, indiscretions, and blunders were splashed all over the front page? I can't throw stones. Jesus was absolutely right you know. He seems to have this way of making you look inside yourself.'

'I know.' Josh smiled.

'Josh, are you laughing at me?' She rolled Richard over, the way she had been shown, and started pummelling his back.

'No, quite the opposite. I'm smiling, because ... because I can see you changing.'

'How am I changing?'

'Well, a few months ago, when I first met you, you wouldn't have thought twice about running that story.'

Jemma shrugged.

'You said it yourself, you're just biding your time here until you're snapped up by the dailies. You said you were waiting for one sniff of a great story and you'd be off like a shot. You were the restless one, always wanting to move up, move out. What happened?'

'That was then.'

'What changed?'

'I ... I don't know.'

'Yes you do. I can see something different in you – a dignity, a stillness.'

'Well, I met you for a start.'

'I thought you made a point of listening to everything I said and then doing the complete opposite.'

'Am I that bad?'

Josh took her hand and laughed. 'Terrible!'

'I mean it, Josh. Am I really a bad person?'

'We're all bad people.'

'You're not.'

'Yes, I am.'

'But you do good things. I've never known you to do bad things. The worst thing you've ever done to me is told me the truth.'

'Is that why you threw your drink over me?'

'Perhaps.'

'"Why do you call me good? No one is good except God alone."' Josh went to the window and looked out. Richard appeared to be asleep.

'Is that from the Bible?' Jemma joined him at the window. She could see the river in the distance.

'Yes, Jesus said it.'

'Well, if he isn't good, I don't know who is.'

'Exactly, it's one of the things he said that make us sure he is God.'

'Isn't that a bit weird. Going around saying you are God. Even if you are.'

'That's one of the reasons the religious leaders at the time wanted him killed. It was uncomfortable for them. They found his words offensive.'

'But he only said kind things, forgave people, and healed them, didn't he?'

'Oh, he had some pretty harsh words for the hypocritical religious leaders who said one thing and did another. They were oppressive, sanctimonious, and corrupt. They forced people to follow impossible rules, then punished them when they failed. But they claimed to have the monopoly on God. The ordinary folk didn't have a look in. As you said, they weren't "good" enough.'

'So how can anyone be good enough? The religious leaders couldn't do it and the ordinary people couldn't do it, so what chance do we stand?'

'None at all. That's why Jesus had to die.'

'What do you mean, *had* to die? I thought it was all a ghastly mistake.'

'No. It was a bit like a hostage situation. As you said, we've all done and thought wrong things. In a way we can't help it; we're born like it. None of us deserve to be with God. It is as if Jesus said, "I can take it. I'll stand in for you." He died so we don't have to.'

Jemma gave a little snort. 'But we all still die.'

'Our bodies do, but there's the essence of us that lives on. Call it what you like, soul, spirit, consciousness. And we choose where that essence will spend eternity. Forever with God, or forever separated from him.'

Richard groaned in his sleep. Jemma crossed the room and took his hand.

'Does he still have his "essence"? Has it left him, or will we ever see the real Richard again?'

'I believe it's still in there. He just can't communicate with us at the moment. I've been praying that he'll recover.'

'Then why hasn't he?' Jemma's breathing was getting faster; she could feel her cheeks burning. Tears began to sting her eyes. 'If God is as powerful as you say, why doesn't Richard get better? Haven't you prayed hard enough? Don't you believe enough? Haven't you said the right words? What's gone wrong, Josh? Oh, it all sounds fine in theory, but it doesn't work, does it?' She was shouting now. 'Make him better! Then I'll know that everything you've been saying is true.'

Josh looked very weary. 'I can't. I don't know why he's still sick. But I know I must keep praying.'

'Do what you like! Say your magic words, wave your Bible at him.' She stroked Richard's hair. 'Look at him. What's the point, Josh? What is the point?'

'We've got to have hope. We can't give up on that.'

'Yeah, right.'

Jemma stormed out of the room, slamming the door so hard a nurse came scurrying up the corridor. She ran downstairs and fled into the hospital car park. It was no good. She just couldn't stand it any more. She had spent over six months of her life at Richard's bedside. She had seen more of him recently than she had in the whole of the previous two years. She didn't even know why she was spending so much time with him. After all he had left her for another woman. Whoever this 'other woman' was, she hadn't stayed on the scene once Richard had been injured. She hadn't shown up, not even once.

Jemma had been to Richard's last address, a B&B in Maidstone, but there was no clue to her identity. Whether it was helping to pull him out of the river or a bizarre sense of loyalty, Jemma just knew she had to be there for him. Things had cooled off with Josh. It was as if her emotions had shut down. She was just doing what had to be done. She went to work, she rehearsed the mystery plays, she wrote her column, and she visited Richard. She had no time or energy for anything more. She hadn't seen Lou for months; she hadn't even visited her grandfather in York during the holidays. Instead, she spent the best part of Christmas day with Josh at Richard's bedside.

That morning Mohan had told her she was looking tired and haggard and she should get some early nights because her sour face was putting him off his Danish. She couldn't be bothered to work out whether it was supposed to be some kind of joke, but it had cut deep. She had lost weight. She was having trouble sleeping, and her concentration span was ...

What was she thinking? She found a bench, sat down, and put her head in her hands as the tears came. 'Why?' she shouted. 'Why did you let this happen, God? Why isn't he getting better? Don't you listen? Don't you care?' Jemma fished in her bag for a tissue and wiped her eyes. 'I can't believe I'm doing this. I don't even believe in you, but I'm talking to you. If you can hear me, if you are real, show me. Show me tonight that you care.'

She felt a hand on her shoulder that made her jump.

'Josh!'

'Sorry, I didn't mean to scare you. I bought you this.' He handed her a coffee. 'It's the real stuff, from the restaurant, not the machine.'

'Thanks.' She took the cup. Josh sat on the bench next to her and took a swig of his own cup of coffee.

'Are you okay?'

'Josh, don't laugh, but I was praying.'

'Why should I laugh? It's the best thing you could do. What were you praying about?'

'I asked God to show me that he cared, right before you turned up with the coffee.'

'So God knew that you really needed a coffee and sent me to you.'

Jemma shook her head and smiled. 'Coincidence.'

They sat in silence watching the ambulances. A relay of smokers, some staff, some patients, joined them, sucking their cigarettes as if their lives depended on them before flicking the ends into the row of nearby scrubby bushes.

A male nurse hurried towards them. 'Are you Richard Sutton's friend Jemma?'

'Yes. What's happened?' Jemma gripped Josh's hand.

'You'd better come up.'

'Is he all right?'

'He's asking for you.'

Scene Three

'OY! WILL YOU LOT JUST STAND STILL!' RONNIE BELLOWED. HIS NORMALLY crispy, clipped syllables replaced by an inflection that wouldn't have been out of place on a vegetable stall in Maidstone market. 'I said, stand still!' His exasperated voice rang through the hall, echoing Ruth's thoughts.

'I've got parrots chatting among themselves, apes scratching, sloths yawning, and I'm not even saying what the rabbits seem to be getting up to. Think, people! Each time you step onto this stage you're acting – even when you're not speaking to the audience. Think about what's happening. React; provide background; if all else fails, just stand still. Whatever you do, don't just switch off, or worse still, have a chat about last night's episode of *Coronation Street*!' Ronnie paused to wipe his forehead with a yellow silk handkerchief. Little beads of spittle had collected at the corners of his mouth and his face was beetroot red.

'God, Noah, his wife and sons have lines. The rest of you animals still have to act. I know the stage is small and you're all a little cramped, but there's nothing that can be done about it at the moment. You will have more space on the day and you'll be in costume, but you must start to think about your character now. Eagles, look majestic, and tigers, you are fierce predators, not pussycats waiting for your next tin of Whiskers. Oh, for goodness sake! You silly cows over there, come forward – you won't be seen there behind the gorillas.'

Ruth hid a smile as two rather affronted middle-aged women emerged from behind former Kent middleweight wrestling champion, Ken (Grappler) Morell and his good lady 'Battleaxe.' During a production, Ronnie was very fond of calling actors by their character names. Although Hamlet, Lear, or Lady Macbeth may be acceptable, and in some cases flattering, referring to the actors as dogs, pigs, or even cows was more than likely to earn Ronnie a slap on the face. He had, rather mischievously, sat down and likened each actor's looks or character to an animal. He and Ruth had giggled over people's facial characteristics, mannerisms, and personality traits to match them up with various creatures.

The whole cast was involved in the Noah scenes. Ronnie and Ruth had made that decision early on, if only to prevent the actors who were appearing later, in the New Testament section, from spending the early part of the evening in the pub. The thought of having to trek down the High Street and through the doors of the saloon bar of the Queen's Head to separate half a dozen disciples from their pints of Old Jack's Bone Cracker filled Ruth with trepidation.

Alistair sat down next to Ruth. 'Look at this – shambolic.'

Ronnie pretended not to hear and went to give the actors a piece of his mind.

'I told you, casting pearls before swine!' Alistair continued.

'What do you mean?'

'Well, letting sacred things fall into the hands of the hoi polloi. Some of the Monksford residents are hardly what you'd call respectable.'

'And we are?'

'I don't know what you mean.'

'Don't give me that, Alistair. The difference is I don't pretend to be something I'm not.'

He tried to take her hand, but she snatched it away.

'It's a community play, not just something performed by a nice little groups of Christians, but an opportunity for everyone in Monksford to be drawn into God's love story with humankind. Christians don't have a monopoly on God. Besides, some of the grants specify community involvement.'

A scuffle broke out between some goats and a sheep they claimed was upstaging them. Ronnie beckoned to Ruth, and she clambered on to the stage to help him sort it out and ended up moving the sheep to the other side of the stage, near the lioness. When she returned to her seat, Alistair had gone.

Ruth noticed quite a few faces missing from the tableau among them, the male lion – played by Josh, and the dove – Jemma. It was unlike them to be late, and they usually rang if they couldn't make a rehearsal. She hoped nothing had happened to Jemma's ex in hospital.

She was relieved that Alistair Fry had disappeared so she would not have to watch him on stage. When it came to choosing a suitable animal for Alistair, she admitted she wasn't feeling altogether impartial. A snake would have been a suitable choice, or a toad, maybe a pig or a leech. Ronnie had eventually taken over, choosing an ox, owing, she suspected, to Alistair's robust physique and craggy features.

Ronnie looked stressed and weary.

Back in the autumn, she had dreaded having to tell him about the music. 'I'm sorry Ronnie, I just don't think it's appropriate.'

He looked downcast. 'So it's going to all be that hideous cacophony performed by those nauseatingly smiley pubescent bobby-soxers, I suppose.'

'No Ronnie. I've found some better music, the kind they use in York. Some instrumental, some choral. I'm talking to Harlan too.'

'So there's not even a chance of a little something from Jesus Christ Superstar?'

'No, I'm afraid not.'

'C'est la vie!'

And that was the last they had spoken of it.

Her discussion with Harlan had been a lot steamier.

'What?' she shrieked. 'After all the work I've put in. I never thought I'd say this but you, Reverend Wells, are totally heartless.'

And she refused to speak to Ruth for the rest of the evening.

'She'll come round,' Ronnie said. 'It would kill her if she wasn't involved. She'd simply explode with envy.'

That night in bed, a tumult of worries and anxieties prevented her sleeping. There was so much still to consider, the catering, the programmes, the complex and sometimes fraught relationships – Harlan and Ronnie, Jemma, Josh, and Richard, and of course Alistair and her.

Ruth had tried to leave some breathing space between them, but she couldn't put him off forever. They were running the nativity scene tomorrow, and she would have to be there.

Bleary-eyed from lack of sleep, she stepped through the door of the hall the next day and saw Ronnie heading towards her. 'How are ticket sales going?'

The plays had reached the stage that every producer dreads, a sort of pivotal point of no return when the initial excitement of the casting has worn off and first-night euphoria seems a distant and implausible prospect.

'Well, there's the Scouts, and the Tuesday afternoon tea club – oh, and Peter, the Bishop, will definitely try to make it.'

'That's about eight in the audience, then,' said Ronnie. 'And half of those stand some chance of staying awake.'

'Oh, Ronnie, why are we doing this?' A mischievous thought struck her. 'Shall we cancel the whole show and cut our losses?'

'Let's steal the ticket money and run away to Kathmandu,' Ronnie said.

Ruth rattled the cash box. 'We might get as far as Dover.'

He placed his hands gently on her shoulders. 'We'll do it.'

'You know the old adage "it will be all right on the night".'

Ronnie smiled. 'We just need to grit our teeth and hang in there. You're the one with all the faith.'

Ruth felt her faith trickling away. She patted him on the shoulder and took her position at the back of the hall.

Ronnie turned his attention to the actors on the stage. 'Right,' Ronnie said, 'finally you're in the correct positions. That's how I want you. Stay there. You'll have a piece of music playing; you will have taken up your positions for the flood sequence, and you hold it. You stand still! Does anyone have a problem with that?'

No one seemed to.

'Okay. Let's take the scene from the beginning. Noah, I've got the pieces and the frame. I'd like you to have a go at fitting them together as you speak. A bit of multitasking for you. Do you think you can manage that?'

Noah nodded.

'Right. All you animals, off the stage. Remember stay in character. Off you go. Now, God … "When I made this world …"'

God spoke of his heartbreak at a perfect creation gone bad and his hope of a new world through one family in a floating menagerie. His reassurance that he would help the painfully inadequate Noah in his task and guide his hands to build the ark made Ruth feel very small. It was only through God's grace that these mystery plays were happening at all. So many pitfalls, hazards, and circumstances had threatened the production that hearing God's reassurances to Noah made her very grateful and not a little weepy.

'No, no, no, Noah!' Ronnie bellowed at the poor little man as he struggled to slot the large pieces of wood to the timber framework to make the ark. Ronnie demonstrated how to slide the section in, then hopped down from the stage and whispered, 'I tell you, Ruthie dear, never get into a car with that man; I'm sure he has trouble walking and breathing at the same time.'

Ruth suppressed a giggle.

The rest of the scene didn't go any more smoothly, but the animals did indeed behave slightly better this time. Mrs Hobson-Brown's snide comments about the other performers demonstrated exactly why she had been cast as the female dog.

After a fairly dismal second run through, Ruth persuaded Ronnie to call it a day. The cast had filed out to the car park, and Harlan left without saying goodbye. Ruth and Ronnie were stacking chairs when the doors swung open crashing against the wall with the force.

'Ruth, I must speak to you ...' Alistair's face was dark with emotion.

'I think I'd better be going.' Ronnie slung his canary yellow sweater around his shoulders like a stole.

'Please stay.' Ruth's eyes grew wide imploring Ronnie not to leave her alone with Alistair. To her relief he nodded and pulled up three chairs. Alistair sat silent. Ruth waited. She wasn't going to compromise on this, and Alistair knew why. Ronnie, bless him, in a rare moment of diplomacy jumped up and walked towards the door leading to the kitchen.

'I'll just slip out and feng-shui the kitchen.' He opened the serving hatch and kept vigil as Alistair poured his heart out to Ruth.

'I'm losing her, Ruth. I'm sitting here watching while my marriage is slipping through my fingers. And there doesn't seem to be a thing I can do about it.'

'What makes you think that?' Ruth's voice sounded harsh in her ears.

'She hardly speaks to me. She's always out. She's taken no interest in the mystery plays. And – ' he pulled his chair closer and lowered his voice ' – we haven't, you know, made love for weeks.'

'I'm not a marriage guidance counsellor,' Ruth snapped. Her chair screeched on the floor as she pulled away from him.

'I know, but I thought you were my friend.'

'Just how I, who have never been married, can advise you, who seem to be something of an expert on failed marriages, I'm not quite sure.' Ruth folded her arms.

'Ouch!'

'I'm sorry, Alistair, but I don't know what you expect me to say. Have you tried talking to her?'

Alistair gave a snort. 'I'm the last person she wants to talk to at the moment.'

'Why?'

'She thinks ...' He shot a glance towards the kitchen. 'She thinks I'm having an affair.'

Ruth kept her gaze steady. 'And are you?'

'You know I'm not,' he hissed.

'I know you're not having one with me,' she whispered.

'Please, Ruth ...'

'Please what?'

'Please help me. Talk to her. Convince her that nothing happened.'

'I can't do that because something did happen. You kissed me, and that kiss changed me, and however much I want to, I can't seem to change back.' She stood up. He took her hand.

'Ruth, can we at least discuss this like adults. Come for a drink with me ... or we could go back to your place.'

'What are we going to talk about? How your wife doesn't understand you?' She strode towards the door, and as much as she hated leaving Ronnie in the lurch, she needed to make her exit before she changed her mind.

She drove straight home and, abandoning her car in the drive, rushed gratefully into the vicarage and slammed the heavy front door shut. She leant against it breathing hard.

Trembling slightly, she filled the kettle. The phone rang, making her jump. She watched it suspiciously for a few seconds, then, steeling herself, she picked up the receiver.

'Hello?' Her voice sounded hoarse.

'Ruth, dear, it's Ronnie. Just calling to see if you are all right.'

'Thanks, Ronnie. I'm fine. Look, I'm sorry to rush off like that.'

'I locked up for you. Would you like me to drop the key in tonight?'

'Er ... Alistair left?'

'Well, I didn't lock him in the church hall, did I?'

'No, Ronnie. Don't worry. I'll collect the key in the morning.'

'It's no skin off my nose. Look, Ruth, I don't know what's going on with you and our esteemed Councillor, and, as much as I'd love to have all the juicy goss, I know when to keep my sticky little beak out ... It's just that before he left he muttered something about getting this sorted out ... and I'm concerned he may be making his way over to the vicarage. I'm just saying, if you'd like me to come over ...'

Ruth smiled at Ronnie's uncharacteristic display of chivalry.

'It's very sweet of you, Ronnie, but I'll be fine. I'm going to bed now, so if he does come round, he'll just have to go away again.'

'Just as long as you're okay.'

'Thanks, Ronnie.'

Ruth took extra care to lock up and switched the phone ringer off. The answering machine could take care of any calls. She glanced into the vicarage garden and, despite the warm night, made sure that both the windows and the curtains were firmly shut.

RUTH WOKE WITH A START. THE CLOCK FACE SHOWED TWENTY PAST EIGHT. IT was strange not to be jolted awake by the half past six alarm, and it took her several minutes to wake up fully. A whole three weeks leave stretched before her – two before the plays, one after.

She pulled on her dressing gown, yawned, and opened the curtains. A dark blue Mercedes was parked across her drive. She drew the curtains again. Why had Alistair left his car outside her house? She half wished she had taken Ronnie up on his offer. Her first instinct would be to sneak out of the back door and escape through the fields. She realised that if she was going to do anything useful today, visit Eliza in hospital for instance, she would have to take her car, which was stuck in the drive, and that would mean confronting Alistair.

She showered and dressed carefully, choosing a sapphire blue blouse and a coordinating flowered skirt; she would forgo the dog collar and be off duty today. She had recently taken to applying a little lipstick and mascara before going out.

Switching on the coffee percolator, she took two croissants out of the freezer. She heated them, ate hers with jam, no butter, sipped her coffee, and poured herself a glass of orange juice. She set a tray and went out to the front garden. Net curtains twitched in the house opposite. Alistair lay in the driver's seat with his eyes closed. She noticed his pale face, his mouth lolling open, and for one horrible moment she thought he was dead, until she heard the unmistakable sound of snoring.

She balanced the tray in one hand and knocked on the window. Alistair opened his eyes and rubbed a hand across his stubbled chin. He hauled himself into an upright position and squinted at her through the tinted glass.

'Open the window. I've brought you breakfast.'

He obligingly turned the key and pressed a button. The window purred down, and she handed him the tray. He struggled to sit upright.

'Ruth, couldn't I come in?'

'No need. I've brought everything out.'

'Can we talk?'

'I'm afraid not. I have to go out now.'

'But I need to use the bathroom.'

'Now that is a difficult one.' She pretended to scratch her head. 'Yes, I've got it. Perhaps you could go home.'

'She's locked me out.' He looked crestfallen.

'So you thought you'd try your luck here?'

'I thought you were my friend.'

'Alistair. Don't pull that one on me. Just finish your breakfast and go. Sort things out with Amanda. Oh, and can you move the car up a little, please? You're blocking my drive.'

She returned to her Fiesta and proceeded to reverse rapidly down the drive, hoping that he'd had the sense to move his car. Her heart was pounding. What had he told Amanda? She slowed her breathing and focused on her driving as she negotiated her way through the rush-hour traffic on the bypass.

By the time she reached Hope Farm, she had calmed down. Bram Griffin seemed more relaxed than he had been the last time she visited him. He had just made tea for Raj. Ruth sat next to Bram on a straw bale and gratefully sipped the steaming brew. 'So how's it going, Bram? Not too much disruption, I hope.'

'Nope. Not a bit of it. I must admit that I've been more apprehensive than a porcupine on his wedding night, but that Raj bloke has been great. I've had no trouble, and when I've had to bring the cows through here for milking, he's had them all stop work, so there's no noise to scare them. How's that for consideration?'

'Yes, Raj is a good sort.'

Raj waved, put down his clipboard, and walked over.

'Hello, Raj.' He shook her solemnly by the hand. 'How is everything?'

'Do you mean, "Is my wife pregnant yet"?' He shook his head. 'They were talking about in vitro fertilisation, but we didn't want to go down that route.'

'I'm so sorry.'

'I had high hopes but it was not to be. Then quite out of the blue, we saw a poster about fostering and adoption. Well, the long and short of it is that we've been approved as foster carers. If we can't have our child the normal way, we can love and care for a child who needs a home. A child who's having it tough. We've had the training, and we're waiting for the first child to come to us.'

'That's fantastic!' Ruth hugged him.

'You have a saying that "God moves in mysterious ways"?'

Ruth nodded. 'He certainly does.'

A lorry with a trailer full of scaffolding poles pulled into the yard. Raj made his excuses and ran over to supervise the delivery.

'Now, Bram, can I have a proper tour this time?'

'Anything for you, Ruth. Shall we start in the upper field then go down to the abbey?' He gestured towards a mud-spattered green Land Rover. She hitched up her skirt and climbed in. They jolted across the farmyard, and Ruth hopped down to open the gate to the upper field. The sky was clear and azure blue. She stood in the field breathing in the soft summer air. The disembodied voice of a lark sang somewhere above her. The breeze stroked her skin.

'Grass needs mowing, of course. I'll have the lads do that before next week. And – ' he wiped his boot on a tussock – 'I think I need to have someone clear up the manure.'

Ruth looked down, the perfect moment ruined. 'That should be fine. Are we all right to go down to the lower field, by the abbey today? You haven't been spraying again, have you?'

'Er, no ... It's all clear this time.'

Ruth studied his face and fancied she saw the hint of a blush rising up from his shirt collar.

They left the Land Rover at the top of the hill and stumbled through the coarse tufty grass to the stage area at the bottom.

'It's not very big, is it? I know the plays would most likely have been performed on waggons, even so, if we have people all the way up the hill, they're not going to see much.'

'That's what your Rajinder bloke put up.'

Ruth shrugged. 'So we're going to have the seating area cordoned off down here and the portable toilets set up at the top of the hill. What about the generators?'

'Down here, near the stage.'

'What about the noise?'

'You won't hear it. It'll be behind the speakers, and we've got a fair humdinger of a PA system. It's so powerful that you'll be able to hear a mosquito sneeze. All the equipment arrived last week, and we've got the boys installing it at the weekend, ready for the dress rehearsal.'

Bram helped Ruth over the stile that linked the upper to the lower field. Despite holding his arm, and despite his stream of advice that sounded as if he was instructing his fork-lift driver how to stack the hay bales, she still caught her skirt on a piece of barbed wire and twisted her ankle climbing down. She rubbed her ankle and examined her skirt, muttering curses much milder than the ones she was thinking.

'Good, so you're okay, then.' He scratched the back of his head, causing his trademark white Stetson to tilt over one eye. 'Listen, I've just got to mosey on up and check on something in the upper field. I'll be back in two ticks.'

Ruth shook her head as he strode up the hill. Gathering herself, she limped to the abbey ruins where three vertical scaffolding poles had been erected, pointing upwards like fingers. She shivered as she imagined the crosspiece being hauled into position. She had heard from other actors who had played Christ that there was no problem simulating agony in crucifixion scenes. However the actor is attached, with ropes or harnesses, the experience of hanging on the cross is excruciatingly painful.

She suddenly felt sorry for Josh. It had been a difficult six months – first the fire, then the situation with Jemma and Richard. She watched him sometimes in church, and it was evident he had taken on a huge burden. Apart from the physical exertion of rehearsing the plays, he seemed to be under mental stress. He would stop suddenly during a hymn, unable to sing the words, the prayers often brought a mist of sweat to his forehead. His enthusiasm for helping others seemed boundless. Every spare moment was spent at the old people's home or at the school or with troubled youngsters. She knew he was praying for Richard and visited him daily. She told him to slow down, to take some time for himself, but he did not heed her advice. Something was driving him, and it was stronger than either of them.

As for Jemma, Ruth felt sure she could see the first signs of a growing interest in the Christian faith, or was it a growing interest in Josh? She had started attending evensong, sitting close to Josh who attentively found every page in the hymnbooks and advised her when to kneel, when to stand, and when to join in with the responses. Ruth had felt a pang of jealousy – no man had ever shown her that degree of chivalry. She felt the familiar evangelical obligation to do an altar call, get Jemma to 'sign on the dotted line'. However, one of the things she had learnt about Jemma was that she didn't like being put on the spot. So, instead, she had committed to praying for Jemma and asking God for the right people and the right opportunities to present themselves.

As the sun stood high over the abbey ruins, Ruth looked up at the triple arches – all that remained of the south wall – and felt the need to pray. Finally, and in spite of Alistair's sojourn outside her house, the stillness had returned, and Ruth felt profoundly grateful.

'I said, are you ready to go?' Bram's voice jarred her back to the real world. 'Looks like you were away with the fairies just then.'

'Actually, I was praying,' Ruth said, rather haughtily.

'Nice one, Vicar, send a couple up for me.'

Ruth wandered over to the fence that separated the lower field from the river. 'Er ... as I said, time's getting on – people to go, places to see.' Bram shuffled anxiously from one foot to the other.

Ruth forced a smile. She looked at the field, just grass and a barn. Nothing, as far as she could see, that warranted spraying.

'I have, um ... an important appointment, with my ... accountant, and I really need to be getting back.'

'What's that smell?' Ruth wrinkled her nose at the faint but sickening odour.

'Nothing! Um ... it must be coming from the river. Look, I really must insist we go home now.'

Ruth started walking ahead as they returned across the field to where the Land Rover was parked. She stopped at the stile and looked back towards the abbey.

'Bram, what is in that field?'

'Grass,' he said, shaking his head.

'No, I mean what else?'

'Nothing. I'm planning to graze it. I had to spray against mastitis.'

'Oh, but what about that smell?'

'What smell? I can't smell anything.'

Ruth sighed. Trying to get information out of Bram was like trying to get an old lady at a bus stop not to tell you about her latest operation – pointless and extremely frustrating.

The Land Rover bounced them back to the farmhouse and Ruth disembarked. Her ankle was stiff, and she would have to buy some blue sewing thread. She limped back to her own car. Bram was now in a slightly less ebullient mood.

'It will be all right, Ruth. It'll all be all right.' She wasn't sure if he was trying to reassure him or herself.

Back in the sedate and slightly stuffy calm of the vicarage, Ruth couldn't help thinking about that smell. It was foul and putrid. She had smelt it before. But where?

She made herself a coffee and meandered, cup in hand, around the vicarage garden, dead-heading the Rambling Rector roses on her way. Her mother bought them as a joke when they moved in. She sniffed the scent, trying to expel that rank odour from her nostrils. It didn't seem to be working. As she threw the rose heads on the compost heap there was a scrambling and scuttling noise. She instinctively jumped back. Mice!

On the day that she and Mother had moved into the vicarage she remembered being greeted by the same scuttling and squeaking. That night, she had lain awake with the covers pulled up tight around her chin, listening for the signs that those vile little creatures were holding a welcome party. The next morning, she had hotfooted it to the hardware shop, bought up Mr Lightowler's entire stock of mouse-bait, and declared war on the vicarage's rodent population. She then spent the most nauseating week sweeping up tiny corpses from every nook and cranny.

Shortly after that, they decided to acquire a cat. It was only after Dimitri had arrived in the parish that she had managed to locate the sources of the stench to the bottom of the spare-room wardrobe, behind the boiler pipes in the kitchen, and the tinder pile in the drawing room log box.

It had been the same smell that had just turned her stomach in Bram's field. There was no escape from it; there was something dead and rotting in that field. Somehow she didn't think it was mice.

Scene Four

MOHAN WAS SMILING. HE WAS ACTUALLY SMILING. 'WELL DONE, JEMMA,' he said.

She smiled back. 'Thank you, Mohan.'

Six months ago she would have given her right arm plus several other vital body parts to hear him say that. Now there were other things on her mind. Every day at work she felt like an android, a robohack automatic writing machine. Every day she counted the seconds until she could get back to the hospital to find out what gem, what nugget, what fresh revelation had emerged from Richard's fledgling memory banks. She glanced at her watch.

'Am I keeping you?' Mohan tapped his foot against his desk drawer.

'Sorry,' said Jemma.

'Are you going to see Richard?'

Jemma nodded.

'Okay, I won't delay you. I just wanted you to know. This has been one of the paper's most successful columns. Our readership and our advertising revenue are both up. Of course, I can't put it all down to your work, but judging by reader letters and the amount of businesses that have backed these mystery plays, you've done a good job. He shuffled some printed emails on his desk. Even the "powers that be" have noticed.'

Jemma started edging towards the door.

'If we decided to appoint a new senior reporter, your name's in the frame.'

'Thanks.'

'Give my regards to Richard, won't you?'

'Of course. He'd like to see you some time, you know.'

'Yes, yes, I promise. It's just so difficult to get away. You know what it's like.'

Jemma nodded, then scuttled out of Mohan's office, right into the path of Saffy Walton. Although, with Josh's encouragement, she had pledged to be nicer to Saffy, now was neither the time nor the place.

'Jemma, I wonder if you have a moment.'

If this were my last moment on earth, I would rather spend it being savaged by a rabid gerbil than spend it with you, Jemma thought. She composed her features into a sweet facsimile of a smile. Josh would have been so proud of her.

'Of course, Saffy. I am in rather a hurry, but a minute or two won't make any difference. What can I do for you?'

'Well, I've always admired your fashion sense, and you know I've always looked up to you when it comes to style.'

This was news to Jemma. Saffy always seemed to have dressed using the leftovers from the Girl Guides Jumble Sale.

'So I wanted to ask your opinion on this.' Saffy began to pull up her jumper and pull down the waistband of her trousers, exposing rather too much of the top of her thong for Jemma's liking. Jemma fought the urge to yell, 'Stop!' before Saffy undressed any further. Looking carefully, she could see a cluster of little blue butterflies, tattooed at the top of Saffy's right buttock.

If there was one thing Jemma hated, it was tattoos, especially on women. Human graffiti – ugly, common, and invariably carried out by mindless morons high on drink or drugs. Judging by the redness and inflammation, it was a recent acquisition. What to say? Fortunately, Saffy couldn't see Jemma's initial reaction of disgust. By the time she had rearranged her clothing, Jemma's expression was back to normal.

'They're butterflies,' explained Saffy, unnecessarily. 'Butterflies mean birth, freedom, beauty, and nature.'

'Really!'

'Yes, and some ancient Mexican tribes use it to symbolise a good harvest in the summer. I chose the purples, greens, and blues because they're my favourite colours. Air and water colours – that's me.'

A complete airhead and a bit of a drip, thought Jemma. She searched for the nicest thing she could think of to say. 'Saffy, I can honestly say, that if I was thinking of having a tattoo, I would have one exactly like that.'

'You would?' Saffy's eyes were shining.

'You bet!' said Jemma. 'Now, I'm sorry, but I really must go.'

'Of course.'

Jemma glanced at her watch as she jogged up the stairs to the car park. She had hoped to be there by now. Richard would be expecting her.

She thrust her car into gear and put her foot down. The tyres gave a little squeak of protest as she accelerated out of the car park. She wound down the window, then wound it back up again as she passed the meat-processing factory. Goodness knows what kind of meat they were producing; she wouldn't be eating any of it.

Richard, dressed in jogging pants and a T-shirt, was sitting in a chair when she entered his room. He smiled and tried painfully to get up. She waved him back down.

'Hi, how was your day?' She gave him a peck on the cheek.

'Oh, the usual exciting stuff.' His speech was still slightly slurred. 'This morning was ...' His brow furrowed as he searched for the word.

'Physio?' Jemma offered.

'Physio,' he concurred. 'Then my mum came and pushed me round the grounds for a while. Then ...' He paused again, retrieving items from his short-term memory was a tortuous process. 'I had a rest and watched television.'

'What did you watch?'

'It was a camera – I mean a film. It was about a sportsman who got cancer.'

'What sport did he play?'

'It was ... Oh, what is the name of it?'

Jemma sat patiently as Richard thumped the arm of the chair with his good left hand in frustration. This time she couldn't help him with the word. She could see that he was almost weeping with frustration but the questioning was neither idle curiosity, not deliberate cruelty, but mental exercises on the advice of his doctors, the cerebral equivalent of the physiotherapy intended to restore the use of the muscles on his weakened right side.

'It doesn't matter,' she said. 'Did you enjoy the film?'

'It was sad. He died at the end.'

'That is sad,' Jemma agreed.

'Sometimes it's better to die.'

'What do you mean?'

'If you are very sick or injured.'

'Some people get well again.' Jemma could feel panic rising.

'Some don't. Perhaps it is better to die than to stay ... alive.'

'Richard, what are you getting at?'

'Jemma, do you think I should have died?'

'Of course not! Whatever made you say that?'

He picked up his weakened arm and let it drop in his lap.

'But you're getting better! Every day you can do more, remember more, you're getting stronger and better and more like the old Richard ...' She took his weak hand and massaged it.

'No, the old Richard died, Richard the journalist, Richard the sportsman. What you've got now is a new person, weak as anything, and who can't even put a sentence together.'

'That's not true! The old Richard is still there, underneath. You will get well again, I know it.'

'You don't understand. I've changed. What it feels like to be me is different. Sometimes it's as if this is all there has ever been – as if the last thirty years never existed.' He looked close to tears. His frustration was almost palpable. 'I can't trust myself any more. I can't trust my body and I can't trust my mind.' He turned his head away, breathing deeply. 'I'm tired now. I think you need to go.'

Jemma said nothing but didn't move.

'I said, you can go!'

Richard turned back to look at her as tears coursed down her face.

He reached towards her with his good hand, but she didn't grasp it. 'I lost you once when you left me,' she said. 'Now I'm losing you again. You have no idea what that feels like.' She rose to her feet and gazed out of the window, blinking back her tears.

'You're right. I have no idea. I have no idea about a lot of things. I have no idea how I got like this.'

'You still don't remember anything? Even what you were doing by the river.'

'Nothing.'

'You can't remember if you were coming to see me.' She took a tissue from the box on his bedside locker and wiped her eyes.

He shook his head. 'Nothing.'

'Do you think it was an accident then? The police were convinced that someone did this to you.'

'I told you, I can't remember anything. Did the police find the murder weapon ... I mean a weapon.'

She smiled. 'They looked along the banks, and a couple of policemen searched the bushes, but because you were too ... stubborn to get murdered and insisted on staying alive, they didn't look that hard.'

'Did I make the front page?'

'We thought you'd prefer page two.'

'Did you write it or did ... what's his name?'

'Mohan?'

'That's it.'

'I wrote it. It was the hardest thing I've ever written.'

'Tell me again how you found me.'

Jemma recited the story of how she and Josh had heard the splash, saw something floating in the river, and pulled out what they thought was a corpse. Even though Jemma told the story every time she visited, it still gave her shivers, like drops of icy water down her back.

'Is Josh coming today?'

Jemma looked down at her hands. 'I'm not sure. He's working late, and we've got a three-line-whip for a costume fitting later. You'll never believe it but the costume designer is a patient here in the hospital, and we're sneaking into her room to try on costumes.'

'What's wrong with her? Why is she in hospital?'

'She's got cancer. Terminal, I think. But it's her dying wish to be involved in these plays. That's what Ruth says, anyway.'

Richard's brow furrowed. 'Oh, I see. Who's Ruth?'

'Ruth's the vicar I told you about. She's the one who is organising the plays. Do you remember?' She sat on the bed and took his hand.

'A vicar, now that's the same as a ... priest? That's right, isn't it?'

'Yes, and she's very nice. She said she might visit you, now that you're better. Is that all right?'

'I suppose so. A priest. She won't give me last rights, will she?'

Jemma smiled. 'Of course not! Anyway she's here to see the costume lady. She's the one who's ill.'

'And that's why she's in hospital.'

'That's right.'

Jemma stood up and straightened her skirt. 'Richard, I need to go now. I must have something to eat. Everyone at the *Monksford Gazette* sends their regards. Bye now. Sleep well.' She opened the door to leave.

'Speed skating.'

'Pardon?' Jemma halted in the doorway.

'The sportsman in the film was a speed skater.'

'TRY TO MAKE IT LOOK AS IF YOU'RE AN ORDINARY VISITOR,' RUTH'S NOTE HAD read. Jemma dashed into the hospital shop, grabbed a basket of rather sad-looking fruit, and took it to the equally sad-looking cashier.

'Four pounds fifty,' she said.

'What, for an orange, a couple of apples and an overripe banana?'

'Overheads,' the woman mumbled.

Jemma paid, reluctantly. She supposed a hospital shop had a monopoly: Contrite customers who callously omitted to purchase inspiring gifts, wishing to assuage their guilty consciences are a captive audience, will pay ridiculous prices for poor quality merchandise just to avoid adding to their loved one's suffering.

Armed with her paltry offering, she tracked down Eliza Feldman's ward. She took a deep breath, not sure what to expect in the frail old woman's room. What she didn't expect was the cross between a department store changing area and a sweatshop clothing factory. Costumes in various states of completion covered every available surface. They were draped over the bed, suspended on hangers from the doors, and arrayed over the backs of the chairs.

There were two elderly women, one next to the door and one in the corner. Both were stitching furiously and chatting merrily. Sitting up in bed, queening it over the others was Mrs Feldman, tubes, drips, and drains attached. No oxygen mask this time, and sparky as ever, and had a scarlet chiffon headdress across her arm. She was stitching on tiny gold beads.

She looked up. 'Which one are you?'

Before Jemma could answer, there was a curt knock on the door. To avoid becoming a casualty herself, she tucked herself into the corner beside the sink. The door flew open and Ruth blustered in.

'Hello, Eliza, sorry I'm late. You're looking much better today.'

'Thank you, dear. They say I can go home in a few days, don't they?' The two old women nodded in agreement. 'After a week they've had enough of me – that must be a good sign.' Again the two women agreed, in unison, like the dog ornaments that adorn the dashboards of motorists with no sense of taste.

Ruth moved the red costume to one side and perched on the bed. 'So the doctors have sorted you out then?'

'Yes, I'm feeling much better. They just have to cure the cancer now, and I'll be hunky-dory.'

'I'm sorry, Eliza, I didn't mean …'

'I know you didn't, dear. Have I introduced you to my friends?' She pointed to the thinner of the women who wore too much make up and smelt of vapour rub. 'This is Rebekkah Amos, and this – ' she indicated the plump woman who was wearing a smocklike creation that looked as if it had been made from a shower curtain – 'is Judy Williams.' The two women nodded again to acknowledge Ruth, then recommenced their sewing. 'They're helping me with the costumes. We've got a veritable little production line going, here. The nurses aren't too happy about it so I'm having to be a bit subtle, but they're nearly finished.'

Ruth took the costume and ran the fabric between her fingers. 'I expect Jemma will be here soon.'

Jemma coughed and gave a little wave from her station behind the door. Ruth gasped. 'Oh, Jemma. I didn't see you there!'

'Come out so we can get a proper look at you.'

'This,' said Ruth, gathering herself, 'is Jemma Durham, our Mary Magdalene.'

'Oh, Ruth, she's even lovelier than you said, but oh so skinny. Over here, my dear. Don't be afraid, I won't bite you.'

Jemma was taken aback. It had been a long time since anyone other than her grandfather had called her skinny, and even longer since anyone had thought she was afraid. She stepped forwards.

'Go on then, turn around. What are you, thirty-four, twenty-five, thirty-five?'

'About that,' agreed Jemma.

'You've lost weight then, those are not the measurements you gave me last November.'

'Sorry!'

'I should think so too.' The other old ladies shook their heads and tutted. 'That means I'll have to take it all in! As if I haven't got enough to do!' She threw Jemma the bundle of red linen, which Jemma caught one-handed. 'You might as well try it on, I suppose. I need to see how much work I've got to do.'

Judy Williams, suddenly shot to her feet. 'Nurse approaching!' she whispered. Ruth, Eliza, and Mrs Amos were galvanised into action, stuffing the half-completed costumes into huge bags that they secreted around the room. Jemma stood there, mouth open.

'Come on,' shouted Rebekkah Amos. She bundled Ruth and Jemma into the tiny bathroom.

So this was being subtle? Jemma stood in the shower, trying to breathe quietly as Ruth perched on the toilet lid clutching a rainbow of fabrics.

Jemma heard the murmur of low voices; then a door slammed shut.

'All clear!' Judy Williams said in a stage whisper.

Giggling like schoolgirls at a midnight feast, the women burst out of the bathroom.

'That was a close one,' breathed Rebekkah Amos. She fanned herself with a magazine. 'Blood pressure and temperature!'

'Well, go and try it on then, girl. Goodness knows what you've been doing in there!' Eliza said.

What did they expect her to do? There was hardly enough room to turn around in that bathroom, and it was more crowded than the Victoria line in the rush hour!

'Okay, give me a second.' Jemma left for the bathroom again. She struggled with the garment, a long flowing skirt with so many buttons! Admitting defeat, she emerged in her underwear to shrieks of laughter from the brood of women who clucked like hens.

'Oh, come here girl!' said Rebekkah Amos, not altogether unkindly.

Jemma held up her arms like a child as Ruth, Mrs Amos, and Mrs Williams gently tugged the scarlet costume over her head and Ruth fastened the zip and hooks. She felt like a bride being dressed for her wedding. When the dress was in place she looked down at her figure, giving a little twirl to demonstrate how the fabric hung. Despite it being slightly too large, she loved the way it had been cut to cling to her frame, showing off her bust and waist and slender hips. Eliza made delighted cooing noises. She put a ring of fabric with a scarlet veil on Jemma's head.

'So what do you think, Jemma?' Ruth asked.

Jemma caught a glimpse of herself in the bathroom mirror. The costume was cut very low across the bodice, it skimmed the hips, and the eight-panelled skirt flowed down onto the floor. The neck and sleeves were trimmed with gold braid, and the row of tiny buttons ran down the front and the sleeves. The back was laced with black cords, which Eliza proceeded to tug tight. It was beautiful and feminine – and all in harlot red.

'It's – it's ... stunning.'

'It's called a "Cotehardie". The style dates from the mid-fourteenth century. Very courtly.'

There was a tap on the door, tentative at first, then louder and more insistent. Mrs Amos shushed everyone, and they froze, ready to take flight to the safety of the bathroom again. Mrs Williams opened the door a crack, and Jemma could have sworn she heard her say, 'Who goes there?'

'It's Joshua Wood. Have I got the right place?'

She opened the door a little more and Josh squeezed in.

He spotted Jemma and his jaw dropped. 'Hey, you look ...'

'Fantastic?' Jemma said.

Josh nodded dumbly.

'Just the effect I wanted.' Eliza settled back against her pillow with a smug smile.

'I hope I won't be too distracted to remember my lines,' he said.

'Close your mouth, there's a bus coming.' Jemma tugged at the neckline of her top, trying to cover up. She pulled the headscarf piece over her dark hair and blinked coyly in her veiled modesty. Josh stood there grinning. The elderly ladies exchanged nudges and knowing looks. Eliza Feldman pinched and pulled at Jemma's costume, deftly inserting pins where seams needed to be altered.

Mrs Amos dug Josh's costume out of a large stripy shopping bag, and he slipped into the bathroom. Rather than the usual flowing robes, Eliza had used Ruth's medieval designs to create a tunic effect in pale green with a cape, of sorts, flowing behind.

The old ladies made comments as if Josh wasn't there, or rather, as if he was there but was about three years old. Josh played up to their comments, laughing along with their remarks about the musculature of his legs or the breadth of his chest. They flirted in the way only elderly women can get away with. Jemma blushed, knowing that if she had made comments of that kind, the gossip among Mrs Amos, Mrs Williams, and Mrs Feldman would have been currency for weeks to come.

'So, what do you think?' Josh did what could almost be described as a twirl. Jemma looked at the floor, wondering where the coyness that never used to be part of her nature had originated.

'Come on,' goaded Josh. 'I've given my opinion of your costume.'

'It's ... *okay.*' Jemma wrinkled her nose.

'What's wrong? Is it too long, too short, too tight ... does it make my bum look big?'

The ladies laughed.

'The costume's fine.' Jemma tried to hide a smirk.

'What is it then?'

'Well, it's the beard.'

'What's wrong with the beard? I'll have you know that I've invested a lot of time and effort in this beard.'

'It's just a bit, I dunno, crooked.'

'Which bit?'

'There, under your chin and, it's kind of bushier on that side and the sideburns aren't even.'

The ladies nodded their agreement.

'Do you realise how difficult it is to trim a beard?'

'Oddly, no.' Jemma suspected, looking at Mrs Amos' chin, that the old woman knew exactly how difficult it was.

Josh propelled Jemma to Eliza's bed and sat her down. 'Well, I'll enlighten you then. Firstly, one's eyes are here in the front of one's head.' He pointed unnecessarily. 'And one's sideburns are here – ' again he pointed – 'on the sides of one's head.'

Jemma giggled.

'I'll have you know this is no laughing matter, young lady. Unless one is some kind of chameleon with swivelly eyes, it is well nigh impossible to see what one is doing with the old trimmer.'

'If you were a chameleon, you wouldn't have a beard in the first place.'

'And it would be extremely unlikely that I'd be in the play.'

'And if you were, we'd have trouble seeing you, because you'd keep blending into the scenery.'

They laughed at the silliness.

'Come on, you two. I can't sit here all day listening to you schmoozing. I have better things to be getting on with. Now go and change out of your costumes, and leave me in peace.'

She undid the hooks and zips, and Jemma ducked into the bathroom first. She slipped out of the red dress as quickly and painlessly as she could without dislodging the pins. She only pricked herself twice, but one pin left a scratch, a perforated line down her upper arm. She emerged to find Josh already changed.

'That was quick.'

'Typical! What were you doing in there, washing your hair, having a manicure, perming your eyebrows?'

Josh held the door open for her, and they went out into the corridor.

'Are you seeing Richard again tonight?'

'I thought I might drop in. He's had a pretty rough day. The police have been here.'

'Why? What happened?'

'They heard he was conscious, and they're stepping up the investigation. But I doubt he's been able to tell them anything.'

Josh shrugged.

'Are you coming too? He'll be pleased to see you.'

He looked embarrassed. 'Yeah, I'll see him. Um ... could we get a coffee first? There's something I need to talk to you about.'

They made their way up to the canteen. The plastic chairs in primary colours and the grey floor tiles would have given the place a pleasant sixties retro feel if the chairs and tiles had not actually been there since the sixties. Josh ordered two coffees, and they sat opposite each other on vicious red chairs across a grey Formica table.

'This sounds serious.' Jemma forced a smile.

Josh took her hands.

'Jemma, when the play is over, I'm leaving.'

'What do you mean, leaving?'

'I'm getting away from Monksford.'

'Why?' Jemma felt as if she'd been punched in the stomach. 'Is it me? What have I done?'

'It's not you ...'

How many times had she heard the 'it's not you, it's me' and 'I just need some space' speeches? 'No! You can't leave now.' Jemma snatched her hands away and stood up.

She ran out into the corridor. She didn't know where she was going, just away. Away from those words. Josh found her standing near the lifts. Her eyes stung. She blinked away the tears.

'Why did you tell me now? It isn't a good time.'

'Would there ever be a good time?'

'But here at the hospital. Why couldn't you wait until I was at home?'

'I didn't want you to be on your own. Especially if you were upset. Ruth's here.'

'Too right I'm upset!' Jemma's cheeks flared. 'Anyway, why should I want to talk to Ruth about it?'

'I just thought …'

'Well, don't think.'

The lift arrived and the doors slid open. Jemma stepped inside and pressed the button for the fifth floor. Josh followed her.

'Jemma, I'm sorry.'

'I don't understand, Josh. Where are you going? What are you going to do? Why do you have to go?'

Josh shrugged. 'I just have to leave, that's all. I wasn't going to tell you … but …'

'And I thought we were getting on so well.'

'We were – we are.'

'Then why?'

'I feel God is calling me.'

'God!'

With a ping the lift reached its destination. The doors slid open again. Josh was blocking her way. She pushed past him.

'Yes, God. At least, that's what I think.'

'Then that's it then. I surrender! I can't compete with God, can I? Why couldn't it have been a job, or a girl … anything. Then I would have stood a chance. But God! How am I supposed to argue against God?'

'You'll understand, one day. I'm sure you will.' He put a hand on her shoulder. With a shudder she collected herself. She tried to steady her voice, sound matter of fact. After all, she was getting quite good at being left alone. She tried to sound sensible, rational, as if he was going on holiday.

'Will you write? We'll keep in touch?'

'Best not. Things will be less … complicated.'

'I thought we were friends. What's complicated about that?'

'Jemma, you know …'

'Yes. I suppose it is – ' she let out a sigh – 'complicated.'

'Anyway, what's to stop you moving on?' he asked.

'I thought you were trying to curb my wandering spirit. I never thought you were a hypocrite.'

'I'm not. We all have to change. For someone who lives on a boat, your feet seem mighty firmly planted here in Monksford. You could "weigh anchor" any time you wanted and set off.'

Jemma smiled, fighting her tears. 'Can I tell you a secret?'

Josh moved close.

'It's all a fake, a sham. The *Ebony Hog* won't go anywhere. I bought her, a bargain so I thought, from an old naval man, Admiral Wainwright. He was very tall, with a white beard, a veritable "Captain Birdseye". I fell in love with the *Hog* at first sight, her colour, her smell, her name, and the fact that she was the only boat I'd viewed that I didn't need to bend double to get in. I bought her in the depths of winter, but in the spring of the first year I had her, I planned to sail her up north, to see my granddad. I didn't even get as far as Monksford lock. The footbridge that goes over just before the lock is too low. The *Hog*'s cabin won't fit under it, even in low water – I tried again at the end of the summer. It's the same down river towards Maidstone. The Red Bridge would decapitate her. She'd had her cabin modified, to suit Admiral Wainright's physique, but I hadn't realised that it meant that she couldn't do the one thing real boats are meant to do – sail. So we're stranded here, the *Hog* and I, our destiny to remain stuck in the Monksford mud.'

'You could take a hacksaw to her.'

'I couldn't do that. It would hurt too much,' said Jemma.

'But she would be able to fulfil her destiny.'

'Don't spin me that "cruel to be kind" line. The *Hog* stays here, and so do I.' She searched his brown eyes. 'Josh, stay too ...'

Scene Five

'WE'RE WAITING FOR ALISTAIR.' RUTH SAT ON ELIZA'S BED AND CHECKED HER watch. He was late as usual, and as usual she would forgive him. It was at times like these that she didn't like Alistair very much. He was like the tissue in the pocket of the coloured wash of life, deeply irritating and impossible to get rid of. She might not like him, but deep down, and very much against her will, she knew she loved him.

Josh and Jemma had disappeared, she presumed, to see Richard. Ruth sat twiddling her thumbs, then deciding that her thumbs could be far more usefully employed, she searched for a needle and thread then sat down to sew on buttons.

She promised herself that she would see Richard today. Later, this very evening. While she was here in the hospital. She would definitely do it today. She made herself promise. Although she was busy, there was no excuse for neglecting her pastoral duties. She would force herself to like Richard, even though she would rather see Jemma with Josh.

Eliza had nodded off, her face almost as pale as her pillow. When she was chatting and laughing and working, it was easy to forget just how sick she was. Mrs Williams and Mrs Amos had scuttled home in time for the six o'clock news.

Ruth sat in the silence and closed her eyes. It would take a miracle for the mystery plays to finally come together. Again, her thoughts travelled to another time, another place. She saw a man in the blue

208

Houppelande coat standing at the first station, Shepherd's Cross, near the Black Bull at the end of the High Street.

'Master Thomas Barker, make haste! It is near sunup.'

Guildsmen scuttled around their waggons, making their final preparations. A queue of waggons lined up behind the Barkers Guild. The Plasterers, Cardmakers, and Fullers, and so on until the Mercers and their final judgement. A scuffle broke out between some Vintners and Ironmongers, who accused them of stealing from their waggon.

'Ah, dog! The devil drown thee!'

'I care not for your waggon or the players!'

The man in blue strode towards them. 'Sires, be merry. Wit you not that this is a Holy day? Calm yourselves, I pray you. Be about your business and grieve me no more.'

With a flourish, a fine horse galloped across the dusty ground, sending soil flying with its hooves. His fine attire marked the rider out as a Goldsmith, one of the wealthiest guilds.

'Good day, Master.' The man in blue removed his hat and made a low bow. He took the reins and led him to the waggon where Herod and the Magi were passing round a flagon of ale and a piece of bread.

Crowds were already gathering. Farm workers, children, women in homespun clothes, merchants in fine embroidered tunics, and chaperons, their ladies in cotehardies and elaborate headdresses.

She heard them gasp as Lucifer fell, and hiss as Satan tempted Eve. They wept with Abraham as he prepared to sacrifice his only son and cheered Moses as he begged Pharaoh to let the Israelites go.

God's story played out before their eyes.

The spectators stood still and let the pageant wind its way through old Monksford, stopping to perform at the appointed stations.

A knock on the door brought her back from her reverie. But her thoughts remained caught in the wonder of the pageant.

For people whose only contact with the sacred was through robed priests and Latin liturgy, this lively, funny and very human portrayal of Bible stories must have been utterly overwhelming. She hoped that the modern equivalent of the medieval audience, spoiled rotten with television, Hollywood, and the Internet, would be equally overwhelmed.

Another knock. This time louder. Ruth blinked as Alistair's craggy face appeared around the doorframe and he crept into the room.

'You're late,' Ruth whispered.

'Yes,' he agreed with no sign of remorse. 'I didn't have my car. It's being valeted.'

Ruth prickled. 'You've left me hanging around here for nearly an hour.'

'I got held up. Council business.'

'As if I haven't got anything better to do.'

'Perhaps you should have gone and done it.'

'What?' She was still half in a dream.

'Whatever better things you have to do.'

This was not the time to play games. 'That would look good; I disappear and you creep into an old lady's sickroom and start taking your clothes off!'

'Shhhh, that journalist will hear! I'll be spread over the front pages. And we wouldn't want that, now would we?' He took a step towards her. 'Ruth,' he cupped her cheek in his hand, 'I've missed you.'

She brushed his hand away and side-stepped his advance. Eliza Feldman stirred in her sleep. Ruth bustled around the bed and hoisted up a carrier bag. She struggled to make her voice sound normal.

'Um ... the costume's in this bag. You can use that bathroom. Just make sure the tunic fits.' She thrust the bag to him across the bed. Eliza sat up and yawned.

'Oh, I didn't know I had another visitor. You must be Alistair.' She looked him up and down as if trying to decide if she liked what she saw. 'I've been expecting you.'

He smiled half-heartedly, put his hand in the bag, and pulled out a dark brown long-sleeved coat, a light brown hat with a long plume-like piece, and a leather belt. Last to come out were the boots. He glanced at Jemma's dress on the bed. 'Why do you ladies get to wear all the bright colours? Don't forget, we're peacocks at heart.'

'Do you need help with the chaperon?' Eliza asked.

'Chaperon?'

'The hat that looks like a dead chicken.'

He disappeared into the bathroom to change. Peacocks, indeed! Ruth had intended to spend the duration of the play alongside the rank and file of Monksford, dressed as a medieval peasant.

Alistair emerged in his tunic and chaperon, which did indeed look like a dead chicken, holding a cloth moneybag – Judas's purse. The thought made Ruth shudder. Alistair gave his imaginary moustache a twirl. In costume, he looked every inch a villain.

'Very ... dapper.' Ruth said.

'Oy! You do look pernicious, Mr Fry. Do the face,' Eliza said.

Alistair gave a little sneer. This wasn't how Ruth had imagined Judas. This parody, this pantomime villain would have fooled no one.

'No, Alistair. The whole point of Judas was that he didn't look like a bad guy. He was plausible. Right up to the moment of betrayal, they would have had full confidence in him. The disciples trusted him with their money; he was their treasurer. They thought he was one of them – honest, God fearing, and genuine.'

'I know.' Alistair waggled his eyebrows.

'Alistair, I'm serious. I don't want you hamming it up.'

'Would I?'

'I don't know.' She shook her head. 'I just don't know.'

'He'll be just fine. If we can boo and hiss at King Herod, why can't we do the same to him?' Eliza said.

'Ruth, you know I would never do anything to thwart your plays. It was just my little joke. I'm sorry if I upset you. You do trust me, don't you?' He looked pleadingly at her. 'Friends?'

'Get changed, Alistair. I've got to go now. You can sort out any alterations with Eliza.' She gave Eliza a peck on the cheek. 'You'll be all right, won't you? I promised to see someone in another part of the hospital. I'll call in again before I go home.'

'Ruth, wait,' Alistair called. 'I'll come with you.'

She sighed as he seized his clothes and rushed into the bathroom to change.

Eliza settled into her pillows. 'Are you going to see that young friend of Jemma's? The one that was in the coma?'

'Yes,' Ruth said quietly, 'but I'm not sure I particularly want Alistair tagging along. I don't know what's got into him lately.'

'You'd look good together, Ruth. It's a pity he's married.'

For the time being. Whatever happened, she desperately wanted to remain friends. She would just have to be careful. She shook her head. 'I don't think that would – '

Alistair appeared, panting slightly. 'Ready?'

Ruth said her goodbyes again and started up the stairs, Alistair following like a puppy.

'What's wrong with the lift?'

'Exercise,' Ruth said. They reached the fifth floor and Ruth paused to catch her breath.

'Do you want to wait here?'

'Why, are you going to do something confidential and "vicary"?'

'No, not at all. Just paying a visit on a young man who is recovering from a very nasty injury.'

'Do you mind then?'

'It doesn't bother me, but I'd better check that he doesn't.'

Ruth knocked and went in. Josh and Richard were playing chess, Josh on a plastic chair and Richard fully dressed but sprawled on the bed. Jemma sat near the window, pretending to read a magazine. She flipped the pages noisily.

'I hope I'm not disturbing you.'

'Not at all,' Josh said. Jemma and Richard exchanged glances.

'I have a friend with me.'

'The more the merrier!' Jemma said.

Ruth leaned out and beckoned to Alistair. He entered like a man at a job interview. He smiled and acknowledged the others in the room. Jemma looked away. She slung her magazine back on the pile on her way to the door. 'Sorry to break up the party, I've got an early start tomorrow.'

She kissed Richard on the cheek and said a perfunctory goodbye to Ruth and Alistair. She ignored Josh, who didn't look up when she let the door slam shut.

'Richard,' Josh said, 'this is Ruth, the vicar who's been praying for you. She's producing the mystery plays.'

Richard held out his hand, and Ruth shook it warmly. 'How are you feeling?'

'Getting better, thanks.' Richard swung his legs over the side of the bed.

'And this is Alistair. He's in the plays too.'

The smile froze on Richard's face. His eyebrows lowered. Alistair took out his handkerchief and mopped at his palms. He held his hand out. Richard didn't take it.

'What's the matter?' asked Ruth.

'I thought ...' began Richard.

'Do you know each other?' Ruth looked from one to the other.

'No,' Alistair said.

'It's you.' Richard pointed at Alistair, his eyes wild. 'It is. It's you!'

'I don't know what you're talking about.' Alistair backed away. 'What's wrong with him?'

'You! It's all your fault!' Richard's face reddened and the veins in his neck protruded like cables. 'You did this to me!' he spat.

'This is ridiculous; I've never seen him before.'

'What's going on?' Ruth said. 'Is he all right?'

'I don't know how you thought you'd get away with it.' Richard elbowed Josh in the stomach and staggered towards Alistair.

Alistair looked astounded. 'I don't know what you mean.'

Josh gripped Richard by the upper arms as he lunged again towards Alistair, who took a step backwards, nearly tripping over a chair.

'What is going on?' Ruth said.

'I think you'd better leave,' said Josh.

'Did you think you'd get away with this? Did you think I wouldn't remember?' Richard struggled to release Josh's grip.

'You must have mistaken me for someone else,' protested Alistair.

'Get a doctor!' Ruth flung the door open and pushed Alistair backwards towards the open doorway.

'You tried to kill me!' Richard screamed as Alistair stumbled into the corridor. 'You tried to kill me!'

Scene Six

JEMMA BLINKED TWICE, RUBBED HER EYES, THEN TRIED TO GET THE SCREEN back into focus. It was only ten to eleven. Not even coffee time. She was tired. Tired from rehearsing the mystery plays, tired from visiting Richard, tired from coming to terms with her relationship, or lack of, with Josh, and here at work her fatigue had just caught up with her. Had she been at home, she could have curled up on her bed for a ten minute power nap. That might have been enough to see her through, allowed her to finish the article, but today she had felt obliged to show her face in the office. Last Friday Mohan had asked for a photograph of her. She had puzzled for a while, wondering if he needed it for the editorial page, eventually asking why.

'So I can remember what you look like!'

It took her several minutes to work out what he meant. Even his witty repartee was completely lost in her tired brain. There was no doubt her work was suffering. When she was this close to exhaustion, her ability to express herself was severely compromised. Words became curt and functional. They fulfilled their purpose of conveying meaning at some primitive level, but it was as if her articles were built of breeze-blocks – functional but aesthetically unpleasant. Writers need to play with words – to experiment with their shape, sound, and effect. A word can trigger associations and a seemingly innocent word can become taboo overnight. She remembered writing a piece one Christmas Eve where she had described a young band as a 'Tsunami of Talent.' She loved the alliteration, the exotic, overwhelming sound of the word. She had even looked it up in the dictionary to check the spelling. When she returned to work after Christmas, she had to re-write the piece. Her word, her lovely word, had become synonymous with tragedy, devastation, and death. It had been stolen from her, and she wasn't sure she would ever get it back.

Some words, she had decided, are intrinsically funny. She couldn't even type the words *gusset* and *kinkajou* without smiling. Other words – *deadline* and *sombre* – just sounded serious. Even the word *gravity* sounded heavy.

Also, she had been too tired to read. Most days she struggled through the weightier newspapers. Yesterday she had only managed the television page and the cartoons. Her writing was suffering from this lack of stimulation. Wonderful words, she knew, sparked off each other, kindled into brilliance. Now her words stumbled onto the page last place in the marathon – no victory, just relief. Weary words, spent words.

Her mobile started playing its irksome tune. She pressed the but-ton quickly before it disturbed her colleagues.

'Jemma Durham.'

'Jemma, where did you get to last night?' Josh was speaking fast, tripping over his words.

'Home. I wasn't in the mood.'

'And your phone?'

'It must have fallen out of my bag in the car. I found it under the passenger seat. Why, did you try to get hold of me?'

'Can you take a tea break?'

She looked around. Everyone was heads down. Working, or pre-tending to. She glanced over at Mohan's office.

'No!'

'Jemma, I need to talk to you.'

'We have nothing to say.'

'I'm sorry about last night. I didn't mean to upset you.'

'Okay. You didn't mean to upset me. I am not upset. Can I get on with my work?'

'Jemma, please, this is important. It's about Richard.'

'I'll see what I can do.'

Ten minutes later, in leather armchairs in Donatello's, Jemma sat wide-eyed over her cappuccino opposite Josh as he relayed the events at the hospital.

'Poor Richard. How is he?'

'The doctor gave him a sedative. He was sleeping when I left. Ruth said she was taking Alistair home.'

Jemma shook her head. 'But he was getting so much better. He was more rational, he was making sense, his memory was returning – now this. I really thought he was getting it together. I'll try to see him at lunchtime.'

'He was quite adamant that Alistair had tried to kill him.'

'Perhaps he did,' she whispered.

'Pardon?' said Josh.

'It doesn't matter.' Jemma waved her hand, dismissing her comment.

'I've never seen him that agitated. I didn't think I could hold him back for much longer. He was ready to attack Alistair. Do you think the brain injury caused it?'

'Could be. He's not a violent man. Unless … unless he's telling the truth.'

'What do you mean?'

'Alistair. Could he have hurt Richard?'

'And seeing him triggered the memory?' Josh scratched his chin.

'Do you think there's any truth in these allegations?'

'Who knows? Somebody did it – that's for sure. Perhaps that somebody was Alistair Fry.'

Jemma shook her head, unable to assimilate the thought.

'Josh, what are we going to do?'

DETECTIVE SERGEANT MORRISEY TOOK OFF HIS GLASSES, POLISHED THEM ON his tie, regarded Jemma and Josh through the screen, and deciding they posed no threat of violence or infection, opened a door and escorted them through to an interview room.

'Sorry, I just need to make a quick call.' Jemma fished in her bag.

DS Morrisey looked heavenward. He reminded Jemma of a weary basset hound. She finished her call to Mohan and stowed her phone. DS Morrisey indicated a desk with two chairs facing each other. He took one and Josh indicated that Jemma should sit on the other. He stood behind her with his arms folded. She craned round. They must have looked like a Victorian photograph.

'So, what do you think you need to tell me?'

'Well,' Jemma began, 'when the policeman interviewed me, after we found Richard, he said any piece of information, no matter how small was important.'

'Go on.' DS Morrisey glanced at his watch and tapped his foot impatiently.

'The thing is, Richard has accused Alistair Fry of trying to kill him.'

'I know,' DS Morrisey said. 'The doctor rang me. We sent an officer up there, but in view of Mr Sutton's serious injury and the resulting memory loss, he was unable to give us any more information.'

'Isn't that enough?' Jemma rose to her feet, but Josh's hand on her arm prompted her to sit down again.

'Miss Durham, can you tell me anything we don't already know?'

She had the distinct impression she was coming between a man and his coffee break.

'So, have you talked to Alistair Fry?' Josh asked.

'We are talking to anyone we think may have any involvement in this case.'

'Is that a yes or a no?' Jemma pressed.

'Not yet. We have no substantive evidence to link Councillor Fry to the incident.'

'Apart from the victim telling you Fry did it.'

'In view of Mr Sutton's "illness" we need to consider the reliability of the information before dragging in all and sundry for questioning.'

'He's not ill,' Jemma said. 'He was whacked on the head. And he's telling you who did it. I can't believe you haven't even talked to Alistair Fry!'

Josh placed his hand on her arm again to calm her. This time she shrugged it off.

'Look, we will speak to him, in time, and in the light of any corroborating evidence.' He stood up. 'Thank you for coming in; we'll keep you informed of developments.'

'Wait,' Jemma said. 'There was a car, by the river. On the night it happened I was waiting for Josh and I saw a car. I think it was dark blue. It parked in the car park and the driver sat there with the headlamps on. You saw it too, didn't you, Josh? You must have parked near it.'

'I . . . I don't remember. I was in a hurry to see you.'

'Was it there when you returned to the car park later, Mr Wood?'

'No. No, I'm sure the car park was almost empty. I can't really remember.'

'So whoever it was drove away after Richard was attacked.' Jemma couldn't help thumping the table with her fist.

'Or happened to leave some time that evening. Really, Miss Durham, there must be hundreds of dark blue cars in Monksford. Now DC Ives has got your contact details, if there is anything else we need to ask, we know where to find you.' He stood and held the door open for them to exit.

As they left the police station, Jemma glanced back at the blue lamp above the door.

'I can't believe that. They just didn't want to know.'

'It was difficult. Richard can hardly be called a reliable witness.'

Jemma grabbed Josh's hand and dragged him down the High Street. 'Come on. I've got an idea.'

They both set off at a jog, Jemma stopping by the pillared portico of Monksford Town Hall. She bent over, her hands on her knees, panting from the unexpected exercise. Josh was hardly out of breath.

'Jemma, you're not going in there to confront him? Tell me you're not.'

'I'm not going in there at all.' Jemma ducked through the archway and up a side alley to a small rectangle of asphalt. There was a sign. 'Parking for Council Members Only'. Half a dozen cars, one a Daimler with a flag on the front, filled up a quarter of the spaces in the car park. There were no dark blue cars.

'Perhaps he's not here today,' said Jemma.

'Of course not. He'll be at work.'

'True. We can't hang around here until the next council sitting. I think he's a solicitor, but I don't know where he works. I can find out at the *Gazette*'s office. Come on. I told Mohan I'd be back before twelve.'

'Just a second. I've got an idea.' Josh pulled out his mobile phone and flicked the cover open. He pressed buttons. 'Ruth, hi, it's Josh. I know this is a bit of a strange question, but do you happen to know what car Alistair Fry drives?' There was a pause. 'Okay, thanks.' And he closed the cover.

'Well?' said Jemma.

'Alistair Fry drives an estate car, a Mercedes. And it's midnight blue.'

JEMMA LAY IN BED LISTENING TO ALL THE SOUNDS OF THE NIGHT – THE WATER lapping, the occasional screech of a barn owl, and the rumble of the traffic on the bypass. There was an unpleasant smell. She wanted to close the windows, but the heat on the steel and wooden structure that had built up during the day threatened to turn the *Hog* into a nighttime sauna. She threw back the covers and flipped over, searching for a cool spot. She climbed out of the bunk, put on her slippers, padded into the galley, and opened the fridge. She poured herself a drink of cold water and sat down at the table. She opened her laptop and started typing all her questions and theories about Richard's attack. The police were right, apart from Richard's accusation, there was nothing to indicate that Alistair Fry was involved. Why would a Councillor, a pillar of the community and a member of the Church, hit someone on the head, then dump them in the river and leave them for dead? Was the blue car a coincidence? Why was Richard near the river in the first place?

She typed these unanswered and unanswerable questions as they sprang into her mind. The police seemed reluctant to investigate. As far as they were aware Councillor Fry had nothing to do with it. But she knew things about Fry that the police didn't know. She knew he was not the upright citizen everyone thought him to be. She knew about Alistair and Ruth. He was certainly a philanderer, but did that make him a potential murderer?

She poured herself another drink. Perhaps cooling down and getting this multitude of questions outside her head would help to calm her and permit her to sleep. She unlocked the cabin door and stepped onto the deck. She breathed the night air and looked up at the stars. Light pollution from Monksford and nearby Tunbridge Wells and Maidstone diffused a sickly orange glow and overwhelmed all but the brightest constellations. The crackle of tyres on gravel caught her attention, but she couldn't see any headlamps in the car park. She froze, listening and waiting. The river was in darkness. She reached down slowly and her fingers gripped the textured plastic handle of the torch.

Footsteps. The crunch of gravel on the towpath. Coming closer. She ducked into the doorway. A faint flicker of torchlight. She held her breath. The footsteps passed. They crossed the bridge. She twisted to see. The footsteps continued along the path on the opposite bank of the river, the faint beam just visible under some overhanging willow branches. She grasped the torch and crept down the ramp, jumping over the gravel path and landing softly on the grass. She stole across to the car park and shone her flashlight around, half expecting to see a midnight blue Mercedes.

Before today she would never have suspected Alistair, but now she could imagine him sneaking around the river in the pitch dark and she could imagine him being connected with mysterious things that go splash in the night. Her own car sat there, looking a little sorry for itself, and Ray Jones' 2 CV. There was an unfamiliar car, but it wasn't blue, nor was it a Mercedes. It was a slightly battered and extremely muddy Land Rover. She peered through the mud-spattered window. There was a crumpled newspaper and some pieces of baler twine and some empty crisp packets. She walked around and peeped in the back. More rubbish. She peered closely at the tyres, muddy and worn. The khaki-green bodywork was scratched and dented.

Fry would never drive anything like this. Perhaps she had made a mistake and it belonged to a visitor to one of the boats. She straightened up and yawned. She would go back to bed now. Everything would become clearer in the morning. She could even ask around the boat owners to see if anyone knew about the Land Rover.

It was then that she heard the splash.

She took off, running not towards the safety of the *Hog*, but towards the bridge and the direction of the footsteps. She brandished her torch and screamed at the figure.

'What are you doing? I can see you. I'm calling the police!'

The man didn't answer but ran towards the bridge shining his torch into her face, temporarily blinding her. He pushed roughly past and ran back in the direction of the car park. Jemma gave chase, but he was taller and faster. She cursed her fluffy bunny slippers as she tripped over a tussock and sprawled on the grass. She picked herself up and followed the man.

The Land Rover's engine revved and Jemma directed her torch beam through the windscreen. The driver held up his hand to shield his eyes. Jemma caught a glimpse of green waxed jacket – the sort worn by farmers. He let up the clutch and drove towards her. For a moment she froze, then sprinted for the trees. Even with a Land Rover, he couldn't follow. The tyres skidded on the gravel as he braked, then she heard the engine whine as he thrust it into reverse. Then he was gone.

Jemma put her hand to her chest. Her heart felt as if it would burst out of her ribcage. For a moment she couldn't move. Then, trembling, she made her way back to the boat.

She picked up her phone to call the police, but she thought of DS Morrisey, his lackadaisical attitude and his basset-hound eyes. DS Morrisey had wanted evidence, and she had none. She didn't know who the man was, she had no idea what he had dropped in the water, and she hadn't thought to take the registration number of the Land Rover. As far as she knew, no crime had been committed, and no connection to Richard, or Alistair. She paused, her fingers hovering over the keypad. She dialled Josh's number. A voice thick with sleep answered.

'Did I wake you?'

'Jemma, it's half past three.'

'Sorry. Josh, can you come over?'

'What's happened?'

'I'll explain when you get here. Oh, and have you got a net, a landing net or something, or a long pole?'

'I won't ask.'

Fifteen minutes later, Josh and Jemma sat in the *Hog's* tiny galley, drinking tea and waiting for the sun to rise.

'It'll be light enough to see what we're doing but too early for nosy onlookers,' she said.

'Tell me again, exactly what we are looking for?'

'Whatever he dropped in the river. He was keen to get rid of something.'

'Could be anything. What if he's a murderer, and he's disposing of a dismembered body?'

Jemma grimaced in disgust. 'That would give DS Morrisey something to get his teeth into – metaphorically speaking.'

A raft of ducks swam past, quacking emphatically, and a crow in a field began its raucous cry. Jemma glanced at the clock. A watery sun, pale and insipid, was rising above the line of poplars on the ridge.

'Come on.' She stood and deposited her mug in the sink. Josh did the same.

Jemma pulled on her coat and trainers and grabbed her boat hook, while Josh rummaged around for an old landing net. Within minutes they had made their way across the bridge to the opposite bank of the river. She wrinkled her nose; there was that smell again.

Jemma knelt down in the place where she had seen the man. First she scrutinised the reeds, searching for a bent leaf or a disturbance in the surface. Everything looked normal. She stood and walked a little farther along, inspecting the river's surface and the towpath. A pair of mallard made a clumsy take-off, sprinting along the surface and flapping their wings until they became airborne.

They had made their way to a bend a little farther downstream when Jemma spotted a neon orange fishing float.

'I wish those anglers would learn to take their gear home with them. I know we don't have the carnage caused by the lead weights any more, but if they'd seen waterfowl tangled in discarded line ... We did an article on it once. The line gets wrapped round their bills and stops them feeding. They lose legs, their wings get damaged.'

She reached out to scoop up the float. It seemed to be caught. She tugged harder, but it did not give. There seemed to be something heavy on the end of the line. She looked at Josh.

'I think we've found something.'

She took the long pole with the brass hook on the end and delved around among the reeds. She hooked something twice, but as she heaved it towards the surface, it slipped off the hook. Finally she snared it and managed to hoist it out of the water. Josh caught it in the net, let some of the water drain away, and deposited it on the bank. It was a package, about the size of a football, wrapped securely in black plastic and tied up with orange twine. Josh took a penknife from his pocket and gave it to Jemma. She started to cut the wet string.

'Do you want me to do this?'

Jemma felt suddenly squeamish. He had been joking about body parts, hadn't he? It would explain the smell. She shook her head, then carefully unwrapped the layers of black plastic. Inside that were several supermarket carrier bags and inside them a translucent plastic lunchbox. Perhaps someone didn't like their egg sandwiches. Inside the lunchbox she could see a brown envelope. She dried her hands on her jeans and pulled the lid off the lunchbox. She extracted the envelope and tore it open.

'Money!' A wad of ten- and twenty-pound notes, held together with more orange twine.

'There must be hundreds of pounds here.' Josh's eyes were wide. 'What are we going to do?'

'We should take it to the police. If someone has gone to these lengths to conceal the money, there must be something dodgy going on.'

'I agree.' Josh stuffed the money back in the envelope.

DETECTIVE SERGEANT MORRISEY WAS OFF DUTY WHEN JOSH AND JEMMA arrived so they were received indifferently by the laconic WPC Patel, who sat behind the reception desk, reading a newspaper. She reluctantly put down her paper and took the package across the counter. This time they were not going to have the courtesy of the interview room. Jemma recounted the story of how they found the money.

'Fine, we'll keep it until it is claimed,' WPC Patel said.

'This isn't just lost property, you know,' protested Jemma.

'What do you think it is?' she asked.

'I don't know. It could be anything, stolen during a robbery, a ransom payment, drug money ... anything!'

'When you find out, come back and tell us.'

'But that's your job – to find out.'

'We investigate crimes. If you see a crime being committed, notify us and we will investigate.'

'We could be in danger.'

'How?'

'Because of what I've seen. The man, last night. He dropped something – the money in the river, then ran to his car. First he pushed past me on the bridge, then he tried to run me down. I had to jump into the hedge to get away.'

'Did you see him throw the money?' WPC Patel chewed the end of her pencil.

'No,' said Jemma, 'but I heard the splash.'

'So you can't be sure he was involved with the money at all?'

'It was at the same spot,' said Josh.

'Did you see anything, Sir?'

'No, Jemma called me later, but I helped fish the money out.'

'I'm sorry, but I don't see that there's much we can do.'

Outside the police station, Jemma let out a scream of frustration. 'I don't believe it; the police here are useless! They just don't want to know. What possible reason is there for hiding money in the river unless it's linked with a criminal activity?'

'One way to find out,' said Josh.

'What's that?' asked Jemma.

'We'll have to keep our eyes open and find some way of monitoring that part of the river. Like the policewoman said, wait until someone comes to claim it.'

Scene Seven

RUTH WAS NOT THE SORT OF PERSON WHO MADE LISTS. NORMALLY SHE HAD no trouble at all remembering what she had to do or to whom she had to speak. She nudged Dimitri off her desk and wrote at the top of the list,

> Buy cat food

Then she wrote,

> Phone Raj
> Check sound equipment
> Collect costumes
> Spare scripts
> Notify press
> Write to Mr Giddings
> Call Alistair

She wondered if she ought to add eat, sleep, and go to the toilet to the list as she didn't seem to have got round to doing any of those things lately. As if she didn't have enough to think about with the dress rehearsal, she had the added worry of Alistair – and Richard Sutton's bizarre reaction to him. Alistair seemed as bewildered as anyone else. She had bundled him out of the room while Josh held Richard down; then she drove him home.

'So what just happened in there?' Ruth struggled to keep her eyes on the road.

'Search me.'

'Why would he accuse you out of the blue like that?'

'I told you, I've absolutely no idea. I've never seen him before in my life.'

'Perhaps you reminded him of the man who attacked him. Maybe you have a double.'

'Or perhaps it's a symptom, caused by the bang on the head.'

'Do you think the police will want to talk to you?'

'I don't see why they should. I couldn't tell them anything.'

The rest of the journey took place in strained silence. Ruth had made a promise that she wouldn't let herself be alone with Alistair. She watched his hand in case he tried to touch her. It felt even more dangerous now. This new Alistair, the one that might have attacked Richard, was altogether unknown and threatening. When they had first met, he had seemed so solid, so sound and dependable, the perfect Councillor and model churchgoer. Now she wondered what he was hiding.

The doorbell rang, making her jump. She padded downstairs, opened the door to the postman, and signed for a parcel. She scooped up the *Monksford Gazette* from the doormat and made her way into the kitchen to make some tea and toast, a quick breakfast. She glanced at the clock. It was almost seven. It would have to be a very quick breakfast. Dimitri made figures of eight around her legs. She scooped him up and deposited him outside the back door. He would have to find his own breakfast until she had been to the shop.

The front page of the *Gazette* boasted the headline 'New Homes Boost for Monksford'. 'Where are they going to build them, on stilts in the river?' Ruth muttered. She scanned the article and shuddered as she read the line 'Councillor Alistair Fry plans to oppose the building of fifty-five new homes on greenbelt land in Monksford.' First the business park and the road, now a new housing estate. Alistair had opposed them all, but they had all gone ahead despite his opposition. When she first met him, she had imagined him powerful and influential. Now he seemed weak and ineffectual.

The toast popped up and the kettle boiled. She switched on the radio, as the announcer was summarising the seven o'clock news.

'... Monksford Councillor Alistair Fry is helping police with their enquiries following the attack on a journalist last year in the town. Now over to Karl for our sports and weather ...'

She stood, frozen, butter knife in hand. She let out a groan. What if they kept him there all day, or worse, arrested him? Today was the dress rehearsal. How could the play go ahead at Corpus Christi with no Judas? She stopped, shocked that a play had become more important to her than a man's well being and career. She prayed quickly, then threw the toast in the bin, abandoned the tea, and jumped in the car. The show, as they say, must go on.

She parked her car in the farmyard and set off for the upper field, where the first scenes would take place. She glanced at the sky. At least it wasn't raining.

When she arrived, a throng of people, anxious harbingers of gossip and bad news, gathered around her and asked if she had heard about Alistair. She managed to sound calm and reassuring. 'He's just helping the police, you know, answering questions. I'm sure he'll come as soon as he is finished.'

She brushed them aside and found Josh, still in his jeans and T-shirt.

'You heard?'

He nodded. 'What do you think will happen?'

'I hope he'll answer their questions to their satisfaction and get here in time for his scene.'

'I meant, what will happen if they find he was involved? Will he go to prison?'

'I know that's what you meant. I was trying not to think about it.'

'Sorry. I'm not a pessimist, but this could be serious.'

Ruth felt the urge to scream rising from her stomach. She pushed it down and patted Josh's arm. 'Don't worry. Everything will be all right.'

She tried to force herself to believe her own words. Her only option was to focus on the rest of the play. If there was a problem when they reached Alistair's scenes, she would concern herself with it then. She wished she had drunk that cup of tea, or something stronger.

The technicians and sound engineers were still running around securing cables and checking microphones.

'One, two. One, one, two.'

She couldn't help wondering if sound technicians knew how to count any higher. She pulled out her list, checked off the items, then headed for the marquee with a large green trefoil where the actors changed into their costumes. It was hardly luxurious, but it was warm and dry and had been divided with screens, one area for the men and another for the women, plus a general area, a 'green room' with a tea urn.

It wasn't exactly a room, but the grass floor did indeed make it glow green. She deposited the last few costumes on the hanging rail in the women's section and ran her hand along the rainbow colours. She wished that Eliza could be there. She had phoned the hospital immediately after she got up. Eliza had not had a good night. Her temperature was up, and the doctors did not know why. She had promised to drive Eliza home as soon as they agreed to discharge her, but that would not be today.

Three young mums from St Sebastian's were acting as dressers. They were standing in a huddle, laughing and chatting. Ruth wanted to shake them. Didn't they realise how important today was? It was everyone's last chance to get it right before the performance. She took a couple of deep breaths, trying to calm her jangling nerves, to reassure herself that everything was going to be all right. She felt a sweaty hand on her shoulder. 'Don't look so worried. Everything's going to be fine.'

She spun round. 'Ronnie!'

'Sorry, sweetheart. Didn't mean to make you jump.'

'I was miles away.'

'It really will be okay, you know.'

'Thanks Ronnie.' She squeezed his elbow. Despite his reassurances, the knot in her stomach was getting tighter. She was concerned about Eliza, about Josh, about Richard and his accusations, Raj and Surinder and the adoption process, and Bram who had become more taciturn each day. Especially, and most painfully, she was worried about Alistair.

'You heard the news?'

Ronnie nodded. 'A bad business. But we must keep busy.'

'Keep busy, keep busy,' Ruth muttered to herself as a mantra. She found a technician and persuaded him to allow her to use a microphone to speak to the actors and crew. Her voice, resounding across the fields, took her aback, but she was pleased that when she spoke, people stopped what they were doing, stood still and listened.

'Would everyone please take up their positions for scene one, "The Creation"? Anyone not involved in this scene may choose either to watch or to sit in the green room or the scouts' marquee in the upper field. But please, if you watch, don't distract the actors. When we transfer the location to the farmyard, I would like as many of you as possible, in costume, to act as ushers, to make sure that, on the day, the real audience can find its way around the site.

'I want to press on with the Old Testament section now, so I'll let you carry on uninterrupted. We'll break at twelve for lunch then resume the New Testament at one. Have a good one everybody. Break a leg!' She fervently hoped that nobody would break anything. She had enough problems. She returned the microphone and took her folding chair, ready to settle herself to watch the play. The orchestra struck up the opening chords and tingles ran up her spine. 'We're going to do it. We're actually going to do it!'

To Ruth's amazement, the first four scenes passed without a hitch. The only cloud on the horizon was exactly that, a large black cloud drifting over from the direction of Maidstone. If it did rain, it would test their waterproofing. Ruth was getting good at looking on the bright side.

'What are you going to do about it, Ruth? It's just not good enough.'

Harlan Westacre descended like a bat in a black velvet cape and silver jewelry. *Goth is not a good look for the over fifties*, thought Ruth.

'Harlan!' She forced a smile. 'What's the problem?'

'The dressing area is too small, the stage is the wrong shape, and it's going to rain.'

Ruth processed the complaints. Nothing she could do about the third. The second, tough. Harlan would have to cope. 'I'll see what I can do about the dressing room,' she breezed. And headed towards the marquee before Harlan could find anything else to object to. She spent the rest of the morning watching the action on stage, sorting out technical problems and keeping the actors and crew supplied with tea. By lunchtime, she was ready to drop, and they still had the longer section of the cycle to do.

The cast and crew milled round the farm. Some stayed in the upper field with their lunches, making a picnic of it, others gathered in the farmyard, and Ruth busied herself checking the props and the stable. Herod's armies were mounted on a variety of nags from the local riding stables, and one of the wise men had somehow obtained a llama from a nearby farm, which he had dressed up to look like a camel. Once she was confident all was ready, she allowed herself a brief sit down on a bale of hay. She leant against the side of the stable and sat perfectly still with the sun warming her upturned face. She closed her eyes, enjoying a moment's stolen peace until she heard footsteps on the concrete of the yard.

'I bring sustenance.'

Ronnie proffered a Roquefort-and-onion sandwich. Ruth waved it away as politely as she could. It would have been difficult to eat had she felt hungry, but considering the queasy apprehension that had haunted her all morning, it might just finish her off.

She checked her watch. Half past twelve. Alistair must have finished at the police station. He had already been there for hours, perhaps overnight. She hesitated, then pressed the keys on her mobile phone. It connected but went straight to voicemail. If his phone was switched off, it could mean he was still being questioned or that he had been arrested. Alternatively, it could be that he was driving or simply that the battery needed charging. They would have to proceed without him. Ruth called a young actor who had played one of Noah's sons and handed him a script. They would just have to manage.

She was just about to call everyone to order to start again when a bowlegged elderly man in a tweed jacket, huge glasses, and a flat cap stood squarely in front of her.

'I need to talk to you most urgently.'

The old man almost plucked at her sleeve, his face contorted with pleading. Ruth was not in the mood for another distraction.

'Ah, Mr Giddings. You're here again. Why don't I get my diary? We can make an appointment so we can talk this through. Or you could write me another letter.'

He held up his hand. 'This blasphemy must stop. Stop now, or the consequences will be most dire. I have tried to warn you but you have not listened. Hear me now. Turn from this wickedness.'

'Mr Giddings, I do appreciate your feelings, but as I explained to you before, and as I said in my letter – '

'You are still not listening! "On the wicked he will rain fiery coals and burning sulphur; a scorching wind will be their lot."' Ruth was concerned for both his physical health, fearing the anxiety might bring on a heart attack or a stroke, and his mental health, as his campaign had been relentless and verging on paranoid. But there was something unsettling about his assertion that the plays were blasphemous and his desperate insistence that they should be cancelled. He had claimed in his letter that he had a dream, and in this dream he saw God's punishment, which he described in graphic detail. She had shown Alistair the letter, but he had dismissed it as the ranting of a slightly peculiar old man. She had agreed, too readily perhaps, without giving Mr Giddings a proper hearing.

'"If you do not listen, and if you do not set your heart to honour my name," says the LORD Almighty, "I will send a curse upon you, and I will curse your blessings. Yes, I have already cursed them, because you have not set your heart to honour me." Cursed, did you hear that?'

Cursed. A week ago she would have laughed at the idea, but with the accusations against Alistair and Eliza Feldman's deterioration she was starting to wonder.

'Yes, Mr Giddings, I heard. But can't you see how these plays can be a good thing? They're bringing the Bible to people in a form they can understand, just like those waggon-play performers hundreds of years ago.'

A small crowd of teenage reprobates, dressed as first-century Palestinian reprobates, was starting to gather. The lads that Ruth had first met in the church. They were hiding smirks and giggles. One of them shouted, 'Tell us another one, Granddad!'

Mr Giddings was not listening. He was too busy quoting from the book of Jeremiah. '"O LORD, you deceived me, and I was deceived; you overpowered me and prevailed. I am ridiculed all day long; everyone mocks me. Whenever I speak, I cry out proclaiming violence and destruction. So the word of the LORD has brought me insult and reproach all day long."'

Sensing trouble, Harlan and Josh approached. Josh diverted the teenagers, and Harlan and Ruth took an arm each and escorted Mr Giddings, who was still spouting Scripture, towards the farmyard. Ronnie brought a folding chair, and they sat Mr Giddings down, talking quietly to reassure him. He fell silent, but behind the large glasses, tears threatened to spill from his eyes. One of the dressers offered to fetch a glass of water from the farmhouse while another offered to phone Mr Giddings' daughter. Ruth took a deep breath and started to walk back to the field. She prayed as she walked.

'Have I got this all wrong, Father? Are these difficulties a sign from you that you don't want these plays to be performed? Should I call it all off now? All this time, money, and effort – but for what? Am

I neglecting my real calling as pastor of your flock, for this ... play-acting? Will it make one iota of difference to people's lives? Speak to me, Father. Why do you seem so far away? What can I do, how can I change to serve you better? Help me to know your will.'

She crossed the road as a blue Mercedes narrowly missed her. Alistair. He was back, just in time. A sign? Despite her doubts, the rehearsal would go ahead.

Everyone was gathered in the farmyard. She wrestled a microphone from a reluctant engineer and called for attention. Actors and crew filed over to the stable where the annunciation and nativity scenes would take place. She handed the microphone to Harlan.

'Could you take over for a moment? There's something I need to do.'

Harlan was only too delighted to comply.

With Harlan in control, Ruth went out to the small field being used as a car park. Alistair, still wearing his solicitor's suit, looked tired and despondent as he trudged across the rough grass. He had a growth of black stubble and his hair was unkempt.

'You're back! I'm so relieved you made it. We've just started the second act.' She realised she was babbling and stopped herself. 'Is everything all right?'

'Not really. I just spent the evening and most of the night at the police station.'

'What happened?'

'They just wanted to ask me a few questions. That's what they said. Spent hours incarcerated in an interview room with the enchanting Detective Sergeant Morrisey and the equally charming Detective Inspector Reid.'

'They let you go eventually.'

'Theoretically, I could have left at any time, but they might have thought I had something to hide.'

'Which you haven't.'

'Of course not!'

'So what time did you get away?'

'About eight this morning. I've been driving round since, trying to make sense of it all.'

'So you've had no sleep and no breakfast; you must be shattered. Oh, Alistair, why don't you go home to Amanda? We'll manage here; I've appointed an understudy.'

'There's no point in going home.' He rubbed his hand over his face, temporarily rearranging the crags and smoothing out the lines. 'Amanda's left me.'

She felt a surge of compassion. 'That's awful. I'm so sorry.' She was going to add, 'If there's anything I can do ...' but thought better of it. There were some things she couldn't do. 'The more reason not to be here.'

'I'd rather be here with my ... with friends.'

'All the same ...'

'I've decided. Where are we getting changed? And where can I get a coffee? I have a need for caffeine that borders on the clinical.'

Ruth directed him to the marquee and left the three women fussing and brooding over him. If she could have found a solid brick wall she would have hit her head against it. The whole day was taking on a surreal, nightmarish quality. She headed back to the farmyard. Ronnie came jogging up behind her, puffing like an overweight pug dog.

'Ruth, if you have a moment ...'

'Ronnie, this isn't a good time.'

He looked crestfallen. 'I just wanted to show you something. You see, I had this idea – well, I'll show you.'

He led Ruth towards the abbey. As they passed a small copse of trees, he pointed.

'Look, there.'

She squinted through the tree trunks. There, twisting gently left and right, was an unclothed male mannequin, suspended from a branch by a rope around its neck. Ruth snorted a laugh.

'What is that supposed to be?'

'That,' huffed Ronnie, 'is Judas Iscariot.'

'But he's naked.'

'I know he is at the moment, but once dear Alistair has finished his little exposé in the Garden of Gethsemane, he can whip off his costume, we'll dress the dummy and behold – one hanged Judas.'

'Gruesome!'

'All we have to do is put a sign up here saying "Potter's Field". It all adds to the authenticity of the performance.'

'Marvellous! Shall we see if I can get some animal guts to spread around for the bit where "he fell headlong, his body burst open and all his intestines spilled out"?'

'Great idea!'

'Ronnie, these are supposed to be the renaissance of the medieval mystery play tradition. They are intended to point people towards God. They're not some kind of gore fest.'

'Point taken.' He looked despondent.

Ruth thought for a moment. They were going to be using half a gallon of stage blood on poor Josh for the flogging. What could be more grisly than the crucifixion itself? She looked at Ronnie's crushed expression. 'Okay, the dummy stays, but hang it well back into the copse. We don't want to frighten the children.'

By the time she arrived at the farmyard, the wise men had been and gone, Herod had slaughtered the innocents, and the boy Jesus had been lost and found in the temple. She sidled up to Harlan for an update. The only hitches were a nasty buzzing sound from the speakers and an indignant yelping from the Archangel Gabriel following a llama bite.

After a tea break around four, complete with homemade cakes, the cast and crew shifted location once again to the lower field, then to the abbey for the crucifixion and resurrection scenes. The final judgement scene would take place back at the farmyard. Ruth looked at her watch. They were an hour and a half behind schedule. The rain that had held off all day looked certain to make an appearance. The air was still and heavy. Clouds of gnats gathered around the actor's heads, and a dog on the farm began howling. Worst of all, the stench in the field by the river had got worse – a rotting stink of putrefying flesh that made Ruth's stomach heave. She would mention it again to Bram and hoped that there would be a strong wind, blowing away from the audience.

Ruth made careful notes during the trial-before-Pilate scenes. Here she had amalgamated several of the original plays but wondered if she should cut it further. Perhaps John Grisham could keep people enthralled through a lengthy courtroom drama, but she was not sure the same could be said for the amateur actors of Monksford.

She found the next part of the play difficult to watch, even in rehearsal. Ronnie, Harlan, and Ruth had discussed at length how to stage the flogging scene. The four soldiers, dressed as medieval knights, describe in curt, graphic sentences, how they would flog him with reeds and a flail. 'Let us drive at him hard with our dashes, All red with our blows we array him and rend him.'

They tried it with Josh, hands bound with the knights thrashing him with small canes, but they couldn't use enough force to make it look authentic without injuring Josh. One knight got carried away and swished a little too hard. Josh cried out and stumbled forward.

'Stop!' she shouted.

'No … no, carry on. Let's get to the end of the scene.' His back showed stripes of red.

'I said, stop.' The knights untied him. Ruth took Josh a drink of water and handed him his shirt.

The sheer horror of watching a man stripped and vulnerable, mocked, and scourged was more than Ruth could bear.

'We'll have to take the beating out of view,' Ruth decreed.

'But it's a powerful scene,' Harlan said.

'Why don't we have his hands tied around a large pillar? That would obscure most of his body, then he could wear protective padding on his back and the knights can thrash away to their hearts' content.' Ronnie said.

Josh agreed.

'It looks totally ridiculous,' Harlan said, 'as if he's hugging a tree.'

'Why don't we have the scourging offstage with Mary the mother of Jesus and Mary Magdalene on stage reacting to what they hear? That way we get the drama and the sound effects, without Josh getting hurt.'

They nodded in agreement. 'Works for me,' Josh said.

The musicians began their sombre tune, and Jemma and the woman playing Mary, the mother of Jesus, took up their positions. There was a distant rumble of thunder. Josh's face was intense with concentration. Ruth was captivated by the scene. Josh's performance was worthy of the professional theatre, playing a man so beaten and abused, yet with such dignity. As the forty lashes hit their mark harmlessly on a chair, Josh's cries of pain grew louder, then diminished, like a man numbed and semiconscious. She watched Jemma's face. At first she was acting, acting proficiently but obviously acting. Then Ruth noticed that her distress was real. Tears flowed, and her cries to stop became almost hysterical. The woman playing Mary looked pleadingly at Ruth. She had no choice but to stop the scene. She rushed to the stage area and gathered Jemma in her arms like a child. Jemma clung to her until the sobs subsided. Josh ran from backstage and seeing Jemma, knelt next to Ruth and stroked Jemma's hair.

'It's all my fault. It's all my fault,' choked Jemma.

'What happened?' he asked Ruth.

Ruth shook her head and shrugged.

Eventually, she was calm enough for Harlan to take her to the green room and revive her with sweet tea. The actors had started to disperse, and Ruth made an executive decision as she called for them to return.

'We have to rehearse the crucifixion scene. I was not at all happy about it the last time, and we must practise with the actual crossbeam, and in costume. We'll just walk through the part where Christ carries the cross, but we must do the tying, nailing, and hoisting tonight.'

She dismissed those not directly involved and sent a runner to let Harlan know she wasn't calling Jemma again. The first spots of rain started to fall. Large, heavy drops that meant business. There was a flash that lit up the Monksford skyline and another rumble of thunder.

'We'll have to hurry,' Ruth called to the actors.

Josh was shivering as he carried the solid wooden cross from the mockup of Pilate's courtyard to where the scaffolding poles stood. Once again the knights took up their callous banter, complaining about the weight and the pain in their shoulders. 'For great pain is gripping me, my shoulder is torn from its socket.'

The scene required them to hoist, fail to locate the cross, then hoist again. Josh delivered his lines through gritted teeth, the ropes securing his arms, chafing against his skin and biting into his flesh. The wind whipped up the grass, and the rain started to fall more heavily. Ruth would have to admit defeat. Perhaps they would have another opportunity to run through the final scenes before Saturday's performance.

'Okay, get him down!'

Thunder rumbled overhead. It was as dark as night.

The knights lowered Josh to the ground and untied the ropes. Josh massaged the life back into his arms and shoulders, and Ronnie placed a jacket on him.

'Let's call it a day,' Ruth said.

There was a blinding flash and a sound like an explosion. Ruth was thrown off her feet. She lay stunned. Her ears were ringing and a green light persisted when she blinked. She looked round. Ronnie, Josh and the knights lay on the ground. They were not moving. The grass at the foot of the cross was smoking.

'Oh no!' she moaned. She climbed unsteadily to her feet. 'Oh, please, God, no.'

She staggered towards the first knight. She felt his neck for a pulse. He opened his eyes and looked up at her. 'What was that?'

'L – lightning, I think,' stammered Ruth. The others slowly sat up. Ronnie climbed unsteadily to his feet, and Josh rubbed his head.

Ruth ran from one to another. No one seemed to be injured, just knocked off their feet and stunned.

'Perhaps the scaffolding wasn't such a good idea,' Josh said.

Ronnie looked at Ruth. 'Dear, do you think the Almighty is trying to tell us something?'

Scene Eight

JEMMA SLEPT BADLY. THE STORM HADN'T HELPED. SHE FELT PARTICULARLY vulnerable on the boat. Even though the worst of the storm had passed by mid-evening, the crashes and flashes had been far too close for her liking. When it rumbled off into the distance she lay in bed, the storm inside her raging as mightily as ever.

Before the last peal died away, at around six, there was a knock at her door. As soon as she saw Josh's face, she knew something had happened. He recounted the evening's events.

'Do you think God was trying to hit you or miss you?' she said.

'I think he would have hit me if he had wanted to.'

'So, was it a warning?'

'No, it was weather ... and that doesn't mean you can justify running it on the weather page of your rag.'

She smiled and made him some tea. They sat together in the cabin and listened to the thunder.

'I came to see if you were all right. You seemed pretty upset earlier.'

'I thought I had seen it all, that I was tough. I've attended coroner's courts, inquests, and scenes of violence and crime. I've seen court photographs that would make your stomach turn, but this – it was brutal. I couldn't bear seeing them do that to you ... to him.'

'It's just a play.'

'But it isn't, is it?'

'Well, no.'

242

She found her Bible. After Jemma had given up on the Old Testament, Ruth had pointed her to Psalms and the book of Isaiah, and her heart had started to melt.

> He was despised and rejected by men,
>> a man of sorrows, and familiar with suffering.
> Like one from whom men hide their faces
>> he was despised, and we esteemed him not.
> Surely he took up our infirmities
>> and carried our sorrows,
> yet we considered him stricken by God,
>> smitten by him, and afflicted.
> But he was pierced for our transgressions,
>> he was crushed for our iniquities;
> the punishment that brought us peace was upon him,
>> and by his wounds we are healed.

'What does it mean?' she had asked Josh.

'It was Jesus' willingness to give up his life, so that we, who are so helpless and corrupt, can be forgiven.'

'So he suffered all that for us – for me?'

'That's right.'

'All that beating and flogging and abuse and when he was strung up on a cross ...'

'That too. He went through it all. He died for you.'

'But that's ... unbelievable.' The storm had returned, and a flash from outside lit up his face.

'Ah, well,' Josh said, 'there comes the crunch. That's our side of the bargain – we have to believe it.'

Jemma had shaken her head. It was too difficult to accept. Why would any person, least of all, one that was supposed to be God, put himself through all that? Yet the words 'by his wounds we are healed' kept going through her mind. As she witnessed the scene, as she heard the lashes, she wanted to cry out, to scream. She just wanted it to stop.

They had talked long into the night. Josh finally went home, the thunder grew distant, and Jemma finally drifted off in the early hours.

She groaned at the screeching alarm, dragged herself out of bed, and peered into the mirror at her reflection. She was still getting thinner. At first, it had suited her, but now she looked gaunt with dark circles under her eyes, and her hair had lost its shine.

She showered and pulled on the first clothes that came to hand, jeans and a black T-shirt. One of the kitten-heeled boots fell out of the wardrobe. A few months ago they had been the most important things in her life. She had been devastated when they got dirty. Having them cleaned would have cost nearly as much as she paid. She had anticipated that those heels by now would be clicking up the cultured pavements of Fleet Street on her way to her job on a national daily. The boot was still stained with mud, grass, cow pat, and a splash of tea. She flung it back in the wardrobe and dragged on some trainers.

MOHAN WAS POURING HIMSELF A COFFEE WHEN JEMMA ENTERED THE OFFICE. She didn't need to look at him to know that he disapproved of her attire. She plugged in her laptop. It was before eight; at least he couldn't complain that she was late. She planned to ask for some leave but not until she had done a bit of digging to find out more about Alistair Fry and to see whether the police had traced the money to its owner. Just thinking about him made her shudder. How could Ruth even consider ...

She dialled the police station.

'Can I speak to WPC Patel, please?'

She was immediately put on hold. On the third time of listening to Pachelbel's Canon, she was about to give up.

'Patel here. Who is it?'

'It's Jemma Durham, from the *Gazette*. Can you confirm you have been holding Alistair Fry?'

'I'm sorry. I can't give any information about an ongoing inquiry. You will have to contact the press officer for any details about Councillor Fry.'

Jemma clicked into the local radio website for their latest take on the case. All it said was that Councillor Fry had gone voluntarily to the police station to answer questions relating to an alleged assault. As Jemma had seen him at yesterday's rehearsal, she was more up-to-date than her sources.

She closed her eyes in frustration. She knew there was something going on, something potentially devastating.

'Let sleeping dogs lie,' she muttered. But it was no good. This was big – bigger than a stolen kiss, bigger than a community play – and Jemma's metaphorical dog was determined to unearth its bone.

She had no alternative, she would have to go and see Fry herself. But she needed an excuse. She lifted the receiver to dial Josh's number, then changed her mind and replaced it. She could hear his sensible voice in her mind, trying to dissuade her from talking to Fry. She was not in a sensible mood.

She consulted the contact list Ruth had passed to all the actors and crew. Fry's address and telephone number were below hers, just under half way down. For the second time she picked up the phone to dial, then changed her mind.

'For goodness sake!' Mohan shouted. 'Will you show a bit of decisiveness? Are you going to use that phone or not?'

'Er . . . yes. I mean no. Mohan, would it be all right if I slipped out for a while? I'll be back for the nine-thirty meeting, promise.' She slid out of the door before he could answer. She wanted the element of surprise when she called on Fry.

She drove first to the council chambers, but it was only eight thirty and the Town Hall did not open to the public till nine. Next, she stopped by his office. She knocked, and a woman in a green dress informed her that Mr Fry was on leave for a few days. Finally, she went to his house. Once again, all was locked up, but his car was in the drive. She knocked again. There was still no reply. She returned to her car and unlocked the door.

She was about to drive off when she noticed Fry walking along the road. He was striding quickly and seemed to be wiping his hands on a cloth. She climbed out of the driver's seat.

He balked when he saw her, but quickly recovered his composure. 'Oh, hello, Jemma. I wasn't expecting to see anyone this early in the morning. How can I help you?'

'Sorry, it is rather early. I have to get back to work. I didn't want to bother you, but do you have a minute? It's about the play.'

He looked her up and down. 'I am rather busy.'

'Please, Alistair.'

'You'd better come in.'

He unlocked the front door, and the smell of stale air and Chinese takeaways hit her.

'Sorry, it's a bit of a mess. I haven't had time to clear up. Amanda's ... away.'

He cleared a place on the sofa and she sat down. 'Don't apologise. I know the problem.'

'And you probably heard, the police wanted to ask me questions following Mr Sutton's little outburst the other night.'

'Yes, I had heard. Was everything cleared up?'

'I assume so. After keeping me all night, they said thank you and let me go. Of course, I could have left at any time,' he added quickly.

'I see,' said Jemma.

'So what did you want to discuss with me about the play?'

'It was the scene where Judas is describing Jesus' visit to Simon's house ...' She pretended to fumble in her bag for her copy of the script. 'So, what questions did the police ask you?'

'Oh, just where I was, and had I seen anyone. Go on, Simon's house.'

'That's right.' She flicked her script open. 'I was wondering if, in this part, as Judas is describing the woman pouring perfume on Jesus' feet, Josh and I should be acting it out. To one side. Making the scene a little more … authentic.'

'Possibly. What does Ruth think?'

'I haven't discussed it with her yet.'

'Harlan?'

'Or Harlan. I wanted to know what you thought.'

'Doesn't matter much to me one way or another. I would have thought that the directors would be the ones to ask.'

'Yes, of course … and I was going to do that. It's just that …' She started to simper just a little. 'I thought that as it's basically your scene, I wanted to check that it was okay with you first. I didn't want to make things difficult.'

'It's fine with me. Do what you like.' He opened the front door. 'If that's all, I'm afraid I have some housekeeping to do.'

'There was one more thing …' Jemma hesitated. Fry looked apprehensive.

'Yes, what is it?'

Jemma struggled to find a way of asking that wouldn't antagonise him further.

'Cat got your tongue, girl? Don't be scared. Ask away. Or are you worried that curiosity killed the cat?'

'My editor wouldn't let me get away with clichés like that.' She gave a little light laugh. He was standing in front of the door. She glanced behind her, looking for an alternative route in case things turned nasty.

'So, that's what all this is about.' Fry stood with his hands on his hips. He was a solidly built man and was at least six feet tall. 'Your editor told you to use your connections and persuade me to give your grimy little rag an exclusive interview?'

Jemma wished she had thought of that one. It would have been far more convincing than 'It's about the play.'

'Well, tell your editor – no comment.' He stood aside from the door.

Jemma stumbled into the front garden, then paused and turned around. 'Alistair, what do you know about the money in the river?' She watched an almost imperceptible tightening of his jaw, a glint of fear in his eyes, and she fancied his face paled just a little.

'What money in the river? I don't know what you're talking about.'

'My mistake,' she said. 'Sorry to have bothered you. See you at the play.' Jemma walked calmly back to her car and started the engine. She pulled smoothly away and drove round the corner, where she pulled over and sat until she had stopped shaking. The flicker of emotion on Fry's face had been tiny, but unmistakable. Now she knew, beyond doubt, that he was involved. But what was his connection, and how could she prove it?

JEMMA RETURNED TO THE OFFICE, ONLY FIFTEEN MINUTES LATE FOR THE WEEKLY team briefing.

'Glad you could grace us with your presence,' Mohan said.

He caught her gazing out of the window, her pen in her hand and an empty notebook on her lap.

'Jemma, will you stop clicking that blasted ball-pen. You're driving me crazy!' He put his hand to his forehead in frustration. 'Just go home now, will you? You can turn in your column tonight via email. Your mind is obviously miles away. I'll ring you if anything important comes up.'

'If ... if you're sure.'

'I'm sure.' Then he added kindly. 'Take care.'

Jemma nodded, taken slightly aback by the gentleness of his words. 'Thanks, Mohan.'

She rang Josh and arranged to meet for coffee back at the *Hog*.

'I need your help. There's something going on, and ... well, just come round.'

'ARE YOU MAD?' JOSH SAID. 'HAVE YOU GOT SOME KIND OF DEATH WISH? WHAT were you thinking, going round to Alistair's house – on your own – to confront him.'

'It's called investigative journalism. I know what I'm doing, Josh.'

'Do you? We have no idea what that man is capable of. He's had the police round asking questions. You think he's got something to do with the money in the river, and Richard is convinced he tried to kill him. Jemma, this is not some school fête, you know.'

'Don't patronise me.'

'So where do we go from here? Do you want to set up camp in Alistair's garden? Or would you rather just wait until one night when you're alone in bed when it will be whack, splash, goodbye Jemma?'

She looked around the berth. The *Hog*'s walls suddenly seemed insubstantial, and she felt vulnerable. 'You're being ridiculous.'

'Am I? You're the one with all the bright ideas.'

'We go back to the police.'

'And tell them what? We don't know any more than we did before. They are not going to want to know. But meanwhile, you've tipped Alistair off. Now he knows we're on to him. Sorry, Jemma, I've got to get back to work.'

'No, wait.' Jemma chewed her lip thoughtfully. 'I've been watching to see if anyone has been hanging around the river or looking as if they've lost something.'

'And have you seen anything?'

She shook her head.

'You haven't exactly had the area under twenty-four-hour surveillance?'

'Of course not. I can't be here all day, and I can't watch all night. I have to sleep.'

'So you've hardly been watching at all. Basically when you're at work or asleep, Hannibal and all his elephants could have marched down the riverbank, and you would have been none the wiser.'

It was true, all true. She had not been able to keep the area under observation, she had failed to collect any more information to help the police, she had annoyed Alistair, and even worse, let him know she suspected him, and put herself and Josh in danger in the process. She clutched her head and groaned. 'What are we going to do?'

'Of course, there's one thing we haven't considered,' Josh said, 'and that is the reasons behind it.'

'What do you mean?'

'Well, a respected solicitor, who is also a Town Councillor and a church member, would have to have a pretty good reason for bopping someone on the head and running away. And if the money we found in the river is connected to Alistair in some way, we need to know how.'

'Isn't that a job for the police?'

'Exactly,' said Josh. 'So why don't we leave them to it.'

'Because we have left it to them for the last seven months and nothing's happened.'

'But they talked to Alistair yesterday.'

'That was only because of what Richard told them. And if it hadn't been for us, going to the police and insisting, they'd have dismissed it all as the delusions of an amnesiac.'

'But we know Alistair isn't connected with the money,' said Josh, 'because the car was wrong. You said it was a green Land Rover that tried to hit you. I can't imagine Alistair being seen dead in a dirty old thing like that.'

'You're right.'

'So who would drive that kind of car?' He grinned. 'I've driven past schools in the mornings and all the mums dropping off their children seem to be driving enormous four-wheel-drive monstrosities. But they are always showroom shiny.'

'It looks more like the kind of thing a farmer might drive, especially with mud spattered all over it.'

'That doesn't narrow it down much. There have to be four or five farms just within a ten-mile radius of Monksford. The Land Rover could have come from anywhere in Kent – or farther afield. It's a pity you didn't get the number.'

'Well, I do apologise. He was trying to mow me down. Sorry, I didn't think to stop to get my notebook out. How remiss of me.'

'I suppose we could ask Bram. He probably knows all the other farmers around here.'

She mimed holding a telephone. 'Oh, yes, "Hello, Bram. Do you happen to know a farmer who drives a green Land Rover?"'

'Well, have you got any better ideas?'

'No. Ideas are the one commodity I'm really short of this week. It's just so frustrating. I know there's something going on. Something involving Richard and Alistair and the plays and the money and the driver of the green car. I just wish I knew what.'

'And when you do find out, won't it make a great story?'

Jemma shifted on her chair and pulled her phone out of her jeans' pocket. 'Excuse me.' She flipped open the cover.

The voice on the phone was Mohan's. 'Jemma, you might want to come in. There's something breaking. It's big – and it will affect you.'

Josh mouthed, 'I'm going,' and pointed to the hatch.

'What?' She waved to Josh.

Mohan sounded irritated. 'Just get here.'

She scrambled to her feet and followed Josh off the boat. 'Wait! Something's happening. Can you come with me?'

'No, I've got to get back.'

'But this sounds important.'

'They'll sack me!'

'Let them. You're leaving anyway.'

He paused, searching her face. 'Get in the van.'

The van rocked like a ship at sea along the Monksford lanes into town. Josh drove through the industrial estate and left the van in a side street while they cut through an ally to reach the *Gazette*'s offices.

Mohan thrust a photograph into Jemma's hands. It showed three men, all in green wax jackets. One was wearing a white hat.

'What's this?'

'Don't you recognise him?'

Jemma squinted. 'That's Bram Griffin.'

'Who are the other two guys with him?' asked Josh.

'Fred Bartlett, the vet, and an inspector from DEFRA,' said Mohan.

'What's DEFRA?' Josh pulled a face. 'Sounds like something James Bond would tangle with.'

'Only if James Bond had foot-and-mouth disease,' Jemma said. 'DEFRA is the Department for the Environment, Food, and Rural Affairs.'

'Foot-and-mouth,' said Josh. 'Isn't that serious?'

'Very, but we haven't had it confirmed. A veterinary nurse in Bartlett's practice tipped us off, so I sent Saffy down there with a camera, and these are what she came back with.'

Jemma took the photographs from Mohan and flipped through them – the one of Bartlett and the inspector, rinsing their boots in disinfectant, the one of them tying a notice to the gate.

'But the play,' said Jemma. 'Does Ruth know?'

'I'll ring her. Outside.' Josh hurried out to the corridor.

'I can't believe it,' Jemma said.

'It's true, you've seen the evidence,' said Mohan.

'What are we going to do?' Jemma felt dazed. These plays united a community. Six-hundred-year-old plays had brought two-thousand-year-old stories to life. They had done more than that. They had allowed her to catch a glimpse of God. And now it was all over.

'We'll go with the front page,' Mohan said. 'Can you give it a the-atrical twist? Something like, "Curtain Down" or "The Show Can't Go On"?'

'Can't it? Why?'

'Jemma, have you been listening to a word I've been saying?'

'Yes!'

'Well, if they've got an outbreak of foot-and-mouth at Hope Farm, they can't have hundreds of people trouping around. DEFRA will slap a ban on people entering or leaving the farm, and they'll have to slaughter the infected livestock.'

'But you said the outbreak hadn't been confirmed.'

'Not yet. But they aren't taking any chances. So, will you write the article?'

'Yes. Yes, I'll do it.' She gathered up Josh on her way out. 'What did Ruth say?'

'No answer.'

Jemma climbed into the van. 'We'll have to find her before she finds Bram.'

JEMMA BATTERED THE VICARAGE DOOR WITH HER FISTS. THERE WAS NO REPLY.

'The church?' Josh suggested, but Ruth wasn't there either.

'What shall we do? We can't just chase around the countryside all day.'

'I'll drop you back at the *Hog*, and we'll keep trying to ring.'

St Sebastian's clock struck twelve. Jemma stood on the deck and gazed at the river. 'I bet you could tell some stories.' But the river kept its secret hidden in its silent depths. She needed to walk. She could think more clearly on the move. The late-spring sunshine warmed her back, and a lark's disembodied song accompanied the droning bees.

The abbey ruins cast cool shadows, and Jemma, too idle to walk to the gate, slipped through the wire fence surrounding the abbey. She stopped. She could hear a woman sobbing.

Scene Nine

RUTH WAS SITTING ON A PATCH OF GRASS. HER WORLD WAS ENDING. SHE hugged the notice to her chest, rocking gently back and forth. She felt a hand on her shoulder and turned instinctively. Jemma sat next to her on the soft green turf.

Ruth lifted her head and met Jemma's eyes. 'It's all over, finished,' she said, and the tears splashed down on the ancient stones.

'I'm sorry,' Jemma said. 'How did you find out?'

Ruth held up the notice. 'It was on the gate.'

Jemma embraced her in an awkward hug.

'I feel as if I've let you all down. All that hard work, and for nothing.'

'You're not giving up?' Jemma's eyes were wide and incredulous. She fumbled in her bag for a tissue. 'I can't believe that after all this, you're just throwing in the towel!'

'I'm not even sure it's ... right.'

'What do you mean, right?'

'That it might not be God's will that we revive the mystery plays. After all, so much has gone wrong lately ...'

She thought Jemma might explode. 'Not God's will!' She stood up. 'I don't believe you, Ruth. After all we've done. Did you think to send up an application to the heavenly planning committee or whatever it is you do?'

Ruth was taken aback. 'Of course. We prayed for a whole year before we decided to go ahead, not to mention all the practical work and the time spent in modernising the plays.'

'So any time in the past twenty months, God could have told one of us – any of us – if he didn't want the plays to go ahead.'

'Well, yes. I suppose so. But God doesn't always work like that.'

'Then I'm finished!' Jemma threw up her hands in a gesture of defeat. 'If that's what God is like … the kind of God who lets you do all that work then stops you in your tracks, then I don't want to know.'

'What do you mean?' Ruth felt the panic rising.

'I was starting to think there was something in it. When I heard Josh saying those words, it made it all real somehow. I knew Jesus was a person – a man who laughed with his friends, ate and drank, got tired and frustrated … and … and I could relate to that. Then, when I saw the flogging scene, all I could think was that he did all that for me.'

'He did.' Ruth spoke softly. 'The plays have changed me too.' They had made her rely on God in ways she never had before.

'Well, come on, then! Are you going to deny everyone in Monksford the opportunity of seeing it for themselves, the opportunity to be a part of it?'

'It's not that easy.'

'Of course it's not easy.' Jemma gave a harsh laugh. 'But the test of something of value is not whether it is simple. Nothing worthwhile is easy, and anything easy is seldom worthwhile.'

Ruth waved the notice in Jemma's face. 'No one is going on or off the farm until the restrictions are lifted. That could take days … or weeks. It won't work. It's too late.'

'Then we find somewhere else to do it! I thought you Christians were supposed to persevere. All I've heard so far is moaning and whining and defeatism. These plays really can change people. They bring people face-to-face with Jesus. Isn't that worth fighting for? Come on, Ruth.'

It was as if a hand of hope had reached down into her misery. This was the girl who took the part under sufferance. She was everything Ruth wasn't; confident, attractive, self-assured. But she could see in Jemma the beginnings of faith, and this, surely, was the point.

This was the point – of the mystery plays and of her life. And if God could do it in one person's life, he could do it for the whole town. She wiped her eyes and attempted a smile. 'You're right. Absolutely right! Whatever we have to do, these plays will be performed on Saturday to celebrate Corpus Christi.'

'Okay,' Jemma said. 'Here's the plan. You go visit Alistair and see if the council can find us somewhere else to perform. I'll call Josh and ask him to take down the posters, then he can join me at the farm. I'll go and see Bram Griffin. Even if we have to use megaphones, we need to talk. Tell everyone to "watch this space".'

Jemma took off towards the car park. 'Are you coming?'

'Just give me a moment.' Ruth took a deep breath. The words of an old hymn, one of her favourites, came to her as she prayed.

> O let me hear thee speaking in accents clear and still,
> Above the storms of passion, the murmurs of self-will.
> O speak to reassure me, to hasten or control;
> O speak, and make me listen, thou guardian of my soul.

She was glad to be in this place, the abbey where everything felt so sure and so simple. 'Father, give me courage and resolution, but most of all, Father, let me hear your "still, small voice".'

AS SHE PULLED UP OUTSIDE ALISTAIR'S HOUSE SHE PRAYED AGAIN. THE curtains were still drawn, and three days milk festered on the doorstep. She pressed the bell. And waited. No one came. She pressed again and listened to the distant ringing inside. Still no one came. She lifted the black metal lion's head and knocked. She pushed past the clematis and jasmine and walked up the path at the side of the house to the back door. The dustbins had disgorged their contents over the patio. She stepped delicately over the strewn rubbish and tried the door handle. It turned. She edged her way into the dark kitchen. Takeaway bags lay scattered on the floor, and the kitchen sink was piled with dirty dishes and cups.

She made her way to the lounge. The curtains were pulled shut; a table lamp shed a dull golden glow. Alistair lay sprawled in an armchair, snoring, a half-empty whisky bottle and a glass by his side. Ruth tugged the curtains open, letting in a flood of sunlight. Alistair grunted and turned away from the brightness. A haze of dust fogged the room. There were newspapers and crisp packets on the floor and streaks of mud on the carpet.

Ruth collected the empty glass and replaced the screw top on the bottle. She put on the kettle and shovelled two large teaspoons of coffee granules and two of sugar into a mug. She took the steaming brew to Alistair and shook his arm. He groaned and grunted again. His clothes were crumpled and his sleeves looked wet, his shoes were caked in mud, he was unshaven and he stank of whisky.

'If you're going to knock it back, I'd choose something a little cheaper than a thirty-five-year-old single malt.'

He opened his eyes, tried to focus, and closed them again. 'What's the time?'

'It's gone one. Time you were up, showered, and changed. Have you been there all night?'

'No. What are you doing here?'

'You're going to help me find a new venue for the mystery plays.'

'What?'

He hauled himself upright. Ruth handed him the coffee. 'That should help,' she said.

He belched, and Ruth took a step backwards, away from the whisky stench. 'Or I could try to fine some antacid.'

AS THE TOWN HALL CLOCK STRUCK TWO, RUTH, RAJ, AND A SLIGHTLY QUEASY-looking Alistair stood in Monksford Park, next to a war memorial with a stone soldier surrounded by geraniums.

'We could use the bandstand as the stable, I suppose, and have the crucifixion under those lime trees.' Ruth pointed to a line of trees, their leaves shining emerald in the sunlight.

'Space will be far more limited, and we have to consider parking,' Alistair said.

'All my surplus scaffolding is at the farm,' Raj said. 'I can't take my lorries on to collect it. The whole farm is quarantined. The rest of the poles and planks are in use. I don't see what we can do.' He stood, hands on hips, surveying the vista. 'It won't be the same.'

'It won't be exactly the same, but in some ways it could be better. Central location. We can try to move the sound system.' Ruth looked from Raj to Alistair with pleading eyes. The next step would be to get onto her knees and beg.

'We would still have to seek permission from the council, and there are health and safety issues. We can't just move it, lock, stock, and barrel. I'm sorry, Ruth. Four days isn't enough time. I think we're going to have to cancel.'

'No!' She was desperate not to let the tears come again. 'There must be a way. There must.'

Ruth stormed back to her car and drove to the top of Thorne Hill. She looked over the town. The haphazard array of red-brick houses, patchwork farms offices, and the livid scar of the bypass – so many people, so many lives, and all the forces seemed to be uniting against her and silencing the story she needed to tell. Nothing would stop these plays being performed. Monksford might not be under attack from Nebuchadnezzar and his Babylonian hoards, but Jeremiah's words came into her mind: 'I am the LORD, the God of all mankind. Is anything too hard for me?'

As she looked over to the west, the hulking, grey slab of Monksford General Hospital rose before her. She hadn't checked on Eliza Feldman today.

Every traffic light seemed to have something against her as she drove up the High Street, hindering her progress and fraying her already tattered nerves. She sat in the car park entrance for another ten minutes waiting for a vacant space, then she didn't have the right change for the machine. She nearly cried again with frustration. Eventually, she made her way to Eliza's room. On her way past the sister's desk, a nurse beckoned to her, and Ruth's heart gave a thud.

'Oh, don't look so worried, it's not bad news. I was just going to say Eliza can go home today. Would you like me to arrange transport or will you take her?'

'I'll give her a lift. Will she be all right at home?'

'We've contacted her neighbour Joan, and she has offered to take care of her, but she doesn't drive.'

Finding a new venue for the plays would have to wait. People first, that was how Ruth always tried to live. She opened the door to find Eliza, fully dressed and beaming, sitting in a wheelchair in the middle of the room.

'I'm ready to go,' said Eliza. 'I have my best frock on, and I'm wearing lipstick.'

'Those young men had better watch out,' Ruth laughed for the first time that day.

"Too right!' Eliza said.

The traffic signals were kinder on the way back to Eliza's doll's house cottage. Eliza, hardly bigger than a doll herself, was strapped in the passenger seat. She turned to Ruth.

'Did you think I was going to make it?'

'What do you mean?'

'Had you written me off, had me measured for my coffin?'

'No! Of course not.'

'Everyone else did.'

'You've just proved them all wrong.'

'I want you to take me to the plays. On Saturday. I want to see the plays.'

Ruth looked away. How could she tell her? 'The thing is ...'

'I know – I'm too old and too sick to sit in a field all day. But Ruth, it's what I want. You won't deny an old lady her dying wish?'

Ruth squeezed her hand. 'How could I do that?'

Scene Ten

JEMMA LEANED OVER JOSH AND PRESSED THE HORN. THE LONG BLAST SENT A pair of wood pigeons flapping into the sky. A dog barked.

'Don't do that!'

'He's not answering the phone, and we can't get through the gate. How else can I attract his attention?'

Josh shrugged.

'Josh, this is not a waste of time. This is important, more important than anything else I've ever done. We've got to get to the bottom of this.'

She climbed out of the van and leant over the gate. The notice was adamant in its black lettering – NO ENTRY. She strained to see the farmhouse. The bargeware milk churns and wheelbarrow were full of neglected-looking bedding plants.

Josh leaned out of the window. 'He's not in.'

'His car's there.' A mud-spattered green Land Rover stood in the drive. Jemma shuddered. It looked very like the one that had almost finished her off in the car park, but they all looked like that.

Jemma climbed back in the van and tried the phone again.

'Let's go.' Josh started the engine.

'Wait!' Jemma pointed to a figure striding across a ridge of land above the lane. She opened the door and waved, calling out. The figure stopped and put one hand up to shield his eyes from the sun. Then it descended a steep path and crossed the lane.

'Mr Griffin!' Jemma called.

'What are you doing here? You can't come in.' His ruddy face bore the lines deeply etched with worry, and his watery blue eyes darted from Jemma to the notice and back again. He had replaced his white Stetson with a more conventional tweed cap. He could have been any one of a hundred anxious farmers, brought to their knees by the last outbreak of this heinous disease. And now it was back, casting a shadow over his livelihood once more.

'I know we can't come in. I just wanted to talk to you.'

'Are you from the paper?'

'Yes, no! I am a reporter for the *Monksford Gazette*, but I'm not here in an official capacity. I'm also supposed to be acting in the mystery plays.'

'Well, you're not any more. At least not on my land.'

Josh climbed out of the van and joined them.

'Who's he?' Bram looked Josh up and down.

Jemma introduced them, and he solemnly shook Josh's hand.

'Jesus and Mary Magdalene, eh? Perhaps you can perform a miracle here.'

'Mr Griffin, will you tell us what happened?'

Bram rubbed his eyes and looked overcome with weariness. 'I can't.'

'Don't you owe us that?' Josh said.

'Can we go somewhere else?' asked Jemma. 'For a coffee or something. We could head into town or go to my boat.'

'I can't show my face in town, or down by the river, and you're not allowed to bring vehicles on the farm.'

'What if we park here and walk?'

'You'll have to disinfect your shoes.'

'Okay.' Bram opened the gate, and Jemma and Josh sloshed through the disinfectant bath and made their way to the farmhouse. Settled in the kitchen with a blue-and-white mug of tea each, Bram looked as if he was about to break down.

'It's all happening again! It's a nightmare and I can't wake up. I'm going to lose it all. What have I been thinking? All this for nothing.'

Josh made to speak but Jemma put her fingers to her lips to silence him.

'I'm not a bad person. You know that, don't you?'

Jemma nodded vigorously. Josh looked puzzled.

'You did what you felt you had to do. The only thing you could do under the circumstances.'

'And these plays. Letting these plays on my farm. I thought it might help. I thought it might ... I dunno, appease God somehow. But now he's punishing me.'

'God doesn't work like that,' Josh said. 'It wasn't your fault. As you said, you did what you thought was best.'

'That's right. I never meant to hurt anyone. I've never committed a crime before in my life.'

Josh's eyes grew wide. Jemma glared at him to keep quiet. She had to win his trust, get him to speak.

'Mr Griffin, I'm sure people will be more sympathetic if they know your side of the story.'

'I'm a stupid, weak, foolish old man.' He slapped his forehead with the heel of his hand. 'And I deserve everything I get.'

'Not everyone will see it like that. Do you want to tell me what happened?'

'You have to promise me you won't put it in the papers ... or go to the police.'

She thought of her Grandfather's words about honesty and integrity.

'You know I can't promise that. If there's been a crime, I can't keep it quiet. It's unfair to ask me to do that. As for the *Gazette*, I promise I will get your permission before I write a word.'

A look of relief washed over him.

'Anyway,' she continued, 'it's not as if you could keep this quiet, even if you wanted to. The notice on the gate is a bit of a giveaway. And it's only fair to tell you that there will be a story about it in Friday's *Gazette*. My boss has already got details from the nurse at the veterinary practice, and there are photographs of you with the vet and the inspector.'

'Thank you. Thank you for being honest with me.'

So far, so good. Now to get to the bottom of this. 'So, what happened?'

He let out a deep sigh. 'Nosy, bloody do-gooders that's what. People interfering. That half-witted hippy girl who lives on one of them boats down on the river.'

'Skye Wortham?' Jemma was stunned. 'What has she done?' Skye was the most innocuous person Jemma had ever met. She lived simply on her eco-friendly houseboat, ate vegan food supplemented by wild fruit from the hedgerows, and took it upon herself to recycle what rubbish she found on the banks. Skye was a human Womble; what could Bram have against her?

'Only gone and reported me, hasn't she?'

'What for?'

'Said she could smell something. Started poking around. Found some stuff in the lower field and called the vet.'

'What kind of stuff?' asked Josh.

'Animal remains. She jumped to conclusions and told the vet I'd had another outbreak, that I was slaughtering the animals myself and burying them. It's not true!' He put his elbows on the table and hid his face in his hands. 'It's not true. I wouldn't do that. Apart from anything, there's no point. The government even changed the compensation system to the farmer's advantage. The irony is, I'd be better off if my herd did have foot-and-mouth.'

Jemma took his mug and poured him another cup of tea.

'So what happened?' asked Josh.

'Well, after the outbreak in 2001, I was just about finished. I was going to change the sign to "Hopeless Farm". Then Alistair came to see me.'

'Alistair Fry?' Jemma just managed to stop her jaw hitting the floor. 'What did he want?'

'He offered me money.'

'What, a grant?'

'Not exactly. Although I suppose you could call it that if you like.'

'Could you call it a bribe?' Josh stood up. 'Jemma, we have to go to the police.'

'Wait,' said Jemma. 'What did he get out of it?'

'Well, if I agreed to sell off some of my land to a developer, for the bypass and the new industrial estate, he would make sure I had enough money to restock and start again. I still had plenty of land. It would be a smaller venture, but I would keep the farm. It seemed like a good idea at the time.'

'But Alistair opposed the road and the business park. How could he offer you money for it?'

'He made everyone believe he was against it. He led all the protests, made a big noise in the papers and the local media, but behind our backs the developer and some of the business owners must have been lining his pockets.'

Jemma sat open mouthed, shaking her head. 'I can't believe it!'

Josh looked puzzled. He pulled his chair round and sat down again. 'What has this got to do with the animal carcasses on your land?'

'Well, it all worked fine at first. I got my money and Fry got his land, but it didn't stop there. Fry had to pull some strings to get the land redesignated. It was all greenbelt you see. No building allowed. I imagine it cost him a lot more than he was expecting to "influence" the right people. Then he started to ask me for money. Of course, I wasn't in a position to pay him so he offered to broker another deal.'

'What, sell more land?' Jemma asked.

'No, about that time he started to get really twitchy. He thought someone was on to him, so he had to distance himself from any dodgy stuff.'

'I can't believe this. Fry's in it up to his neck.' Jemma took her portable tape player out of the bag. 'Mr Griffin. This is complicated. I need to get the information straight. Please let me record it. Alistair

Fry is the villain here. You can help the police. You can get him locked up.'

'What about me? I'm in on it too. I'll be finished. If the Department of the Environment finds I've been contaminating my land, we're talking hundreds of thousands in fines. Perhaps even prison.'

'Not necessarily. If you go to the police voluntarily, it can only reflect well on you. What Fry has done is pure evil, and you can't let him get away with it.'

Bram's shoulders sagged. 'It can't get any worse, I suppose. Switch your machine on. Right, where was I?'

'You were telling us about the animal remains,' Josh said.

'There is a factory on the industrial estate, meatpackers.'

'I know it,' said Jemma.

'Well, there are very strict rules about disposal of animal waste, the bones, and all that. The factory usually pays to have them prop erly disposed of, and the local authority checks to see that it's done. As you can imagine, it's expensive, and Colin Riley, the factory owner, will do whatever he can to cut costs. Riley was one of those in on the original deal with Fry to get the new road and business park built. Fry suggested that I dispose of the carcasses. Riley paid me, and I paid Fry, to keep it anonymous.'

Jemma's head was starting to ache.

'How did you pay him?' Josh collected their empty cups and de-posited them in the sink.

'The money came in cash, and I couldn't exactly march into his office or the council chambers and hand it over the desk. Besides, he was sure he was being watched. Riley would bring the carcasses at night. I roped off the field and built a barn. Then I got the digger down there and buried them early in the morning. It was fine at first. I dug a deep pit, covered it all up, and nobody was any the wiser. Then the deliveries became more frequent. The trouble is, there were so many of them I couldn't keep up. I buried them when and where I could, but I couldn't get them so deep and the smell began to get worse. That's when that hippie woman came nosing around.

She assumed the foot-and-mouth had struck again and those were my critters I'd buried.'

'You didn't put Skye straight?' Josh shifted in his chair.

Bram Griffin shook his head. 'I didn't want it all coming out. I didn't expect this.'

'What about the money?' Jemma planted her elbows on the table and looked into Bram's eyes.

'We devised an arrangement. Riley gave me the money when he dropped off the waste. To keep it all away from the farm, Riley's factory, and the Town Hall, we found a quiet spot on the river, and I hid the money there. We started by wrapping it up and leaving it under a tree or in the long grass, but "flower child" was so hot on her rubbish clearance that I was worried she'd find it. Then I came up with the idea of hiding it in the water. I put the notes in an envelope, wrapped it all up – '

' – in black plastic and tied a fishing float to it to mark the spot,' Josh filled in.

'You know about it?'

'We found the last lot,' Josh said.

Bram stared at him for a moment without speaking. 'Fry must be going nuts. He's supposed to have picked it up.'

'So that was the splashing I heard.' Jemma glanced at Josh. 'I knew it wasn't sandwiches.'

'Sandwiches?' Bram gave her a quizzical look.

'Just a theory,' Josh said.

A shiver ran through her. The muddy green Land Rover in the car park. Her leap into the trees. 'Then it was you that drove at me! You tried to kill me!'

'You were the idiot shining the torch beam in my eyes. I couldn't see a thing. I nearly hit a tree.'

'So,' Josh said, 'what is Alistair going to do when he finds out the police have his money?'

'Won't be long before the police bring in Fry,' Jemma said. 'Will you come with us if we take the tape to the police?'

'But they'll arrest him!' Josh said.

'Dur, yeah. That is the general idea. But don't you see, if there's no foot-and-mouth, there's nothing to stop the Monksford Mysteries going ahead as planned. And to do the plays we need Alistair.'

'We can't withhold this information – that's a crime in itself.' Josh ran his fingers through his hair.

'We're not withholding it, just delaying. We owe it to Ruth, after all the effort she's put into the plays.' Jemma felt like screaming with frustration.

'I suppose we're only talking about a couple of days, and this has been going on for months. Mr Griffin, will you ring the vet and the Department, see if they'll accept your explanation? Then we'll all go to the police station. You can call Ruth later and give her the good news.'

Jemma felt drained. She was certain things would be far less complicated in Fleet Street.

Scene Eleven

RUTH SAT IN HER MOTHER'S CHAIR. DIMITRI PUSHED HIS HEAD AGAINST HER legs as if he understood. She lifted him up to her lap and stroked hard, running her hands up and down his stripy back. He dug his claws into her thighs. She didn't mind the pain; it distracted her. Today was Corpus Christi, the day when the ancient plays would have been performed in an age when weekends and Bank Holidays had no meaning. After what seemed like centuries, the phone rang. It was Bram.

'Well?' Ruth could feel her heart thumping.

'DEFRA weren't happy about the contamination of the land. They've informed the Department of the Environment who say it will have to be sealed off and properly cleared, but they're happy that it poses no danger to the public.'

Ruth's heart was beating so loudly she was sure Bram could hear it. 'And ...'

'The vet could find no trace of the disease among the cattle or sheep and the results of the blood tests aren't through yet, but he's satisfied my animals are in first class health.'

'So that means – '

'That means they've lifted the ban. The plays can go ahead.'

Ruth gave a whoop of joy and blew kisses to Bram down the phone. Then she found her address sheet and passed on the good news. She saved Alistair's call until last. After all he'd been through recently, he deserved some good news. She rang his house several times, but he wasn't in. She tried his mobile phone. His voice, when he answered was snatched away by the wind, which made the phone crackle and buzz.

'Alistair, where are you?'

'By the river. I thought I'd go for a walk to clear my head.'

'Can I join you? I've got some news.' For once she didn't care if they were alone together. She didn't even care if he kissed her. She longed to see him, to be with him. She wanted to see his smile, to take his hand, and walk with him beside the river.

'Better not. I don't think we should see each other, just for a while.'

It felt as if he had punched her. 'What do you mean?'

His voice sounded strained. 'Ruth, I'm trying to protect you. After all I've done to hurt you, surely you can let me do that.'

'I don't understand.' She had spent months keeping him at arms length. Now, finally, she admitted to herself that she loved him, and he was pushing her away.

'What with Amanda, and my little brush with the law.'

'I thought you were just helping the police.'

'I was, but now that Amanda's gone, it still wouldn't look good for you, a vicar.'

Ruth laughed. 'After all we've been through, now you start to get all prissy.'

'Believe me. I've got your best interests at heart. Now, what did you want to tell me about the plays?'

When she had finished, he merely said, 'That is good news.'

Ruth felt the information warranted a little more enthusiasm. After all, Alistair was almost as much part of the mysteries as she was. 'Alistair, what's wrong?'

'It would be easier to tell you what's right.' He sighed, and Ruth detected a profound sadness and weariness in his voice that made her long to reach out. Now they were both single, perhaps ... perhaps.

His phone went dead. Ruth waited for him to return her call, but he didn't. Her first instinct was to go and find him, but whatever his reasons, he had made it perfectly clear that he needed to be alone.

Overwhelmed by 'things that needed doing', Ruth sat on the chair again, stalled by a kind of inertia. Dimitri jumped on her lap again, and she stoked his soft ears.

'I have to help Alistair,' she said. 'I don't know if there's anything I can do, but I have to try.'

Dimitri looked up with his cold, green eyes. Life was so simple for him – eat, sleep, and receive a little affection now and again, that was all he required. Not for the first time, Ruth wished that they could exchange places.

The person that seemed to hold the key to Alistair's fate was Richard Sutton. She set off for the hospital determined to set things straight. She felt guilty for not visiting Richard since his outburst. With time to compose himself, Ruth was optimistic that the misunderstanding could be resolved and that Alistair could be free of any blemish on his reputation. Perhaps she could make use of her status as vicar to open doors. After all, people trusted the clergy.

Richard was not in his room when Ruth arrived, which sent her spinning for a moment. She calmed herself and asked a nurse where he was. The nurse shrugged.

'Have you tried the day room?'

Ruth found it eventually, an overly cheerful room, painted in yellow and lime green, with blinding sunlight streaming through the picture window.

Richard, dressed in jogging pants and sweatshirt, sat in a chair with a newspaper spread on his lap. Ruth knocked and went in. He didn't appear to notice her. She sat beside him.

'Hello, how are you feeling?'

'Okay.' He didn't look up.

'Do you remember me?'

'Yes. You're ...' He finally met her eyes.

'Ruth Wells. I'm vicar at St Sebastian's, and I'm a friend of Josh's.'

'Why are you here?'

'I was concerned about you. You seemed very upset the last time I was here. You were shouting things about Alistair Fry.'

'I know.'

'I think I should tell you that Mr Fry spent the whole night at the police station answering questions.'

'Really.' His voice was indifferent, but Ruth could see his hands were trembling.

'I ... I wanted to find out why you made those wild accusations.'

Richard shook his head.

Ruth spoke gently. 'It's just that Alistair has a lot on his plate at the moment. He's a very busy man. Apart from acting in the mystery plays, he's a respected town Councillor, a lawyer, church council member – '

'Is that supposed to make it any better?'

'What?'

'What he did to me.'

'Exactly what did he do to you?'

Richard's brows furrowed. 'I ... can't ... remember.'

'Then how can you possibly make these accusations?' Her tone betrayed her frustration.

'I don't know. I just saw him and ...' Richard wiped his hand across his face.

'Do you have any idea how much damage you could have caused?'

'I'm sorry.'

Ruth took his hand. 'I know you've been through a lot, but you can't just go accusing innocent people of hurting you. I hope they catch who did this. I really do.'

'So do I,' Richard said.

Outside the hospital she heaved a sigh of relief. As far as she could see, Alistair's slate was clean, his copybook unblotted, and his character freer from stain than a shirt in a washing-powder commercial. Now she could concentrate on the business of the mystery plays. She made a mental list of things to do and felt overwhelmed again.

'One thing at a time,' she told herself. 'One thing at a time.'

She had to visit the farm and iron out the final creases, but in a rash moment she decided to telephone the local radio station first. As far as they were concerned this was news, and as far as she was concerned, it was good publicity. The presenter, Damien Crow, agreed to interview her live on air, and she would have the opportunity to reassure the people of Monksford that their plays would go ahead. She found herself waiting with the receiver pressed tightly against her ear. She could hear the radio programme being broadcast. It was worse than the Muzak insurance companies inflict on you while they are holding your call. Finally she heard the presenter's voice.

'And on the show today, we are privileged to be speaking to Canon Ruth Welsh, founder of the Monksford Mystery Players. Tell us Canon Welsh – whodunnit?'

'Actually, Damien, I'm Ruth Wells and I'm just Reverend.'

'Okay, Reverend. Tell us why you decided to treat us to this performance. Don't we get all the mystery we need watching *Inspector Morse* and *Prime Suspect?*'

'Well, it's not really that kind of mystery, Damien. We're performing medieval religious plays.'

'That sounds like a lot of fun.'

Ruth riled at his sarcasm. 'We've had a very eventful few months rehearsing, and now we have nothing short of a spectacle.'

'Really! Now I understand the performance was under threat.'

'That's right. We were due to be performing at Hope Farm, but the Department nearly shut the farm down due to rumours of a foot-and-mouth outbreak.'

'And the last thing you'd want is to give the entire population of Monksford foot-and-mouth. Although my producer, Steve, says I suffer from foot-*in*-mouth all the time.' He played a clashing cymbal sound effect to complete the joke.

'Thankfully, we have been given the "all clear", and the plays will go ahead tomorrow as planned.' Ruth struggled on bravely, explaining the background and the significance of the plays. She had the impression Damien hadn't heard a word she said.

'So, people of Monksford and all the surrounding villages, if you really want to get to the heart of the mystery, tomorrow at Home Farm, Monksford, from 8.30 a.m. join Reverend Welsh and her Mystery Players. You'll be glad you did.'

'Hope Farm. It's Hope Farm ...' Ruth said. But it was too late. Damien had started the next track – 'Sweet Little Mystery' by Wet Wet Wet.

Ruth put the phone down. If anyone could work out what it was all about from that interview, she'd eat her dog collar.

The phone rang. It was Josh. 'Ruth, I need to talk to you.'

'What's the matter?'

'I'm not sure I can go through with this.'

Ruth sighed. A deep, cold weariness overwhelmed her. All she needed now was for Josh to get cold feet.

'Don't worry. I'll sort Alistair out, and Bram.'

'It's not that.'

'Is it because of the lightning?'

'Not really, though it did scare the pants off me.'

'Shall I come round?'

'How about if I meet you tonight at St Seb's. Ten o'clock.'

JOSH WAS STANDING IN THE GRAVEYARD WHEN RUTH ARRIVED TO UNLOCK St Sebastian's. She went to embrace him, but he took a step back. His face looked full of torment.

'Ruth, would you pray with me?'

'Of course.'

They entered the church and sat down together on a pew. Ruth placed her hand on his shoulder and prayed about the plays, and for

Josh, committing him into God's care. She noticed his breathing was becoming laboured and that he was shaking.

'Whatever's wrong?'

'Ruth, I've been seeing things.' His eyes were wild.

'What kind of things?'

'Shadows, and things in the shadows. Oh, I know that makes me sound like I'm losing it, but I can't sleep, I can hardly eat ... It's as if someone's following me.'

'Have you called the police?'

'No. The thing is, I'm not even sure if what I'm seeing is real or not.'

'It sounds to me like you should see a doctor.'

'Perhaps ... but it will all be over tomorrow. Then maybe what-ever it is will go away.'

'Do you think it could be something spiritual? Some kind of attack?'

'I don't know!' He stood up, glancing nervously around him. 'I just don't know,' he repeated, quietly this time. 'I feel as if I'm in danger – as if someone, or some *thing* is trying to kill me.'

'It's probably just a stress reaction. You and Jemma have been through a lot recently.'

'Don't tell Jemma. Promise me you won't tell Jemma.' He snatched at her hands.

'I won't say anything. We've got the press coming to the farm at two. Will you be there?'

'I'll try.'

'And I think you should talk to Jemma. She'll understand.'

Scene Twelve

JEMMA WOKE TO THE SOUND OF THE DAWN CHORUS COMPETING WITH THE shrill tones of her alarm clock. She reached over and killed the alarm, then rolled back and bathed in the birdsong. The sharp sunlight cut through the crack in the curtains illuminating a slice through the berth.

She flung the curtains apart and opened the window. The air was sweet with grass and pollen. There was no sign of the unpleasant odour that had alerted Skye Wortham to Bram Griffin's misdemeanours. She breathed deeply, filled with contentment. The plays were going ahead, she had the evidence to get Fry arrested and to get a good story out of it. She knew her lines and relished performing in front of an audience again. The only cow pat on the meadow of her contentment was Josh and his intention to leave.

At the press conference yesterday, Saffy took the publicity shots. Jemma was particularly pleased of the one of Josh and her as Jesus and Mary Magdalene. She was delighted and not a little surprised that the plays had generated so much interest. Ruth had been on the radio, and a reporter from the local television news had shown up.

Josh had been quiet through it all.

'Would you like to come over later? A little last-minute rehearsal.'

'Er, no thanks. Not tonight.' He looked preoccupied.

'Why not? Just a cup of tea. No pressure.'

'It's not that. I'm just tired.'

He had not mentioned again his plans to leave. She decided not to bring up the subject. Perhaps if they didn't talk about it, it wouldn't happen.

She didn't know how she could face his leaving. They had become close over the past few months. They had spent time together with Richard. She had seen him laugh, and he had held her when she cried; she had brought him dinner when he had a cold, and he always just happened to phone her when she was feeling low. More than that, he had opened something in her spirit, the possibility of something beyond work, even beyond family and friends, something eternal.

She shook herself out of her daydream and pulled on her jeans and T-shirt then she went to the bathroom and used the tiny mirror to apply makeup. She spread the foundation more thickly than usual and made up her eyes with dark liner to accentuate them on stage.

'Break a leg!' The cheery voice came from the galley. She followed the sound and found Ray Jones bent almost double peering through her doorway. 'Today's the day, isn't it?'

'Certainly is,' Jemma said.

'I'll be there, cheering you on from the wings, as it were. I've got all the chaps from work coming. We've been reading your paper.'

'Thanks, Ray.'

'Cheerio and good luck.'

Then it hit home. Today was the day! Her stomach churned, and the butterflies would not allow her to eat breakfast. As she forced down a cup of coffee, she clutched her rolled-up script, as if the words would ooze through the pages and permeate her skin and embed themselves in her brain.

She found herself praying on the way to the farm. She gripped the steering wheel fiercely and bombarded God with her list of orders and requests for the day. To her surprise, he seemed to have acquiesced to her demand for a jam-free journey, and she wondered what she had done to get on the Almighty's good side. He was equally compliant with her request for a parking place near the 'Green Room' marquee.

The dew was thick on the grass, but the sun was warm and it promised to be a beautiful day. The actors were milling around, laughing, chatting, and drinking steaming tea from enamel mugs. She spotted Josh standing apart from the crowd, and she walked over to him, suddenly feeling a little shy. As she got closer, she could see his ashen face and sunken, troubled eyes. He greeted her with a kiss on the cheek, then said, 'I've been sick twice this morning.'

'Thank you for sharing that.'

'Sorry.'

She took his hand. 'Don't worry, you'll be fine. Just take deep breaths and speak slowly.'

'Jemma, I don't want to do it.' He was trembling.

'Everyone feels like that; it's just stage fright. The minute you start acting it will be gone. You'll just be concentrating on remembering the words and standing in the right place.'

'I'm afraid.'

'Of course you are, but I promise you – '

'I'm afraid of the crucifixion.'

The abrupt statement drove a chill through Jemma. She was afraid of the crucifixion too. Josh might have been afraid of the physical pain of having his arms stretched out and tied with rough rope; he may even have been afraid of another bolt of lightning, but the raw reminder of the suffering of one man for many two thousand years ago sent fear resounding through her soul.

She gave a little laugh, trying to lighten the mood. 'You will be all right,' she repeated. 'I'll be there.'

'You just don't understand, do you?' Josh shook his head and turned away from her. 'I'm going to find somewhere quiet to think and pray. Will you find me before the Noah's ark scene?'

Jemma didn't know whether to be furious or to cry. She couldn't have felt the pain more acutely if Josh had slapped her face. She wanted to understand, but she couldn't and he wasn't helping. Her failure to comprehend it just seemed to make him angry, and she resented him for it. He had something that she didn't.

A feeling squeezed a knot in her guts, a feeling she hadn't experienced since childhood, and that feeling was jealousy. She concentrated on her breathing, swallowing down the reaction, locking it into the pit of her stomach. She rearranged her features into an amiable smile and tried again.

'Josh, I don't see everything the way you do, but I am trying, and I am your friend. Whatever happens, I'll never leave you. You're not on your own.'

To her astonishment he laughed. Not an ironic smile or a little snigger, but a full-blown belly laugh. She felt her face redden. She turned her back on him and stalked off to join the rest of the group. She noticed Fry, talking raucously with a group of men, the apostles. Astonished by his audacity, she approached the group. He turned and the smile froze on his lips. 'Well, well, if it isn't our tame newshound. Hello, Jemma, I trust everything is going well.'

'The articles have proved very popular, thank you, Alistair.'

'Not exactly Fleet Street, but she does her best with what passes for excitement on the streets of Monksford.' The men sniggered.

'That's right, Alistair. But that could all be about to change, couldn't it?'

'Really! Have milk bottles mysteriously vanished from doorsteps again? Is the baker passing off the day-old bread as fresh?'

'Bram has told me all about your little "fishing trips".'

He took hold of Jemma's arm, pinching the flesh, and marched her away from the group. 'What do you know?'

'Enough to get you locked up for a very long time.'

'So why haven't you gone to the police?'

'And wreck all Ruth's hard work? You may not care about how you use her, but she has been good to Josh and me, and I'm not going to let anything ruin her day. What I have will wait until tonight. You weren't planning on leaving early were you?'

His mouth was a hard line. 'If you, or Josh, ever say anything to anyone, I'll finish you off. And this time I'll do the job properly.'

'You wouldn't dare!'

'Just try me.' He squeezed her arm hard. She felt his fingers digging into her muscle and bruising her skin. For a moment, they were eye to eye.

'Please, everyone, if you could just gather round!' Ruth's voice sounded strained, and the dark circles under her eyes hinted at the stress of the last few days.

Alistair gave Jemma's arm a final twist before releasing it as if to ensure she received the message. He marched off to the far side of the crowd as Jemma rubbed the bruise.

What did he mean he would 'do the job properly'? Could he mean Richard? That would be for the police to sort out. She would have to make sure he didn't sneak away. Meanwhile, it was up to her to carry on as if nothing had happened. She was here to act, after all. She turned her attention to Ruth.

'Before we start, I just wanted to ask a blessing on the performance.' She prayed briefly and movingly.

'Three cheers for the vicar!'

The crowd of actors and crew cheered heartily and would have continued had Ruth not held up her hands to silence them.

'And you'll be delighted to know, we've sold enough pre-booked tickets to break even plus make a substantial profit. It looks as if the whole town is turning out.'

Another cheer.

'Anyway, back to work. Beginners for act one, the Creation, the Fall, etcetera, need to go and make your final checks for wardrobe and props; then see Darren here to have your microphones put on.' She indicated a spotty young man in a heavy-metal T-shirt holding a crate of electronic bric-a-brac. 'The rest of you, those in the later scenes and act two – can I remind you? – need to be dressed as towns-people and act as ushers. Don't forget to sell as many programmes as possible, and as you know the toilets and refreshments are here, and here.'

Ruth pointed like a flight attendant indicating the emergency exits.

'Right folks! To your starting positions, please. We are just about to open the gates.'

Jemma dried her palms on the rough red linen of her costume. Her eyes scanned around for Josh, but she couldn't see him. She needed to warn him about Fry, but that would have to wait until later.

Someone handed her a batch of programmes and a leather bag full of change, which she tied around her waist. She made her way to the gate of Hope Farm, where the entire population of Monksford, it seemed, was waiting to enter. There were old men in straw hats and blazers and women in bright skirts or jeans. There were school children and Scout packs, dog-collared clergy with their entire congregations in tow. Bram Griffin opened the gate, and the throng rushed to take the spot with the best view. The team of peasant-ushers did their best to contain the flow and invited the audience to spread their picnic rugs and pitch their deckchairs starting from the back of the far side of the field. The audience ignored them and sat where they liked. Jemma stepped over toddlers, wheelchairs, hampers, and rugs, selling the programmes where and when she could.

The system for people filling up from the back wasn't working. Those who had complied with instructions would not be able to see past the deckchairs in front of them.

Jemma made her way to the front and with as much voice as she could muster, she shouted, 'Good gentlefolk of Monksford, I pray you, if you have a deckchair or, forsooth a baby buggy, I do earnestly entreat you to convey yourself towards the nether reaches of the field, for to permit all to view the performance.'

A snigger went through the crowd. Jemma wondered how long she could keep up the cod-Shakespearean. She made a dash towards a man who was erecting a fold-up chair and tried to snatch it.

'Oh, no, thou doesn't!'

They ended up in a slapstick tussle. The man eventually released his grip and with a good-natured grin, admitted defeat, and took his chair to the back of the crowd. Jemma flapped at and threatened an elderly couple and a young family, as if she was shooing chickens. Both complied and moved their pitch, others began to follow.

'Thank thee, good master,' Jemma said to a man with a large stripy canvas contraption.

A voice called out from behind her. 'What is this, "ham it up Hamlet"?'

Jemma turned to see Ronnie Mardle strutting across the field. 'They moved, didn't they?' All she needed now was advice from this pompous pantomime character.

'I never imagined you as a bouncer, but now I look more carefully … Hmm, very dominant. I like that in a woman.'

He sidled up and stood too close. Jemma could smell his cloying aftershave.

'You know we'll be auditioning for "Seven Brides for Seven Brothers" next week. If you play your cards right …'

Over my dead body! 'No, thanks,' she said lightly. Ronnie opened his bottle of mineral water and placed it to his pink, moist lips. Jemma watched with disgust as it dribbled down his lilac polo shirt and khaki cargo pants that fitted tightly around his substantial rump. He wiped the back of his hand across his mouth. The realisation hit her that he had remained totally unmoved by the mystery plays. She felt contempt rising. *This is just a show to you, a theatrical performance, just another day out for your directorial ego.*

'Sorry, I have to sell these programmes.'

'Perhaps we should have gone the whole hog and given you a tray of ice creams.'

Jemma tried to hide her loathing. This is not a concert party; it is creation and judgement, rescue and sacrifice, hope and despair, birth, life, death, and resurrection, and when today is over, my Josh

is going to leave, and I may never see him again. She felt like crying.
'No, I don't want a part in your amateur musical.'

'Only trying to be friendly,' Ronnie said. 'We have some very competent performers in the Monksford Operatic and Dramatic Society. Mrs Wilkinson once auditioned for RADA.'

He stuck his nose in the air and flounced off to where Harlan Westacre was having a run-in with a sound technician. Jemma continued to sell programmes and reposition audience members until the introduction music, a composition for sackbut, fife, and drum, heralded the start of the performance.

She hunted around with her eyes, searching for Josh. He had looked so pale and vulnerable. He wove his way through the crowd, still wearing jeans and a T-shirt.

'Good pray?'

'No, it was dreadful. I don't want to do this, but I must.'

'Did God tell you to?'

'Don't mock me, Jemma.'

This was more than method acting, and as much as she was furious with Ronnie for taking the performance too lightly, she was just as mad at Josh for taking it too seriously. He'd been behaving very strangely, almost paranoid.

'I mean it, Josh, identifying with Christ as a character is all very well, but it's almost as if you're becoming delusional. What happened to him isn't going to happen to you.'

'Messiah complex, do you mean? No, I could never measure up to him.'

'What are you afraid of then?'

'What do you think? The real threat comes from a source much closer to home.'

She rubbed the bruise on her arm. 'But even Fry wouldn't be desperate enough to try to harm you here in public.'

'Are you sure about that, Jemma, absolutely sure?'

He shook his head and carried on towards the green room. The stream of people became a trickle. Jemma cast her eye over the upper field. It was difficult to estimate numbers in the sea of people, with rugs and picnic baskets, deckchairs and parasols. Jemma estimated close to a thousand people, she had sold nearly two hundred programmes already, and she knew of four other programme sellers. She replenished her supply from a large cardboard box near the entrance.

Ruth, dressed in the plain brown linen of a medieval peasant, stood next to Eliza Feldman, in a pale yellow silk tunic with a bourrelet of gold and blue, covering her white hair. The old lady looked frail in her wheelchair. She smiled and chatted to everyone who passed.

'How do I look?' she asked. 'I'm lady of the manor.'

'Splendid.' Jemma kissed her on both cheeks, then turned to Ruth. 'A good number.'

'Yes,' Ruth agreed. 'I'm delighted. The *Gazette* seems to have drawn in people from farther afield, Leaton Maynard and Todbourn Heath, even some from Maidstone and Tunbridge Wells.'

'Have you seen Josh?' Jemma asked.

'Last time I saw him he was headed towards the abbey. Poor lamb, he's got himself very worked up about this performance.'

'I know.'

The music stopped and Ruth bristled. 'It's starting.'

Jemma found a space and sat on the grass. A chant followed by an explosion and a flash of pyrotechnics. Then God spoke and his voice echoed across the field.

> I am gracious and great, God without beginning,
> I am maker unmade, all power is in me ...

And the plays began. Jemma sat captivated as the ancient tales sprung to life before her eyes. She watched Lucifer being cast into the fiery pit. She could hardly tear herself away, but she needed to put on her dove costume and prepare for the Noah's ark play, so she headed to the marquee. She expected to see Josh, with his lion mask, but he wasn't there.

A moment's panic hit her. What if Alistair had found him and threatened him, or worse. After all, if he could hurt her, there was no telling what he might do to Josh. But Fry was too clever for that. As much as she feared him, she knew he cared deeply for Ruth and would do nothing to spoil her finest day. It was afterwards she would have to be vigilant. She put on her white robe and feathered mask.

She had a few minutes before she had to be ready. Looking out of the marquee, she saw actors and technicians, parents taking their children to the toilet, people buying cups of tea, but no Josh. She picked up the skirt of her robe so that it didn't drag in the long grass and circumnavigated the tent.

She was about to give up when she heard a sound and spotted Josh under a rowan tree. She approached but he seemed deep in thought.

'Josh?'

He moved, turning his back to her. 'Er ... just give me a minute, will you.'

'What's wrong.' She took a step towards him, but he held out his hand to stop her.

'Nothing! Nothing. I was just about to get changed.'

She longed to go to him and hug him, but he seemed determined to push her away.

'I'll see you in a couple of minutes then.' She turned to go. 'There's not much time,' she added.

'I know.' He turned to face her. His eyes were red-rimmed, and she could see he had been crying. 'Jemma, do you love me?'

'You know I do. You're my best friend. I'd do anything for you.'

'If anything happens to me, you will go to the police and tell them everything. You will tell them about Alistair.'

'Of course. Josh, what's the matter?'

'Nothing ... I can't say.'

'Have you seen Fry?'

Josh was silent.

'Tell me!'

'Just keep watch.'

'Come on, Josh. I'll stay with you. You need to get changed now.' She held out her hand and he took it in his.

They arrived in their positions, just in time. Jemma was enchanted as the audience laughed along with Noah as he sparred with his stubborn wife. Any doubts she had that a modern audience could relate to these ancient texts evaporated. She could tell the actors playing Noah and 'uxor' were enjoying their roles. She couldn't deny that Ronnie had worked wonders with a shy little plumber and a petulant florist from Ashford.

As Jemma stood on the stage, she permitted herself to do something she didn't normally do – look at the audience. She stood very still in what Ronnie had assured her was a suitably dovelike pose. She glanced across the stage at Josh.

Noah spoke,

> Another fowl I see
> Our messenger shall be;
> Dove, I command you,
> Our encouragement to increase.

And Jemma performed her 'scouting' expedition. She refused to flap – Josh had laughed at her in rehearsal, saying she looked like a demented chicken. So, with graceful dance steps, she glided around the stage to retrieve the olive branch. Finally the music soared, and the broad ribbons, red, orange, yellow, green, blue, indigo, and violet, fell from the ark's mast-top. Seven actors caught a ribbon each, Jemma took the violet and raced out towards the audience and up the hill, spreading the rainbow above their heads as they ran. Jemma grinned at the shouts of delight and the applause.

She quickly changed into her peasant costume, then while Abraham narrowly escaped sacrificing his son and Moses led the Israelites to sanctuary through the Red Sea, she directed people up to the farmyard for the nativity scene.

She packed them in like sardines on Raj Rajinder's surprisingly solid scaffolding-raked seating. Those without seats sat on the ground in the dusty farmyard. Fry, already wearing his Judas costume, seemed to scowl at her. She looked away, though her heart pounded. She tried to remind herself that his hours were numbered and that she was just glad she knew where he was and what he was up to. It didn't help. As long as he was nearby, her heart refused to settle into a normal rhythm.

Josh seemed a little more relaxed when Jemma met him coming out of the green room marquee. They didn't speak, but he gave her a grin and she gave him a thumbs-up sign. She changed into her scarlet cotehardie, and the women dressers helped fasten the hooks and pull the laces tight. She shook her hair loose and applied extra red lipstick – not very medieval, but if she was playing a harlot, she wanted to feel like one.

She screamed in pain as her 'accusers' gripped her arms and dragged her before Jesus. They threw her to the ground at his feet and wrenched the sleeve of her dress from her shoulder. She cried out and pulled it up; all these people staring at her nakedness and shame. Her breathing grew rapid, and she didn't dare meet Jesus' eye.

Here, in front of the crowd, sitting in the dust, she had never felt more vulnerable, more exposed. She thought of the one-night stands, the drunken fumble, and the string of casual relationships.

'Whore,' they shouted.

'Slut!'

'Tart!'

She wanted to cover her ears, to block out the shame. They named her lovers, one by one, and her face burned with humiliation. Tom, Joe, Neil, even Richard – she had used him as much as he had used her. Whatever his reasons for leaving, she felt cheap and discarded.

'Stone her!'

She longed for death, anything to escape the dishonour. She hauled herself to her feet, ready to take her punishment, but the man kneeling, writing in the dust, spoke gently.

'He that is without sin among you, let him first cast a stone at her.'

'He shows up my misdeeds more, I leave you here, alone with him,' said one of her accusers and each, stung by his own guilt, drifted away.

'Lord, no man has condemned me,' she said. Could it be, they all had something to feel guilty about?

'And because of me, be ashamed no longer. Of all your sins I make you free. Look no more to sin's assent,' he answered.

A weight lifted from her and she smiled, clean and free. Something had changed, deep inside. Could she be forgiven for all those bad choices and for her refusal to admit they were bad?

'He that will not forgive his enemy and use meekness with heart and hand will never see the kingdom.'

She walked away, her heart singing. She was clean, she was free, and she was forgiven.

Backstage, a dresser stood ready with a shapeless blue robe, and Jemma lifted her arms up like a child. The woman dropped the loose-fitting garment over Jemma's head and secured it with a girdle. She placed a blue hood over her hair. Hardly time to draw breath and she was back on stage, this time, mourning for her brother. The grief overwhelmed her. She threw herself at Josh. Tears streamed down her face as she said. 'Lord, if you had been here, my brother would not have died.'

To her astonishment, he was weeping too. 'Where have you laid him?'

As the stone was lifted away, a shrouded Lazarus stepped blinking into the blinding sunlight. Jemma ran forward and peeled off his grave clothes. Her grief turned to tears of joy.

A miracle. How could this be? People who died couldn't come back to life, but Jesus had restored the one thing most precious to her. She hugged her brother, hugged Jesus, and shouted her praise to God.

The crowd gasped and applauded.

'Here may men find a faithful friend that thus has cured us of our cares,' she cried out.

Jemma slipped off her costume again backstage. She couldn't help smiling. Now she understood the meaning of Jesus' words to Martha, 'I am the resurrection and the life. He who believes in me will live, even though he dies; and whoever lives and believes in me will never die.'

In a blur, Jemma moved to the front of the stage again and helped direct the crowds to 'Jerusalem' down by the abbey. People lined the route and cheered as Josh, riding a donkey, passed by. They threw palm branches. Trumpets and voices reached a crescendo. She saw a face in the crowd. Fry. He was looking straight at her, his mouth a grim line and hatred in his eyes. She shivered.

Then started the conspiracy. All kinds of false accusations against Jesus flew, and Pilate, Annas, and Caiaphas – dressed in medieval priest's vestments – plotted to destroy him. They had their stooge, a willing ally in the disciple Judas Iscariot.

Jemma removed her hood, and as Fry described the scene at Simon the Leper's house, she poured her perfumed oil on Josh's feet then wiped them with her hair.

A chill went through her again at Judas' words of betrayal. 'Take care, then to catch that coward, the one that I kiss.'

The scenes flashed before her eyes. A table and thirteen friends eating a traditional memorial meal. The start of a new promise, rumours of betrayal, denial and rash pledges. A man in utter torment and desolation, going to a garden to plead for his life. She watched as Josh knelt, and she waited as he made the most arduous decision of his life. She watched him sweat and weep as he battled with his Father, eventually submitting. As he wept, Jemma wept too.

The crowd was silent as the knights marched up and encircled the garden. Fry seemed to tower over him.

'I would ask you a kiss master, if you will, for all my love and my favour is upon you.' He took Josh's face in his broad hands and kissed him on both cheeks. The ultimate kiss of betrayal. The friends who had promised to be with him to the bitter end ran away, leaving him alone and vulnerable. Leaving him alone to face death.

Jemma couldn't bring herself to watch the trial scene. She found a quiet spot to sit and rest, behind the abbey ruins. The thought of unjust prosecution, the wrongful conviction of an innocent man, affronted every ounce of her integrity. The irony of the Cutlers' Guild play was not lost on her – the authorities, Roman and Jewish, were all too eager to stick the knife in. Time blurred, and she was there in the crowd outside Pilate's chambers. Bribery, corruption, and crowd-pleasing speeches seemed as prevalent then as they did today.

'Hello, Jemma. Taken a quiet moment to write up the final entry in the column, have you?' Mohan's voice made Jemma jump.

'What are you doing here?'

'You made it all sound so vivid I thought I'd better come and see it for myself.'

'And what do you think?'

'The acting is competent. The directing could be better, and I could have got you a much better printing deal on the programmes, but on the whole it's not bad for an amateur pantomime.'

'Pantomime! All this stuff is real. It really happened.'

'It's a play. A medieval play.'

'No, the events ... they happened.'

'I never had you down as a religious historian. Anyway, they have never proved Jesus existed. Archaeologists have excavated the area extensively, but they never found a body.'

Jemma laughed. 'Of course they didn't. That's the whole point!'

'What, that Jesus didn't die?'

'No, that he did die, but he came back to life again – the resurrection on Easter Sunday.'

'What utter rubbish. No one can come back to life. Hogwash. One chance, that's all you get.' He took Jemma by the hand. 'When I suggested that you get involved in these plays, I didn't expect to find you'd been brainwashed.'

'But I haven't.'

'You'll be telling me next that you've become one of these "born again" Christians.'

'What other kinds of Christians are there?' Jemma was genuinely puzzled.

'I dunno, proper Christians. The ones who are kind to animals and watch *Songs of Praise* on Sunday evenings. The sort who don't take it too far.'

'Mohan, I've got absolutely no idea what you're talking about, but I know these plays have changed the way I see things.'

He shrugged. 'Each to their own.'

'Look, Mohan, I'm glad you're here. Is Saffy with you?'

'Of course. With a whole roll of 35 mm film in her funny little one-legged camera.'

'Good.'

'Why? I'm intrigued now.'

'Something big is going to happen this evening.'

Mohan laughed. Jemma clutched his jacket. 'No, I'm serious. Deadly serious. You have to stay to the end. I can't say anything yet, but it's going to cover the *Gazette*'s front pages for months to come.'

Mohan raised an eyebrow.

'I have to go,' said Jemma. 'I'm needed for the crucifixion.'

Mohan rejoined the crowd, and the impact of Jemma's words hit her. She was an integral part of the crucifixion. She walked to the front of the stage area and gasped with revulsion. Josh was standing motionless, bowed and bloodied, between two Roman soldiers who were dressed as medieval knights. Each breath rasped and he stood naked except for a cloth around his waist.

'Stop!' she cried, but her voice was lost among the crowd baying for his blood. A handful of teenage boys were making the most noise, swearing and shouting the vilest insults. She ran up to them.

'Get out,' she shouted. 'You can't say those things.'

'Of course, we can, you stupid cow. We can say what we like.'

'Yeah, and we're getting paid for the privilege.'

They laughed in her face. She wanted to run away from the horror of it all. She just wanted to get some water and wash away the stage blood, to take Josh home and make him tea and wipe away the tears. She stood frozen until she realised the ushers were moving the crowd on again.

They passed a little wooded area where deep among the trees Ruth's little departure into 'Madame Tussauds' territory hung from a tree branch, swinging gently in the breeze.

'Come and see where Judas hanged himself.'

Spectators gawked at the grisly sight, parents shielding their children's eyes, hurrying them past. They reached the lower field. She spotted a tense-looking Bram Griffin standing by the open gate.

'Come on. Get the best seats for the crucifixion,' a knight called. 'It will all be over by sunset.'

A peasant waved the crowd to the front of the arena. 'Sit at the front for the best view.'

'Souvenir loaves and fishes.' A woman with a basket handed out scraps of bread.

An old hag shouted, 'Come and watch the criminals die – agony guaranteed.'

And the crowd picked up its chairs and blankets and picnic baskets and jostled laughing and chatting, for the best view.

Jemma felt sick. She ran towards the stage where a knight had laid a scarlet robe on Josh's back, and she saw them push a crown of thorns on Josh's head. The blood ran down his face. The knights jostled him laughing and spitting at him. Josh just stood there, letting them. She ran forward. 'No! Stop, you can't do this, you're hurting him!' She reached out to snatch the crown from his head, but sharp thorns punctured her hand.

'Hey, those are real thorns!' Two knights dragged her away. She struggled to get loose, but they held her arms. She collapsed, sobbing on the woman playing Mary, Christ's mother.

'What is happening?' Jemma cried. The woman held her and stroked her hair. Josh, stripped of his red robe, but still wearing that vile crown, was struggling along the rough track carrying a heavy wooden cross. Every few steps, his knees buckled, but no one came to help him.

The crowd shouted and jeered.

'Supposed to be a king. He can hardly walk!'

'He's healed all those people, looks like he needs a doctor himself.'

'Come on, Messiah, save us from this Roman filth.'

Again Jemma covered her ears. The two women clung to each other as they followed as closely behind the cross as the knights would allow. Josh stumbled. Exhausted, he could clearly go no farther, so the knights dragged an actor out of the crowd and put the heavy cross on his shoulders. They pulled Josh roughly to his feet and marched him to the front of the three huge arches of Monksford Abbey.

The sun cast long shadows, and the heat of the day was draining away.

The procession arrived at Golgotha. Two crosses already stood in place, with their criminal residents. Four knights manhandled Josh to the ground. Then, one by one, in curt, sharp comments, they grumbled and mumbled about the task in hand. They complained that the nail holes were in the wrong place and fumbled the ropes to tie him on the cross. The knights complained at the 'snail's pace' at which they were working as the audience, drawn in to their banter, laughed and shouted 'helpful' suggestions. All the while, Josh was silent.

Finally, they secured Josh to the cross and with a knight at his head, one at his foot and one to either side, they lifted the cross and placed the foot into an indentation in the ground. Walking forward, they raised it to an upright position. Rocking it, they complained bitterly at the weight, until with a thud, the foot located deep into the hole.

Josh cried out as his shoulders were jolted by the impact. He hung there, still and silent. Why didn't he perform another miracle? Why didn't he call upon God and all his angels to rescue him? Why did he let these wicked men have their own way? Why did he just hang there like some stupid, dumb animal … like a sheep at the abattoir? Like the guilty sheep in that Bible story. It died so the person could be forgiven.

The crowd that had been laughing and jeering fell silent, shocked that they had become part of the baying pack. Shocked at their guilt.

Jemma let out a sob. She put her hand to her mouth and clung more tightly to Mary. Oblivious of Josh's pain, the knights gambled for his clothes. The thief on the cross to the left jeered at him, while the other protested his innocence.

There was a loud cry, '*Heloy, heloy!* My God, my God, *Lama zabatanye,* Why did you forsake me?' Then he spoke directly to his mother, commending her to the care of his friend, John.

Finally he cried out again, 'My father, hear my plea, for now this thing is done. My spirit I send to you now into your safe hands.' Then he hung his head.

Jemma felt weak and spent with grief. She sat on the floor, unable to cry any more, and watched. The knights broke the other prisoners' legs. Then she watched with horror as one of them picked up a spear to jab into his side. In rehearsals, she had held her breath every time, as the knight thrust it at him and the trick blade slid harmlessly into the shaft.

Something was amiss. The hairs on the back of her neck stood up and her scalp began to prickle. Was it the way he lifted it, or some instinct, a voice inside her? She ran forward, ducked through the cordon of ushers and wrenched the spear out of the knight's hand.

'Wait! There's something wrong.'

The other knights hurried to pull her away.

'Look,' she hissed. 'The blade, it doesn't look right. If you stick that into him, you really will kill him.'

The knight examined it carefully, testing it by jabbing it into his palm. Then he looked at her.

She held her breath as blood dripped from the puncture in his hand onto the grass.

Someone had tampered with the stage prop. A small sliver of wood locked the retractable steel blade into place, and the tip had been sharpened.

'What on earth … How did this happen,' the knight muttered.

'I have a good idea,' Jemma said. 'Carry on before anyone notices.'

He took another spear and made feeble jabbing movements towards Josh's side, delivering his lines in a slightly shaky voice.

Someone had tried to kill Josh.

She looked over her shoulder. They were taking him down from the cross, and Mary, his mother, was weeping over the body. Jemma knew she didn't have long. Her next scene was the resurrection.

She stumbled to the green room, hunting for Fry. That bully, that cheat, that … Judas. His clothes were in a pile. She felt in the pocket and took his car keys. 'He won't get far,' she whispered.

'What are you doing?'

'Harlan! You made me jump.'

'Stealing from people's wallets.'

'I wasn't.'

'I'm calling the police.' Harlan reached into her handbag and pulled out her phone.

'Good idea. Go ahead.'

'What?'

'Call them. We'll need them soon.' Harlan stood with her phone in her hand and her mouth open.

Jemma held her scrawny shoulders. 'Harlan, listen to me. This is really important. I need to find Alistair Fry and stop him getting away.'

'Why, what has he done?'

Where do I start? 'Look, Harlan, I need to get back on stage. If you see him, don't say anything just ring the police.'

She crossed the field to the abbey, half running, half stumbling. Still no sign of him. She searched outside, behind the trees, but there wasn't time to reach the farmyard.

She arrived as they were carrying Josh to the cave-tomb and joined the other women. It could have been Josh who died. She found herself weeping with the other women.

'Oh, if only I could die too, No one, surely no one could ever be as sorrowful to have seen the things that I have seen ... to have loved and lost so much ...' She paused. These were not the words she had learnt. These were the thoughts of her heart, gushing from her lips in a torrent. She returned to her script. 'That Christ my Master most of might, is dead and gone from me.'

The angel appeared and sent the women to tell the disciples the literally earth-shattering news of the resurrection. Jemma wept alone by the tomb.

She heard footsteps approaching and looked up. There was a man dressed in a hard-hat, jeans, and wearing a yellow vest with a Monksford council crest. He carried a rake and a broom.

'Sir, I have looked both far and near to find my Lord – I cannot find him,' she said.

'Woman, weep not, but mend your cheer, I know full well where he was brought,' he said.

'Sweet sir, if you have taken him away. Tell me so and lead me there.'

'Mary, do not grieve; see my wounds; it is I. For mankind's sins I shed my blood, and all this bitter pain did bear.'

He lifted off the hat and showed his face, washed clean of the blood. But his hands still bore red marks, the imprint of the nails. She reached out to embrace him.

> Touch me not, my love, let be,
> Mary, my daughter sweet.
> To my Father in Trinity
> For I ascend not yet.

296 | THE ART OF STANDING STILL

A sense of hope filled her, the restoration of what was lost and the longing for what is yet to come. Josh's eyes were so full of love and pain that she longed to cling to him, but she obeyed and watched as he walked away across the field.

Tired, yet elated, she found Ruth and Eliza. The mystery plays were over for her, and she could concentrate on her next role – that of a journalist exposing an evil, corrupt, and murderous man.

'Have you seen Alistair?' she asked.

They shook their heads. 'Not since the garden of Gethsemane.'

She had his keys; he couldn't get far. She scanned the crowd. He was bound to turn up for the curtain call. She sat with them as she watched the final judgement. Josh, the blood washed from his face, stood majestic in a white robe, on the stage to the right of the throne. God commanded the angels to summon the 'good' and 'bad' souls.

It had been Ronnie's idea to plant these representatives of the entire human race in the crowd. The actors, dressed in plain contemporary clothing, mingled with the audience until summoned for judgement. Then they were assigned either to paradise or the fiery pit. Ruth had turned down Ronnie's suggestion for a working hell-mouth, belching smoke and real flame, due to the fire hazard.

'That's what they had in the middle ages,' he said.

Despite the lack of real fire and brimstone, the effect was electrifying. People looked shocked; some laughed and some looked close to tears as the bad souls were sent away to destruction and the good souls welcomed to Christ's presence. The impact was even greater because those being judged were people like them, not actors in medieval costume. They were judged on what they did for the hungry, the sick, the naked, and the imprisoned. 'When any that had need, night or day, asked your help and had it soon.'

Jemma felt her heart flip. At last she understood. She saw what Josh meant, she knew why Ruth needed to tell this story, and she knew what had kept Eliza Feldman alive against all the odds. She wanted to sing, to shout, to tell everyone of the life-changing, soul-changing message of how one man's death could liberate everyone.

She could feel Ruth nudging her. It was time to take a bow, a curtain call – if there had been a curtain.

She took her place between the disciples Peter and John and gave a curtsey. She looked up the line at Josh. He was smiling, relief all over his face. It was finished.

But it wasn't finished for Fry. She looked to the place where he should be, but she couldn't see him. Panic started to rise. What if he had gone? What if he had run away and escaped from the police? He could be anywhere. She broke away from the line as the applause died away and ran to the ruins to search for him.

Scene Thirteen

JEMMA CREPT ALONG THE PATH TO THE STAGE ON THE OTHER SIDE OF THE abbey, Pilate's residence. It was deserted. She looked into the green room again. It was empty. The dressers had joined most of the cast and crew by the abbey.

She ran to the car park. The dark blue Mercedes stood, just as it had this morning – so he didn't have spare keys. Good. At least he hadn't escaped. Unless he had gone on foot or had an accomplice to transport him.

She walked back to the green room and changed into her jeans, carefully hanging up the beautiful cotehardie and wondering what would happen to all the costumes. Several possibilities had been batted around, including an exhibition at the Town Hall and potentially reviving the plays each year. Everyone groaned at the last suggestion. Jemma wondered if her nerves could stand it. But to her the plays had come alive; they had existence beyond scripts and costumes and church hall rehearsals. They were living, breathing, life-changing things.

As she grabbed her bag from the chair, she noticed that Fry's clothes were still folded neatly on the pile. So was his spare costume. That was odd. He was supposed to have changed out of his Judas costume and put it on the hanging dummy. He must have brought extra clothes, perhaps some kind of disguise to slip away unnoticed.

She stopped to think, puzzled. That didn't make sense. He didn't know he had been discovered until she confronted him this morning. He must have planned this all along, to slide away at the end of his scene. Everyone else would still be on stage or occupied. It was the perfect cover. He could change clothes, abandon his car, and slip away.

She rifled through his clothes. His wallet and phone were hidden neatly underneath his folded jumper. Perhaps he had stolen someone else's clothes, perhaps he'd planned a new identity. Unless . . .

Jemma took off at a run. The lower field was emptying. She pushed her way through the crowds with their baskets and chairs and buggies. She caught Josh by the hand.

'Come with me, quickly.'

'What's happened?'

She didn't answer.

'Alistair, is it Alistair? Where is he?'

Together they ran to the path. Mohan saw her face and started running with them. The three reached the copse and stopped.

There was a creaking noise coming from the branch as the hanging figure, head tilted grotesquely to one side, twisted slowly, clockwise, then anticlockwise. Judas in his final indignity.

'Wicked!' Four teenage boys skidded to a halt beside them and stood transfixed by the grisly scene.

Jemma and Mohan waited at the edge of the wooded area, but Josh kept running towards the figure. Jemma paused for a moment, leaning against a tree to catch her breath. Then she pushed through the brambles farther into the copse. The first thing she noticed was the naked mannequin on the ground.

'Call an ambulance,' Josh shouted.

Jemma stared at him, rooted to the spot.

'And the police. Now!'

Two of the men who had played the disciples ran past her, one of them knocking her against the tree. She dashed forward as Josh and one of the men held Fry around the knees and lower legs, slackening the rope around his neck. The other man tried to slip the rope off the branch.

'A knife! We need something to cut the rope.' Josh shouted over his shoulder.

Someone ran to try to borrow one from the caterers. Bram Griffin appeared from the other side of the copse and began hacking at the rope with his penknife. The final strands of rope gave, and they man-handled Fry's body to the ground.

Scene Fourteen

RUTH PUSHED HER WAY THROUGH THE GATHERING CROWD. 'WHAT'S HAPPENING?'
She saw Jemma's pale face and wide eyes.

'Have you called that ambulance yet?' Josh searched for a pulse.

'Ambulance? Has someone been hurt?' Ruth felt a tightness in her chest.

'N – n-no.' Jemma fumbled for her phone.

'Tell me! It's Alistair, isn't it?'

Bram, Mohan, and the other men stood watching, helpless, as Josh frantically pumped Alistair's chest. His face was livid and his eyes bulged. Ruth knew they were too late. Josh shook his head and stood up. The blood seemed to drain to Ruth's feet, and she thought she would pass out. She looked on in horror, unable to tear her eyes from Alistair's distorted face and twisted body.

She felt a hand on her shoulder, turning her away from the scene.

'No! I have to ...'

'Come on, there's nothing you can do,' Jemma said. 'The ambulance and police will be here soon. Let's go over to the marquee and I'll make you some tea.'

'No, I can't leave him.'

'I'm so sorry. I did everything I could,' Josh said. 'But he's gone.'

With Jemma on one side and Josh on the other, Ruth walked in a daze across the road. Jemma found a chair and Josh boiled the kettle.

'I don't understand what happened.' Her voice was weak and hoarse. 'Was it an accident or did someone kill him?'

Josh took her hand. 'I don't know. The police will be here soon. It looks as if he might have . . .'

'Suicide?'

Josh nodded.

'Oh, no! Please, no.' Ruth felt her heart would break. 'If only he had talked to me. There must be something I could have done. I pushed him away when he needed me most.'

'It's my fault. I should have acted sooner. I should have gone to the police,' Jemma said

'Why?' Ruth looked hard at Jemma, studying her perfect face and long, sleek hair.

'I found out some things . . . Oh, Ruth, I didn't think it would end like this.'

'What things?' Ruth asked quietly.

'Things about Alistair. You don't want to know.'

'Yes, I do. I need to understand. What did he do?'

'Not now.' Jemma's eyes pleaded.

Ruth was determined. Whatever Jemma had to say couldn't make her feel any worse. 'Yes now.'

Jemma took a deep breath. 'Corruption, fraud, blackmail . . . and I think it really was Alistair that attacked Richard.'

Ruth laughed.

'It's true!'

'Then why didn't you tell the police?'

'I wanted to wait until after the plays. I didn't want to spoil things for you.'

'Spoil things? You stupid girl!' Ruth rose to slap her. Jemma thought she knew best, knew everything – stupid, meddling, arrogant . . .

Josh moved between them and put his arm round Jemma's shoulders.

'I'm sorry. I didn't know this would happen.' Tears flowed down Jemma's cheeks, but Ruth couldn't cry. She wanted to shout, to hit out. Maybe she had been wrong about God, that he did punish people for their thoughts and actions in this life. At last she had found something – someone – special. And now he had been snatched away.

'Did he leave a note? Was there a message for me?' Ruth's voice was small and wretched. Didn't he know that he was the only man she ever loved? She thought he had loved her. Perhaps she was just another person he had betrayed.

'I don't know.' Jemma couldn't look her in the eye. 'The police will be here soon. They might find something.'

The sound of sirens ripped through the quiet farmland. When Josh and the two women emerged from the marquee, the crowds had all but disbursed, unaware of the new source of drama in the small copse.

'What's up?' Joan pushed Eliza Feldman's wheelchair across the rough grass. She gathered the yellow folds of her dress into her lap so they didn't drag along the ground.

'There's been an accident,' Jemma said.

'For a moment I thought they were coming to take me away!' Eliza laughed. Ruth stood by the gate, hesitating.

'You don't have to go back over there.'

'Yes, I do.' Ruth took a deep breath to steady herself.

'So, who's the stiff,' Eliza asked. Josh put his finger to his lips to try to silence her.

'I'm afraid it's Alistair,' Jemma said.

'Never liked him ... nasty piece of work.'

'Would you like me to find someone to drive you and Joan home?' Ruth asked.

'No, my dear, I'll stay. I want to make the most of the day.'

'You don't understand, something terrible has happened.' Ruth ran her hand over her face.

'"See now that I myself am He! There is no God besides me. I put to death and I bring to life, I have wounded and I will heal, and no one can deliver out of my hand,"' said Eliza. 'That's from the Torah. What could be more terrible and more wonderful than life and death? And it's all in God's hand.'

Scene Fifteen

MOHAN CAUGHT UP WITH JEMMA BY THE AMBULANCE. HIS EYES WERE SHINING. 'This is amazing! And right on our doorstep. You've got all the details, naturally.'

'Mohan! This isn't the play; it's real life. You can't treat people as ... stories, as front-page fodder, as paycheques!'

Saffy put a hand on Jemma's shoulder. 'But all the stuff he was involved in – corruption, attempted murder.'

'That doesn't mean he deserved this.' She waved her hand towards the ambulances and police cars.

'He was in it up to his neck.' Saffy glanced at the end of the rope dangling limply. 'Oh sorry, what I meant was ...'

Jemma turned slowly to look at Saffy. 'You knew about this?'

Saffy nodded. 'I've got files.'

'But how?'

'Richard gave them to me. For safe keeping.'

'Richard?' Mohan looked stunned.

'He'd been investigating some kind of corruption in Monksford Town Hall. He'd stumbled on something, a deal relating to the bypass and the new industrial estate. He was about to run the story, then Alistair Fry found out and started making threats. That's when Richard moved away.'

'That's why he left so suddenly.' The scribbled note, the late-night calls, not giving his address. It was all making sense. Richard had been a fugitive, hiding from Alistair. There had been no 'other woman'.

'Why didn't he go to the police?' asked Mohan.

'He didn't have enough evidence. And I guess he wanted the *Gazette* to run the story first.'

'Then why didn't you say anything, if he'd given you all that information?' asked Jemma, feeling hurt that it had been Saffy and not her that Richard had trusted.

'He told me not to. He gave me the files and told me to hide them. So I did. He said he needed one last fragment of evidence, the last piece of the puzzle. That was the night you found him in the river.'

'Why didn't you come forward then?'

'Richard said that I was only to let anyone see the file in the event of his death. He was quite adamant. Made me swear it.'

'But he nearly died!' Jemma's voice squeaked with incredulity.

'He survived. And I thought it might make things worse for him. For us all.'

'We'd better speak to the police now.' Mohan directed Jemma and Saffy to the waiting car, and Jemma asked to be taken to the police station to see Detective Sergeant Morrisey.

Monksford Gazette   *Thursday 22 June*

BETRAYED

By Jemma Durham

The town of Monksford is reeling following the death of local Councillor, Alistair Fry. Fry died last Saturday after his portrayal of Judas Iscariot at a production of the Monksford Mystery Plays. A coroner's inquest is due to open next week to establish the cause of death of Mr Fry, who was found hanging from a tree by other cast members. They attempted to revive him, but he was found to be dead on arrival at Monksford General Hospital.

Councillor Fry had been at the forefront of the campaign against the Monksford bypass but had more recently been linked with financial irregularities and had been helping the Monksford police with their inquiries regarding the attack on journalist Richard Sutton last year.

'Mr Fry will be remembered for his tireless work on behalf of the people of Monksford,' said friend and Monksford vicar, Ruth Wells. 'He will be missed.'

The police are appealing for witnesses to the incident to contact DS Morrisey at Monksford police station.

Scene Sixteen

RUTH GROANED AS THE DOORBELL RANG FOR THE FOURTH TIME THAT AFTERNOON. The last five days and been a nightmare, an ordeal made worse by well-meaning people who wouldn't leave her alone with their incessant phone calls, visits, letters. If it hadn't been well-wishers, it was press and television crews. First Josh, then Harlan and Ronnie, the *Gazette*, the *Daily Mail*, the BBC.

She opened the door a crack. The wind threatened to tear it out of her hand.

'Ruth, how are you?' Jemma shuffled uncomfortably on the vicarage doorstep. Her hair blew in her face.

'I'm all right.'

'Really?'

'Why do people do that?' Ruth turned and walked away, leaving Jemma in the hallway. Jemma shut the door and followed her into the lounge, which was full of flowers. 'Do what?'

'Ask if you're all right, then question it when you say you're fine?'

'Because they think you're not.'

'Then why ask in the first place?' Ruth sat in her favourite armchair and drew up her knees. The wind roared down the chimney.

'People say they're all right. Sometimes they're just trying to cope.'

'Well, I think I am fine. But if I'm not, that makes me deluded, which is even worse.'

'I'm sorry.'

'Look, Jemma, I do appreciate your concern, and I didn't mean to snap. What I mean is, I'm not all right but I'm coping.'

If 'coping' meant crying herself to sleep at night, if it meant imagining she saw his car whenever she looked out the window, if it meant not eating or sleeping or even praying – then Ruth was coping.

'I understand.'

'If you say so.' She forced a smile. 'Anyway, how are you?'

'Josh left.'

'I know. He dropped in to say goodbye.'

'More than he said to me.'

'I'm sorry. I tried to persuade him to call you before he left. If it's any consolation, he looked pretty distraught.'

Dimitri stretched his paws up to Ruth, jabbing his claws into her leg. She picked him up and rubbed her cheek against his soft fur. Jemma sat down opposite her.

'Where did Josh go?'

'He wouldn't tell me.'

'Great!' Jemma let out a sigh.

'Were you in love with him?'

Jemma looked stunned. 'Love? I don't know. He was my friend, my mentor, the person I went to with all my good and bad news. His was the first voice I wanted to hear in the morning and the last one I wanted to hear at night.'

'It affected him very badly, you know. Not just Alistair, but the whole thing. It shook his faith.'

'Why?'

'I suppose it brought it all into such close focus. Reading about it is one thing, but acting it out ...'

'Watching it, being part of it, certainly made me realise the sheer ... magnitude. What Josh went through, what Jesus suffered. All that pain and humiliation.' Jemma looked ready to cry again. '"And being found in appearance as a man, he humbled himself and became obedient to death – even death on a cross!" That's from the Bible.'

'I know.'

Ruth clung on to her faith by her fingertips. Raging at God had turned into pleading with God, which was slowly becoming acceptance. In her grief, her faith was the still point around which everything spun uncontrollably.

Ruth felt weary: 'What are your plans? Will you stay in Monksford?'

'There's plenty of work at the paper at the moment what with ...'

Ruth's eyes misted over.

'I mean, now that the plays are over. Mohan seemed pleased with the column, and the Chief Reporter's job is still vacant. I plan to take some time off first, go up to Yorkshire, and visit my grandfather.'

Ruth nodded. *Go, just go.*

'And Richard will be home in a few weeks. He'll be staying with his parents. I need to see, you know, where we stand. And then there's Josh.'

'He promised ... I made him promise ... to get in touch with you. When he's settled.'

'Thanks.' Jemma wrung the strap of her handbag. 'I don't know if I'll ever see him again. Even if I don't, I'll never forget what we had ... what we almost had.'

They sat in silence for a moment.

Jemma tugged at the catch on her bag. 'I don't know if you want to see these.' She pulled out a package. 'Photographs from the mysteries. Our press photographer took them.'

Ruth forced a smile. 'I'd love to see them.' *Anything, just to see his face again.*

Jemma handed the package to Ruth. As she flicked through the prints, her eyes misted again. The faces, happy and smiling, stared from the rectangles of glossy paper. And there among them, smiling, was Alistair. He looked so ... untroubled.

'Was it worth it?'

'What do you mean?' Jemma asked.

'The plays – everything.'

Jemma shook her head. 'It was worth it for me.'

Jealousy shot through Ruth like an electric current. Jemma had a new-fledged faith, not battered and scarred and war-torn like hers, and Jemma still had her man. Any journalist worth her salt could track Josh down no matter where he was.

'But we've both lost so much,' Ruth said. 'Josh has gone, and Alistair ...' The tears started. 'I loved him, you understand. Although he was wrong and corrupt and he hurt people, I loved him.'

'I know.' Jemma stood up and fetched a box of tissues from the sideboard.

Ruth felt as if a lorry had struck her. 'How do you know?'

'One day, by the river. I saw you. I saw you and Alistair kiss.'

Ruth covered her eyes. So she hadn't got away with it. 'You knew! All that time and you didn't tell anyone. You didn't put it in the paper?'

'I didn't tell anyone else, only Josh. It wouldn't have been fair. My granddad was a journalist of the old school. "Be truthful, accurate, and fair," he says.'

'That's a good adage.'

'He also said, "Integrity – that's what matters, and it's even more important when you work in the town where you live." Too many people would have got hurt if I'd splashed it all over the front page. I couldn't do it.'

'Thank you.' Ruth nearly laughed. 'Not that it really matters now. I would write it across the sky if I thought it would bring him back. Will you say anything?'

'No. There's no reason.'

Ruth shook her head. She didn't know whether to laugh or cry. She had misjudged Jemma, but if Jemma had gone to press, perhaps Alistair would have been alive now. 'You're right, what is the point of raking it up? We were friends. I'm even happy for everyone to think he duped me, but what we had, or what I thought we had ... oh, Jemma, it was something special. You see ... this sounds so stupid

... I'd never been in love before. And even now, knowing all that he did, I love him and I forgive him.'

'What will you do?'

'Carry on, I suppose. I'm good at carrying on. That's what I do best. I carried on after my mother died; I'll do the same after Alistair.'

'Will you take a break, a holiday?'

'I think I need to get back to parish life as soon as possible. I feel as if I've been standing still for the past few weeks. It's time to move on.'

'Standing still is good sometimes.'

'I know. Perhaps we don't do enough of it.'

'Come with me.'

IN THE DYING LIGHT, THE TWO WOMEN STOOD TOGETHER ON THE COLLAPSED chapel wall. The three arches were silhouetted against the sky. The abbey ruins were desolate and barren, but the grass smelled fresh from the summer rain. The wind whipped up from the river and tore at their hair, ruffled their clothes and snatched their breath.

Ruth took Jemma's hand, and they stood in silence with their eyes closed.

A gust channelled through the arched windows, whistling and buffeting them and threatening to knock them off their feet, but they leant against it, solid and firm, and refused to let it displace them.

Author's Note

THE YORK MYSTERY PLAYS

Monksford is a fictional town in Kent. It is presumed, however, that many medieval towns would have held performances of Mystery Plays for Corpus Christi. I based *The Art of Standing Still* on the York cycle of plays, the most complete text still in existence. Here are my sources, if you are interested to know more about these beautiful, powerful, compelling dramas.

TEXTS OF THE YORK MYSTERY PLAYS

- Richard Beadle and Pamela M. King, *York Mystery Plays: A Selection in Modern Spelling* (Oxford Paperbacks, Oxford World's Classics, 1999).
- An electronic version of the original text of the York plays at the University of Michigan: *http://www.hti.umich. edu/cgi/c/cme/cme-idx?type=header&idno=York*

THE STORY OF THE MODERN MYSTERY PLAYS IN YORK

- *http://www.yorkmysteryplays.org/index_highres.htm*
- The revived waggon plays, performed in July 2006, and information about the York guilds: *http://www.yorkstories.fsnet. co.uk/york-mystery-plays/index.htm*
- An open-air play on the Life of Christ, performed on a farm near Guildford, Surrey: *http://www.wintershall-estate.com/*

Theodora's Diary

Faith, Hope and Chocolate

Penny Culliford

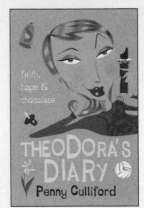

Saturday 8th May. Emergency!

It is 11:30 p.m. and I am suffering from an incredibly intense chocolate craving that will not leave me in spite of prayer, distraction activities and half a loaf of bread and butter. Got out of bed and searched the flat. No luck. Not even a bourbon biscuit. Not even a cream egg left from Easter. All the shops are closed so no nipping out to replenish supplies. Nothing else for it. I'm reduced to the chocoholic's equivalent of meths – cooking chocolate.

It's been one of those days for Theodora. Her mother has become the Greek equivalent of Delia Smith, her boyfriend would rather watch 22 men kick a ball around a field than go shopping with her, and chintzy Charity Hubble wants to pray for her. And of course, the crowning insult is her utter lack of chocolate. Join in her daily life with all of its challenges and joys, tears and laughter.

> "Theodora's Diary is a hilarious and realistic peek into the life of a sprightly Christian sister living 'across the pond.' I found myself laughing out loud and thinking, 'Yes, life is just like this!' Penny Culliford is a welcome new voice in inspirational fiction."
> – ANGELA HUNT, AUTHOR OF *THE DEBT*.

Softcover: 0007110014

Pick up a copy today at your favorite bookstore!

Theodora's Wedding

Faith, Love, and Chocolate

Penny Culliford

I've actually done it! I've kept up my diary for over a year.

I may not have grown very much spiritually, nor have I been hailed as the next British supermodel, but I have gained a fiancé, even if he is football mad. And to cap it all, I weigh half a stone less than I did this time last year.

Welcome back to Theodora's world. Now a bit older but not much wiser, thirty-something Theodora Llewellyn begins her second year as a diarist. And as usual, the results are endearing, hilarious and delightfully human.

Joy, bliss, ecstasy! Have just tried my holiday clothes on and they are actually too big! What a fabulous excuse to go and buy some new ones. Unfortunately, bank account doesn't agree. Saving to get married is such a nuisance.

In her search for life, love and a plentiful supply of chocolate, Theodora discovers that the course of true love never runs smoothly, especially when a voice from the past precipitates a crisis. But fear not – Theodora's humor and wit are up to the challenge. In the end, just one question remains unanswered: Exactly how much vitamin C is there in a chocolate orange?

Softcover: 0310250390

Pick up a copy today at your favorite bookstore!

ZONDERVAN®
.com

Theodora's Baby

Penny Culliford

"I'm not sure I'm cut out for parenthood. It's not in my plan. All right, I haven't actually got a plan, but if I had one, this wouldn't be in it. I don't even like babies – nasty, small, noisy, smelly things that take over your life. But this is a different baby. This is not just a baby; this is our baby …"

Newlywed Theodora discovers a slight oversight she and Kevin made on their honeymoon. Now she's gained an important new subject for her famous diary – but at such a cost!

"Tom opened the oven door and got out the most enormous chocolate pudding and placed it on the table in front of me. 'Especially for you, dear sister,' said

Ariadne. I swallowed hard a few times then took off for the bathroom. Ariadne looked at Tom and said, 'I told you so.'"

What? Theodora sick (literally) of chocolate? How will she survive without her favorite food group? Answer: with typical irrepressible humour that finds much to laugh at about marital bliss, faith, friendships, and the foibles of pregnancy. But will she be reunited with her lost love? Never fear – Theodora and chocolate can't be separated forever.

Softcover: 0-310-26558-4

Pick up a copy today at your favorite bookstore!